PRAISE FOR PATRICIA HIGHSMITH

"A border zone of the macabre, the disturbing, the not quite accidental. . . . Highsmith achieves the effect of the occult without any recourse to supernatural machinery."
—*The New York Times Book Review*

"The deadly games of pursuit played in [Highsmith's] novels dig down very deeply into the roots of personality. . . . She has produced work as serious in its implications and as subtle in its approach as anything being done in the novel today." —Julian Symons

"To call Patricia Highsmith a thriller writer is true but not the whole truth: her books have stylistic texture, psychological depth, mesmeric readability."
—*The Sunday Times* (London)

"Highsmith . . . conveys a firm, unshakable belief in the existence of evil—personal, psychological and political. . . . The genius of Highsmith's writing is that it is at once deeply disturbing and exhilarating."
—*Boston Phoenix*

"Murder, in Patricia Highsmith's hands, is made to occur almost as casually as the bumping of a fender or a bout of food poisoning. This downplaying of the dramatic . . . has been much praised, as has the ordinariness of the details with which she depicts the daily lives and mental processes of her psychopaths. Both undoubtedly contribute to the domestication of crime in her fiction, thereby implicating the reader further in the sordid fantasy that is being worked out."
—Roberts Towers,
The New York Review of Books

"Patricia Highsmith is often called a mystery or crime writer, which is a bit like calling Picasso a draftsman." —*The Plain Dealer*

Patricia Highsmith

THE TALENTED MR. RIPLEY

Patricia Highsmith was born in Texas, spent much of her life in England, France, and Switzerland. Among her more than twenty books are *Strangers on a Train*, *The Cry of the Owl*, and four other novels featuring Tom Ripley. She died in 1995.

ALSO BY PATRICIA HIGHSMITH

Novels

Short Stories

THE TALENTED MR. RIPLEY

THE TALENTED MR. RIPLEY

Patricia Highsmith

Vintage Crime/Black Lizard

VINTAGE BOOKS

A DIVISION OF RANDOM HOUSE, INC.

NEW YORK

FIRST VINTAGE OPEN MARKET EDITION, NOVEMBER, 1999

Copyright © 1955, copyright renewed 1983 by Patricia Highsmith

All rights reserved under International and Pan-American Copyright Conventions. Published in the United States of America by Vintage Books, a division of Random House, Inc., New York. Originally published by Coward-McCann, Inc., New York, in 1955. Published here by arrangement with Diogenes Verlag AG, Zurich.

Vintage is a registered trademark and Vintage Crime/Black Lizard and colophon are trademarks of Random House, Inc.

The Library of Congress Cataloging-in-Publication Data
Highsmith, Patricia, 1921-1995
The talented Mr. Ripley/Patricia Highsmith
—1st Vintage crime/Black Lizard ed.
p. cm. —(Vintage crime/Black Lizard)
I. Title. II. Series.
PS3558.I366T33 1992
813'.54—dc20 92-53511
CIP

VINTAGE OPEN-MARKET ISBN: 0-375-70824-3

www.vintagebooks.com

Printed in Canada
10 9 8 7 6 5 4 3 2 1

THE TALENTED MR. RIPLEY

1

TOM GLANCED BEHIND him and saw the man coming out of the Green Cage, heading his way. Tom walked faster. There was no doubt the man was after him. Tom had noticed him five minutes ago, eyeing him carefully from a table, as if he weren't *quite* sure, but almost. He had looked sure enough for Tom to down his drink in a hurry, pay and get out.

At the corner Tom leaned forward and trotted across Fifth Avenue. There was Raoul's. Should he take a chance and go in for another drink? Tempt fate and all that? Or should he beat it over to Park Avenue and try losing him in a few dark doorways? He went into Raoul's.

Automatically, as he strolled to an empty space at the bar, he looked around to see if there was anyone he knew. There was the big man with red hair, whose name he always forgot, sitting at a table with a blonde girl. The red-haired man waved a hand, and Tom's hand went up limply in response. He slid one leg over a stool and faced the door challengingly, yet with a flagrant casualness.

'Gin and tonic, please,' he said to the barman.

Was this the kind of man they would send after him? Was he, wasn't he, was he? He didn't look like a policeman or a detective at all. He looked like a businessman, somebody's father, well-dressed, well-fed, greying at the temples, an air of uncertainty about him. Was that the kind they sent on a job like this, maybe to start chatting with you in a bar, and then *bang!* — the hand on the shoulder, the other hand displaying a policeman's badge. *Tom Ripley, you're under arrest.* Tom watched the door.

Here he came. The man looked around, saw him and immediately looked away. He removed his straw hat, and took a place around the curve of the bar.

My God, what did he want? He certainly wasn't a *pervert*, Tom thought for the second time, though now his tortured brain groped and produced the actual word, as if the word could protect him, because he would rather the man be a pervert than a policeman. To a pervert, he could simply say, 'No, thank you,' and smile and walk away. Tom slid back on the stool, bracing himself.

Tom saw the man make a gesture of postponement to the barman, and come around the bar towards him. Here it was! Tom stared at him, paralysed. They couldn't give you more than ten years, Tom thought. Maybe fifteen, but with good conduct— In the instant the man's lips parted to speak, Tom had a pang of desperate, agonized regret.

'Pardon me, are you Tom Ripley?'

'Yes.'

'My name is Herbert Greenleaf. Richard Greenleaf's father.' The expression on his face was more confusing to Tom than if he had focused a gun on him. The face was friendly, smiling and hopeful. 'You're a friend of Richard's, aren't you?'

It made a faint connection in his brain. Dickie Greenleaf. A tall blond fellow. He had quite a bit of money, Tom remembered. 'Oh, Dickie Greenleaf. Yes.'

'At any rate, you know Charles and Marta Schriever. They're the ones who told me about you, that you might – uh— Do you think we could sit down at a table?'

'Yes,' Tom said agreeably, and picked up his drink. He followed the man towards an empty table at the back of the little room. Reprieved, he thought. Free! Nobody was going to arrest him. This was about something else. No matter what it was, it wasn't grand larceny or tampering with the mails or whatever they called it. Maybe Richard was in some kind of jam. Maybe Mr. Greenleaf wanted help, or advice. Tom knew just what to say to a father like Mr. Greenleaf.

'I wasn't quite sure you were Tom Ripley,' Mr. Greenleaf said. 'I've seen you only once before, I think. Didn't you come up to the house once with Richard?'

'I think I did.'

'The Schrievers gave me a description of you, too. We've all been trying to reach you, because the Schrievers wanted us to meet at their house. Somebody told them you went to the Green Cage bar now and then. This is the first night I've tried to find you, so I suppose I should consider myself lucky.' He smiled. 'I wrote you a letter last week, but maybe you didn't get it.'

'No, I didn't.' Marc wasn't forwarding his mail, Tom thought. Damn him. Maybe there was a cheque there from Auntie Dottie. 'I moved a week or so ago,' Tom added.

'Oh, I see. I didn't say much in my letter. Only that I'd like to see you and have a chat with you. The Schrievers seemed to think you knew Richard quite well.'

'I remember him, yes.'

'But you're not writing to him now?' He looked disappointed.

'No, I don't think I've seen Dickie for a couple of years.'

'He's been in Europe for two years. The Schrievers spoke very highly of you, and thought you might have some influence on Richard if you were to write to him. I want him to come home. He has responsibilities here – but just now he ignores anything that I or his mother try to tell him.'

Tom was puzzled. 'Just what did the Schrievers say?'

'They said – apparently they exaggerated a little – that you and Richard were very good friends. I suppose they took it for granted you were writing him all along. You see, I know so few of Richard's friends any more—' He glanced at Tom's glass, as if he would have liked to offer him a drink, at least, but Tom's glass was nearly full.

Tom remembered going to a cocktail party at the Schrievers' with Dickie Greenleaf. Maybe the Greenleafs were more friendly with the Schrievers than he was, and that was how it had all come about, because he hadn't seen the Schrievers more than three or four times in his life. And the last time, Tom thought, was the night he had worked out Charley Schriever's income tax for him. Charley was a TV director, and he had been in a complete muddle with his freelance accounts. Charley had thought he was a genius for having doped out his tax and made it lower than the one Charley had arrived at, and perfectly legitimately lower. Maybe that was what had prompted Charley's recommendation of him to Mr. Greenleaf. Judging him from that night, Charley could have told Mr. Greenleaf that he was intelligent, level-headed, scrupulously honest, and very willing to do a favour. It was a slight error.

'I don't suppose you know of anybody else close to Richard who might be able to wield a little influence?' Mr. Greenleaf asked rather pitifully.

There was Buddy Lankenau, Tom thought, but he didn't want to wish a chore like this on Buddy. 'I'm afraid I don't,' Tom said, shaking his head. 'Why won't Richard come home?'

'He says he prefers living over there. But his mother's quite ill right now— Well, those are family problems. I'm sorry to annoy you like this.' He passed a hand in a distraught way over his thin, neatly combed grey hair. 'He says he's painting. There's no harm in that, but he hasn't the talent to be a painter. He's got great talent for boat designing, though, if he'd just put his mind to it.' He looked up as a waiter spoke to him. 'Scotch and soda, please. Dewar's. You're not ready?'

'No, thanks,' Tom said.

Mr. Greenleaf looked at Tom apologetically. 'You're the first of Richard's friends who's even been willing to listen. They all take the attitude that I'm trying to interfere with his life.'

Tom could easily understand that. 'I certainly wish I could help,' he said politely. He remembered now that Dickie's money came from a shipbuilding company. Small sailing boats. No doubt his father wanted him to come home and take over the family firm. Tom smiled at Mr. Greenleaf, meaninglessly, then finished his drink. Tom was on the edge of his chair, ready to leave, but the disappointment across the table was almost palpable. 'Where is he staying in Europe?' Tom asked, not caring a damn where he was staying.

'In a town called Mongibello, south of Naples. There's not even a library there, he tells me. Divides his time between sailing and painting. He's bought a house there. Richard has his own income – nothing huge, but enough to live on in Italy, apparently. Well, every man to his own taste, but I'm sure I can't see the attractions of the place.' Mr. Greenleaf smiled bravely. 'Can't I offer you a drink, Mr. Ripley?' he asked when the waiter came with his Scotch and soda.

Tom wanted to leave. But he hated to leave the man sitting alone with his fresh drink. 'Thanks, I think I will,' he said, and handed the waiter his glass.

'Charley Schriever told me you were in the insurance business,' Mr. Greenleaf said pleasantly.

'That was a little while ago. I—' But he didn't want to say he was working for the Department of Internal Revenue, not now. 'I'm in the accounting department of an advertising agency at the moment.'

'Oh?'

Neither said anything for a minute. Mr. Greenleaf's eyes were fixed on him with a pathetic, hungry expression. What on earth could he say? Tom was sorry he had accepted the drink. 'How old is Dickie now, by the way?' he asked.

'He's twenty-five.'

So am I, Tom thought. Dickie was probably having the time of his life over there. An income, a house, a boat. Why should he want to come home? Dickie's face was becoming clearer in his memory: he had a big smile, blondish hair with crisp waves in it, a happy-go-lucky face. Dickie was lucky. What was he himself doing at twenty-five? Living from week to week. No bank account. Dodging cops now for the first time in his life. He had a talent for mathematics. Why in hell didn't they pay him for it, somewhere? Tom realized that all his muscles had tensed, that the matchcover in his fingers was mashed sideways, nearly flat. He was bored, God-damned bloody bored, bored, bored! He wanted to be back at the bar, by himself.

Tom took a gulp of his drink. 'I'd be very glad to write to Dickie, if you give me his address,' he said quickly. 'I suppose he'll remember me. We were at a weekend party once out on Long Island, I remember. Dickie and I went out and gathered mussels, and everyone had them for breakfast.' Tom smiled. 'A couple of us got sick, and it wasn't a very good party. But I remember Dickie talking that weekend about going to Europe. He must have left just—'

'I remember!' Mr. Greenleaf said. 'That was the last weekend Richard was here. I think he told me about the mussels.' He laughed rather loudly.

'I came up to your apartment a few times, too,' Tom went on, getting into the spirit of it. 'Dickie showed me some ship models that were sitting on a table in his room.'

'Those are only childhood efforts!' Mr. Greenleaf was beaming. 'Did he ever show you his frame models? Or his drawings?'

Dickie hadn't, but Tom said brightly, 'Yes! Of course he did. Pen-and-ink drawings. Fascinating, some of them.' Tom had never seen them, but he could see them now, precise draughtsman's drawings with every line and bolt and screw labelled, could see Dickie smiling, holding them up for him to look at, and he could have gone on for several minutes describing details for Mr. Greenleaf's delight, but he checked himself.

'Yes, Richard's got talent along those lines,' Mr. Greenleaf said with a satisfied air.

8

'I think he has,' Tom agreed. His boredom had slipped into another gear. Tom knew the sensations. He had them sometimes at parties, but generally when he was having dinner with someone with whom he hadn't wanted to have dinner in the first place, and the evening got longer and longer. Now he could be maniacally polite for perhaps another whole hour, if he had to be, before something in him exploded and sent him running out of the door. 'I'm sorry I'm not quite free now or I'd be very glad to go over and see if I could persuade Richard myself. Maybe I could have some influence on him,' he said, just because Mr. Greenleaf wanted him to say that.

'If you seriously think so – that is, I don't know if you're planning a trip to Europe or not.'

'No, I'm not.'

'Richard was always so influenced by his friends. If you or somebody like you who knew him could get a leave of absence, I'd even send them over to talk to him. I think it'd be worth more than my going over, anyway. I don't suppose you could possibly get a leave of absence from your present job, could you?'

Tom's heart took a sudden leap. He put on an expression of reflection. It was a possibility. Something in him had smelt it out and leapt at it even before his brain. Present job: nil. He might have to leave town soon, anyway. He wanted to leave New York. 'I might,' he said carefully, with the same pondering expression, as if he were even now going over the thousands of little ties that could prevent him.

'If you did go, I'd be glad to take care of your expenses, that goes without saying. Do you really think you might be able to arrange it? Say, this fall?'

It was already the middle of September. Tom stared at the gold signet ring with the nearly worn-away crest on Mr. Greenleaf's little finger. 'I think I might. I'd be glad to see Richard again – especially if you think I might be of some help.'

'I do! I think he'd listen to you. Then the mere fact that you don't know him very well— If you put it to him strongly why you think he ought to come home, he'd know you hadn't any axe to grind.' Mr. Greenleaf leaned back in his chair, looking at Tom with approval. 'Funny thing is, Jim Burke and his wife – Jim's my partner – they went by Mongibello last year when they were on a cruise. Richard promised he'd come home when the winter began. Last winter. Jim's given him up. What boy of twenty-five listens to an old man of sixty or more? You'll probably succeed where the rest of us have failed!'

'I hope so,' Tom said modestly.

'How about another drink? How about a nice brandy?'

2

IT WAS AFTER midnight when Tom started home. Mr.
Greenleaf had offered to drop him off in a taxi, but Tom had
not wanted him to see where he lived – in a dingy brownstone
between Third and Second with a ROOMS TO LET sign hanging out. For the last two and a half weeks Tom had been living
with Bob Delancey, a young man he hardly knew, but Bob had
been the only one of Tom's friends and acquaintances in New
York who had volunteered to put him up when he had been
without a place to stay. Tom had not asked any of his friends up
to Bob's, and had not even told anybody where he was living.
The main advantage of Bob's place was that he could get his
George McAlpin mail there with the minimum chance of
detection. But the smelly john down the hall that didn't lock,
that grimy single room that looked as if it had been lived in by a
thousand different people who had left behind their particular
kind of filth and never lifted a hand to clean it, those slithering
stacks of *Vogue* and *Harper's Bazaar* and those big chi-chi
smoked-glass bowls all over the place, filled with tangles of
string and pencils and cigarette butts and decaying fruit! Bob
was a freelance window decorator for shops and department
stores, but now the only work he did was occasional jobs for
Third Avenue antique shops, and some antique shop had given
him the smoked-glass bowls as a payment for something. Tom
had been shocked at the sordidness of the place, shocked that he
even knew anybody who lived like that, but he had known that
he wouldn't live there very long. And now Mr. Greenleaf had
turned up. Something always turned up. That was Tom's
philosophy.

Just before he climbed the brownstone steps, Tom stopped and looked carefully in both directions. Nothing but an old woman airing her dog, and a weaving old man coming around the corner from Third Avenue. If there was any sensation he hated, it was that of being followed, by *anybody*. And lately he had it all the time. He ran up the steps.

A lot the sordidness mattered now, he thought as he went into the room. As soon as he could get a passport, he'd be sailing for Europe, probably in a first-class cabin. Waiters to bring him things when he pushed a button! Dressing for dinner, strolling into a big dining-room, talking with people at his table like a gentleman! He could congratulate himself on tonight, he thought. He had behaved just right. Mr. Greenleaf couldn't possibly have had the impression that he had wangled the invitation to Europe. Just the opposite. He wouldn't let Mr. Greenleaf down. He'd do his very best with Dickie. Mr. Greenleaf was such a decent fellow himself, he took it for granted that everybody else in the world was decent, too. Tom had almost forgotten such people existed.

Slowly he took off his jacket and untied his tie, watching every move he made as if it were somebody else's movements he were watching. Astonishing how much straighter he was standing now, what a different look there was in his face. It was one of the few times in his life that he felt pleased with himself. He put a hand into Bob's glutted closet and thrust the hangers aggressively to right and left to make room for his suit. Then he went into the bathroom. The old rusty showerhead sent a jet against the shower curtain and another jet in an erratic spiral that he could hardly catch to wet himself, but it was better then sitting in the filthy tub.

When he woke up the next morning Bob was not there, and Tom saw from a glance at his bed that he hadn't come home. Tom jumped out of bed, went to the two-ring burner and put on coffee. Just as well Bob wasn't home this morning. He didn't want to tell Bob about the European trip. All that crummy bum would see in it was a free trip. And Ed Martin, too, probably, and Bert Visser, and all the other crumbs he knew. He wouldn't tell any of them, and he wouldn't have anybody seeing him off. Tom began to whistle. He was invited to dinner tonight at the Greenleafs' apartment on Park Avenue.

Fifteen minutes later, showered, shaved, and dressed in a suit and a striped tie that he thought would look well in his passport photo, Tom was strolling up and down the room with a cup of black coffee in his hand, waiting for the morning mail. After the mail, he would go over to Radio City to take care of the passport business. What should he do this afternoon? Go to some art exhibits, so he could chat about them tonight with the Greenleafs? Do some research on Burke-Greenleaf Watercraft, Inc., so Mr. Greenleaf would know that he took an interest in his work?

The whack of the mailbox came faintly through the open window, and Tom went downstairs. He waited until the mailman was down the front steps and out of sight before he took the letter addressed to George McAlpin down from the edge of the mailbox frame where the mailman had stuck it. Tom ripped it open. Out came a cheque for one hundred and nineteen dollars and fifty-four cents, payable to the Collector of Internal Revenue. Good old Mrs. Edith W. Superaugh! Paid without a whimper, without even a telephone call. It was a good omen. He went upstairs again, tore up Mrs. Superaugh's envelope and dropped it into the garbage bag.

He put her cheque into a manila envelope in the inside pocket of one of his jackets in the closet. This raised his total in cheques to one thousand eight hundred and sixty-three dollars and fourteen cents, he calculated in his head. A pity that he couldn't cash them. Or that some idiot hadn't paid in cash yet, or made out a cheque to George McAlpin, but so far no one had. Tom had a bank messenger's identification card that he had found somewhere with an old date on it that he could try to alter, but he was afraid he couldn't get away with cashing the cheques, even with a forged letter of authorization for whatever the sum was. So it amounted to no more than a practical joke, really. Good clean sport. He wasn't stealing money from anybody. Before he went to Europe, he thought, he'd destroy the cheques.

There were seven more prospects on his list. Shouldn't he try just one more in these last ten days before he sailed? Walking home last evening, after seeing Mr. Greenleaf, he had thought that if Mrs. Superaugh and Carlos de Sevilla paid up, he'd call it quits. Mr. de Sevilla hadn't paid up yet – he needed a good scare by telephone to put the fear of God into him, Tom thought – but Mrs. Superaugh had been so easy, he was tempted to try just *one* more.

Tom took a mauve-coloured stationery box from his suitcase in the closet. There were a few sheets of stationery in the box, and below them a stack of various forms he had taken from the Internal Revenue office when he had worked there as a stockroom clerk a few weeks ago. On the very bottom was his list of prospects – carefully chosen people who lived in the Bronx or in Brooklyn and would not be too inclined to pay the New York office a personal visit, artists and writers and free-lance people who had no withholding taxes, and who made from seven to twelve thousand a year. In that bracket, Tom figured that people seldom hired professional tax men to compute their taxes, while they earned enough money to be logically accused of having made a two- or three-hundred-dollar error in their tax computations. There was William J. Slatterer, journalist; Philip Robillard, musician; Frieda Hoehn, illustrator; Joseph J. Gennari, photographer; Frederick Reddington, artist; Frances Karnegis – Tom had a hunch about Reddington. He was a comic-book artist. He probably didn't know whether he was coming or going.

He chose two forms headed NOTICE OF ERROR IN COMPUTATION, slipped a carbon between them, and began to copy rapidly the data below Reddington's name on his list.

14

Income: $11,250. Exemptions: 1. Deductions: $600. Credits: nil. Remittance: nil. Interest: (he hesitated a moment) $2.16. Balance due: $233.76. Then he took a piece of typewriter paper stamped with the Department of Internal Revenue's Lexington Avenue address from his supply in his carbon folder, crossed out the address with one slanting line of his pen, and typed below it:

Dear Sir:

Due to an overflow at our regular Lexington Avenue office, your reply should be sent to:

>Adjustment Department
>**Attention of** George McAlpin
>187 E. 51 Street
>New York 22, New York.

Thank you.

>Ralph F. Fischer
>Gen. Dir. Adj. Dept.

Tom signed it with a scrolly, illegible signature. He put the other forms away in case Bob should come in suddenly, and picked up the telephone. He had decided to give Mr. Reddington a preliminary prod. He got Mr. Reddington's number from information and called it. Mr. Reddington was at home. Tom explained the situation briefly, and expressed surprise that Mr. Reddington had not yet received the notice from the Adjustment Department.

'That should have gone out a few days ago,' Tom said. 'You'll undoubtedly get it tomorrow. We've been a little rushed around here.'

'But I've *paid* my tax,' said the alarmed voice at the other end. 'They were all—'

'These things can happen, you know, when the income's earned on a freelance basis with no withholding tax. We've been over your return very carefully, Mr. Reddington. There's no mistake. And we wouldn't like to slap a lien on the office you work for or your agent or whatever—' Here he chuckled. A friendly, personal chuckle generally worked wonders. '– but we'll have to do that unless you pay within forty-eight hours. I'm sorry the notice hasn't reached you before now. As I said, we've been pretty—'

'Is there anyone there I can talk to about it if I come in?' Mr. Reddington asked anxiously. 'That's a hell of a lot of money!'

'Well, there is, of course.' Tom's voice always got folksy at this point. He sounded like a genial old codger of sixty-odd, who might be as patient as could be if Mr. Reddington came in, but who wouldn't yield by so much as a red cent, for all the talking and explaining Mr. Reddington might do. George McAlpin represented the Tax Department of the United States of America, suh. 'You can talk to *me*, of course,' Tom drawled, 'but there's absolutely no mistake about this, Mr. Reddington. I'm just thinking of saving you your time. You can come in if you want to, but I've got all your records right here in my hand.'

Silence. Mr. Reddington wasn't going to ask him anything about records, because he probably didn't know what to begin asking. But if Mr. Reddington were to ask him to explain what it was all about, Tom had a lot of hash about net income versus accrued income, balance due versus computation, interest at six per cent per annum accruing from due date of the tax until paid on any balance which represents tax shown on original return, which he could deliver in a slow voice as incapable of interruption as a Sherman tank. So far, no one had insisted in coming in person to hear more of that. Mr. Reddington was backing down, too. Tom could hear it in the silence.

'All right,' Mr. Reddington said in a tone of collapse. 'I'll read the notice when I get it tomorrow.'

'All right, Mr. Reddington,' he said, and hung up.

Tom sat there for a moment, giggling, the palms of his thin hands pressed together between his knees. Then he jumped up, put Bob's typewriter away again, combed his light-brown hair neatly in front of the mirror, and set off for Radio City.

3

'HELLO-O, TOM, MY boy!' Mr. Greenleaf said in a voice that promised good martinis, a gourmet's dinner, and a bed for the night in case he got too tired to go home. 'Emily, this is Tom Ripley!'

'I'm so happy to meet you!' she said warmly.

'How do you do, Mrs. Greenleaf?'

She was very much what he had expected – blonde, rather tall and slender, with enough formality to keep him on his good behaviour, yet with the same naïve good-will-toward-all that Mr. Greenleaf had. Mr. Greenleaf led them into the living-room. Yes, he had been here before with Dickie.

'Mr. Ripley's in the insurance business,' Mr. Greenleaf announced, and Tom thought he must have had a few already, or he was very nervous tonight, because Tom had given him quite a description last night of the advertising agency where he had said he was working.

'Not a very exciting job,' Tom said modestly to Mrs. Greenleaf.

A maid came into the room with a tray of martinis and canapés.

'Mr. Ripley's been here before,' Mr. Greenleaf said. 'He's come here with Richard.'

'Oh, has he? I don't believe I met you, though.' She smiled. 'Are you from New York?'

'No, I'm from Boston,' Tom said. That was true.

About thirty minutes later – just the right time later, Tom thought, because the Greenleafs had kept insisting that he drink another and another martini – they went into a dining-room off the living-room, where a table was set for three with candles, huge dark-blue dinner napkins, and a whole cold chicken in aspic. But first there was céleri rémoulade. Tom was very fond of it. He said so.

'So is Richard!' Mrs. Greenleaf said. 'He always liked it the way our cook makes it. A pity you can't take him some.'

'I'll put it with the socks,' Tom said, smiling, and Mrs. Greenleaf laughed. She had told him she would like him to take Richard some black woollen socks from Brooks Brothers, the kind Richard always wore.

The conversation was dull, and the dinner superb. In answer to a question of Mrs. Greenleaf's, Tom told her that he was working for an advertising firm called Rothenberg, Fleming and Barter. When he referred to it again, he deliberately called it Reddington, Fleming and Parker. Mr. Greenleaf didn't seem to notice the difference. Tom mentioned the firm's name the second time when he and Mr. Greenleaf were alone in the living-room after dinner.

'Did you go to school in Boston?' Mr. Greenleaf asked.

'No, sir. I went to Princeton for a while, then I visited another aunt in Denver and went to college there.' Tom waited, hoping Mr. Greenleaf would ask him something about Princeton, but he didn't. Tom could have discussed the system of teaching history, the campus restrictions, the atmosphere at the weekend dances, the political tendencies of the student body, anything. Tom had been very friendly last summer with a Princeton junior who had talked of nothing but Princeton, so that Tom had finally pumped him for more and more, foreseeing a time when he might be able to use the information. Tom had told the Greenleafs that he had been raised by his Aunt Dottie in Boston. She had taken him to Denver when he was sixteen, and actually he had only finished high school there, but there had been a young man named Don Mizell rooming in his Aunt Bea's house in Denver who had been going to the University of Colorado. Tom felt as if he had gone there, too.

'Specialize in anything in particular?' Mr. Greenleaf asked.

'Sort of divided myself between accounting and English composition,' Tom replied with a smile, knowing it was such a dull answer that nobody would possibly pursue it.

Mrs. Greenleaf came in with a photograph album, and Tom sat beside her on the sofa while she turned through it. Richard taking his first step, Richard in a ghastly full-page colour photograph dressed and posed as the Blue Boy, with long blond curls. The album was not interesting to him until Richard got to be sixteen or so, long-legged, slim, with the wave tightening in his hair. So far as Tom could see, he had hardly changed between sixteen and twenty-three or -four, when the pictures of him stopped, and it was astonishing to Tom how little the bright, naïve smile changed. Tom could not help feeling that Richard was not very intelligent, or else he loved to be photographed and thought he looked best with his mouth spread from ear to ear, which was not very intelligent of him, either.

'I haven't gotten round to pasting these in yet,' Mrs. Greenleaf said, handing him a batch of loose pictures. 'These are all from Europe.'

They were more interesting: Dickie in what looked like a café in Paris, Dickie on a beach. In several of them he was frowning.

'This is Mongibello, by the way,' Mrs. Greenleaf said, indicating the picture of Dickie pulling a rowboat up on the sand. The picture was backgrounded by dry, rocky mountains and a fringe of little white houses along the shore. 'And here's the girl there, the only other American who lives there.'

'Marge Sherwood,' Mr. Greenleaf supplied. He sat across the room, but he was leaning forward, following the picture-showing intently.

The girl was in a bathing suit on the beach, her arms around her knees, healthy and unsophisticated-looking, with tousled, short blonde hair – the good-egg type. There was a good picture of Richard in shorts, sitting on the parapet of a terrace. He was smiling, but it was not the same smile, Tom saw. Richard looked more poised in the European pictures.

Tom noticed that Mrs. Greenleaf was staring down at the rug in front of her. He remembered the moment at the table when she had said, 'I wish I'd never heard of Europe!' and Mr. Greenleaf had given her an anxious glance and then smiled at him, as if such outbursts had occurred before. Now he saw tears in her eyes. Mr. Greenleaf was getting up to come to her.

'Mrs. Greenleaf,' Tom said gently, 'I want you to know that I'll do everything I can to make Dickie come back.'

'Bless you, Tom, bless you.' She pressed Tom's hand that rested on his thigh.

'Emily, don't you think it's time you went in to bed?' Mr. Greenleaf asked, bending over her.

Tom stood up as Mrs. Greenleaf did.

'I hope you'll come again to pay us a visit before you go, Tom,' she said. 'Since Richard's gone, we seldom have any young men to the house. I miss them.'

'I'd be delighted to come again,' Tom said.

Mr. Greenleaf went out of the room with her. Tom remained standing, his hands at his sides, his head high. In a large mirror on the wall he could see himself: the upright, self-respecting young man again. He looked quickly away. He was doing the right thing, behaving the right way. Yet he had a feeling of guilt. When he had said to Mrs. Greenleaf just now. *I'll do everything I can* . . . Well, he meant it. He wasn't trying to fool anybody.

He felt himself beginning to sweat, and he tried to relax. What was he so worried about? He'd felt so well tonight! When he had said that about Aunt Dottie—

Tom straightened, glancing at the door, but the door had not opened. That had been the only time tonight when he had felt uncomfortable, unreal, the way he might have felt if he had been lying, yet it had been practically the only thing he had said that *was* true: *My parents died when I was very small. I was raised by my aunt in Boston.*

Mr. Greenleaf came into the room. His figure seemed to pulsate and grow larger and larger. Tom blinked his eyes, feeling a sudden terror of him, an impulse to attack him before he was attacked.

'Suppose we sample some brandy?' Mr. Greenleaf said, opening a panel beside the fireplace.

It's like a movie, Tom thought. In a minute, Mr. Greenleaf or somebody else's voice would say, 'Okay, *cut!*' and he would relax again and find himself back in Raoul's with the gin and tonic in front of him. No, back in the Green Cage.

'Had enough?' Mr. Greenleaf asked. 'Don't drink this, if you don't want it.'

Tom gave a vague nod, and Mr. Greenleaf looked puzzled for an instant, then poured the two brandies.

A cold fear was running over Tom's body. He was thinking of the incident in the drugstore last week, though that was all over and he wasn't *really* afraid, he reminded himself, not now. There was a drugstore on Second Avenue whose phone number he gave out to people who insisted on calling him again about their income tax. He gave it out as the phone number of the Adjustment Department where he could be reached only between three-thirty and four on Wednesday and Friday afternoons. At these times, Tom hung around the booth in the drugstore, waiting for the phone to ring. When the druggist had looked at him suspiciously the second time he had been there, Tom had said that he was waiting for a call from his girl friend. Last Friday when he had answered the telephone, a man's voice had said, 'You know what we're talking about, don't you? We know where you live, if you want us to come to your place.... We've got the stuff for you, if you've got it for us.' An insistent yet evasive voice, so that Tom had thought it was some kind of a trick and hadn't been able to answer anything. Then, 'Listen, we're coming right over To your *house.*'

Tom's legs had felt like jelly when he got out of the phone booth, and then he had seen the druggist staring at him, wide-eyed, panicky-looking, and the conversation had suddenly explained itself: the druggist sold dope, and he was afraid that Tom was a police detective who had come to get the goods on *him.* Tom had started laughing, had walked out laughing uproariously, staggering as he went, because his legs were still weak from his own fear.

'Thinking about Europe?' Mr. Greenleaf's voice said.

Tom accepted the glass Mr. Greenleaf was holding out to him. 'Yes, I was,' Tom said.

'Well, I hope you enjoy your trip, Tom, as well as have some effect on Richard. By the way, Emily likes you a lot. She told me so. I didn't have to ask her.' Mr. Greenleaf rolled his brandy glass between his hands. 'My wife has leukaemia, Tom.'

'Oh. That's very serious, isn't it?'

'Yes. She may not live a year.'

'I'm sorry to hear that,' Tom said.

Mr. Greenleaf pulled a paper out of his pocket. 'I've got a list of boats. I think the usual Cherbourg way is quickest, and also the most interesting. You'd take the boat train to Paris, then a sleeper down over the Alps to Rome and Naples.'

'That'd be fine.' It began to sound exciting to him.

'You'll have to catch a bus from Naples to Richard's village. I'll write him about you — not telling him that you're an emissary from me,' he added, smiling, 'but I'll tell him we've met. Richard ought to put you up, but if he can't for some reason, there're hotels in the town. I expect you and Richard'll hit it off all right. Now as to money—' Mr. Greenleaf smiled his fatherly smile. 'I propose to give you six hundred dollars in traveller's cheques apart from your round-trip ticket. Does that suit you? The six hundred should see you through nearly two months, and if you need more, all you have to do is wire me, my boy. You don't look like a young man who'd throw money down the drain.'

'That sounds ample, sir.'

Mr. Greenleaf got increasingly mellow and jolly on the brandy, and Tom got increasingly close-mouthed and sour. Tom wanted to get out of the apartment. And yet he still wanted to go to Europe, and wanted Mr. Greenleaf to approve of him. The moments on the sofa were more agonizing than the moments in the bar last night when he had been so bored, because now that break into another gear didn't come. Several times Tom got up with his drink and strolled to the fireplace and back, and when he looked into the mirror he saw that his mouth was turned down at the corners.

Mr. Greenleaf was rollicking on about Richard and himself in Paris, when Richard had been ten years old. It was not in the least interesting. If anything happened with the police in the next ten days, Tom thought, Mr. Greenleaf would take him in. He could tell Mr. Greenleaf that he'd sublet his apartment in a hurry, or something like that, and simply hide out here. Tom felt awful, almost physically ill.

'Mr. Greenleaf, I think I should be going.'

'Now? But I wanted to show you— Well, never mind. Another time.'

Tom knew he should have asked, 'Show me what?' and been patient while he was shown whatever it was, but he couldn't.

'I want you to visit the yards, of course!' Mr. Greenleaf said cheerfully. 'When can you come out? Only during your lunch hour, I suppose. I think you should be able to tell Richard what the yards look like these days.'

'Yes – I could come in my lunch hour.'

'Give me a call any day, Tom. You've got my card with my private number. If you give me half an hour's notice, I'll have a man pick you up at your office and drive you out. We'll have a sandwich as we walk through, and he'll drive you back.'

'I'll call you,' Tom said. He felt he would faint if he stayed one minute longer in the dimly lighted foyer, but Mr. Greenleaf was chuckling again, asking him if he had read a certain book by Henry James.

'I'm sorry to say I haven't, sir, not that one,' Tom said.

'Well, no matter.' Mr. Greenleaf smiled.

Then they shook hands, a long suffocating squeeze from Mr. Greenleaf, and it was over. But the pained, frightened expression was still on his face as he rode down in the elevator, Tom saw. He leaned in the corner of the elevator in an exhausted way, though he knew as soon as he hit the lobby he would fly out of the door and keep on running, running, all the way home.

4

THE ATMOSPHERE OF the city became stranger as the days went on. It was as if something had gone out of New York – the realness or the importance of it – and the city was putting on a show just for him, a colossal show with its buses, taxis, and hurrying people on the sidewalks, its television shows in all the Third Avenue bars, its movie marquees lighted up in broad daylight, and its sound effects of thousands of honking horns and human voices, talking for no purpose whatsoever. As if when his boat left the pier on Saturday, the whole city of New York would collapse with a *poof* like a lot of cardboard on a stage.

Or maybe he was afraid. He hated water. He had never been anywhere before on water, except to New Orleans from New York and back to New York again, but then he had been working on a banana boat mostly below deck, and he had hardly realized he was on water. The few times he had been on deck the sight of the water had at first frightened him, then made him feel sick, and he had always run below deck again, where, contrary to what people said, he had felt better. His parents had drowned in Boston Harbour, and Tom had always thought that probably had something to do with it, because as long as he could remember he had been afraid of water, and he had never learned how to swim. It gave Tom a sick, empty feeling at the pit of his stomach to think that in less than a week he would have water below him, miles deep, and that undoubtedly he would have to look at it most of the time, because people on ocean liners spent most of their time on deck. And it was particularly un-chic to be seasick, he felt. He had never been seasick, but he came very near it several times in those last days, simply thinking about the voyage to Cherbourg.

He had told Bob Delancey that he was moving in a week, but he hadn't said where. Bob did not seem interested, anyway. They saw very little of each other at the Fifty-first Street place. Tom had gone to Marc Priminger's house in East-Forty-fifth Street – he still had the keys – to pick up a couple of things he had forgotten, and he had gone at an hour when he had thought Marc wouldn't be there, but Marc had come in with his new housemate, Joel, a thin drip of a young man who worked for a publishing house, and Marc had put on one of his suave 'Please-do-*just*-as-you-like' acts for Joel's benefit, though if Joel hadn't been there Marc would have cursed him out in language that even a Portuguese sailor wouldn't have used. Marc (his given name was, of all things, Marcellus) was an ugly mug of a man with a private income and a hobby of helping out young men in temporary financial difficulties by putting them up in his two-storey, three-bedroom house, and playing God by telling them what they could and couldn't do around the place and by giving them advice as to their lives and their jobs, generally rotten advice. Tom had stayed there three months, though for nearly half that time Marc had been in Florida and he had had the house all to himself, but when Marc had come back he had made a big stink about a few pieces of broken glassware – Marc playing God again, the Stern Father – and Tom had gotten angry enough, for once, to stand up for himself and talk to him back. Whereupon Marc had thrown him out, after collecting sixty-three dollars from him for the broken glassware. The old tightwad! He should have been an old maid, Tom thought, at the head of a girls' school. Tom was bitterly sorry he had ever laid eyes on Marc Priminger, and the sooner he could forget Marc's stupid, piglike eyes, his massive jaw, his ugly hands with the gaudy rings (waving through the air, ordering this and that from everybody), the happier he would be.

The only one of his friends he felt like telling about his European trip was Cleo, and he went to see her on the Thursday before he sailed. Cleo Dobelle was a tall, slim dark-haired girl who could have been anything from twenty-three to thirty, Tom didn't know, who lived with her parents in Gracie Square and painted in a small way – a *very* small way, in fact, on little pieces of ivory no bigger than postage stamps that had to be viewed through a magnifying glass, and Cleo used a magnifying glass when she painted them. 'But think how convenient it is to be able to carry *all* my paintings in a cigar box! Other painters have to have rooms and rooms to hold their canvases!' Cleo said. Cleo lived in her own suite of rooms with a little bath and kitchen at the back of her parents' section of the apartment, and Cleo's apartment was always rather dark since it had no exposure except to a tiny backyard overgrown with ailanthus trees that blocked out the light. Cleo always had the lights on, dim ones, which gave a nocturnal atmosphere whatever the time of day. Except for the night when he had met her, Tom had seen Cleo only in close-fitting velvet slacks of various colours and gaily striped silk shirts. They had taken to each other from the very first night, when Cleo had asked him to dinner at her apartment on the following evening. Cleo always asked him up to her apartment, and there was somehow never any thought that he might ask her out to dinner or the theatre or do any of the ordinary things that a young man was expected to do with a girl. She didn't expect him to bring her flowers or books or candy when he came for dinner or cocktails, though Tom did bring her a little gift sometimes, because it pleased her so. Cleo was the one person he could tell that he was going to Europe and why. He did.

Cleo was enthralled, as he had known she would be. Her red lips parted in her long, pale face, and she brought her hands down on her velvet thighs and exclaimed, '*Tom*-mie! How too, too marvellous! It's just like out of Shakespeare or something!'

That was just what Tom thought, too. That was just what he had needed someone to say.

Cleo fussed around him all evening, asking him if he had this and that, Kleenexes and cold tablets and woollen socks because it started raining in Europe in the fall, and his vaccinations. Tom said he felt pretty well prepared.

'Just don't come to see me off, Cleo. I don't want to be seen off.'

'Of course not!' Cleo said, understanding perfectly. 'Oh, Tommie, I think that's such fun! Will you write me everything that happens with Dickie? You're the only person I know who ever went to Europe for a *reason*.'

He told her about visiting Mr. Greenleaf's shipyards in Long Island, the miles and miles of tables with machines making shiny metal parts, varnishing and polishing wood, the dry-docks with boat skeletons of all sizes, and impressed her with the terms Mr. Greenleaf had used – coamings, inwales, keel-sons, and chines. He described the second dinner at Mr. Greenleaf's house, when Mr. Greenleaf had presented him with a wrist-watch. He showed the wrist-watch to Cleo, not a fabulously expensive wrist-watch, but still an excellent one and just the style Tom might have chosen for himself – a plain white face with fine black Roman numerals in a simple gold setting with an alligator strap.

'Just because I happened to say a few days before that I didn't own a watch,' Tom said. 'He's really adopted me like a son.' And Cleo, too, was the only person he knew to whom he could say that.

Cleo sighed. 'Men! You have all the luck. Nothing like that could ever happen to a girl. Men're so *free*!'

Tom smiled. It often seemed to him that it was the other way around. 'Is that the lamb chops burning?'

Cleo jumped up with a shriek.

After dinner, she showed him five or six of her latest paint-ings, a couple of romantic portraits of a young man they both

28

knew, in an open-collared white shirt, three imaginary land-scapes of a junglelike land, derived from the view of ailanthus trees out her window. The hair of the little monkeys in the paintings was really astoundingly well done, Tom thought. Cleo had a lot of brushes with just one hair in them, and even these varied from comparatively coarse to ultra fine. They drank nearly two bottles of Medoc from her parents' liquor shelf, and Tom got so sleepy he could have spent the night right where he was lying on the floor – they had often slept side by side on the two big bear rugs in front of the fireplace, and it was another of the wonderful things about Cleo that she never wanted or expected him to make a pass at her, and he never had – but Tom hauled himself up at a quarter to twelve and took his leave.

'I won't see you again, will I?' Cleo said dejectedly at the door.

'Oh, I should be back in about six weeks,' Tom said, though he didn't think so at all. Suddenly he leaned forward and planted a firm, brotherly kiss on her ivory cheek. 'I'll miss you, Cleo.'

She squeezed his shoulder, the only physical touch he could recall her ever having given him. 'I'll miss you,' she said.

The next day he took care of Mrs. Greenleaf's commissions at Brooks Brothers, the dozen pairs of black woollen socks and the bathrobe. Mrs. Greenleaf had not suggested a colour for the bathrobe. She would leave that up to him, she had said. Tom chose a dark maroon flannel with a navy-blue belt and lapels. It was not the best-looking robe of the lot, in Tom's opinion, but he felt it was exactly what Richard would have chosen, and that Richard would be delighted with it. He put the socks and the robe on the Greenleafs' charge account. He saw a heavy linen sport shirt with wooden buttons that he liked very much, that would have been easy to put on the Greenleafs' account, too, but he didn't. He bought it with his own money.

5

THE MORNING OF his sailing, the morning he had looked forward to with such buoyant excitement, got off to a hideous start. Tom followed the steward to his cabin congratulating himself that his firmness with Bob about not wanting to be seen off had taken effect, and had just entered the room when a bloodcurdling whoop went up.

'Where's all the champagne, Tom? We're waiting!'

'Boy, is this a stinking room! Why don't you ask them for something decent?'

'Tommie, take *me*?' from Ed Martin's girl friend, whom Tom couldn't bear to look at.

There they all were, mostly Bob's lousy friends, sprawled on his bed, on the floor, everywhere. Bob had found out he was sailing, but Tom had never thought he would do a thing like this. It took self-control for Tom not to say in an icy voice, 'There *isn't* any champagne.' He tried to greet them all, tried to smile, though he could have burst into tears like a child. He gave Bob a long, withering look, but Bob was already high, on something. There were very few things that got under his skin, Tom thought self-justifyingly, but this was one of them: noisy surprises like this, the riffraff, the vulgarians, the slobs he had thought he had left behind when he crossed the gangplank, littering the very stateroom where he was to spend the next five days!

Tom went over to Paul Hubbard, the only respectable person in the room, and sat down beside him on the short, built-in sofa. 'Hello, Paul,' he said quietly. 'I'm sorry about all this.'

'Oh!' Paul scoffed. 'How long'll you be gone? – What's the matter, Tom? Are you sick?'

It was awful. It went on, the noise and the laughter and the girls feeling the bed and looking in the john. Thank God the Greenleafs hadn't come to see him off! Mr. Greenleaf had had to go to New Orleans on business, and Mrs. Greenleaf, when Tom had called this morning to say good-bye, had said that she didn't feel quite up to coming down to the boat.

Finally, Bob or somebody produced a bottle of whisky, and they all began to drink out of the two glasses from the bathroom, and then a steward came in with a tray of glasses. Tom refused to have a drink. He was sweating so heavily, he took off his jacket so as not to soil it. Bob came over and rammed a glass in his hand, and Bob was not exactly joking, Tom saw, and he knew why – because he had accepted Bob's hospitality for a month, and he might at least put on a pleasant face, but Tom could not put on a pleasant face any more than if his face had been made of granite. So what if they all hated him after this, he thought, what had he lost?

'I can fit in here, Tommie,' said the girl who was determined to fit in somewhere and go with him. She had wedged herself sideways into a narrow closet about the size of a broom closet.

'I'd like to see Tom caught with a girl in his room!' Ed Martin said, laughing.

Tom glared at him. 'Let's get out of here and get some air,' he murmured to Paul.

The others were making so much noise, nobody noticed their leaving. They stood at the rail near the stern. It was a sunless day, and the city on their right was already like some grey, distant land that he might be looking at from mid-ocean – except for those bastards inside his stateroom.

'Where've you been keeping yourself?' Paul asked. 'Ed called up to tell me you were leaving. I haven't seen you in weeks.'

Paul was one of the people who thought he worked for the Associated Press. Tom made up a fine story about an assignment he had been sent on. Possibly the Middle East, Tom said. He made it sound rather secret. 'I've been doing quite a lot of night work lately, too,' Tom said, 'which is why I haven't been around much. It's awfully nice of you to come down and see me off.'

'I hadn't any classes this morning.' Paul took the pipe out of his mouth and smiled. 'Not that I wouldn't have come anyway, probably. Any old excuse!'

Tom smiled. Paul taught music at a girls' school in New York to earn his living, but he preferred to compose music on his own time. Tom could not remember how he had met Paul, but he remembered going to his Riverside Drive apartment for Sunday brunch once with some other people, and Paul had played some of his own compositions on the piano, and Tom had enjoyed it immensely. 'Can't I offer you a drink? Let's see if we can find the bar,' Tom said.

But just then a steward came out, hitting a gong and shouting, 'Visitors ashore, please! All visitors ashore!'

'That's me,' Paul said.

They shook hands, patted shoulders, promised to write postcards to each other. Then Paul was gone.

Bob's gang would stay till the last minute, he thought, probably have to be blasted out. Tom turned suddenly and ran up a narrow, ladderlike flight of stairs. At the top of it he was confronted by a CABIN CLASS ONLY sign hanging from a chain, but he threw a leg over the chain and stepped on to the deck. They surely wouldn't object to a first-class passenger going into second-class, he thought. He couldn't bear to look at Bob's gang again. He had paid Bob half a month's rent and given him a good-bye present of a good shirt and tie. What more did Bob want?

The ship was moving before Tom dared to go down to his room again. He went into the room cautiously. Empty. The neat blue bedcover was smooth again. The ashtrays were clean. There was no sign they had ever been here. Tom relaxed and smiled. This was service! The fine old tradition of the Cunard

Line, British seamanship and all that! He saw a big basket of fruit on the floor by his bed. He seized the little white envelope eagerly. The card inside said:

Bon voyage and bless you, Tom. All our good wishes go with you.
                                        Emily and Herbert Greenleaf

The basket had a tall handle and it was entirely under yellow cellophane – apples and pears and grapes and a couple of candy bars and several little bottles of liqueurs. Tom had never received a bon voyage basket. To him, they had always been something you saw in florists' windows for fantastic prices and laughed at. Now he found himself with tears in his eyes, and he put his face down in his hands suddenly and began to sob.

6

HIS MOOD WAS tranquil and benevolent, but not at all sociable. He wanted his time for thinking, and he did not care to meet any of the people on the ship, not any of them, though when he encountered the people with whom he sat at his table, he greeted them pleasantly and smiled. He began to play a role on the ship, that of a serious young man with a serious job ahead of him. He was courteous, poised, civilized and preoccupied.

He had a sudden whim for a cap and bought one in the haberdashery, a conservative bluish-grey cap of soft English wool. He could pull its visor down over nearly his whole face when he wanted to nap in his deck-chair, or wanted to look as if he were napping. A cap was the most versatile of headgear, he thought, and he wondered why he had never thought of wearing one before? He could look like a country gentleman, a thug, an Englishman, a Frenchman, or a plain American eccentric, depending on how he wore it. Tom amused himself with it in his room in front of the mirror. He had always thought he had the world's dullest face, a thoroughly forgettable face with a look of docility that he could not understand, and a look also of vague fright that he had never been able to erase. A real conformist's face, he thought. The cap changed all that. It gave him a country air, Greenwich, Connecticut, country. Now he was a young man with a private income, not long out of Princeton, perhaps. He bought a pipe to go with the cap.

He was starting a new life. Good-bye to all the second-rate people he had hung around and had let hang around him in the past three years in New York. He felt as he imagined immigrants felt when they left everything behind them in some foreign country, left their friends and relations and their past mistakes, and sailed for America. A clean slate! Whatever happened with Dickie, he would acquit himself well, and Mr. Greenleaf would know that he had, and would respect him for it. When Mr. Greenleaf's money was used up, he might not come back to America. He might get an interesting job in a hotel, for instance, where they needed somebody bright and personable who spoke English. Or he might become a representative for some European firm and travel everywhere in the world. Or somebody might come along who needed a young man exactly like himself, who could drive a car, who was quick at figures, who could entertain an old grandmother or squire somebody's daughter to a dance. He was versatile, and the world was wide! He swore to himself he would stick to a job once he got it. Patience and perseverance! Upward and onward!

'Have you Henry James' *The Ambassador*?' Tom asked the officer in charge of the first-class library. The book was not on the shelf.

'I'm sorry, we haven't, sir,' said the officer.

Tom was disappointed. It was the book Mr. Greenleaf had asked him if he had read. Tom felt he ought to read it. He went to the cabin-class library. He found the book on the shelf, but when he started to check it out and gave his cabin number, the attendant told him sorry, that first-class passengers were not allowed to take books from the cabin-class library. Tom had been afraid of that. He put the book back docilely, though it would have been easy, so easy, to make a pass at the shelf and slip the book under his jacket.

In the mornings he strolled several times round the deck, but very slowly, so that the people puffing around on their morning constitutionals always passed him two or three times before he had been around once, then settled down in his deck-chair for bouillon and more thought on his own destiny. After lunch, he pottered around in his cabin, basking in its privacy and comfort, doing absolutely nothing. Sometimes he sat in the writing-room, thoughtfully penning letters on the ship's stationery to Marc Priminger, to Cleo, to the Greenleafs. The letter to the Greenleafs began as a polite greeting and a thank-you for the bon voyage basket and the comfortable accommodations, but he amused himself by adding an imaginary postdated paragraph about finding Dickie and living with him in his Mongibello house, about the slow but steady progress he was making in persuading Dickie to come home, about the swimming, the fishing, the café life, and he got so carried away that it went on for eight or ten pages and he knew he would never mail any of it, so he wrote on about Dickie's not being romantically inter-ested in Marge (he gave a complete character analysis of Marge) so it was not Marge who was holding Dickie, though Mrs. Greenleaf had thought it might be, etc., etc., until the table was covered with sheets of paper and the first call came for dinner.

On another afternoon, he wrote a polite note to Aunt Dottie:

Dear Auntie [which he rarely called her in a letter and never to her face],

As you see by the stationery, I am on the high seas. An unexpected business offer which I cannot explain now. I had to leave rather suddenly, so I was not able to get up to Boston and I'm sorry, because it may be months or even years before I come back.

I just wanted you not to worry and not to send me any more cheques, thank you. Thank you very much for the last one of a month or so ago. I don't suppose you have sent any more since then. I am well and extremely happy.

Love,
Tom

No use sending any good wishes about her health. She was as strong as an ox. He added:

P.S. I have no idea what my address will be, so I cannot give you any.

That made him feel better, because it definitely cut him off from her. He needn't ever tell her where he was. No more of the snidely digging letters, the sly comparisons of him to his father, the piddling cheques for the strange sums of six dollars and forty-eight cents and twelve dollars and ninety-five, as if she had had a bit left over from her latest bill-paying, or taken something back to a store and had tossed the money to him, like a crumb. Considering what Aunt Dottie might have sent him, with her income, the cheques were an insult. Aunt Dottie insisted that his upbringing had cost her more than his father had left in insurance, and maybe it had, but did she have to keep rubbing it in his face? Did anybody human keep rubbing a thing like that in a child's face? Lots of aunts and even strangers raised a child for nothing and were delighted to do it.

After his letter to Aunt Dottie, he got up and strode around the deck, walking it off. Writing her always made him feel angry. He resented the courtesy to her. Yet until now he had always wanted her to know where he was, because he had always needed her piddling cheques. He had had to write a score of letters about his changes of address to Aunt Dottie. But he didn't need her money now. He would hold himself independent of it, forever.

He thought suddenly of one summer day when he had been about twelve, when he had been on a cross-country trip with Aunt Dottie and a woman friend of hers, and they had got stuck in a bumper-to-bumper traffic jam somewhere. It had been a hot summer day, and Aunt Dottie had sent him out with the thermos to get some ice water at a filling station, and suddenly the traffic had started moving. He remembered running between huge, inching cars, always about to touch the door of Aunt Dottie's car and never being quite able to, because she had kept inching along as fast as she could go, not willing to wait for him a minute, and yelling, 'Come on, come on, slowpoke!' out the window all the time. When he had finally made it to the car and got in, with tears of frustration and anger running down his cheeks, she had said gaily to her friend, 'Sissy! He's a sissy from the ground up. Just like his father!' It was a wonder he had emerged from such treatment as well as he had. And just what, he wondered, made Aunt Dottie think his father had been a sissy? Could she, had she, ever cited a single thing? No.

Lying in his deck-chair, fortified morally by the luxurious surroundings and inwardly by the abundance of well-prepared food, he tried to take an objective look at his past life. The last four years had been for the most part a waste, there was no denying that. A series of haphazard jobs, long perilous intervals with no job at all and consequent demoralization because of having no money, and then taking up with stupid, silly people in order not to be lonely, or because they could offer him something for a while, as Marc Priminger had. It was not a record to be proud of, considering he had come to New York with such high aspirations. He had wanted to be an actor, though at twenty he had not had the faintest idea of the difficulties, the necessary training, or even the necessary talent. He had thought he had the necessary talent and that all he would have to do was show a producer a few of his original one-man skits – Mrs. Roosevelt writing 'My Day' after a visit to a clinic for unmarried mothers for instance – but his first three rebuffs had killed all his courage and his hope. He had had no reserve of money, so he had taken the job on the banana boat, which at least had removed him from New York. He had been afraid that Aunt Dottie had called the police to look for him in New York, though he hadn't done anything wrong in Boston, just run off to make his own way in the world as millions of young men had done before him.

His main mistake had been that he had never stuck to anything, he thought, like the accounting job in the department store that might have worked into something, if he had not been so completely discouraged by the slowness of department-store promotions. Well, he blamed Aunt Dottie to some extent for his lack of perseverance, never giving him credit when he was younger for anything he had stuck to – like his paper route when he was thirteen. He had won a silver medal from the newspaper for 'Courtesy, Service, and Reliability'. It was like looking back at another person to remember himself then, a skinny, snivelling wretch with an eternal cold in the nose, who had still managed to win a medal for courtesy, service, and reliability. Aunt Dottie had hated him when he had a cold; she used to take her handkerchief and nearly wrench his nose off, wiping it.

Tom writhed in his deck-chair as he thought of it, but he writhed elegantly, adjusting the crease of his trousers.

He remembered the vows he had made, even at the age of eight, to run away from Aunt Dottie, the violent scenes he had imagined – Aunt Dottie trying to hold him in the house, and he hitting her with his fists, flinging her to the ground and throttling her, and finally tearing the big brooch off her dress and stabbing her a million times in the throat with it. He had run away at seventeen and had been brought back, and he had done it again at twenty and succeeded. And it was astounding and pitiful how naïve he had been, how little he had known about the way the world worked, as if he had spent so much of his time hating Aunt Dottie and scheming how to escape her, that he had not had enough time to learn and grow. He remembered the way he had felt when he had been fired from the warehouse job during his first month in New York. He had held the job less than two weeks, because he hadn't been strong enough to lift orange crates eight hours a day, but he had done his best and knocked himself out trying to hold the job, and when they had fired him, he remembered how horribly unjust he had thought it. He remembered deciding then that the world was full of Simon Legrees, and that you had to be an animal, as tough as the gorillas who worked with him at the warehouse, or starve. He remembered that right after that, he had stolen a loaf of bread from a delicatessen counter and had taken it home and devoured it, feeling that the world owed a loaf of bread to him, and more.

'Mr. Ripley?' One of the Englishwomen who had sat on the sofa with him in the lounge the other day during tea was bending over him. 'We were wondering if you'd care to join us in a rubber of bridge in the game room? We're going to start in about fifteen minutes.'

Tom sat up politely in his chair. 'Thank you very much, but I think I prefer to stay outside. Besides, I'm not too good at bridge.'

'Oh, neither are we! All right, another time.' She smiled and went away.

Tom sank back in his chair again, pulled his cap down over his eyes and folded his hands over his waist. His aloofness, he knew, was causing a little comment among the passengers. He had not danced with either of the silly girls who kept looking at him hopefully and giggling during the after-dinner dancing every night. He imagined the speculations of the passengers: Is he an American! I *think* so, but he doesn't act like an American, does he? Most Americans are so *noisy*. He's terribly serious, isn't he, and he can't be more than twenty-three. He must have something very important on his mind.

Yes, he had. The present and the future of Tom Ripley.

7

PARIS WAS NO more than a glimpse out of a railroad station window of a lighted café front, complete with rain-streaked awning, sidewalk tables, and boxes of hedges, like a tourist poster illustration, and otherwise a series of long station platforms down which he followed dumpy little blue-clad porters with his luggage, and at last the sleeper that would take him all the way to Rome. He could come back to Paris at some other time, he thought. He was eager to get to Mongibello.

When he woke up the next morning, he was in Italy. Something very pleasant happened that morning. Tom was watching the landscape out of the window, when he heard some Italians in the corridor outside his compartment say something with the word 'Pisa' in it. A city was gliding by on the other side of the train. Tom went into the corridor to get a better look at it, looking automatically for the Leaning Tower, though he was not at all sure that the city was Pisa or that the tower would even be visible from here, but there it was! — a thick white column sticking up out of the low chalky houses that formed the rest of the town, and *leaning*, leaning at an angle that he wouldn't have thought possible! He had always taken it for granted that the leaning of the Leaning Tower of Pisa was exaggerated. It seemed to him a good omen, a sign that Italy was going to be everything that he expected, and that everything would go well with him and Dickie.

He arrived in Naples late that afternoon, and there was no bus to Mongibello until tomorrow morning at eleven. A boy of about sixteen in dirty shirt and trousers and G.I. shoes latched on to him at the railroad station when he was changing some money, offering him God knew what, maybe girls, maybe dope, and in spite of Tom's protestations actually got into the taxi with him and instructed the driver where to go, jabbering on and holding a finger up as if he was going to fix him up fine, wait and see. Tom gave up and sulked in a corner with his arms folded, and finally the taxi stopped in front of a big hotel that faced the bay. Tom would have been afraid of the imposing hotel if Mr. Greenleaf had not been paying the bill.

'Santa Lucia!' the boy said triumphantly, pointing seaward.

Tom nodded. After all, the boy seemed to mean well. Tom paid the driver and gave the boy a hundred-lire bill, which he estimated to be sixteen and a fraction cents and appropriate as a tip in Italy, according to an article on Italy he had read on the ship, and when the boy looked outraged, gave him another hundred, and when he still looked outraged, waved a hand at him and went into the hotel behind the bellboys who had already gathered up his luggage.

Tom had dinner that evening at a restaurant down on the water called Zi' Teresa, which had been recommended to him by the English-speaking manager of the hotel. He had a difficult time ordering, and he found himself with a first course of miniature octopuses, as virulently purple as if they had been cooked in the ink in which the menu had been written. He tasted the tip of one tentacle, and it had a disgusting consistency like cartilage. The second course was also a mistake, a platter of fried fish of various kinds. The third course – which he had been sure was a kind of dessert – was a couple of small reddish fish. Ah, Naples! The food didn't matter. He was feeling mellow on the wine. Far over on his left, a three-quarter moon drifted above the jagged hump of Mount Vesuvius. Tom gazed at it calmly, as if he had seen it a thousand times before. Around the corner of land there, beyond Vesuvius, lay Richard's village.

He boarded the bus the next morning at eleven. The road followed the shore and went through little towns where they made brief stops – Torre del Greco, Torre Annunciata, Castellammare, Sorrento. Tom listened eagerly to the names of the towns that the driver called out. From Sorrento, the road was a narrow ridge cut into the side of the rock cliffs that Tom had seen in the photographs at the Greenleafs'. Now and then he caught glimpses of little villages down at the water's edge, houses like white crumbs of bread, specks that were the heads of people swimming near the shore. Tom saw a boulder-sized rock in the middle of the road that had evidently broken off a cliff. The driver dodged it with a nonchalant swerve.

'*Mongibello!*'

Tom sprang up and yanked his suitcase down from the rack. He had another suitcase on the roof, which the bus boy took down for him. Then the bus went on, and Tom was alone at the side of the road, his suitcases at his feet. There were houses above him, straggling up the mountain, and houses below, their tile roofs silhouetted against the blue sea. Keeping an eye on his suitcases, Tom went into a little house across the road marked POSTA, and inquired of the man behind the window where Richard Greenleaf's house was. Without thinking, he spoke in English, but the man seemed to understand, because he came out and pointed from the door up the road Tom had come on the bus, and gave in Italian what seemed to be explicit directions how to get there.

'Sempre seeneestra, seeneestra!'

Tom thanked him, and asked if he could leave his two suitcases in the post office for a while, and the man seemed to understand this, too, and helped Tom carry them into the post office.

He had to ask two more people where Richard Greenleaf's house was, but everybody seemed to know it, and the third person was able to point it out to him – a large two-storey house with an iron gate on the road, and a terrace that projected over the cliff's edge. Tom rang the metal bell beside the gate. An Italian woman came out of the house, wiping her hands on her apron.

'Mr. Greenleaf?' Tom asked hopefully.

The woman gave him a long, smiling answer in Italian and pointed downward toward the sea. 'Jew,' she seemed to keep saying, 'Jew.'

Tom nodded. 'Grazie.'

Should he go down to the beach as he was, or be more casual about it and get into a bathing suit? Or should he wait until the tea or cocktail hour? Or should he try to telephone him first? He hadn't brought a bathing suit with him, and he'd certainly have to have one here. Tom went into one of the little shops near the post office that had shirts and bathing shorts in its tiny front window, and after trying on several pairs of shorts that did not fit him, or at least not adequately enough to serve as a bathing suit, he bought a black-and-yellow thing hardly bigger than a G-string. He made a neat bundle of his clothing inside his raincoat, and started out of the door barefoot. He leapt back inside. The cobblestones were hot as coals.

'Shoes? Sandals?' he asked the man in the shop.

The man didn't sell shoes.

Tom put on his own shoes again and walked across the road to the post office, intending to leave his clothes with his suitcases, but the post office door was locked. He had heard of this in Europe, places closing from noon to four sometimes. He turned and walked down a cobbled lane which he supposed led toward the beach. He went down a dozen steep stone steps, down another cobbled slope past shops and houses, down more steps, and finally he came to a level length of broad sidewalk slightly raised from the beach, where there were a couple of cafés and a restaurant with outdoor tables. Some bronzed adolescent Italian boys sitting on wooden benches at the edge of the pavement inspected him thoroughly as he walked by. He felt mortified at the big brown shoes on his feet and at his ghost-white skin. He had not been to a beach all summer. He hated beaches. There was a wooden walk that led half across the beach, which Tom knew must be hot as hell to walk on, because everybody was lying on a towel or something else, but he took his shoes off anyway and stood for a moment on the hot wood, calmly surveying the groups of people near him. None of the people looked like Richard, and the shimmering heat waves kept him from making out the people very far away. Tom put one foot out on the sand and drew it back. Then he took a deep breath, raced down the rest of the walk, sprinted across the sand, and sank his feet into the blissfully cool inches of water at the sea's edge. He began to walk.

Tom saw him from a distance of about a block – unmistakably Dickie, though he was burnt a dark brown and his crinkly blond hair looked lighter than Tom remembered it. He was with Marge.

'Dickie Greenleaf?' Tom asked, smiling.

Dickie looked up. 'Yes?'

'I'm Tom Ripley. I met you in the States several years ago. Remember?' Dickie looked blank.

'I think your father said he was going to write you about me.'

'Oh, yes!' Dickie said, touching his forehead as if it was stupid of him to have forgotten. He stood up. 'Tom *what* is it?'

'Ripley.'

'This is Marge Sherwood,' he said. 'Marge, Tom Ripley.'

'How do you do?' Tom said.

'How do you do?'

'How long are you here for?' Dickie asked.

'I don't know yet,' Tom said. 'I just got here. I'll have to look the place over.'

Dickie was looking him over, not entirely with approval, Tom felt. Dickie's arms were folded, his lean brown feet planted in the hot sand that didn't seem to bother him at all. Tom had crushed his feet into his shoes again.

'Taking a house?' asked Dickie.

'I don't know,' Tom said undecidedly, as if he had been considering it.

'It's a good time to get a house, if you're looking for one for the winter,' the girl said. 'The summer tourists have practically all gone. We could use a few more Americans around here in winter.'

Dickie said nothing. He had reseated himself on the big towel beside the girl, and Tom felt that he was waiting for him to say good-bye and move on. Tom stood there, feeling pale and naked as the day he was born. He hated bathing suits. This one was very revealing. Tom managed to extract his pack of cigarettes from his jacket inside the raincoat, and offered it to Dickie and the girl. Dickie accepted one, and Tom lighted it with his lighter.

'You don't seem to remember me from New York,' Tom said.

'I can't really say I do,' Dickie said. 'Where did I meet you?'

'I think— Wasn't it at Buddy Lankenau's?' It wasn't, but he knew Dickie knew Buddy Lankenau, and Buddy was a very respectable fellow.

'Oh,' said Dickie, vaguely. 'I hope you'll excuse me. My memory's rotten for America these days.'

'It certainly is,' Marge said, coming to Tom's rescue. 'It's getting worse and worse. When did you get here, Tom?'

'Just about an hour ago. I've just parked my suitcases at the post office.' He laughed.

'Don't you want to sit down? Here's another towel.' She spread a smaller white towel beside her on the sand.

Tom accepted it gratefully.

'I'm going in for a dip to cool off,' Dickie said, getting up.

'Me too!' Marge said. 'Coming in, Tom?'

Tom followed them. Dickie and the girl went out quite far – both seemed to be excellent swimmers – and Tom stayed near the shore and came in much sooner. When Dickie and the girl came back to the towels, Dickie said, as if he had been prompted by the girl, 'We're leaving. Would you like to come up to the house and have lunch with us?'

'Why, yes. Thanks very much.' Tom helped them gather up the towels, the sunglasses, the Italian newspapers.

Tom thought they would never get there. Dickie and Marge went in front of him, taking the endless flights of stone steps slowly and steadily, two at a time. The sun had enervated Tom. The muscles of his legs trembled on the level stretches. His shoulders were already pink, and he had put on his shirt against the sun's rays, but he could feel the sun burning through his hair, making him dizzy and nauseous.

'Having a hard time?' Marge asked, not out of breath at all. 'You'll get used to it, if you stay here. You should have seen this place during the heat wave in July.'

Tom hadn't breath to reply anything.

Fifteen minutes later he was feeling better. He had had a cool shower, and he was sitting in a comfortable wicker chair on Dickie's terrace with a martini in his hand. At Marge's suggestion, he had put his swimming outfit on again, with his shirt over it. The table on the terrace had been set for three while he was in the shower, and Marge was in the kitchen now, talking in Italian to the maid. Tom wondered if Marge lived here. The house was certainly big enough. It was sparsely furnished, as far as Tom could see, in a pleasant mixture of Italian antique and American bohemian. He had seen two original Picasso drawings in the hall.

Marge came out on the terrace with her martini. 'That's my house over there.' She pointed. 'See it? The square-looking white one with the darker red roof than the houses just beside it.'

It was hopeless to pick it out from the other houses, but Tom pretended he saw it. 'Have you been here long?'

'A year. All last winter, and it was quite a winter. Rain every day except one for three whole months!'

'Really!'

'Um-hm.' Marge sipped her martini and gazed out contentedly at her little village. She was back in her bathing suit, too, a tomato-coloured bathing suit, and she wore a striped shirt over it. She wasn't bad-looking, Tom supposed, and she even had a good figure, if one liked the rather solid type. Tom didn't, himself.

'I understand Dickie has a boat,' Tom said.

'Yes, the *Pipi*. Short for *Pipistrello*. Want to see it?'

She pointed at another indiscernible something down at the little pier that they could see from the corner of the terrace. The boats looked very much alike, but Marge said Dickie's boat was larger than most of them and had two masts.

Dickie came out and poured himself a cocktail from the pitcher on the table. He wore badly ironed white duck trousers and a terra cotta linen shirt the colour of his skin. 'Sorry there's no ice. I haven't got a refrigerator.'

Tom smiled. 'I brought a bathrobe for you. Your mother said you'd asked for one. Also some socks.'

'Do you know my mother?'

'I happened to meet your father just before I left New York, and he asked me to dinner at his house.'

'Oh? How was my mother?'

'She was up and around that evening. I'd say she gets tired easily.'

Dickie nodded. 'I had a letter this week saying she was a little better. At least there's no particular crisis right now, is there?'

'I don't think so. I think your father was more worried a few weeks ago.' Tom hesitated. 'He's also a little worried because you won't come home.'

'Herbert's always worried about something,' Dickie said.

Marge and the maid came out of the kitchen carrying a steaming platter of spaghetti, a big bowl of salad, and a plate of bread. Dickie and Marge began to talk about the enlargement of some restaurant down on the beach. The proprietor was widening the terrace so there would be room for people to dance. They discussed it in detail, slowly, like people in a small town who take an interest in the most minute changes in the neighbourhood. There was nothing Tom could contribute.

He spent the time examining Dickie's rings. He liked them both: a large rectangular green stone set in gold on the third finger of his right hand, and on the little finger of the other hand a signet ring, larger and more ornate than the signet Mr. Greenleaf had worn. Dickie had long, bony hands, a little like his own hands, Tom thought.

'By the way, your father showed me around the Burke-Greenleaf yards before I left,' Tom said. 'He told me he'd made a lot of changes since you've seen it last. I was quite impressed.'

'I suppose he offered you a job, too. Always on the lookout for promising young men.' Dickie turned his fork round and round, and thrust a neat mass of spaghetti into his mouth.

'No, he didn't.' Tom felt the luncheon couldn't have been going worse. Had Mr. Greenleaf told Dickie that he was coming to give him a lecture on why he should go home? Or was Dickie just in a foul mood? Dickie had certainly changed since Tom had seen him last.

Dickie brought out a shiny espresso machine about two feet high, and plugged it into an outlet on the terrace. In a few moments there were four little cups of coffee, one of which Marge took into the kitchen to the maid.

'What hotel are you staying at?' Marge asked Tom.

Tom smiled. 'I haven't found one yet. What do you recommend?'

'The Miramare's the best. It's just this side of Giorgio's. The only other hotel is Giorgio's, but—'

'They say Giorgio's got pulci in his beds,' Dickie interrupted.

'That's fleas. Giorgio's is cheap,' Marge said earnestly, 'but the service is—'

'Non-existent,' Dickie supplied.

'You're in a fine mood today, aren't you?' Marge said to Dickie, flicking a crumb of gorgonzola at him.

'In that case, I'll try the Miramare,' Tom said, standing up. 'I must be going.'

Neither of them urged him to stay. Dickie walked with him to the front gate. Marge was staying on. Tom wondered if Dickie and Marge were having an affair, one of those old, faute de mieux affairs that wouldn't necessarily be obvious from the outside, because neither was very enthusiastic. Marge was in love with Dickie, Tom thought, but Dickie couldn't have been more indifferent to her if she had been the fifty-year-old Italian maid sitting there.

'I'd like to see some of your paintings sometime,' Tom said to Dickie.

'Fine. Well, I suppose we'll see you again if you're around,' and Tom thought he added it only because he remembered that he had brought him the bathrobe and the socks.

'I enjoyed the lunch. Good-bye, Dickie.'

'Good-bye.'

The iron gate clanged.

8

TOM TOOK A room at the Miramare. It was four o'clock by the time he got his suitcases up from the post office, and he had barely the energy to hang up his best suit before he fell down on the bed. The voices of some Italian boys who were talking under his window drifted up as distinctly as if they had been in the room with him, and the insolent, cackling laugh of one of them, bursting again and again through the pattering syllables, made Tom twitch and writhe. He imagined them discussing his expedition to Signor Greenleaf, and making unflattering speculations as to what might happen next.

What was he doing here? He had no friends here and he didn't speak the language. Suppose he got sick? Who would take care of him?

Tom got up, knowing he was going to be sick, yet moving slowly because he knew just when he was going to be sick and that there would be time for him to get to the bathroom. In the bathroom he lost his lunch, and also the fish from Naples, he thought. He went back to his bed and fell instantly asleep.

When he awoke groggy and weak, the sun was still shining and it was five-thirty by his new watch. He went to a window and looked out, looking automatically for Dickie's big house and projecting terrace among the pink and white houses that dotted the climbing ground in front of him. He found the sturdy reddish balustrade of the terrace. Was Marge still there? Were they talking about him? He heard a laugh rising over the little din of street noises, tense and resonant, and as American as if it had been a sentence in

American. For an instant he saw Dickie and Marge as they crossed a space between houses on the main road. They turned the corner, and Tom went to his side window for a better view. There was an alley by the side of the hotel just below his window, and Dickie and Marge came down it, Dickie in the white trousers and terra cotta shirt, Marge in a skirt and blouse. She must have gone home, Tom thought. Or else she had clothes at Dickie's house. Dickie talked with an Italian on the little wooden pier, gave him some money, and the Italian touched his cap, then untied the boat from the pier. Tom watched Dickie help Marge into the boat. The white sail began to climb. Behind them, to the left, the orange sun was sinking into the water. Tom could hear Marge's laugh, and a shout from Dickie in Italian toward the pier. Tom realized he was seeing them on a typical day – a siesta after the late lunch, probably, then the sail in Dickie's boat at sundown. Then apéritifs at one of the cafés on the beach. They were enjoying a perfectly ordinary day, as if he did not exist. Why should Dickie want to come back to subways and taxis and starched collars and a nine-to-five job? Or even a chauffeured car and vacations in Florida and Maine? It wasn't as much fun as sailing a boat in old clothes and being answerable to nobody for the way he spent his time, and having his own house with a good-natured maid who probably took care of everything for him. And money besides to take trips, if he wanted to. Tom envied him with a heartbreaking surge of envy and of self-pity.

Dickie's father had probably said in his letter the very things that would set Dickie against him, Tom thought. How much better it would have been if he had just sat down in one of the cafés down at the beach and struck up an acquaintance with Dickie out of the blue! He probably could have persuaded Dickie to come home eventually, if he had begun like that, but this way it was useless. Tom cursed himself for having been so heavy-handed and so humourless today.

Nothing he took desperately seriously ever worked out. He'd found that out years ago.

He'd let a few days go by, he thought. The first step, anyway, was to make Dickie like him. That he wanted more than anything else in the world.

9

TOM LET THREE days go by. Then he went down to the beach on the fourth morning around noon, and found Dickie alone, in the same spot Tom had seen him first, in front of the grey rocks that extended across the beach from the land.

'Morning!' Tom called. 'Where's Marge?'

'Good morning. She's probably working a little late. She'll be down.'

'Working?'

'She's a writer.'

'Oh.'

Dickie puffed on the Italian cigarette in the corner of his mouth. 'Where've you been keeping yourself? I thought you'd gone.'

'Sick,' Tom said casually, tossing his rolled towel down on the sand, but not too near Dickie's towel.

'Oh, the usual upset stomach?'

'Hovering between life and the bathroom,' Tom said, smiling. 'But I'm all right now.' He actually had been too weak even to leave the hotel, but he had crawled around on the floor of his room, following the patches of sunlight that came through his windows, so that he wouldn't look so white the next time he came down to the beach. And he had spent the remainder of his feeble strength studying an Italian conversation book that he had bought in the hotel lobby.

Tom went down to the water, went confidently up to his waist and stopped there, splashing the water over his shoulders. He lowered himself until the water reached his chin, floated around a little, then came slowly in.

'Can I invite you for a drink at the hotel before you go up to your house?' Tom asked Dickie. 'And Marge, too, if she comes. I wanted to give you your bathrobe and socks, you know.'

'Oh, yes. Thanks very much, I'd like to have a drink.' He went back to his Italian newspaper.

Tom stretched out on his towel. He heard the village clock strike one.

'Doesn't look as if Marge is coming down,' Dickie said. 'I think I'll be going along.'

Tom got up. They walked up to the Miramare, saying practically nothing to each other, except that Tom invited Dickie to lunch with him, and Dickie declined because the maid had his lunch ready at the house, he said. They went up to Tom's room, and Dickie tried the bathrobe on and held the socks up to his bare feet. Both the bathrobe and the socks were the right size, and, as Tom had anticipated, Dickie was extremely pleased with the bathrobe.

'And this,' Tom said, taking a square package wrapped in drugstore paper from a bureau drawer. 'Your mother sent you some nosedrops, too.'

Dickie smiled. 'I don't need them any more. That was sinus. But I'll take them off your hands.'

Now Dickie had everything, Tom thought, everything he had to offer. He was going to refuse the invitation for a drink, too, Tom knew. Tom followed him toward the door. 'You know, your father's very concerned about your coming home. He asked me to give you a good talking to, which of course I won't, but I'll still have to tell him something. I promised to write him.'

Dickie turned with his hand on the doorknob. 'I don't know what my father thinks I'm doing over here – drinking myself to death or what. I'll probably fly home this winter for a few days, but I don't intend to stay over there. I'm happier here. If I went back there to live, my father would be after me to work in Burke-Greenleaf. I couldn't possibly paint. I happen to like painting, and I think it's my business how I spend my life.'

'I understand. But he said he wouldn't try to make you work in his firm if you come back, unless you wanted to work in the designing department, and he said you liked that.'

'Well – my father and I have been over that. Thanks, anyway, Tom, for delivering the message and the clothes. It was very nice of you.' Dickie held out his hand.

Tom couldn't have made himself take the hand. This was the very edge of failure, failure as far as Mr. Greenleaf was concerned, and failure with Dickie. 'I think I ought to tell you something else,' Tom said with a smile. 'Your father sent me over here especially to ask you to come home.'

'What do you mean?' Dickie frowned. 'Paid your way?'

'Yes.' It was his one last chance to amuse Dickie or to repel him, to make Dickie burst out laughing or go out and slam the door in disgust. But the smile was coming, the long corners of his mouth going up, the way Tom remembered Dickie's smile.

'Paid your way! What do you know! He's getting desperate, isn't he?' Dickie closed the door again.

'He approached me in a bar in New York,' Tom said. 'I told him I wasn't a close friend of yours, but he insisted I could help if I came over. I told him I'd try.'

'How did he ever meet you?'

'Through the Schrievers. I hardly know the Schrievers, but there it was! I was your friend and I could do you a lot of good.'

They laughed.

'I don't want you to think I'm someone who tried to take advantage of your father,' Tom said. 'I expect to find a job somewhere in Europe soon, and I'll be able to pay him back my passage money eventually. He bought me a round-trip ticket.'

'Oh, don't bother! It goes on the Burke-Greenleaf expense list. I can just see Dad approaching you in a bar! Which bar was it?'

'Raoul's. Matter of fact, he followed me from the Green Cage.' Tom watched Dickie's face for a sign of recognition of the Green Cage, a very popular bar, but there was no recognition.

They had a drink downstairs in the hotel bar. They drank to Herbert Richard Greenleaf.

'I just realized today's Sunday,' Dickie said. 'Marge went to church. You'd better come up and have lunch with us. We always have chicken on Sunday. You know it's an old American custom, chicken on Sunday.'

Dickie wanted to go by Marge's house to see if she was still there. They climbed some steps from the main road up the side of a stone wall, crossed part of somebody's garden, and climbed more steps. Marge's house was a rather sloppy-looking one-storey affair with a messy garden at one end, a couple of buckets and a garden hose cluttering the path to the door, and the feminine touch represented by her tomato-coloured bathing suit and a bra hanging over a window-sill. Through an open window, Tom had a glimpse of a disorderly table with a typewriter on it.

'Hi!' she said, opening the door. 'Hello, Tom! Where've you been all this time?'

She offered them a drink, but discovered there was only half an inch of gin in her bottle of Gilbey's.

'It doesn't matter, we're going to my house,' Dickie said. He strolled around Marge's bedroom–living-room with an air of familiarity, as if he lived half the time here himself. He bent over a flower pot in which a tiny plant of some sort was growing, and touched its leaf delicately with his forefinger. 'Tom has something funny to tell you,' he said. 'Tell her, Tom.'

Tom took a breath and began. He made it very funny, and Marge laughed like someone who hadn't had anything funny to laugh at in years. 'When I saw him coming in Raoul's after me, I was ready to climb out of a back window!' His tongue rattled on almost independently of his brain. His brain was estimating how high his stock was shooting up with Dickie and Marge. He could see it in their faces.

The climb up the hill to Dickie's house didn't seem half so long as before. Delicious smells of roasting chicken drifted out on the terrace. Dickie made some martinis. Tom showered and then Dickie showered, and came out and poured himself a drink, just like the first time, but the atmosphere now was totally changed.

Dickie sat down in a wicker chair and swung his legs over one of the arms. 'Tell me more,' he said, smiling. 'What kind of work do you do? You said you might take a job.'

'Why? Do you have a job for me?'

'Can't say that I have.'

'Oh, I can do a number of things – valeting, baby-sitting, accounting – I've got an unfortunate talent for figures. No matter how drunk I get, I can always tell when a waiter's cheating me on a bill. I can forge a signature, fly a helicopter, handle dice, impersonate practically anybody, cook – and do a one-man show in a nightclub in case the regular entertainer's sick. Shall I go on?' Tom was leaning forward, counting them off on his fingers. He could have gone on.

'What kind of a one-man show?' Dickie asked.

'Well—' Tom sprang up. 'This for example.' He struck a pose with one hand on his hip, one foot extended. 'This is Lady Assburden sampling the American subway. She's never even been in the underground in London, but she wants to take back some American experiences.' Tom did it all in pantomime, searching for a coin, finding it didn't go into the slot, buying a token, puzzling over which stairs to go down, registering alarm at the noise and the long express ride, puzzling again as to how to get out of the place – here Marge came out, and Dickie told her it was an Englishwoman in the subway, but Marge didn't seem to get it and asked, 'What?' – walking through a door which could only be the door of the men's room from her twitching horror of this and that, which augmented until she fainted. Tom fainted gracefully on to the terrace glider.

'Wonderful!' Dickie yelled, clapping.

Marge wasn't laughing. She stood there looking a little blank. Neither of them bothered to explain it to her. She didn't look as if she had that kind of sense of humour, anyway, Tom thought.

Tom took a gulp of his martini, terribly pleased with himself. 'I'll do another for you sometime,' he said to Marge, but mostly to indicate to Dickie that he had another one to do.

'Dinner ready?' Dickie asked her. 'I'm starving.'

'I'm waiting for the darned artichokes to get done. You know that front hole. It'll barely make anything come to a boil.' She smiled at Tom. 'Dickie's very old-fashioned about some things, Tom, the things *he* doesn't have to fool with. There's still only a wood stove here, and he refuses to buy a refrigerator or even an icebox.'

'One of the reasons I fled America,' Dickie said. 'Those things are a waste of money in a country with so many servants. What'd Ermelinda do with herself, if she could cook a meal in half an hour?' He stood up. 'Come on in, Tom, I'll show you some of my paintings.'

Dickie led the way into the big room Tom had looked into a couple of times on his way to and from the shower, the room with a long couch under the two windows and the big easel in the middle of the floor. 'This is one of Marge I'm working on now.' He gestured to the picture on the easel.

'Oh,' Tom said with interest. It wasn't good in his opinion, probably in anybody's opinion. The wild enthusiasm of her smile was a bit off. Her skin was as red as an Indian's. If Marge hadn't been the only girl around with blonde hair, he wouldn't have noticed any resemblance at all.

'And these – a lot of landscapes,' Dickie said with a deprecatory laugh, though obviously he wanted Tom to say something complimentary about them, because obviously he was proud of them. They were all wild and hasty and monotonously similar. The combination of terra cotta and electric blue was in nearly every one, terra cotta roofs and mountains and bright electric-blue seas. It was the blue he had put in Marge's eyes, too.

'My surrealist effort,' Dickie said, bracing another canvas against his knee.

Tom winced with almost a personal shame. It was Marge again, undoubtedly, though with long snakelike hair, and worst of all two horizons in her eyes, with a miniature landscape of Mongibello's houses and mountains in one eye, and the beach in the other full of little red people. 'Yes, I like that,' Tom said. Mr. Greenleaf had been right. Yet it gave Dickie something to do, kept him out of trouble, Tom supposed, just as it gave thousands of lousy amateur painters all over America something to do. He was only sorry that Dickie fell into this category as a painter, because he wanted Dickie to be much more.

'I won't ever set the world on fire as a painter,' Dickie said, 'but I get a great deal of pleasure out of it.'

'Yes.' Tom wanted to forget all about the paintings and forget that Dickie painted. 'Can I see the rest of the house?'

'Absolutely! You haven't seen the salon, have you?'

Dickie opened a door in the hall that led into a very large room with a fireplace, sofas, bookshelves, and three exposures — to the terrace, to the land on the other side of the house, and to the front garden. Dickie said that in summer he did not use the room, because he liked to save it as a change of scene for the winter. It was more of a bookish den than a living-room, Tom thought. It surprised him. He had Dickie figured out as a young man who was not particularly brainy, and who probably spent most of his time playing. Perhaps he was wrong. But he didn't think he was wrong in feeling that Dickie was bored at the moment and needed someone to show him how to have fun.

'What's upstairs?' Tom asked.

The upstairs was disappointing: Dickie's bedroom in the corner of the house above the terrace was stark and empty – a bed, a chest of drawers, and a rocking chair, looking lost and unrelated in all the space – a narrow bed, too, hardly wider than a single bed. The other three rooms of the second floor were not even furnished, or at least not completely. One of them held only firewood and a pile of canvas scraps. There was certainly no sign of Marge anywhere, least of all in Dickie's bedroom.

'How about going to Naples with me sometime?' Tom asked. 'I didn't have much of a chance to see it on my way down.'

'All right,' Dickie said. 'Marge and I are going Saturday afternoon. We have dinner there nearly every Saturday night and treat ourselves to a taxi or a carrozza ride back. Come along.'

'I meant in the daytime or some weekday so I could see a little more,' Tom said, hoping to avoid Marge in the excursion. 'Or do you paint all day?'

'No. There's a twelve o'clock bus Mondays, Wednesdays, and Fridays. I suppose we could go tomorrow, if you feel like it.'

'Fine,' Tom said, though he still wasn't sure that Marge wouldn't be asked along. 'Marge is a Catholic?' he asked as they went down the stairs.

'With a vengeance! She was converted about six months ago by an Italian she had a mad crush on. Could that man talk! He was here for a few months, resting up after a ski accident. Marge consoles herself for the loss of Eduardo by embracing his religion.'

'I had the idea she was in love with you.'

'With me? Don't be silly!'

The meal was ready when they went out on the terrace. There were even hot biscuits with butter, made by Marge.

'Do you know Vic Simmons in New York?' Tom asked Dickie.

Vic had quite a salon of artists, writers, and dancers in New York, but Dickie didn't know of him. Tom asked him about two or three other people, also without success.

Tom hoped Marge would leave after the coffee, but she didn't. When she left the terrace for a moment Tom said, 'Can I invite you for dinner at my hotel tonight?'

'Thank you. At what time?'

'Seven-thirty? So we'll have a little time for cocktails? – After all, it's your father's money,' Tom added with a smile.

Dickie laughed. 'All right, cocktails and a good bottle of wine. Marge!' Marge was just coming back. 'We're dining tonight at the Miramare, compliments of Greenleaf père!'

So Marge was coming, too, and there was nothing Tom could do about it. After all, it was Dickie's father's money.

The dinner that evening was pleasant, but Marge's presence kept Tom from talking about anything he would have liked to talk about, and he did not feel even like being witty in Marge's presence. Marge knew some of the people in the dining-room, and after dinner she excused herself and took her coffee over to another table and sat down.

'How long are you going to be here?' Dickie asked.

'Oh, at least a week, I'd say,' Tom replied.

'Because—' Dickie's face had flushed a little over the cheek-bones. The chianti had put him into a good mood. 'If you're going to be here a little longer, why don't you stay with me? There's no use staying in a hotel, unless you really prefer it.'

'Thank you very much,' Tom said.

'There's a bed in the maid's room, which you didn't see. Ermelinda doesn't sleep in. I'm sure we can make out with the furniture that's scattered around, if you think you'd like to.'

'I'm sure I'd like to. By the way, your father gave me six hundred dollars for expenses, and I've still got about five hundred of it. I think we both ought to have a little fun on it, don't you?'

'Five hundred!' Dickie said, as if he'd never seen that much money in one lump in his life. 'We could pick up a little car for that!'

Tom didn't contribute to the car idea. That wasn't his idea of having fun. He wanted to fly to Paris. Marge was coming back, he saw.

The next morning he moved in.

Dickie and Ermelinda had installed an armoire and a couple of chairs in one of the upstairs rooms, and Dickie had thumb-tacked a few reproductions of mosaic portraits from St. Mark's Cathedral on the walls. Tom helped Dickie carry up the narrow iron bed from the maid's room. They were finished before twelve, a little lightheaded from the frascati they had been sipping as they worked.

'Are we still going to Naples?' Tom asked.

'Certainly.' Dickie looked at his watch. 'It's only a quarter to twelve. We can make the twelve o'clock bus.'

They took nothing with them but their jackets and Tom's book of traveller's cheques. The bus was just arriving as they reached the post office. Tom and Dickie stood by the door, waiting for people to get off; then Dickie pulled himself up, right into the face of a young man with red hair and a loud sports shirt, an American.

'Dickie!'

'Freddie!' Dickie yelled. 'What're you doing here?'

'Came to see you! And the Cecchis. They're putting me up for a few days.'

'Ch'elegante! I'm off to Naples with a friend. Tom?' Dickie beckoned Tom over and introduced them.

The American's name was Freddie Miles. Tom thought he was hideous. Tom hated red hair, especially this kind of carrot-red hair with white skin and freckles. Freddie had large red-brown eyes that seemed to wobble in his head as if he were cockeyed, or perhaps he was only one of those people who never looked at anyone they were talking to. He was also overweight. Tom turned away from him, waiting for Dickie to finish his conversation. They were holding up the bus, Tom noticed. Dickie and Freddie were talking about skiing, making a date for some time in December in a town Tom had never heard of.

'There'll be about fifteen of us at Cortina by the second,' Freddie said. 'A real bang-up party like last year! Three weeks, if our money holds out!'

'If we hold out!' Dickie said. 'See you tonight, Fred!'

Tom boarded the bus after Dickie. There were no seats, and they were wedged between a skinny, sweating man who smelled, and a couple of old peasant women who smelled worse. Just as they were leaving the village Dickie remembered that Marge was coming for lunch as usual, because they had thought yesterday that Tom's moving would cancel the Naples trip. Dickie shouted for the driver to stop. The bus stopped with a squeal of brakes and a lurch that threw everybody who was standing off balance, and Dickie put his head through a window and called, 'Gino! Gino!'

A little boy on the road came running up to take the hundred-lire bill that Dickie was holding out to him. Dickie said something in Italian, and the boy said, 'Subito, signor!' and flew up the road, Dickie thanked the driver, and the bus started again. 'I told him to tell Marge we'd be back tonight, but probably late,' Dickie said.

'Good.'

The bus spilled them into a big, cluttered square in Naples, and they were suddenly surrounded by push-carts of grapes, figs, pastry, and water-melon, and screamed at by adolescent boys with fountain pens and mechanical toys. The people made way for Dickie.

'I know a good place for lunch,' Dickie said. 'A real Neapolitan pizzeria. Do you like pizza?'

'Yes.'

The pizzeria was up a street too narrow and steep for cars.

Strings of beads hanging in the doorway, a decanter of wine on every table, and there were only six tables in the whole place, the kind of place you could sit in for hours and drink wine and not be disturbed. They sat there until five o'clock, when Dickie said it was time to move on to the Galleria. Dickie apologized for not taking him to the art museum, which had original da Vincis and El Grecos, he said, but they could see that at another time. Dickie had spent most of the afternoon talking about Freddie Miles, and Tom had found it as uninteresting as Freddie's face. Freddie was the son of an American hotel-chain owner, and a playwright — self-styled, Tom gathered, because he had written only two plays, and neither had seen Broadway. Freddie had a house in Cagnes-sur-Mer, and Dickie had stayed with him several weeks before he came to Italy.

'This is what I like,' Dickie said expansively in the Galleria, 'sitting at a table and watching the people go by. It does something to your outlook on life. The Anglo-Saxons make a great mistake not staring at people from a sidewalk table.'

Tom nodded. He had heard it before. He was waiting for something profound and original from Dickie. Dickie was handsome. He looked unusual with his long, finely cut face, his quick, intelligent eyes, the proud way he carried himself regardless of what he was wearing. He was wearing broken-down sandals and rather soiled white pants now, but he sat there as if he owned the Galleria, chatting in Italian with the waiter when he brought their espressos.

'Ciao!' he called to an Italian boy who was passing by.

'Ciao, Dickie!'

'He changes Marge's traveller's cheques on Saturdays,' Dickie explained to Tom.

A well-dressed Italian greeted Dickie with a warm hand-shake and sat down at the table with them. Tom listened to their conversation in Italian, making out a word here and there. Tom was beginning to feel tired.

'Want to go to Rome?' Dickie asked him suddenly.

'Sure,' Tom said. 'Now?' He stood up, reaching for money to pay the little tabs that the waiter had stuck under their coffee cups.

The Italian had a long grey Cadillac equipped with venetian blinds, a four-toned horn, and a blaring radio that he and Dickie seemed content to shout over. They reached the outskirts of Rome in about two hours. Tom sat up as they drove along the Appian Way, especially for his benefit, the Italian told Tom, because Tom had not seen it before. The road was bumpy in spots. These were stretches of original Roman brick left bare to show people how Roman roads felt, the Italian said. The flat fields to left and right looked desolate in the twilight, like an ancient graveyard, Tom thought, with just a few tombs and remains of tombs still standing. The Italian dropped them in the middle of a street in Rome and said an abrupt good-bye.

'He's in a hurry,' Dickie said. 'Got to see his girl friend and get away before the husband comes home at eleven. There's the music hall I was looking for. Come on.'

They bought tickets for the music-hall show that evening. There was still an hour before the performance, and they went to the Via Veneto, took a sidewalk table at one of the cafés, and ordered americanos. Dickie didn't know anybody in Rome, Tom noticed, or at least none who passed by, and they watched hundreds of Italians and Americans pass by their table. Tom got very little out of the music-hall show, but he tried his very best. Dickie proposed leaving before the show was over. Then they caught a carrozza and drove around the city, past fountain after fountain, through the Forum and around the Colosseum. The moon had come out. Tom was still a little sleepy, but the sleepiness, underlaid with excitement at being in Rome for the first time, put him into a receptive, mellow mood. They sat slumped in the carrozza, each with a sandalled foot propped on a knee, and it seemed to Tom that he was looking in a mirror when he looked at Dickie's leg and his propped foot beside him. They were the same height, and very much the same weight, Dickie perhaps a bit heavier, and they wore the same size bathrobe, socks, and probably shirts.

Dickie even said, 'Thank you, Mr. Greenleaf,' when Tom paid the carrozza driver. Tom felt a little weird.

They were in even finer mood by one in the morning, after a bottle and a half of wine between them at dinner. They walked with their arms around each other's shoulders, singing, and around a dark corner they somehow bumped into a girl and knocked her down. They lifted her up, apologizing, and offered to escort her home. She protested, they insisted, one on either side of her. She had to catch a certain trolley, she said. Dickie wouldn't hear of it. Dickie got a taxi. Dickie and Tom sat very properly on the jump seats with their arms folded like a couple of footmen, and Dickie talked to her and made her laugh. Tom could understand nearly everything Dickie said. They helped the girl out in a little street that looked like Naples again, and she said, 'Grazie tante!' and shook hands with both of them, then vanished into an absolutely black doorway.

'Did you hear that?' Dickie said. 'She said we were the nicest Americans she'd ever met!'

'You know what most crummy Americans would do in a case like that — rape her,' Tom said.

'Now where are we?' Dickie asked, turning completely around.

Neither had the slightest idea where they were. They walked for several blocks without finding a landmark or a familiar street name. They urinated against a dark wall, then drifted on.

'When the dawn comes up, we can see where we are,' Dickie said cheerfully. He looked at his watch. ''S only a couple more hours.'

'Fine.'

'It's worth it to see a nice girl home, isn't it?' Dickie asked, staggering a little.

'Sure it is. I like girls,' Tom said protestingly. 'But it's just as well Marge isn't here tonight. We never could have seen that girl home with Marge with us.'

'Oh, I don't know,' Dickie said thoughtfully, looking down at his weaving feet. 'Marge isn't—'

'I only mean, if Marge was here, we'd be worrying about a hotel for the night. We'd be *in* the damned hotel, probably. We wouldn't be seeing half of Rome!'

'That's right!' Dickie swung an arm around his shoulder.

Dickie shook his shoulder, roughly. Tom tried to roll out from under it and grab his hand, 'Dickie-e!' Tom opened his eyes and looked into the face of a policeman.

Tom sat up. He was in a park. It was dawn. Dickie was sitting on the grass beside him, talking very calmly to the policeman in Italian. Tom felt for the rectangular lump of his traveller's cheques. They were still in his pocket.

'Passaporti!' the policeman hurled at them again, and again Dickie launched into his calm explanation.

Tom knew exactly what Dickie was saying. He was saying that they were Americans, and they didn't have their passports because they had only gone out for a little walk to look at the stars. Tom had an impulse to laugh. He stood up and staggered, dusting his clothing. Dickie was up, too, and they began to walk away, though the policeman was still yelling at them. Dickie said something back to him in a courteous, explanatory tone. At least the policeman was not following them.

'We do look pretty cruddy,' Dickie said.

Tom nodded. There was a long rip in his trouser knee where he had probably fallen. Their clothes were crumpled and grass-stained and filthy with dust and sweat, but now they were shivering with cold. They went into the first café they came to, and had caffe latte and sweet rolls, then several Italian brandies that tasted awful but warmed them. Then they began to laugh. They were still drunk.

By eleven o'clock they were in Naples, just in time to catch the bus for Mongibello. It was wonderful to think of going back to Rome when they were more presentably dressed and seeing all the museums they had missed, and it was wonderful to think of lying on the beach at Mongibello this afternoon, baking in the sun. But they never got to the beach. They had showers at Dickie's house, then fell down on their respective beds and slept until Marge woke them up around four. Marge was annoyed because Dickie hadn't sent her a telegram saying he was spending the night in Rome.

'Not that I minded your spending the night, but I thought you were in Naples and anything can happen in Naples.'

'Oh-h,' Dickie drawled with a glance at Tom. He was making Bloody Marys for all of them.

Tom kept his mouth mysteriously shut. He wasn't going to tell Marge anything they had done. Let her imagine what she pleased. Dickie had made it evident that they had had a very good time. Tom noticed that she looked Dickie over with disapproval of his hangover, his unshaven face, and the drink he was taking now. There was something in Marge's eyes when she was very serious that made her look wise and old in spite of the naïve clothes she wore and her windblown hair and her general air of a Girl Scout. She had the look of a mother or an older sister now – the old feminine disapproval of the destructive play of little boys and men. La dee da! Or was it jealousy? She seemed to know that Dickie had formed a closer bond with him in twenty-four hours, just because he was another man, than she could ever have with Dickie, whether he loved her or not, and he didn't. After a few moments she loosened up, however, and the look went out of her eyes. Dickie left him with Marge on the terrace. Tom asked her about the book she was writing. It was a book about Mongibello, she said, with her own photographs. She told him she was from Ohio and showed him a picture, which she carried in her wallet, of her family's house. It was just a plain clapboard house, but it was home, Marge said with a smile. She pronounced the adjective 'Clabbered', which amused Tom, because that was the word she used to describe people who were drunk, and just a few minutes before she had said to Dickie, 'You look absolutely clabbered!' Her speech, Tom thought, was abominable, both her choice of words and her pronunciation. He tried to be especially pleasant to her. He felt he could afford to be. He walked with her to the gate, and they said a friendly good-bye to each other, but neither said anything about their all getting together later that day or tomorrow. There was no doubt about it, Marge was a little angry with Dickie.

10

FOR THREE OR four days they saw very little of Marge except down at the beach, and she was noticeably cooler towards both of them on the beach. She smiled and talked just as much or maybe more, but there was an element of politeness now, which made for the coolness. Tom noticed that Dickie was concerned, though not concerned enough to talk to Marge alone, apparently, because he hadn't seen her alone since Tom had moved into the house. Tom had been with Dickie every moment since he had moved into Dickie's house.

Finally Tom, to show that he was not obtuse about Marge, mentioned to Dickie that he thought she was acting strangely.

'Oh, she has moods,' Dickie said. 'Maybe she's working well. She doesn't like to see people when she's in a streak of work.'

The Dickie–Marge relationship was evidently just what he had supposed it to be at first, Tom thought. Marge was much fonder of Dickie than Dickie was of her.

Tom, at any rate, kept Dickie amused. He had lots of funny stories to tell Dickie about people he knew in New York, some of them true, some of them made up. They went for a sail in Dickie's boat every day. There was no mention of any date when Tom might be leaving. Obviously Dickie was enjoying his company. Tom kept out of Dickie's way when Dickie wanted to paint, and he was always ready to drop whatever he was doing and go with Dickie for a walk or a sail or simply sit and talk. Dickie also seemed pleased that Tom was taking his study of Italian seriously. Tom spent a couple of hours a day with his grammar and conversation books.

Tom wrote to Mr. Greenleaf that he was staying with Dickie now for a few days, and said that Dickie had mentioned flying home for a while in the winter, and that probably he could by that time persuade him to stay longer. This letter sounded much better now that he was staying at Dickie's house than his first letter in which he had said he was staying at a hotel in Mongibello. Tom also said that when his money gave out he intended to try to get himself a job, perhaps at one of the hotels in the village, a casual statement that served the double purpose of reminding Mr. Greenleaf that six hundred dollars could run out, and also that he was a young man ready and willing to work for a living. Tom wanted to convey the same good impression to Dickie, so he gave Dickie the letter to read before he sealed it.

Another week went by, of ideally pleasant weather, ideally lazy days in which Tom's greatest physical exertion was climb-ing the stone steps from the beach every afternoon and his greatest mental effort trying to chat in Italian with Fausto, the twenty-three-year-old Italian boy whom Dickie had found in the village and had engaged to come three times a week to give Tom Italian lessons.

They went to Capri one day in Dickie's sailboat. Capri was just far enough away not to be visible from Mongibello. Tom was filled with anticipation, but Dickie was in one of his pre-occupied moods and refused to be enthusiastic about anything. He argued with the keeper of the dock where they tied the *Pipistrello*. Dickie didn't even want to take a walk through the wonderful-looking little streets that went off in every direction from the piazza. They sat in a café on the piazza and drank a couple of Fernet-Brancas, and then Dickie wanted to start home before it became dark, though Tom would have will-ingly paid their hotel bill if Dickie had agreed to stay overnight. Tom supposed they would come again to Capri, so he wrote that day off and tried to forget it.

A letter came from Mr. Greenleaf, which had crossed Tom's letter, in which Mr. Greenleaf reiterated his arguments for

Dickie's coming home, wished Tom success, and asked for a prompt reply as to his results. Once more Tom dutifully took up the pen and replied. Mr. Greenleaf's letter had been in such a shockingly businesslike tone – really as if he had been checking on a shipment of boat parts, Tom thought – that he found it very easy to reply in the same style. Tom was a little high when he wrote the letter, because it was just after lunch and they were always slightly high on wine just after lunch, a delicious sensation that could be corrected at once with a couple of espressos and a short walk, or prolonged with another glass of wine, sipped as they went about their leisurely afternoon routine. Tom amused himself by injecting a faint hope in this letter. He wrote in Mr. Greenleaf's own style:

... If I am not mistaken, Richard is wavering in his decision to spend another winter here. As I promised you, I shall do everything in my power to dissuade him from spending another winter here, and in time – though it may be as long as Christmas – I may be able to get him to stay in the States when he goes over.

Tom had to smile as he wrote it, because he and Dickie were talking of cruising around the Greek islands this winter, and Dickie had given up the idea of flying home even for a few days, unless his mother should be really seriously ill by then. They had talked also of spending January and February, Mongibello's worst months, in Majorca. And Marge would not be going with them, Tom was sure. Both he and Dickie excluded her from their travel plans whenever they discussed them, though Dickie had made the mistake of dropping to her that they might be taking a winter cruise somewhere. Dickie was so damned open about everything! And now, though Tom knew Dickie was still firm about their going alone, Dickie was being more than usually attentive to Marge, just because he realized that she would be lonely here by herself, and that it was essentially unkind of them not to ask her along. Dickie and

Tom both tried to cover it up by impressing on her that they would be travelling in the cheapest and worst possible way around Greece, cattleboats, sleeping with peasants on the decks and all that, no way for a girl to travel. But Marge still looked dejected, and Dickie still tried to make it up by asking her often to the house now for lunch and dinner. Dickie took Marge's hand sometimes as they walked up from the beach, though Marge didn't always let him keep it. Sometimes she extricated her hand after a few seconds in a way that looked to Tom as if she were dying for her hand to be held.

And when they asked her to go along with them to Herculaneum, she refused.

'I think I'll stay home. You boys enjoy yourselves,' she said with an effort at a cheerful smile.

'Well, if she won't, she won't,' Tom said to Dickie, and drifted tactfully into the house so that she and Dickie could talk alone on the terrace if they wanted to.

Tom sat on the broad window-sill in Dickie's studio and looked out at the sea, his brown arms folded on his chest. He loved to look out at the blue Mediterranean and think of himself and Dickie sailing where they pleased. Tangiers, Sofia, Cairo, Sevastopol . . . By the time his money ran out, Tom thought, Dickie would probably be so fond of him and so used to him that he would take it for granted they would go on living together. He and Dickie could easily live on Dickie's five hundred a month income. From the terrace he could hear a pleading tone in Dickie's voice, and Marge's monosyllabic answers. Then he heard the gate clang. Marge had left. She had been going to stay for lunch. Tom shoved himself off the window-sill and went out to Dickie on the terrace.

'Was she angry about something?' Tom asked.

'No. She feels kind of left out, I suppose.'

'We certainly tried to include her.'

'It isn't just this.' Dickie was walking slowly up and down the terrace. 'Now she says she doesn't even want to go to Cortina with me.'

'Oh, she'll probably come around about Cortina before December.'

'I doubt it,' Dickie said.

Tom supposed it was because he was going to Cortina, too. Dickie had asked him last week. Freddie Miles had been gone when they got back from their Rome trip: he had had to go to London suddenly, Marge had told them. But Dickie had said he would write Freddie that he was bringing a friend along. 'Do you want me to leave, Dickie?' Tom asked, sure that Dickie didn't want him to leave. 'I feel I'm intruding on you and Marge.'

'Of course not! Intruding on what?'

'Well, from her point of view.'

'No. It's just that I owe her something. And I haven't been particularly nice to her lately. *We* haven't.'

Tom knew he meant that he and Marge had kept each other company over the long, dreary last winter, when they had been the only Americans in the village, and that he shouldn't neglect her now because somebody else was here. 'Suppose I talk to her about going to Cortina,' Tom suggested.

'Then she surely won't go,' Dickie said tersely, and went into the house.

Tom heard him telling Ermelinda to hold the lunch because he wasn't ready to eat yet. Even in Italian Tom could hear that Dickie said *he* wasn't ready for lunch, in the master-of-the-house tone. Dickie came out on the terrace, sheltering his lighter as he tried to light his cigarette. Dickie had a beautiful silver lighter, but it didn't work well in the slightest breeze. Tom finally produced his ugly, flaring lighter, as ugly and efficient as a piece of military equipment, and lighted it for him. Tom checked himself from proposing a drink: it wasn't his house, though as it happened he had bought the three bottles of Gilbey's that now stood in the kitchen.

'It's after two,' Tom said. 'Want to take a little walk and go by the post office?' Sometimes Luigi opened the post office at two-thirty, sometimes not until four, they could never tell.

They walked down the hill in silence. What *had* Marge said about him, Tom wondered. The sudden weight of guilt made sweat come out on Tom's forehead, an amorphous yet very strong sense of guilt, as if Marge had told Dickie specifically that he had stolen something or had done some other shameful thing. Dickie wouldn't be acting like this only because Marge had behaved coolly, Tom thought. Dickie walked in his slouching, downhill gait that made his bony knees jut out in front of him, a gait that Tom had unconsciously adopted, too. But now Dickie's chin was sunk down on his chest and his hands were rammed into the pockets of his shorts. He came out of silence only to greet Luigi and thank him for his letter. Tom had no mail. Dickie's letter was from a Naples bank, a form slip on which Tom saw typewritten in a blank space: $500.00. Dickie pushed the slip carelessly into a pocket and dropped the envelope into a wastebasket. The monthly announcement that Dickie's money had arrived in Naples, Tom supposed. Dickie had said that his trust company sent his money to a Naples bank. They walked on down the hill, and Tom assumed that they would walk up the main road to where it curved around a cliff on the other side of the village, as they had done before, but Dickie stopped at the steps that led up to Marge's house.

'I think I'll go up to see Marge,' Dickie said. 'I won't be long, but there's no use in your waiting.'

'All right,' Tom said, feeling suddenly desolate. He watched Dickie climb a little way up the steep steps cut into the wall, then he turned abruptly and started back towards the house.

About half-way up the hill he stopped with an impulse to go down to Giorgio's for a drink (but Giorgio's martinis were terrible), and with another impulse to go up to Marge's house, and, on a pretence of apologizing to her, vent his anger by surprising them and annoying them. He suddenly felt that Dickie was embracing her, or at least touching her, at this minute, and partly he wanted to see it, and partly he loathed the idea of seeing it. He turned and walked back to Marge's gate. He closed the gate carefully behind him, though her house was so far above she could not possibly have heard it, then ran up the steps two at a time. He slowed as he climbed the last flight of steps. He would say, 'Look here, Marge, I'm sorry if *I've* been causing the strain around here. We asked you to go today, and we mean it. *I* mean it.'

Tom stopped as Marge's window came into view: Dickie's arm was around her waist. Dickie was kissing her, little pecks on her cheek, smiling at her. They were only about fifteen feet from him, but the room was shadowed compared to the bright sunlight he stood in, and he had to strain to see. Now Marge's face was tipped straight up to Dickie's, as if she were fairly lost in ecstasy, and what disgusted Tom was that he knew Dickie didn't mean it, that Dickie was only using this cheap, obvious, easy way to hold on to her friendship. What disgusted him was the big bulge of her behind in the peasant skirt below Dickie's arm that circled her waist. And Dickie—! Tom really wouldn't have believed it possible of Dickie!

Tom turned away and ran down the steps, wanting to scream. He banged the gate shut. He ran all the way up the road home, and arrived gasping, supporting himself on the parapet after he entered Dickie's gate. He sat on the couch in Dickie's studio for a few moments, his mind stunned and blank. That kiss – it hadn't looked like a first kiss. He walked to Dickie's easel, unconsciously avoiding looking at the bad painting that was on it, picked up the kneaded eraser that lay on the palette and flung it violently out of the window, saw it arc down and disappear towards the sea. He picked up more erasers from Dickie's table, pen points, smudge sticks, charcoal and pastel fragments, and threw them one by one into corners or out of the windows. He had a curious feeling that his brain remained calm and logical and that his body was out of control. He ran out on the terrace with an idea of jumping on to the parapet and doing a dance or standing on his head, but the empty space on the other side of the parapet stopped him.

He went up to Dickie's room and paced around for a few moments, his hands in his pockets. He wondered when Dickie was coming back? Or was he going to stay and make an afternoon of it, really take her to bed with him? He jerked Dickie's closet door open and looked in. There was a freshly pressed, new-looking grey flannel suit that he had never seen Dickie wearing. Tom took it out. He took off his knee-length shorts and put on the grey flannel trousers. He put on a pair of Dickie's shoes. Then he opened the bottom drawer of the chest and took out a clean blue-and-white striped shirt.

He chose a dark-blue silk tie and knotted it carefully. The suit fitted him. He re-parted his hair and put the part a little more to one side, the way Dickie wore his.

'Marge, you must understand that I don't *love* you,' Tom said into the mirror in Dickie's voice, with Dickie's higher pitch on the emphasized words, with the little growl in his throat at the end of the phrase that could be pleasant or unpleasant, intimate or cool, according to Dickie's mood. 'Marge, stop it!' Tom turned suddenly and made a grab in the air as if he were seizing Marge's throat. He shook her, twisted her, while she sank lower and lower, until at last he left her, limp, on the floor. He was panting. He wiped his forehead the way Dickie did, reached for a handkerchief and, not finding any, got one from Dickie's top drawer, then resumed in front of the mirror. Even his parted lips looked like Dickie's lips when he was out of breath from swimming, drawn down a little from his lower teeth. 'You know why I had to do that,' he said, still breathlessly, addressing Marge, though he watched himself in the mirror. 'You were interfering between Tom and me— No, not that! But there *is* a bond between us!'

He turned, stepped over the imaginary body, and went stealthily to the window. He could see, beyond the bend of the road, the blurred slant of the steps that went up to Marge's house level. Dickie was not on the steps or on the parts of the road that he could see. Maybe they were sleeping together, Tom thought with a tighter twist of disgust in his throat. He imagined it, awkward, clumsy, unsatisfactory for Dickie, and Marge loving it. She'd love it even if he tortured her! Tom darted back to the closet again and took a hat from the top shelf. It was a little grey Tyrolian hat with a green-and-white feather in the brim. He put it on rakishly. It surprised him how much he looked like Dickie with the top part of his head covered. Really it was only his darker hair that was very different from Dickie. Otherwise, his nose – or at least its general form – his narrow jaw, his eyebrows if he held them right—

'What're you *doing*?'

Tom whirled around. Dickie was in the doorway. Tom realized that he must have been right below at the gate when he had looked out. 'Oh – just amusing myself,' Tom said in the deep voice he always used when he was embarrassed. 'Sorry, Dickie.'

Dickie's mouth opened a little, then closed, as if anger churned his words too much for them to be uttered. To Tom, it was just as bad as if he had spoken. Dickie advanced into the room.

'Dickie, I'm sorry if it—'

The violent slam of the door cut him off. Dickie began opening his shirt scowling, just as he would have if Tom had not been there, because this was his room, and what was Tom doing in it? Tom stood petrified with fear.

'I wish you'd get out of my clothes,' Dickie said.

Tom started undressing, his fingers clumsy with his mortification, his shock, because up until now Dickie had always said wear this and wear that that belonged to him. Dickie would never say it again.

Dickie looked at Tom's feet. 'Shoes, too? Are you crazy?'

'No.' Tom tried to pull himself together as he hung up the suit, then he asked, 'Did you make it up with Marge?'

'Marge and I are fine,' Dickie snapped in a way that shut Tom out from them. 'Another thing I want to say, but clearly,' he said, looking at Tom, 'I'm not queer. I don't know if you have the idea that I am or not.'

'Queer?' Tom smiled faintly. 'I never thought you were queer.'

Dickie started to say something else, and didn't. He straightened up, the ribs showing in his dark chest. 'Well, Marge thinks you are.'

'Why?' Tom felt the blood go out of his face. He kicked off Dickie's second shoe feebly, and set the pair in the closet. 'Why should she? What've I ever done?' He felt faint. Nobody had ever said it outright to him, not in this way.

'It's just the way you act,' Dickie said in a growling tone, and went out of the door.

Tom hurried back into his shorts. He had been half concealing himself from Dickie behind the closet door, though he had his underwear on. Just because Dickie liked him, Tom thought, Marge had launched her filthy accusations of him at Dickie. And Dickie hadn't had the guts to stand up and deny it to her!

He went downstairs and found Dickie fixing himself a drink at the bar shelf on the terrace. 'Dickie, I want to get this straight,' Tom began. 'I'm not queer either, and I don't want anybody thinking I am.'

'All right,' Dickie growled.

The tone reminded Tom of the answers Dickie had given him when he had asked Dickie if he knew this person and that in New York. Some of the people he had asked Dickie about were queer, it was true, and he had often suspected Dickie of deliberately denying knowing them when he did know them. All right! Who was making an issue of it, anyway? Dickie was. Tom hesitated while his mind tossed in a welter of things he might have said, bitter things, conciliatory things, grateful and hostile. His mind went back to certain groups of people he had known in New York, known and dropped finally, all of them, but he regretted now having ever known them. They had taken him up because he amused them, but *he* had never had anything to do with any of them! When a couple of them had made a pass at him, he had rejected them – though he remembered how he had tried to make it up to them later by getting ice for their drinks, dropping them off in taxis when it was out of his way, because he had been afraid they would start to dislike him. He'd been an ass! And he remembered, too, the humiliating moment when Vic Simmons had said, *Oh, for Christ sake, Tommie, shut up!* when he had said to a group of people, for perhaps the third or fourth time in Vic's presence, 'I can't make up my mind whether I like men or women, so I'm thinking of giving them *both* up.' Tom had used to pretend he was going to an analyst, because everybody else was going to an analyst, and he had used to spin wildly funny stories about his sessions with his analyst to amuse people at parties, and the line about giving up men and women both had always been good for a laugh, the way he delivered it, until Vic had told him for Christ sake to shut up, and after that Tom had never said it again and never mentioned his analyst again, either. As a matter of fact, there was a lot of truth in it, Tom thought. As people went, he was one of the most innocent and clean-minded he had ever known. That was the irony of this situation with Dickie.

'I feel as if I've—' Tom began, but Dickie was not even listening. Dickie turned away with a grim look around his mouth and carried his drink to the corner of the terrace. Tom advanced towards him, a little fearfully, not knowing whether Dickie would hurl him off the terrace, or simply turn around and tell him to get the hell out of the house. Tom asked quietly, 'Are you in love with Marge, Dickie?'

'No, but I feel sorry for her. I care about her. She's been very nice to me. We've had some good times together. You don't seem to be able to understand that.'

'I do understand. That was my original feeling about you and her — that it was a platonic thing as far as you were concerned, and that she was probably in love with you.'

'She is. You go out of your way not to hurt people who're in love with you, you know.'

'Of course.' He hesitated again, trying to choose his words. He was still in a state of trembling apprehension, though Dickie was not angry with him any more. Dickie was not going to throw him out. Tom said in a more self-possessed tone, 'I can imagine that if you both were in New York you wouldn't have seen her nearly so often — or at all — but this village being so lonely—'

'That's exactly right. I haven't been to bed with her and I don't intend to, but I do intend to keep her friendship.'

'Well, have I done anything to prevent you? I told you, Dickie, I'd rather leave than do anything to break up your friendship with Marge.'

Dickie gave a glance. 'No, you haven't done anything, specifically, but it's obvious you don't like her around. Whenever you make an effort to say anything nice to her, it's so obviously an effort.'

'I'm sorry,' Tom said contritely. He was sorry he hadn't made more of an effort, that he had done a bad job when he might have done a good one.

'Well, let's let it go. Marge and I are okay,' Dickie said defiantly. He turned away and stared off at the water.

Tom went into the kitchen to make himself a little boiled coffee. He didn't want to use the espresso machine, because

Dickie was very particular about it and didn't like anyone using it but himself. He'd take the coffee up to his room, and study some Italian before Fausto came, Tom thought. This wasn't the time to make it up with Dickie. Dickie had his pride. He would be silent for most of the afternoon, then come around by about five o'clock after he had been painting for a while, and it would be as if the episode with the clothes had never happened. One thing Tom was sure of: Dickie was glad to have him here. Dickie was bored with living by himself, and bored with Marge, too. Tom still had three hundred dollars of the money Mr. Greenleaf had given him, and he and Dickie were going to use it on a spree in Paris. Without Marge. Dickie had been amazed when Tom had told him he hadn't had more than a glimpse of Paris through a railroad station window.

While he waited for his coffee, Tom put away the food that was to have been their lunch. He set a couple of pots of food in bigger pots of water to keep the ants away from them. There was also the little paper of fresh butter, the pair of eggs, the paper of four rolls that Ermelinda had brought for their breakfast tomorrow. They had to buy small quantities of everything every day, because there was no refrigerator. Dickie wanted to buy a refrigerator with part of his father's money. He had mentioned it a couple of times. Tom hoped he changed his mind, because a refrigerator would cut down their travelling money, and Dickie had a very definite budget for his own five hundred dollars every month. Dickie was cautious about money, in a way, yet down at the wharf, and in the village bars, he gave generous tips right and left, and gave five-hundred-lire bills to any beggar who approached him.

Dickie was back to normal by five o'clock. He had had a good afternoon of painting, Tom supposed, because he had been whistling for the last hour in his studio. Dickie came out on the terrace where Tom was scanning his Italian grammar, and gave him some pointers on his pronunciation.

'They don't always say "voglio" so clearly,' Dickie said. 'They say "io vo' presentare mia amica Marge, per esempio."' Dickie drew his long hand backwards through the air. He always made gestures when he spoke Italian, graceful gestures as if he were leading an orchestra in a legato. 'You'd better listen to Fausto more and read that grammar less. I picked my Italian up off the streets.' Dickie smiled and walked away down the garden path. Fausto was just coming in the gate.

Tom listened carefully to their laughing exchanges in Italian, straining to understand every word.

Fausto came out on the terrace smiling, sank into a chair, and put his bare feet up on the parapet. His face was either smiling or frowning, and it could change from instant to instant. He was one of the few people in the village, Dickie said, who didn't speak in a southern dialect. Fausto lived in Milan, and he was visiting an aunt in Mongibello for a few months. He came, dependably and punctually, three times a week between five and five-thirty, and they sat on the terrace and sipped wine or coffee and chatted for about an hour. Tom tried his utmost to memorize everything Fausto said about the rocks, the water, politics (Fausto was a Communist, a card-carrying Communist, and he showed his card to Americans at the drop of a hat, Dickie said, because he was amused by their astonishment at his having it), and about the frenzied, catlike sex-life of some of the village inhabitants. Fausto found it hard to think of things to talk about sometimes, and then he would stare at Tom and burst out laughing. But Tom was making great progress. Italian was the only thing he had ever studied that he enjoyed and felt he could stick to. Tom wanted his Italian to be as good as Dickie's, and he thought he could make it that good in another month, if he kept on working hard at it.

11

TOM WALKED BRISKLY across the terrace and into Dickie's studio. 'Want to go to Paris in a coffin?' he asked.

'*What?*' Dickie looked up from his watercolour.

'I've been talking to an Italian in Giorgio's. We'd start out from Trieste, ride in coffins in the baggage car escorted by some Frenchman, and we'd get a hundred thousand lire apiece. I have the idea it concerns dope.'

'Dope in the coffins? Isn't that an old stunt?'

'We talked in Italian, so I didn't understand everything, but he said there'd be three coffins, and maybe the third has a real corpse in it and they've put the dope into the corpse. Anyway, we'd get the trip plus the experience.' He emptied his pockets of the packs of ship's store Lucky Strikes that he had just bought from a street pedlar for Dickie. 'What do you say?'

'I think it's a marvellous idea. To Paris in a coffin!'

There was a funny smile on Dickie's face, as if Dickie were pulling his leg by pretending to fall in with it, when he hadn't the least intention of falling in with it. 'I'm serious,' Tom said. 'He really is on the lookout for a couple of willing young men. The coffins are supposed to contain the bodies of French casualties from Indo–China. The French escort is supposed to be the relative of one of them, or maybe all of them.' It wasn't exactly what the man had said to him, but it was near enough. And two hundred thousand lire was over three hundred dollars, after all, plenty for a spree in Paris. Dickie was still hedging about Paris.

Dickie looked at him sharply, put out the bent wisp of the Nazionale he was smoking, and opened one of the packs of

Luckies. 'Are you sure the guy you were talking to wasn't under the influence of dope himself?'

'You're so damned cautious these days!' Tom said with a laugh. 'Where's your spirit? You look as if you don't even believe me! Come with me and I'll show you the man. He's still down there waiting for me. His name's Carlo.'

Dickie showed no sign of moving. 'Anybody with an offer like that doesn't explain all the particulars to you. They get a couple of toughs to ride from Trieste to Paris, maybe, but even that doesn't make sense to me.'

'Will you come with me and talk to him? If you don't believe me, at least look at him.'

'Sure.' Dickie got up suddenly. 'I might even do it for a hundred thousand lire.' Dickie closed a book of poems that had been lying face down on his studio couch before he followed Tom out of the room. Marge had a lot of books of poetry. Lately Dickie had been borrowing them.

The man was still sitting at the corner table in Giorgio's when they came in. Tom smiled at him and nodded.

'Hello, Carlo,' Tom said. 'Posso sedermi?'

'Si, si,' the man said, gesturing to the chairs at his table.

'This is my friend,' Tom said carefully in Italian. 'He wants to know if the work with the railroad journey is correct.' Tom watched Carlo looking Dickie over, sizing him up, and it was wonderful to Tom how the man's dark, tough, callous-looking eyes betrayed nothing but a polite interest, how in a split second he seemed to take in and evaluate Dickie's faintly smiling but suspicious expression, Dickie's tan that could not have been acquired except by months of lying in the sun, his worn, Italian-made clothes and his American rings.

A smile spread slowly across the man's pale, flat lips, and he glanced at Tom.

'Allora?' Tom prompted, impatient.

The man lifted his sweet martini and drank. 'The job is real, but I do not think your friend is the right man.'

Tom looked at Dickie. Dickie was watching the man alertly, with the same neutral smile that suddenly struck Tom as contemptuous. 'Well, at least it's true, you see!' Tom said to Dickie.

'Mm-m,' Dickie said, still gazing at the man is if he were some kind of animal which interested him, and which he could kill if he decided to.

Dickie could have talked Italian to the man. Dickie didn't say a word. Three weeks ago, Tom thought, Dickie would have taken the man up on his offer. Did he have to sit there looking like a stool pigeon or a police detective waiting for reinforcements so he could arrest the man? 'Well,' Tom said finally, 'you believe me, don't you?'

Dickie glanced at him. 'About the job? How do I know?'

Tom looked at the Italian expectantly.

The Italian shrugged. 'There is no need to discuss it, is there?' he asked in Italian.

'No,' Tom said. A crazy, directionless fury boiled in his blood and made him tremble. He was furious at Dickie. Dickie was looking over the man's dirty nails, dirty shirt collar, his ugly dark face that had been recently shaven though not recently washed, so that where the beard had been was much lighter than the skin above and below it. But the Italian's dark eyes were cool and amiable, and stronger than Dickie's. Tom felt stifled. He was conscious that he could not express himself in Italian. He wanted to speak both to Dickie and to the man.

'Niente, grazie, Berto,' Dickie said calmly to the waiter who had come over to ask what they wanted. Dickie looked at Tom. 'Ready to go?'

Tom jumped up so suddenly his straight chair upset behind him. He set it up again, and bowed a good-bye to the Italian. He felt he owed the Italian an apology, yet he could not open his mouth to say even a conventional good-bye. The Italian nodded good-bye and smiled. Tom followed Dickie's long white-clad legs out of the bar.

Outside, Tom said, 'I just wanted you to see that it's true at least. I hope you see.'

'All right, it's true,' Dickie said, smiling. 'What's the matter with you?'

'What's the matter with *you*?' Tom demanded.

'The man's a crook. Is that what you want me to admit? Okay!'

'Do you have to be so damned superior about it? Did he do anything to you?'

'Am I supposed to get down on my knees to him? I've seen crooks before. This village gets lot a of them.' Dickie's blond eyebrows frowned. 'What the hell *is* the matter with you? Do you want to take him up on his crazy proposition? Go ahead!'

'I couldn't now if I wanted to. Not after the way you acted.'

Dickie stopped in the road, looking at him. They were arguing so loudly, a few people around them were looking, watching.

'It could have been fun,' Tom said, 'but not the way you chose to take it. A month ago when we went to Rome, you'd have thought something like this was fun.'

'Oh, no,' Dickie said, shaking his head. 'I doubt it.'

The sense of frustration and inarticulateness was agony to Tom. And the fact that they were being looked at. He forced himself to walk on, in tense little steps at first, until he was sure that Dickie was coming with him. The puzzlement, the suspicion, was still in Dickie's face, and Tom knew Dickie was puzzled about his reaction. Tom wanted to explain it, wanted to break through to Dickie so he would understand and they would feel the same way. Dickie had felt the same way he had a month ago. 'It's the way you acted,' Tom said. 'You didn't have to act that way. The fellow wasn't doing you any harm.'

'He looked like a dirty crook!' Dickie retorted. 'For Christ sake, go back if you like him so much. You're under no obligation to do what I do!'

Now Tom stopped. He had an impulse to go back, not necessarily to go back to the Italian, but to leave Dickie. Then his tension snapped suddenly. His shoulders relaxed, aching, and his breath began to come fast, through his mouth. He wanted to say at least, 'All right Dickie,' to make it up, to make Dickie forget it. He felt tongue-tied. He stared at Dickie's blue eyes that were still frowning, the sun-bleached eyebrows white and the eyes themselves shining and empty, nothing but little pieces of blue jelly with a black dot in them, meaningless, without relation to him. You were supposed to see the soul through the eyes, to see love through the eyes, the one place you could look at another human being and see what really went on inside, and in Dickie's eyes Tom saw nothing more now than he would have seen if he had looked at the hard, bloodless surface of a mirror. Tom felt a painful wrench in his breast, and he covered his face with his hands. It was as if Dickie had been suddenly snatched away from him. They were not friends. They didn't know each other. It struck Tom like a horrible truth, true for all time, true for the people he had known in the past and for those he would know in the future: each had stood and would stand before him, and he would know time and time again that he would never know them, and the worst was that there would always be the illusion, for a time, that he did know them, and that he and they were completely in harmony and alike. For an instant the wordless shock of his realization seemed more than he could bear. He felt in the grip of a fit, as if he would fall to the ground. It was too much: the foreignness around him, the different language, his failure, and the fact that Dickie hated him. He felt surrounded by strangeness, by hostility. He felt Dickie yank his hands down from his eyes.

'What's the matter with you?' Dickie asked. 'Did that guy give you a shot of something?'

'No.'

'Are you sure? In your drink?'

'No.' The first drops of the evening rain fell on his head. There was a rumble of thunder. Hostility from above, too. 'I want to die,' Tom said in a small voice.

Dickie yanked him by the arm. Tom tripped over a doorstep. They were in the little bar opposite the post office. Tom heard Dickie ordering a brandy, specifying Italian brandy because he wasn't good enough for French, Tom supposed. Tom drank it off, slightly sweetish, medicinal-tasting, drank three of them, like a magic medicine to bring him back to what his mind knew was usually called reality: the smell of the Nazionale in Dickie's hand, the curlicued grain in the wood of the bar under his fingers, the fact that his stomach had a hard pressure in it as if someone were holding a fist against his navel, the vivid anticipation of the long steep walk from here up to the house, the faint ache that would come in his thighs from it.

'I'm okay,' Tom said in a quiet, deep voice. 'I don't know what was the matter. Must have been the heat that got me for a minute.' He laughed a little. That was reality, laughing it off, making it silly, something that was more important than anything that had happened to him in the five weeks since he had met Dickie, maybe that had ever happened to him.

Dickie said nothing, only put the cigarette in his mouth and took a couple of hundred-lire bills from his black alligator wallet and laid them on the bar. Tom was hurt that he said nothing, hurt like a child who has been sick and probably a nuisance, but who expects at least a friendly word when the sickness is over. But Dickie was indifferent. Dickie had bought him the brandies as coldly as he might have bought them for a stranger he had encountered who felt ill and had no money. Tom thought suddenly, *Dickie doesn't want me to go to Cortina.* It was not the first time Tom had thought that. Marge was going to Cortina now. She and Dickie had bought a new giant-sized thermos to take to Cortina the last time they had been in Naples. They hadn't asked him if he had liked the thermos, or anything else. They were just quietly and gradually leaving him out of their preparations. Tom felt that Dickie expected him to take off, in fact, just before the Cortina trip. A couple of weeks ago, Dickie had said he would show him some of the ski trails around Cortina that were marked on a map that he had. Dickie had looked at the map one evening, but he had not talked to him.

'Ready?' Dickie asked.

Tom followed him out of the bar like a dog.

'If you can get home all right by yourself, I thought I'd run up and see Marge for a while,' Dickie said on the road.

'I feel fine,' Tom said.

'Good.' Then he said over his shoulder as he walked away, 'Want to pick up the mail? I might forget.'

Tom nodded. He went into the post office. There were two letters, one to him from Dickie's father, one to Dickie from someone in New York whom Tom didn't know. He stood in the doorway and opened Mr. Greenleaf's letter, unfolded the typewritten sheet respectfully. It had the impressive pale green letterhead of Burke-Greenleaf Watercraft, Inc., with the ship's-wheel-trademark in the centre.

10 Nov., 19——

My dear Tom,

In view of the fact you have been with Dickie over a month and that he shows no more sign of coming home than before you went, I can only conclude that you haven't been successful. I realize that with the best of intentions you reported that he is considering returning, but frankly I don't see it anywhere in his letter of October 26th. As a matter of fact, he seems more determined than ever to stay where he is.

I want you to know that I and my wife appreciate whatever efforts you have made on our behalf, and his. You need no longer consider yourself obligated to me in any way. I trust you have not inconvenienced yourself greatly by your efforts of the past month, and I sincerely hope the trip has afforded you some pleasure despite the failure of its main objective.

Both my wife and I send you greetings and our thanks.

Sincerely,

H. R. Greenleaf

It was the final blow. With the cool tone – even cooler than his usual businesslike coolness, because this was a dismissal and he had injected a note of courteous thanks in it – Mr. Greenleaf had simply cut him off. He had failed. 'I trust you have not inconvenienced yourself greatly...' Wasn't that sarcastic? Mr. Greenleaf didn't even say that he would like to see him again when he returned to America.

Tom walked mechanically up the hill. He imagined Dickie in Marge's house now, narrating to her the story of Carlo in the bar, and his peculiar behaviour on the road afterward. Tom knew what Marge would say: 'Why don't you get *rid* of him, Dickie?' Should he go back and explain to them, he wondered, force them to listen? Tom turned around, looking at the inscrutable square front of Marge's house up on the hill, at its empty, dark-looking window. His denim jacket was getting wet from the rain. He turned its collar up. Then he walked on quickly up the hill towards Dickie's house. At least, he thought proudly, he hadn't tried to wheedle any more money out of Mr. Greenleaf, and he might have. He might have, even with Dickie's co-operation, if he had ever approached Dickie about it when Dickie had been in a good mood. Anybody else would have, Tom thought, anybody, but he hadn't, and that counted for *something*.

He stood at the corner of the terrace, staring out at the vague empty line of the horizon and thinking of nothing, feeling nothing except a faint, dreamlike lostness and aloneness. Even Dickie and Marge seemed far away, and what they might be talking about seemed unimportant. He was alone. That was the only important thing. He began to feel a tingling fear at the end of his spine, tingling over his buttocks.

He turned as he heard the gate open. Dickie walked up the path, smiling, but it struck Tom as a forced, polite smile.

'What're you doing standing there in the rain?' Dickie asked, ducking into the hall door.

'It's very refreshing,' Tom said pleasantly. 'Here's a letter for you.' He handed Dickie his letter and stuffed the one from Mr. Greenleaf into his pocket.

Tom hung his jacket in the hall closet. When Dickie had finished reading his letter – a letter that had made him laugh out loud as he read it – Tom said, 'Do you think Marge would like to go up to Paris with us when we go?'

Dickie looked surprised. 'I think she would.'

'Well, ask her,' Tom said cheerfully.

'I don't know if I should go up to Paris,' Dickie said. 'I wouldn't mind getting away somewhere for a few days, but Paris—' He lighted a cigarette. 'I'd just as soon go up to San Remo or even Genoa. That's quite a town.'

'But Paris – Genoa can't compare with Paris, can it?'

'No, of course not, but it's a lot closer.'

'But when *will* we get to Paris?'

'I don't know. Any old time. Paris'll still be there.'

Tom listened to the echo of the words in his ears, searching their tone. The day before yesterday, Dickie had received a letter from his father. He had read a few sentences aloud and they had laughed about something, but he had not read the whole letter as he had a couple of times before. Tom had no doubt that Mr. Greenleaf had told Dickie that he was fed up with Tom Ripley, and probably that he suspected him of using his money for his own entertainment. A month ago Dickie would have laughed at something like that, too, but not now, Tom thought. 'I just thought while I have a little money left, we ought to make our Paris trip,' Tom persisted.

'You go up. I'm not in the mood right now. Got to save my strength for Cortina.'

'Well – I suppose we'll make it San Remo then.' Tom said, trying to sound agreeable, though he could have wept.

'All right.'

Tom darted from the hall into the kitchen. The huge white form of the refrigerator sprang out of the corner at him. He had wanted a drink, with ice in it. Now he didn't want to touch the thing. He had spent a whole day in Naples with Dickie and Marge, looking at refrigerators, inspecting ice trays, counting the number of gadgets, until Tom hadn't been able to tell one refrigerator from another, but Dickie and Marge had kept at it with the enthusiasm of newlyweds. Then they had spent a few more hours in a café discussing the respective merits of all the refrigerators they had looked at before they decided on the one they wanted. And now Marge was popping in and out more often than ever, because she stored some of her own food in it, and she often wanted to borrow ice. Tom realized suddenly why he hated the refrigerator so much. It meant that Dickie was staying put. It finished not only their Greek trip this winter, but it meant Dickie probably never would move to Paris or Rome to live, as he and Tom had talked of doing in Tom's first weeks here. Not with a refrigerator that had the distinction of being one of only about four in the village, a refrigerator with six ice trays and so many shelves on the door that it looked like a supermarket swinging out at you every time you opened it.

Tom fixed himself an iceless drink. His hands were shaking. Only yesterday Dickie had said, 'Are you going home for Christmas?' very casually in the middle of some conversation, but Dickie knew damned well he wasn't going home for Christmas. He didn't have a home, and Dickie knew it. He had told Dickie all about Aunt Dottie in Boston. It had simply been a big hint, that was all. Marge was full of plans about Christmas. She had a can of English plum pudding she was saving, and she was going to get a turkey from some contadino. Tom could imagine how she would slop it up with her saccharine sentimentality. A Christmas tree, of course, probably cut out of cardboard. 'Silent Night'. Eggnog. Gooey presents for Dickie. Marge knitted. She took Dickie's socks home to darn all the time. And they'd both slightly, politely, leave him out. Every friendly thing they would say to him would be a painful effort. Tom couldn't bear to imagine it. All right, he'd leave. He'd do something rather than endure Christmas with them.

12

MARGE SAID SHE didn't care to go with them to San Remo. She was in the middle of a 'streak' on her book. Marge worked in fits and starts, always cheerfully, though it seemed to Tom that she was bogged down, as she called it, about seventy-five per cent of the time, a condition that she always announced with a merry little laugh. The book must stink, Tom thought. He had known writers. You didn't write a book with your little finger, lolling on a beach half the day, wondering what to eat for dinner. But he was glad she was having a 'streak' at the time he and Dickie wanted to go to San Remo.

'I'd appreciate it if you'd try to find that cologne, Dickie,' she said. 'You know, the Stradivari I couldn't find in Naples. San Remo's bound to have it, they have so many shops with French stuff.'

Tom could see them spending a whole day looking for it in San Remo, just as they had spent hours looking for it in Naples one Saturday.

They took only one suitcase of Dickie's between them, because they planned to be away only three nights and four days. Dickie was in a slightly more cheerful mood, but the awful finality was still there, the feeling that this was the last trip they would make together anywhere. To Tom, Dickie's polite cheerfulness on the train was like the cheerfulness of a host who has loathed his guest and is afraid the guest realizes it, and who tries to make it up at the last minute. Tom had never before in his life felt like an unwelcome, boring guest. On the train, Dickie told Tom about San Remo and the week he had spent there with Freddie Miles when he first arrived in Italy.

San Remo was tiny, but it had a famous name as an inter-national shopping centre, Dickie said, and people came across the French border to buy things there. It occurred to Tom that Dickie was trying to sell him on the town and might try to persuade him to stay there alone instead of coming back to Mongibello. Tom began to feel an aversion to the place before they got there.

Then, almost as the train was sliding into the San Remo station, Dickie said, 'By the way, Tom – I hate to say this to you, if you're going to mind terribly, but I really would prefer to go to Cortina d'Ampezzo alone with Marge. I think she'd prefer it, and after all I owe something to her, a pleasant holiday at least. You don't seem to be too enthusiastic about ski-ing.'

Tom went rigid and cold, but he tried not to move a muscle. Blaming it on Marge! 'All right,' he said. 'Of course.' Nervously he looked at the map in his hands, looking desper-ately around San Remo for somewhere else to go, though Dickie was already swinging their suitcase down from the rack. 'We're not far from Nice, are we?' Tom asked.

'No.'

'And Cannes. I'd like to see Cannes as long as I'm this far. At least Cannes is France,' he added on a reproachful note.

'Well, I suppose we could. You brought your passport, didn't you?'

Tom had brought his passport. They boarded a train for Cannes, and arrived around eleven o'clock that night.

Tom thought it beautiful – the sweep of curving harbour extended by little lights to long thin crescent tips, the elegant yet tropical-looking main boulevard along the water with its rows of palm trees, its row of expensive hotels. France! It was more sedate than Italy, and more chic, he could feel that even in the dark. They went to a hotel on the first back street, the Gray d'Albion, which was chic enough but wouldn't cost them their shirts, Dickie said, though Tom would gladly have paid what-ever it cost at the best hotel on the ocean front. They left their suitcases at the hotel, and went to the bar of the Hotel Carlton, which Dickie said was the most fashionable bar in Cannes. As he had predicted, there were not many people in the bar, because there were not many people in Cannes at this time of year. Tom proposed a second round of drinks but Dickie declined.

They breakfasted at a café the next morning, then strolled down to the beach. They had their swimming trunks on under their trousers. The day was cool, but not impossibly cool for swimming. They had been swimming in Mongibello on colder days. The beach was practically empty – a few isolated pairs of people, a group of men playing some kind of game up the embankment. The waves curved over and broke on the sand with a wintry violence. Now Tom saw that the group of men were doing acrobatics.

'They must be professionals,' Tom said. 'They're all in the same yellow G-strings.'

Tom watched with interest as a human pyramid began building, feet braced on bulging thighs, hands gripping fore-arms. He could hear their 'Allez!' and their 'Un – deux!'

'Look!' Tom said. 'There goes the top!' He stood still to watch the smallest one, a boy of about seventeen, as he was boosted to the shoulders of the centre man in the three top men. He stood poised, his arms open, as if receiving applause. 'Bravo!' Tom shouted.

The boy smiled at Tom before he leapt down, lithe as a tiger.

Tom looked at Dickie. Dickie was looking at a couple of men sitting near by on the beach.

'Ten thousand saw I at a glance, nodding their heads in sprightly dance,' Dickie said sourly to Tom.

It startled Tom, then he felt that sharp thrust of shame, the same shame he had felt in Mongibello when Dickie had said, *Marge thinks you are.* All right, Tom thought, the acrobats were fairies. Maybe Cannes was full of fairies. So what? Tom's fists were clenched tight in his trouser pockets. He remembered

Aunt Dottie's taunt: *Sissy! He's a sissy from the ground up. Just like his father!* Dickie stood with his arms folded, looking out at the ocean. Tom deliberately kept himself from even glancing at the acrobats again, though they were certainly more amusing to watch than the ocean. 'Are you going in?' Tom asked, boldly unbottoning his shirt, though the water suddenly looked cold as hell.

'I don't think so,' Dickie said. 'Why don't you stay here and watch the acrobats? I'm going back.' He turned and started back before Tom could answer.

Tom buttoned his clothes hastily, watching Dickie as he walked diagonally away, away from the acrobats, though the next stairs up to the sidewalk were twice as far as the stairs nearer the acrobats. Damn him anyway, Tom thought. Did he have to act so damned aloof and superior all the time? You'd think he'd never seen a pansy! Obvious what was the matter with Dickie, all right! Why didn't he break down, just for once? What did he have that was so important to lose? A half-dozen taunts sprang to his mind as he ran after Dickie. Then Dickie glanced around at him coldly, with distaste, and the first taunt died in his mouth.

They left for San Remo that afternoon, just before three o'clock, so there would not be another day to pay on the hotel bill. Dickie had proposed leaving by three, though it was Tom who paid the 430-franc bill, ten dollars and eight cents American, for one night. Tom also bought their railroad tickets to San Remo, though Dickie was loaded with francs. Dickie had brought his monthly remittance cheque from Italy and cashed it in francs, figuring that he would come out better converting the francs back into lire later, because of a sudden recent strengthening of the franc.

Dickie said absolutely nothing on the train. Under a pretence of being sleepy, he folded his arms and closed his eyes. Tom sat opposite him, staring at his bony, arrogant, handsome face, at his hands with the green ring and the gold signet ring. It crossed Tom's mind to steal the green ring when he left. It would be easy: Dickie took it off when he swam. Sometimes he took it off even when he showered at the house. He would do it the very last day, Tom thought. Tom stared at Dickie's closed eyelids. A crazy emotion of hate, of affection, of impatience and frustration was swelling in him, hampering his breathing. He wanted to kill Dickie. It was not the first time he had thought of it. Before, once or twice or three times, it had been an impulse caused by anger or disappointment, an impulse that vanished immediately and left him with a feeling of shame. Now he thought about it for an entire minute, two minutes, because he was leaving Dickie anyway, and what was there to be ashamed of any more? He had failed with Dickie, in every way. He hated Dickie, because, however he looked at what had happened, his failing had not been his own fault, not due to anything he had done, but due to Dickie's inhuman stubbornness. And his blatant rudeness! He had offered Dickie friendship, companionship, and respect, everything he had to offer, and Dickie had replied with ingratitude and now hostility. Dickie was just shoving him out in the cold. If he killed him on this trip, Tom thought, he could simply say that some accident had happened. He could— He had just thought of something brilliant: he could become Dickie Greenleaf himself. He could do everything that Dickie did. He could go back to Mongibello first and collect Dickie's things, tell Marge any damned story, set up an apartment in Rome or Paris, receive Dickie's cheque every month and forge Dickie's signature on it. He could step right into Dickie's shoes. He could have Mr. Greenleaf, Sr., eating out of his hand. The danger of it, even the inevitable temporariness of it which he vaguely realized, only made him more enthusiastic. He began to think of *how*.

The water. But Dickie was such a good swimmer. The cliffs. It would be easy to push Dickie off some cliff when they took a walk, but he imagined Dickie grabbing at him and pulling *him* off with him, and he tensed in his seat until his thighs ached and his nails cut red scallops in his thumbs. He would have to get the other ring off, too. He would have to tint his hair a little lighter. But he wouldn't live in a place, of course, where anybody who knew Dickie lived. He had only to look enough like Dickie to be able to use his passport. Well, he did. If he—

Dickie opened his eyes, looking right at him, and Tom relaxed, slumped into the corner with his head back and his eyes shut, as quickly as if he had passed out.

'Tom, are you okay?' Dickie asked, shaking Tom's knee.

'Okay,' Tom said, smiling a little. He saw Dickie sit back with an air of irritation, and Tom knew why: because Dickie had hated giving him even that much attention. Tom smiled to himself, amused at his own quick reflex in pretending to collapse, because that had been the only way to keep Dickie from seeing what had been a very strange expression on his face.

San Remo. Flowers. A main drag along the beach again, shops and stores and French and English and Italian tourists. Another hotel, with flowers in the balconies. Where? In one of these little streets tonight? The town would be dark and silent by one in the morning, if he could keep Dickie up that long. In the water? It was slightly cloudy, though not cold. Tom racked his brain. It would be easy in the hotel room, too, but how would he get rid of the body? The body had to *disappear*, absolutely. That left only the water, and the water was Dickie's element. There were boats, rowboats and little motor-boats, that people could rent down at the beach. In each motor-boat, Tom noticed, was a round weight of cement attached to a line, for anchoring the boat.

'What do you say we take a boat Dickie?' Tom asked, trying not to sound eager, though he did, and Dickie looked at him, because he had not been eager about anything since they had arrived here.

They were little blue-and-white and green-and-white motor-boats, about ten of them, lined up at the wooden pier, and the Italian was anxious for customers because it was a chilly and rather gloomy morning. Dickie looked out at the Mediterranean, which was slightly hazy though not with a presage of rain. This was the kind of greyness that would not disappear all day, and there would be no sun. It was about ten-thirty – that lazy hour after breakfast, when the whole long Italian morning lay before them.

'Well, all right. For an hour around the port,' Dickie said, almost immediately jumping into a boat, and Tom could see from his little smile that he had done it before, that he was looking forward to remembering, sentimentally, other mornings or some other morning here, perhaps with Freddie, or Marge. Marge's cologne bottle bulged the pocket of Dickie's corduroy jacket. They had bought it a few minutes ago at a store very much like an American drugstore on the main drag.

The Italian boatkeeper started the motor with a yanked string, asking Dickie if he knew how to work it, and Dickie said yes. And there was an oar, a single oar in the bottom of the boat, Tom saw. Dickie took the tiller. They headed straight out from the town.

'Cool!' Dickie yelled, smiling. His hair was blowing.

Tom looked to right and left. A vertical cliff on one side, very much like Mongibello, and on the other a flattish length of land fuzzing out in the mist that hovered over the water. Offhand he couldn't say in which direction it was better to go.

'Do you know the land around here?' Tom shouted over the roar of the motor.

'Nope!' Dickie said cheerfully. He was enjoying the ride.

'Is that thing hard to steer?'

'Not a bit! Want to try it?'

Tom hesitated. Dickie was still steering straight out to the open sea. 'No, thanks.' He looked to right and left. There was a sailboat off to the left. 'Where're you going?' Tom shouted.

'Does it matter?' Dickie smiled.

No, it didn't.

Dickie swerved suddenly to the right, so suddenly that they both had to duck and lean to keep the boat righted. A wall of white spray rose up on Tom's left, then gradually fell to show the empty horizon. They were streaking across the empty water again, towards nothing. Dickie was trying the speed, smiling, his blue eyes smiling at the emptiness.

'In a little boat it always feels so much faster than it is!' Dickie yelled.

Tom nodded, letting his understanding smile speak for him. Actually, he was terrified. God only knew how deep the water was here. If something happened to the boat suddenly, there wasn't a chance in the world that they could get back to shore, or at least that *he* could. But neither was there a chance that anybody could see anything that they did here. Dickie was swerving very slightly towards the right again, towards the long spit of fuzzy grey land, but he could have hit Dickie, sprung on him, or kissed him, or thrown him overboard, and nobody could have seen him at this distance. Tom was sweating, hot under his clothes, cold on his forehead. He felt afraid, but it was not of the water, it was of Dickie. He knew that he was going to do it, that he would not stop himself now, maybe *couldn't* stop himself, and that he might not succeed.

'You dare me to jump in?' Tom yelled, beginning to unbutton his jacket.

Dickie only laughed at this proposal from him, opening his mouth wide, keeping his eyes fixed on the distance in front of the boat. Tom kept on undressing. He had his shoes and socks off. Under his trousers he wore his swimming trunks, like Dickie. 'I'll go in if you will!' Tom shouted. 'Will you?' He wanted Dickie to slow down.

'Will I? Sure!' Dickie slowed the motor abruptly. He released the tiller and took off his jacket. The boat bobbed, losing its momentum. 'Come on,' Dickie said, nodding at Tom's trousers that were still on.

Tom glanced at the land. San Remo was a blur of chalky white and pink. He picked up the oar, as casually as if he were playing with it between his knees, and when Dickie was shoving his trousers down, Tom lifted the oar and came down with it on the top of Dickie's head.

'Hey!' Dickie yelled, scowling, sliding half off the wooden seat. His pale brows lifted in groggy surprise.

Tom stood up and brought the oar down again, sharply, all his strength released like the snap of a rubber band.

'For God's sake!' Dickie mumbled, glowering, fierce, though the blue eyes wobbled, losing consciousness.

Tom swung a left-handed blow with the oar against the side of Dickie's head. The edge of the oar cut a dull gash that filled with a line of blood as Tom watched. Dickie was on the bottom of the boat, twisted, twisting. Dickie gave a groaning roar of protest that frightened Tom with its loudness and its strength. Tom hit him in the side of the neck, three times, chopping strokes with the edge of the oar, as if the oar were an axe and Dickie's neck a tree. The boat rocked, and water splashed over his foot that was braced on the gunwale. He sliced at Dickie's forehead, and a broad patch of blood came slowly where the oar had scraped. For an instant Tom was aware of tiring as he raised and swung, and still Dickie's hands slid towards him on the bottom of the boat, Dickie's long legs straightened to thrust him forward. Tom got a bayonet grip on the oar and plunged its handle into Dickie's side. Then the prostrate body relaxed, limp and still. Tom straightened, getting his breath back painfully. He looked around him. There were no boats, nothing, except far, far away a little white spot creeping from right to left: a speeding motor-boat heading for the shore.

He stopped and yanked at Dickie's green ring. He pocketed it. The other ring was tighter, but it came off, over the bleeding scuffed knuckle. He looked in the trousers pockets. French and Italian coins. He left them. He took a keychain with three keys. Then he picked up Dickie's jacket and took Marge's cologne package out of the pocket. Cigarettes and Dickie's silver lighter, a pencil stub, the alligator wallet and several little cards in the inside breast pocket. Tom stuffed it all into his own corduroy jacket. Then he reached for the rope that was tumbled over the white cement weight. The end of the rope was tied to the metal ring at the prow. Tom tried to untie it. It was a hellish, water-soaked, immovable knot that must have been there for years. He banged at it with his fist. He had to have a knife.

He looked at Dickie. Was he dead? Tom crouched in the narrowing prow of the boat watching Dickie for a sign of life. He was afraid to touch him, afraid to touch his chest or his wrist to feel a pulse. Tom turned and yanked at the rope frenziedly, until he realized that he was only making it tighter.

His cigarette lighter. He fumbled for it in the pocket of his trousers on the bottom of the boat. He lighted it, then held a dry portion of the rope over its flame. The rope was about an inch and a half thick. It was slow, very slow, and Tom used the minutes to look all round him again. Would the Italian with the boats be able to see him at this distance? The hard grey rope refused to catch fire, only glowed and smoked a little, slowly parting, strand by strand. Tom yanked it, and his lighter went out. He lighted it again, and kept on pulling at the rope. When it parted, he looped it four times around Dickie's bare ankles before he had time to feel afraid, and tied a huge, clumsy knot, overdoing it to make sure it would not come undone, because he was not very good at tying knots. He estimated the rope to be about thirty-five or forty feet long. He began to feel cooler, and smooth and methodical. The cement weight should be just enough to hold a body down, he thought. The body might drift a little, but it would not come up to the surface.

Tom threw the weight over. It made a *ker-plung* and sank through the transparent water with a wake of bubbles, disappeared, and sank and sank until the rope drew taut on Dickie's ankles, and by that time Tom had lifted the ankles over the side and was pulling now at an arm to lift the heaviest part, the shoulders, over the gunwale. Dickie's limp hand was warm and clumsy. The shoulders stayed on the bottom of the boat, and when he pulled, the arm seemed to stretch like rubber, and the body not to rise at all. Tom got down on one knee and tried to heave him out over the side. It made the boat rock. He had forgotten the water. It was the only thing that scared him. He would have to get him out over the stern, he thought, because the stern was lower in the water. He pulled the limp body towards the stern, sliding the rope around the gunwale. He could tell from the buoyancy of the weight in the water that the weight had not touched bottom. Now he began with Dickie's head and shoulders, turned Dickie's body on its belly and pushed him out little by little. Dickie's head was in the water, the gunwale cutting across his waist, and now the legs were in a dead weight, resisting Tom's strength with their amazing weight, as his shoulders had done, as if they were magnetized to the boat bottom. Tom took a deep breath and heaved. Dickie went over, but Tom lost his balance and fell against the tiller. The idling motor roared suddenly.

Tom made a lunge for the control lever, but the boat swerved at the same time in a crazy arc. For an instant he saw water underneath him and his own hand outstretched towards it, because he had been trying to grab the gunwale and the gunwale was no longer there.

He was in the water.

He gasped, contracting his body in an upward leap, grabbing at the boat. He missed. The boat had gone into a spin. Tom leapt again, then sank lower, so low the water closed over his head again with a deadly, fatal slowness, yet too fast for him to get a breath, and he inhaled a noseful of water just as his eyes sank below the surface. The boat was farther away. He had seen such spins before: they never stopped until somebody climbed in and stopped the motor, and now in the deadly emptiness of the water he suffered in advance the sensations of dying, sank threshing below the surface again, and the crazy motor faded as the water *thugged* into his ears, blotting out all sound except the frantic sounds that he made inside himself, breathing, struggling, the desperate pounding of his blood. He was up again and fighting automatically towards the boat, because it was the only thing that floated, though it was spinning and impossible to touch, and its sharp prow whipped past him twice, three times, four, while he caught one breath of air.

He shouted for help. He got nothing but a mouthful of water. His hand touched the boat beneath the water and was pushed aside by the animal-like thrust of the prow. He reached out wildly for the end of the boat, heedless of the propeller's blades. His fingers felt the rudder. He ducked, but not in time. The keel hit the top of his head, passing over him. Now the stern was close again, and he tried for it, fingers slipping down off the rudder. His other hand caught the stern gunwale. He kept an arm straight, holding his body away from the propeller. With an unpremeditated energy, he hurled himself towards a stern corner, and caught an arm over the side. Then he reached up and touched the lever.

The motor began to slow.

Tom clung to the gunwale with both hands, and his mind went blank with relief, with disbelief, until he became aware of the flaming ache in his throat, the stab in his chest with every breath. He rested for what could have been two or ten minutes, thinking of nothing at all but the gathering of strength enough to haul himself into the boat, and finally he made slow jumps up and down in the water and threw his weight over and lay face down in the boat, his feet dangling over the gunwale. He rested, faintly conscious of the slipperiness of Dickie's blood under his fingers, a wetness mingled with the water that ran out of his own nose and mouth. He began to think before he could move, about the boat that was all bloody and could not be returned, about the motor that he would have to get up and start in a moment. About the direction.

About Dickie's rings. He felt for them in his jacket pocket. They were still there, and after all what could have happened to them? He had a fit of coughing, and tears blurred his vision as he tried to look all around him to see if any boat was near, or coming towards him. He rubbed his eyes. There was no boat except the gay little motor-boat in the distance, still dashing around in wide arcs, oblivious of him. Tom looked at the boat bottom. *Could* he wash it all out? But blood was hell to get out, he had always heard. He had been going to return the boat, and say, if he were asked by the boatkeeper where his friend was, that he had set him ashore at some other point. Now that couldn't be.

Tom moved the lever cautiously. The idling motor picked up and he was afraid even of that, but the motor seemed more human and manageable than the sea, and therefore less frightening. He headed obliquely towards the shore, north of San Remo. Maybe he could find some place, some little deserted cove in the shore where he could beach the boat and get out. But if they found the boat? The problem seemed immense. He tried to reason himself back to coolness. His mind seemed blocked as to how to get rid of the boat.

Now he could see pine trees, a dry empty-looking stretch of tan beach and the green fuzz of a field of olive trees. Tom cruised slowly to right and left of the place, looking for people. There were none. He headed in for the shallow, short beach, handling the throttle respectfully, because he was not sure it wouldn't flare up again. Then he felt the scrape and jolt of earth under the prow. He turned the lever to FERMA, and moved another lever that cut the motor. He got out cautiously into about ten inches of water, pulled the boat up as far as he could, then transferred the two jackets, his sandals, and Marge's cologne box from the boat to the beach. The little cove where he was – not more than fifteen feet wide – gave him a feeling of safety and privacy. There was not a sign anywhere that a human foot had ever touched the place. Tom decided to try to scuttle the boat.

He began to gather stones, all about the size of a human head because that was all he had the strength to carry, and to drop them one by one into the boat, but finally he had to use smaller stones because there were no more big ones near enough by. He worked without a halt, afraid that he would drop in a faint of exhaustion if he allowed himself to relax even for an instant, and that he might lie there until he was found by somebody. When the stones were nearly level with the gunwale, he shoved the boat off and rocked it, more and more, until water slopped in at the sides. As the boat began to sink, he gave it a shove towards deeper water, shoved and walked with it until the water was up to his waist, and the boat sank below his reach. Then he ploughed his way back to the shore and lay down for a while, face down on the sand. He began to plan his return to the hotel, and his story, and his next moves: leaving San Remo before nightfall, getting back to Mongibello. And the story there.

13

AT SUNDOWN, JUST the hour when the Italians and everybody else in the village had gathered at the sidewalk tables of the cafés, freshly showered and dressed, staring at everybody and everything that passed by, eager for whatever entertainment the town could offer, Tom walked into the village wearing only his swimming shorts and sandals and Dickie's corduroy jacket, and carrying his slightly bloodstained trousers and jacket under his arm. He walked with a languid casualness because he was exhausted, though he kept his head up for the benefit of the hundreds of people who stared at him as he walked past the cafés, the only route to his beachfront hotel. He had fortified himself with five espressos full of sugar and three brandies at a bar on the road just outside San Remo. Now he was playing the role of an athletic young man who had spent the afternoon in and out of the water because it was his peculiar taste, being a good swimmer and impervious to cold, to swim until late afternoon on a chilly day. He made it to the hotel, collected the key at the desk, went up to his room and collapsed on the bed. He would allow himself an hour to rest, he thought, but he must not fall asleep lest he sleep longer. He rested, and when he felt himself falling asleep, got up and went to the basin and wet his face, took a wet towel back to his bed simply to waggle in his hand to keep from falling asleep.

Finally he got up and went to work on the blood smear on one leg of his corduroy trousers. He scrubbed it over and over with soap and a nailbrush, got tired and stopped for a while to pack the suitcase. He packed Dickie's things just as Dickie had always packed them, toothpaste and toothbrush in the back left pocket. Then he went back to finish the trouser leg. His own jacket had too much blood on it ever to be worn again, and he would have to get rid of it, but he could wear Dickie's jacket, because it was the same beige colour and almost identical in size. Tom had had his suit copied from Dickie's, and it had been made by the same tailor in Mongibello. He put his own jacket into the suitcase. Then he went down with the suitcase and asked for his bill.

The man behind the desk asked where his friend was, and Tom said he was meeting him at the railroad station. The clerk was pleasant and smiling, and wished Tom 'Buon viaggio'.

Tom stopped in at a restaurant two streets away and forced himself to eat a bowl of minestrone for the strength it would give him. He kept an eye out for the Italian who owned the boats. The main thing, he thought, was to leave San Remo tonight, take a taxi to the next town, if there was no train or bus.

There was a train south at ten-twenty-four, Tom learned at the railroad station. A sleeper. Wake up tomorrow in Rome, and change trains for Naples. It seemed absurdly simple and easy suddenly, and in a burst of self-assurance he thought of going to Paris for a few days.

"Spetta un momento,' he said to the clerk who was ready to hand him his ticket. Tom walked around his suitcase, thinking of Paris. Overnight. Just to see it, for two days, for instance. It wouldn't matter whether he told Marge or not. He decided abruptly against Paris. He wouldn't be able to relax. He was too eager to get to Mongibello and see about Dickie's belongings.

The white, taut sheets of his berth on the train seemed the most wonderful luxury he had ever known. He caressed them with his hands before he turned the light out. And the clean blue-grey blankets, the spanking efficiency of the little black net over his head – Tom had an ecstatic moment when he thought of all the pleasures that lay before him now with Dickie's money, other beds, tables, seas, ships, suitcases, shirts, years of freedom, years of pleasure. Then he turned the light out and put his head down and almost at once fell asleep, happy, content, and utterly, utterly confident, as he had never been before in his life.

In Naples he stopped in the men's room of the railway station and removed Dickie's toothbrush and hairbrush from the suitcase, and rolled them up in Dickie's raincoat together with his own corduroy jacket and Dickie's blood-spotted trousers. He took the bundle across the street from the station and pressed it into a huge burlap bag of garbage that leaned against an alley wall. Then he breakfasted on caffe latte and a sweet roll at a café on the bus-stop square, and boarded the old eleven o'clock bus for Mongibello.

He stepped off the bus almost squarely in front of Marge, who was in her bathing suit and the loose white jacket she always wore to the beach.

'Where's Dickie?' she asked.

'He's in Rome.' Tom smiled easily, absolutely prepared. 'He's staying up there for a few days. I came down to get some of his stuff to take up to him.'

'Is he staying with somebody?'

'No, just in a hotel.' With another smile that was half a good-bye, Tom started up the hill with his suitcase. A moment later he heard Marge's cork-soled sandals trotting after him. Tom waited. 'How's everything been in our home sweet home?' he asked.

'Oh, dull. As usual.' Marge smiled. She was ill at ease with him. But she followed him into the house – the gate was unlocked, and Tom got the big iron key to the terrace door from its usual place, back of a rotting wooden tub that held earth and a half-dead shrub – and they went on to the terrace together. The table had been moved a little. There was a book on the glider. Marge had been here since they left, Tom thought. He had been gone only three days and nights. It seemed to him that he had been away for a month.

'How's Skippy?' Tom asked brightly, opening the refrigerator, getting out an ice tray. Skippy was a stray dog Marge had acquired a few days ago, an ugly black-and-white bastard that Marge pampered and fed like a doting old maid.

'He went off. I didn't expect him to stay.'

'Oh.'

'You look like you've had a good time,' Marge said, a little wistfully.

'We did.' Tom smiled. 'Can I fix you a drink?'

'No, thanks. How long do you think Dickie's going to be away?'

'Well—' Tom frowned thoughtfully. 'I don't really know. He says he wants to see a lot of art shows up there. I think he's just enjoying a change of scene.' Tom poured himself a generous gin and added soda and a lemon slice. 'I suppose he'll be back in a week. By the way!' Tom reached for the suitcase, and took out the box of cologne. He had removed the shop's wrapping paper, because it had had blood smears on it. 'Your Stradivari. We got it in San Remo.'

'Oh, thanks – very much.' Marge took it, smiling, and began to open it, carefully, dreamily.

Tom strolled tensely around the terrace with his drink, not saying a word to Marge, waiting for her to go.

'Well—' Marge said finally, coming out on the terrace. 'How long are you staying?'

'Where?'

'Here.'

'Just overnight. I'll be going up to Rome tomorrow. Probably in the afternoon,' he added, because he couldn't get the mail tomorrow until perhaps after two.

'I don't suppose I'll see you again, unless you're at the beach,' Marge said with an effort at friendliness. 'Have a good time in case I don't see you. And tell Dickie to write a postcard. What hotel is he staying at?'

'Oh – uh – what's the name of it? Near the Piazza di Spagna?'

'The Inghilterra?'

'That's it. But I think he said to use the American Express as a mailing address.' She wouldn't try to telephone Dickie, Tom thought. And he could be at the hotel tomorrow to pick up a letter if she wrote. 'I'll probably go down to the beach tomorrow morning,' Tom said.

'All right. Thanks for the cologne.'

'Don't mention it!'

She walked down the path to the iron gate, and out.

Tom picked up the suitcase and ran upstairs to Dickie's bedroom. He slid Dickie's top drawer out: letters, two address books, a couple of little notebooks, a watchchain, loose keys, and some kind of insurance policy. He slid the other drawers out, one by one, and left them open. Shirts, shorts, folded sweaters and disordered socks. In the corner of the room a sloppy mountain of portfolios and old drawing pads. There was a lot to be done. Tom took off all his clothes, ran downstairs naked and took a quick, cool shower, then put on Dickie's old white duck trousers that were hanging on a nail in the closet.

He started with the top drawer, for two reasons: the recent letters were important in case there were current situations that had to be taken care of immediately, and also because, in case Marge happened to come back this afternoon, it wouldn't look as if he were dismantling the entire house so soon. But at least he could begin, even this afternoon, packing Dickie's biggest suitcases with his best clothes, Tom thought.

Tom was still pottering about the house at midnight. Dickie's suitcases were packed, and now he was assessing how much the house furnishings were worth, what he would bequeath to Marge, and how he would dispose of the rest. Marge could have the damned refrigerator. That ought to please her. The heavy carved chest in the foyer, which Dickie used for his linens, ought to be worth several hundred dollars,

Tom thought. Dickie had said it was four hundred years old, when Tom had asked him about it. Cinquecento. He intended to speak to Signor Pucci, the assistant manager of the Miramare, and ask him to act as agent for the sale of the house and the furniture. And the boat, too. Dickie had told him that Signor Pucci did jobs like that for residents of the village.

He had wanted to take all of Dickie's possessions straight away to Rome, but in view of what Marge might think about his taking so much for presumably such a short time, he decided it would be better to pretend that Dickie had later made a decision to move to Rome.

Accordingly, Tom went down to the post office around three the next afternoon, claimed one interesting letter for Dickie from a friend in America and nothing for himself, but as he walked slowly back to the house again he imagined that he was reading a letter from Dickie. He imagined the exact words, so that he could quote them to Marge, if he had to, and he even made himself feel the slight surprise he would have felt at Dickie's change of mind.

As soon as he got home he began packing Dickie's best drawings and best linens into the big cardboard box he had gotten from Aldo at the grocery store on the way up the hill. He worked calmly and methodically, expecting Marge to drop in at any minute, but it was after four before she came.

'Still here?' she asked as she came into Dickie's room.

'Yes. I had a letter from Dickie today. He's decided he's going to move to Rome.' Tom straightened up and smiled a little, as if it were a surprise to him, too. 'He wants me to pick up all his things, all I can handle.'

'*Move* to Rome? For how long?'

'I don't know. The rest of the winter apparently, anyway.' Tom went on tying canvases.

'He's not coming back all winter?' Marge's voice sounded lost already.

'No. He said he might even sell the house. He said he hadn't decided yet.'

'Gosh!— What happened?'

Tom shrugged. 'He apparently wants to spend the winter in Rome. He said he was going to write to you. I thought you might have got a letter this afternoon, too.'

'No.'

Silence. Tom kept on working. It occurred to him that he hadn't packed up his own things at all. He hadn't even been into his room.

'He's still going to Cortina, isn't he?' Marge asked.

'No, he's not. He said he was going to write to Freddie and cancel it. But that shouldn't prevent your going.' Tom watched her. 'By the way, Dickie said he wants you to take the refrigerator. You can probably get somebody to help you move it.'

The present of the refrigerator had no effect at all on Marge's stunned face. Tom knew she was wondering whether he was going to live with Dickie or not, and that she was probably concluding, because of his cheerful manner, that he was going to live with him. Tom felt the question creeping up to her lips – she was as transparent as a child to him – then she asked: 'Are you going to stay with him in Rome?'

'Maybe for a while. I'll help him get settled. I want to go to Paris this month, then I suppose around the middle of December I'll be going back to the States.'

Marge looked crestfallen. Tom knew she was imagining the lonely weeks ahead – even if Dickie did make periodic little visits to Mongibello to see her – the empty Sunday mornings, the lonely dinners. 'What's he going to do about Christmas? Do you think he wants to have it here or in Rome?'

Tom said with a trace of irritation, 'Well, I don't think here. I have the feeling he wants to be alone.'

Now she was shocked to silence, shocked and hurt. Wait till she got the letter he was going to write from Rome, Tom thought. He'd be gentle with her, of course, as gentle as Dickie, but there would be no mistaking that Dickie didn't want to see her again.

A few minutes later, Marge stood up and said good-bye in an absent-minded way. Tom suddenly felt that she might be going to telephone Dickie today. Or maybe even go up to Rome. But what if she did? Dickie could have changed his hotel. And there were enough hotels in Rome to keep her busy for days, even if she came to Rome to find him. When she didn't find him, by telephone or by coming to Rome, she would suppose that he had gone to Paris or to some other city with Tom Ripley.

Tom glanced over the newspapers from Naples for an item about a scuttled boat's having been found near San Remo. *Barca affondata vicino San Remo*, the caption would probably say. And they would make a great to-do over the bloodstains in the boat, if the bloodstains were still there. It was the kind of thing the Italian newspapers loved to write up in their melodramatic journalese: 'Giorgio di Stefani, a young fisherman of San Remo, yesterday at three o'clock in the afternoon made a most terrible discovery in two metres of water. A little motor-boat, its interior covered with horrible bloodstains ...' But Tom did not see anything in the paper. Nor had there been anything yesterday. It might take months for the boat to be found, he thought. It might never be found. And if they did find it, how could they know that Dickie Greenleaf and Tom Ripley had taken the boat out together? They had not told their names to the Italian boatkeeper at San Remo. The boatkeeper had given them only a little orange ticket which Tom had had in his pocket, and had later found and destroyed.

Tom left Mongibello by taxi around six o'clock, after an espresso at Giorgio's, where he said good-bye to Giorgio, Fausto, and several other village acquaintances of his and Dickie's. To all of them he told the same story, that Signor Greenleaf was staying in Rome for the winter, and that he sent his greetings until he saw them again. Tom said that undoubtedly Dickie would be down for a visit before long.

He had had Dickie's linens and paintings crated by the American Express that afternoon, and the boxes sent to Rome along with Dickie's trunk and two heavier suitcases, to be claimed in Rome by Dickie Greenleaf. Tom took his own two suitcases and one other of Dickie's in the taxi with him. He had spoken to Signor Pucci at the Miramare, and had said that there was a possibility that Signor Greenleaf would want to sell his house and furniture, and could Signor Pucci handle it? Signor Pucci had said he would be glad to. Tom had also spoken to Pietro, the dockkeeper, and asked him to be on the lookout for someone who might want to buy the *Pipistrello*, because there was a good chance that Signor Greenleaf would want to get rid of it this winter. Tom said that Signor Greenleaf would let it go for five hundred thousand lire, hardly eight hundred dollars, which was such a bargain for a boat that slept two people, Pietro thought he could sell it in a matter of weeks.

On the train to Rome Tom composed the letter to Marge so carefully that he memorized it in the process, and when he got to the Hotel Hassler he sat down at Dickie's Hermes Baby, which he had brought in one of Dickie's suitcases, and wrote the letter straight off.

Rome
28 November, 19—

Dear Marge:

I've decided to take an apartment in Rome for the winter, just to have a change of scene and get away from old Mongy for a while. I feel a terrific urge to be by myself. I'm sorry it was so sudden and that I didn't get a chance to say good-bye, but actually I'm not far away, and I hope I'll be seeing you now and then. I just didn't feel like going to pack my stuff, so I threw the burden on Tom.

As to us, it can't harm anything and possibly may improve everything if we don't see each other for a while. I had a terrible feeling I was boring you, though you weren't boring *me*, and please don't think I am running away from anything. On the contrary, Rome should bring me closer to reality. Mongy certainly didn't. Part of my discontent was you. My going away doesn't solve anything, of course, but it will help me to discover how I really feel about you. For this reason, I prefer not to see you for a while, darling, and I hope you'll understand. If you don't – well, you don't, and that's the risk I run. I may go up to Paris for a couple of weeks with Tom, as he's dying to go. That is, unless I start painting right away. Met a painter named Di Massimo whose work I like very much, an old fellow without much money who seems to be very glad to have me as a student if I pay him a little bit. I am going to paint with him in his studio.

The city looks marvellous with its fountains going all night and everybody up all night, contrary to old Mongy. You were on the wrong track about Tom. He's going back to the States soon and I don't care when, though he's really not a bad guy and I don't dislike him. He has nothing to do with us, anyway, and I hope you realize that.

Write me c/o American Express, Rome until I know where I am. Shall let you know when I find an apartment. Meanwhile keep the home fires burning, the refrigerators working and your typewriter also. I'm terribly sorry about Xmas, darling, but I don't think I should see you that soon, and you can hate me or not for that.

All my love,
Dickie

Tom had kept his cap on since entering the hotel, and he had given Dickie's passport in at the desk instead of his own, though hotels, he had noticed, never looked at the passport photo, only copied the passport number which was on the front cover. He had signed the register with Dickie's hasty and rather flamboyant signature with the big looping capitals R and G. When he went out to mail the letter he walked to a drugstore several streets away and bought a few items of make-up that he thought he might need. He had fun with the Italian salesgirl, making her think that he was buying them for his wife who had lost her make-up kit, and who was indisposed in the hotel with the usual upset stomach.

He spent that evening practising Dickie's signature for the bank cheques. Dickie's monthly remittance was going to arrive from America in less than ten days.

14

HE MOVED THE next day to the Hotel Europa, a moderately priced hotel near the Via Veneto, because the Hassler was a trifle flashy, he thought, the kind of hotel that was patronized by visiting movie people, and where Freddie Miles, or people like him who knew Dickie, might choose to stay if they came to Rome.

Tom held imaginary conversations with Marge and Fausto and Freddie in his hotel room. Marge was the most likely to come to Rome, he thought. He spoke to her as Dickie, if he imagined it on the telephone, and as Tom, if he imagined her face to face with him. She might, for instance, pop up to Rome and find his hotel and insist on coming up to his room, in which case he would have to remove Dickie's rings and change his clothing.

'I don't know,' he would say to her in Tom's voice. 'You know how he is – likes to feel he's getting away from everything. He said I could use his hotel room for a few days, because mine happens to be so badly heated. . . . Oh, he'll be back in a couple of days, or there'll be a postcard from him saying he's all right. He went to some little town with Di Massimo to look at some paintings in a church.'

('But you don't know whether he went north or south?')

'I really don't. I guess south. But what good does that do us?'

('It's just my bad luck to miss him, isn't it? Why couldn't he at least have said where he was going?')

'I know. I asked him, too. Looked the room over for a map or anything else that might have shown where he was going.

He just called me up three days ago and said I could use his room if I cared to.'

It was a good idea to practise jumping into his own character again, because the time might come when he would need to in a matter of seconds, and it was strangely easy to forget the exact timbre of Tom Ripley's voice. He conversed with Marge until the sound of his own voice in his ears was exactly the same as he remembered it.

But mostly he was Dickie, discoursing in a low tone with Freddie and Marge, and by long distance with Dickie's mother, and with Fausto, and with a stranger at a dinner party, conversing in English and Italian, with Dickie's portable radio turned on so that if a hotel employee passed by in the hall and happened to know that Signor Greenleaf was alone he would not think him an eccentric. Sometimes, if the song on the radio was one that Tom liked, he merely danced by himself, but he danced as Dickie would have with a girl – he had seen Dickie once on Giorgio's terrace, dancing with Marge, and also in the Giardino degli Orangi in Naples – in long strides yet rather stiffly, not what could be called exactly good dancing. Every moment to Tom was a pleasure, alone in his room or walking the streets of Rome, when he combined sightseeing with looking around for an apartment. It was impossible ever to be lonely or bored, he thought, so long as he was Dickie Greenleaf.

They greeted him as Signor Greenleaf at the American Express, where he called for his mail. Marge's first letter said:

Dickie:

Well, it was a bit of a surprise. I wonder what came over you so suddenly in Rome or San Remo or wherever it was? Tom was most mysterious except to say that he would be staying with you. I'll believe he's leaving for America when I see it. At the risk of sticking my neck out, old boy, may I say that *I* don't like that guy? From my point of view or anybody else's he is using you for what you are worth. If you want to make some changes for your own good, for gosh sakes get *him* away from you. All right, he may not be queer. He's just a nothing, which is worse. He isn't normal enough to have *any* kind of sex life, if you know what I mean. However I'm not interested in Tom but in you. Yes, I can bear the few weeks without you, darling, and even Christmas, though I prefer not to think of Christmas. I prefer not to think about you and – as you said – let the feelings come or not. But it's impossible not to think of you here because every inch of the village is haunted with you as far as I'm concerned, and in this house, everywhere I look there is some sign of you, the hedge we planted, the fence we started repairing and never finished, the books I borrowed from you and never returned. And your chair at the table, that's the worst.

To continue with the neck-sticking, I don't say that Tom is going to do anything actively bad to you, but I know that he has a subtly bad influence on you. You act vaguely ashamed of being around him when you *are* around him, do you know that? Did you ever try to analyse it? I thought you were beginning to realize all this in the last few weeks, but now you're with him again and frankly, dear boy, I don't know what to make of it. If you really 'don't care when' he takes off, for God's sake send him packing! He'll never help you or anybody else to get straightened out about anything. In fact it's greatly to his interest to keep you muddled and string you along and your father too.

Thanks loads for the cologne, darling. I'll save it – or most of it – for when I see you next. I haven't got the refrigerator over to my house yet. You can have it, of course, any time you want it back.

Maybe Tom told you that Skippy skipped out. Should I capture a gecko and tie a string around its neck? I have to get to work on the house wall right away before it mildews completely and collapses on me. Wish you were here, darling – of course.

Lots of love and *write*,

XX
Marge

c/o American Express
Rome
12 Dec. 19——

Dear Mother and Dad:

I'm in Rome looking for an apartment, though I haven't found exactly what I want yet. Apartments here are either too big or too small, and if too big you have to shut off every room but one in winter in order to heat it properly anyway. I'm trying to get a medium-sized, medium-priced place that I can heat completely without spending a fortune for it.

Sorry I've been so bad about letters lately. I hope to do better with the quieter life I'm leading here. I felt I needed a change from Mongibello — as you've both been saying for a long time — so I've moved bag and baggage and may even sell the house and the boat. I've met a wonderful painter called Di Massimo who is willing to give me instruction in his studio. I'm going to work like blazes for a few months and see what happens. A kind of trial period. I realize this doesn't interest you, Dad, but since you're always asking how I spend my time, this is how. I'll be leading a very quiet, studious life until next summer.

Apropos of that, could you send me the latest folders from Burke-Greenleaf? I like to keep up with what you're doing, too, and it's been a long time since I've seen anything.

Mother, I hope you haven't gone to great trouble for my Christmas. I don't really need anything I can think of. How are you feeling? Are you able to get out very much? To the theatre, etc.? How is Uncle Edward now? Send him my regards and keep me posted.

With love,
Dickie

Tom read it over, decided there were probably too many commas, and retyped it patiently and signed it. He had once seen a half-finished letter of Dickie's to his parents in Dickie's typewriter, and he knew Dickie's general style. He knew that Dickie had never taken more than ten minutes writing any letter. If this letter was different, Tom thought, it could be different only in being a little more personal and enthusiastic than usual. He felt rather pleased with the letter when he read it over for the second time. Uncle Edward was a brother of Mrs. Greenleaf, who was ill in an Illinois hospital with some kind of cancer, Tom had learned from the latest letter to Dickie from his mother.

A few days later he was off to Paris by plane. He had called the Inghilterra before he left Rome: no letters or phone calls for Richard Greenleaf. He landed at Orly at five in the afternoon. The passport inspector stamped his passport after only a quick glance at him, though Tom had lightened his hair slightly with a peroxide wash and had forced some waves into it, aided by hair oil, and for the inspector's benefit he had put on the rather tense, rather frowning expression of Dickie's passport photograph. Tom checked in at the Hôtel du Quai-Voltaire, which had been recommended to him by some Americans with whom he had struck up an acquaintance at a Rome café, as being conveniently located and not too full of Americans. Then he went out for a stroll in the raw, foggy December evening. He walked with his head up and a smile on his face. It was the atmosphere of the city that he loved, the atmosphere that he had always heard about, crooked streets, grey-fronted houses with skylights, noisy car horns, and everywhere public urinals and columns with brightly coloured theatre notices on them. He wanted to let the atmosphere seep in slowly, perhaps for several days, before he visited the Louvre or went up the Eiffel Tower or anything like that. He bought a *Figaro*, sat down at a table in the Dôme, and ordered a fine à l'eau, because Dickie had once said that fine à l'eau was his usual drink in France. Tom's French was limited, but so was Dickie's, Tom knew. Some interesting people stared at him through the glass-enclosed front of the café, but no one came in to speak to him.

Tom was prepared for someone to get up from one of the tables at any moment, and come over and say, 'Dickie Greenleaf! Is it really you?'

He had done so little artificially to change his appearance, but his very expression, Tom thought, was like Dickie's now. He wore a smile that was dangerously welcoming to a stranger, a smile more fit to greet an old friend or a lover. It was Dickie's best and most typical smile when he was in a good humour. Tom was in a good humour. It was Paris. *Wonderful* to sit in a famous café, and to think of tomorrow and tomorrow and tomorrow being Dickie Greenleaf! The cuff links, the white silk shirts, even the old clothes – the worn brown belt with the brass buckle, the old brown grain-leather shoes, the kind advertised in *Punch* as lasting a life-time, the old mustard-coloured coat sweater with the sagging pockets, they were all his and he loved them all. And the black fountain pen with little gold initials. And the wallet, a well-worn alligator wallet from Gucci's. And there was plenty of money to go in it.

By the next afternoon he had been invited to a party in the Avenue Kléber by some people – a French girl and an American young man – with whom he had started a conversation in a large café-restaurant on the Boulevard Saint-Germain. The party consisted of thirty or forty people, most of them middle-aged, standing around rather frigidly in a huge, chilly, formal apartment. In Europe, Tom gathered, inadequate heating was a hallmark of chic in winter, like the iceless martini in summer. He had moved to a more expensive hotel in Rome, finally, in order to be warmer, and had found that the more expensive hotel was even colder. In a gloomy, old-fashioned way the house was chic, Tom supposed. There were a butler and a maid, a vast table of pâtés en croûte, sliced turkey, and petits fours, and quantities of champagne, although the up-holstery of the sofa and the long drapes at the windows were threadbare and rotting with age, and he had seen mouseholes in the hall by the elevator. At least half a dozen of the guests he had been presented to were counts and countesses. An American informed Tom that the young man and the girl who had invited him were going to be married, and that her parents were not enthusiastic. There was an atmosphere of strain in the big room, and Tom made an effort to be as pleasant as possible to everyone, even the severer-looking French people to whom he could say little more than 'C'est très agréable, n'est-ce pas?' He did his very best, and won at least a smile from the French girl who had invited him. He considered himself lucky to be there. How many Americans alone in Paris could get themselves invited to a French home after only a week or so in the city? The French were especially slow in inviting strangers to their homes, Tom had always heard. Not a single one of the Americans seemed to know his name. Tom felt completely comfortable, as he had never felt before at any party that he could remember. He behaved as he had always wanted to behave at a party. This was the clean slate he had thought about on the boat coming over from America. This was the real annihilation of his past and of himself, Tom Ripley, who was made up of that past, and his rebirth as a completely new person. One Frenchwoman and two of the Americans invited him to parties, but Tom declined with the same reply to all of them: 'Thank you very much, but I'm leaving Paris tomorrow.'

It wouldn't do to become too friendly with any of these, Tom thought. One of them might know somebody who knew Dickie very well, someone who might be at the next party.

At eleven-fifteen, when he said good-bye to his hostess and to her parents, they looked very sorry to see him go. But he wanted to be at Notre Dame by midnight. It was Christmas Eve.

The girl's mother asked his name again.

'Monsieur Granelafe,' the girl repeated for her. 'Deekie Granelafe. Correct?'

'Correct,' Tom said, smiling.

Just as he reached the downstairs hall he remembered Freddie Miles' party at Cortina. December second. Nearly a month ago! He had meant to write to Freddie to say that he wasn't coming. Had Marge gone, he wondered? Freddie would think it very strange that he hadn't written to say he wasn't coming, and Tom hoped Marge had told Freddie, at least. He must write Freddie at once. There was a Florence address for Freddie in Dickie's address book. It was a slip, but nothing serious, Tom thought. He just mustn't let such a thing happen again.

He walked out into the darkness and turned in the direction of the illuminated, bone-white Arc de Triomphe. It was strange to feel so alone, and yet so much a part of things, as he had felt at the party. He felt it again, standing on the outskirts of the crowd that filled the square in front of Notre Dame. There was such a crowd he couldn't possibly have got into the cathedral, but the amplifiers carried the music clearly to all parts of the square. French Christmas carols whose names he didn't know. 'Silent Night'. A solemn carol, and then a lively, babbling one. The chanting of male voices. Frenchmen near him removed their hats. Tom removed his. He stood tall, straight, sober-faced, yet ready to smile if anyone had addressed him. He felt as he had felt on the ship, only more intensely, full of good will, a gentleman, with nothing in his past to blemish his character. He was Dickie, good-natured, naïve Dickie, with a smile for everyone and a thousand francs for anyone who asked him. An old man did ask him for money as Tom was leaving the cathedral square, and he gave him a crisp blue thousand-franc bill. The old man's face exploded in a smile, and he tipped his hat.

Tom felt a little hungry, though he rather liked the idea of going to bed hungry tonight. He would spend an hour or so with his Italian conversation book, he thought, then go to bed. Then he remembered that he had decided to try to gain about five pounds, because Dickie's clothes were just a trifle loose on him and Dickie looked heavier than he in the face, so he stopped at a bar-tabac and ordered a ham sandwich on long crusty bread and a glass of hot milk, because a man next to him at the counter was drinking hot milk. The milk was almost tasteless, pure and chastening, as Tom imagined a wafer tasted in church.

He came down in a leisurely way from Paris, stopping overnight in Lyon and also in Arles to see the places that Van Gogh had painted there. He maintained his cheerful equanimity in the face of atrociously bad weather. In Arles, the rain borne on the violent mistral soaked him through as he tried to discover the exact spots where Van Gogh had stood to paint from. He had bought a beautiful book of Van Gogh reproductions in Paris, but he could not take the book out in the rain, and he had to make a dozen trips back to his hotel to verify the scenes. He looked over Marseille, found it drab except for the Canebière, and moved on eastward by train, stopping for a day in St. Tropez, Cannes, Nice, Monte Carlo – all the places he had heard of and felt such affinity for when he saw them, though in the month of December they were overcast by grey winter clouds, and the gay crowds were not there, even on New Year's Eve in Menton. Tom put the people there in his imagination, men and women in evening clothes descending the broad steps of the gambling palace in Monte Carlo, people in bright bathing costumes, light and brilliant as a Dufy water-colour, walking under the palms of the Boulevard des Anglais at Nice. People – American, English, French, German, Swedish, Italian. Romance, disappointment, quarrels, reconciliations, murder. The Côte d'Azur excited him as no other place he had yet seen in the world excited him. And it was so tiny, really, this curve in the Mediterranean coastline with the wonderful names strung like beads – Toulon, Fréjus, St. Rafael, Cannes, Nice, Menton, and then San Remo.

There were two letters from Marge when he got back to Rome on the fourth of January. She was giving up her house on the first of March, she said. She had not quite finished the first draft of her book, but she was sending three-quarters of it with all the photographs to the American publisher who had been interested in her idea when she wrote him about it last summer. She wrote:

When am I going to see you? I hate passing up a summer in Europe after I've weathered another awful winter, but I think I'll go home early in March. Yes, I'm *homesick*, finally, *really*. Darling, it would be so wonderful if we could go home on the same boat together. Is there a possibility? I don't suppose there *is*. You're not going back to the U.S. even for a short visit this winter?

I was thinking of sending all my stuff (eight pieces of luggage, two trunks, three boxes of books and miscellaneous!) by slow boat from Naples and coming up through Rome and if you were in the mood we could at least go up the coast again and see Forte dei Marmi and Viareggio and the other spots we like – a last look. I'm not in the mood to care about the weather, which I know will be *horrid*. I wouldn't ask you to accompany me to Marseille, where I catch the boat, but from *Genoa*??? What do you think? . . .

The other letter was more reserved. Tom knew why: he had not sent her even a postcard for nearly a month. She said:

Have changed my mind about the Riviera. Maybe this damp weather has taken away my enterprise or my book has. Anyway, I'm leaving from Naples on an earlier boat – the *Constitution* on 28 Feb. Imagine – back to America as soon as I step aboard. American food, Americans, dollars for drinks and the horseraces— Darling, I'm sorry not to be seeing you, as I gather from your silence you still don't want to see me, so don't give it a thought. Consider me off your hands.

Of course I do hope I see you again, in the States or anywhere else. Should you possibly be inspired to make a trip down to

Mongy before the 28th, you know damned well you are welcome.

As ever,

Marge

P.S. I don't even know if you're still in Rome.

Tom could see her in tears as she wrote it. He had an impulse to write her a very considerate letter, saying he had just come back from Greece, and had she gotten his two postcards? But it was safer, Tom thought, to let her leave without being sure where he was. He wrote her nothing.

The only thing that made him uneasy, and that was not very uneasy, was the possibility of Marge's coming up to see him in Rome before he could get settled in an apartment. If she combed the hotels she could find him, but she could never find him in an apartment. Well-to-do Americans didn't have to report their places of residence at the questura, though, according to the stipulations of the Permesso di Soggiorno, one was supposed to register every change of address with the police. Tom had talked with an American resident of Rome who had an apartment and who had said he never bothered with the questura, and it never bothered him. If Marge did come up to Rome suddenly, Tom had a lot of his own clothing hanging ready in the closet. The only thing he had changed about himself, physically, was his hair, but that could always be explained as being the effect of the sun. He wasn't really worried. Tom had at first amused himself with an eyebrow pencil – Dickie's eyebrows were longer and turned up a little at the outer edges – and with a touch of putty at the end of his nose to make it longer and more pointed, but he abandoned these as too likely to be noticed. The main thing about impersonation, Tom thought, was to maintain the mood and temperament of the person one was impersonating, and to assume the facial expressions that went with them. The rest fell into place.

On the tenth of January Tom wrote Marge that he was back in Rome after three weeks in Paris alone, that Tom had left Rome a month ago, saying he was going up to Paris, and from there to America though he hadn't run into Tom in Paris, and that he had not yet found an apartment in Rome but he was looking and would let her know his address as soon as he had one. He thanked her extravagantly for the Christmas package: she had sent the white sweater with the red V stripes that she had been knitting and trying on Dickie for size since October, as well as an art book of quattrocento painting and a leather shaving kit with his intials, H.R.G., on the lid. The package had arrived only on January sixth, which was the main reason for Tom's letter: he didn't want her to think he hadn't claimed it, imagine that he had vanished into thin air, and then start a search for him. He asked if she had received a package from him? He had mailed it from Paris, and he supposed it was late. He apologized. He wrote:

I'm painting again with Di Massimo and am reasonably pleased. I miss you, too, but if you can still bear with my experiment, I'd prefer not to see you for several more weeks (unless you do suddenly go home in February, which I still doubt!) by which time you may not care to see me again. Regards to Giorgio and wife and Fausto if he's still there and Pietro down at the dock ...

It was a letter in the absent-minded and faintly lugubrious tone of all Dickie's letters, a letter that could not be called warm or unwarm, and that said essentially nothing.

Actually he had found an apartment in a large apartment house in the Via Imperiale near the Pincian Gate, and had signed a year's lease for it, though he did not intend to spend most of his time in Rome, much less the winter. He only wanted a home, a base somewhere, after years of not having any. And Rome was chic. Rome was part of his new life. He wanted to be able to say in Majorca or Athens or Cairo or wherever he was: 'Yes, I live in Rome. I keep an apartment there.' 'Keep' was the word for apartments among the international set. You kept an apartment in Europe the way you kept a garage in America. He also wanted his apartment to be elegant, though he intended to have the minimum of people up to see him, and he hated the idea of having a telephone, even an unlisted telephone, but he decided it was more of a safety measure than a menace, so he had one installed. The apartment had a large living-room, a bedroom, a kind of sitting-room, kitchen, and bath. It was furnished somewhat ornately, but it suited the respectable neighbourhood and the respectable life he intended to lead. The rent was the equivalent of a hundred and seventy-five dollars a month in winter including heat, and a hundred and twenty-five in summer.

Marge replied with an ecstatic letter saying she had just received the beautiful silk blouse from Paris which she hadn't expected *at all* and it fitted to perfection. She said she had had Fausto and the Cecchis for Christmas dinner at her house and the turkey had been divine, with marrons and giblet gravy and plum pudding and blah blah blah and everything but *him*. And what was he doing and thinking about? And was he happier? And that Fausto would look him up on his way to Milan if he sent an address in the next few days, otherwise leave a message for Fausto at the American Express, saying where Fausto could find him.

Tom supposed her good humour was due mostly to the fact that she now thought Tom had departed for America via Paris. Along with Marge's letter came one from Signor Pucci, saying that he had sold three pieces of his furniture for a hundred and fifty thousand lire in Naples, and that he had a prospective buyer for the boat, a certain Anastasio Martino of Mongibello, who had promised to pay the first down payment within a week, but that the house probably couldn't be sold until summer when the Americans began coming in again. Less fifteen per cent for Signor Pucci's commission, the furniture sale amounted to two hundred and ten dollars, and Tom celebrated that night by going to a Roman nightclub and ordering a superb dinner which he ate in elegant solitude at a candlelit table for two. He did not at all mind dining and going to the theatre alone. It gave him the opportunity to concentrate on being Dickie Greenleaf. He broke his bread as Dickie did, thrust his fork into his mouth with his left hand as Dickie did, gazed off at the other tables and at the dancers in such a profound and benevolent trance that the waiter had to speak to him a couple of times to get his attention. Some people waved to him from a table, and Tom recognized them as one of the American couples he had met at the Christmas Eve party in Paris. He made a sign of greeting in return. He even remembered their name, Souders. He did not look at them again during the evening, but they left before he did and stopped by his table to say hello.

'All by yourself?' the man asked. He looked a little tipsy.

'Yes. I have a yearly date here with myself,' Tom replied. 'I celebrate a certain anniversary.'

The American nodded a little blankly, and Tom could see that he was stymied for anything intelligent to say, as uneasy as any small-town American in the presence of cosmopolitan poise and sobriety, money and good clothes, even if the clothes were on another American.

'You said you were living in Rome, didn't you?' his wife asked. 'You know, I think we've forgotten your name, but we remember you very well from Christmas Eve.'

'Greenleaf,' Tom replied. 'Richard Greenleaf.'

'*Oh*, yes!' she said, relieved. 'Do you have an apartment here?'

She was all ready to take down his address in her memory.

'I'm staying at a hotel at the moment, but I'm planning to move into an apartment any day, as soon as the decorating's finished. I'm at the Elisio. Why don't you give me a ring?'

'We'd love to. We're on our way to Majorca in three more days, but that's plenty of time!'

'Love to see you,' Tom said. 'Buona sera!'

Alone again, Tom returned to his private reveries. He ought to open a bank account for Tom Ripley, he thought, and from time to time put a hundred dollars or so into it. Dickie Greenleaf had two banks, one in Naples and one in New York, with about five thousand dollars in each account. He might open the Ripley account with a couple of thousand, and put into it the hundred and fifty thousand lire from the Mongibello furniture. After all, he had two people to take care of.

15

HE VISITED THE Capitoline and the Villa Borghese, explored the Forum thoroughly, and took six Italian lessons from an old man in his neighbourhood who had a tutoring sign in his window, and to whom Tom gave a false name. After the sixth lesson, Tom thought that his Italian was on a par with Dickie's. He remembered verbatim several sentences that Dickie had said at one time or another which he now knew were incorrect. For example, 'Ho paura che non c'è arrivata, Giorgio,' one evening in Giorgio's, when they had been waiting for Marge and she had been late. It should have been 'sia arrivata' in the subjunctive after an expression of fearing. Dickie had never used the subjunctive as often as it should be used in Italian. Tom studiously kept himself from learning the proper uses of the subjunctive.

Tom bought dark-red velvet for the drapes in his living-room, because the drapes that had come with the apartment offended him. When he had asked Signora Buffi, the wife of the house superintendent, if she knew of a seamstress who could make them up, Signora Buffi had offered to make them herself. Her price was two thousand lire, hardly more than three dollars. Tom forced her to take five thousand. He bought several minor items to embellish his apartment, though he never asked anyone up – with the exception of one attractive but not very bright young man, an American, whom he had met in the Café Greco when the young man had asked him how to get to the Hotel Excelsior from there. The Excelsior was on the way to Tom's house, so Tom asked him to come up for a drink. Tom had only wanted to impress him for an hour and then say good-bye to him forever, which he did, after serving him his best brandy and strolling about his apartment discoursing on the pleasure of life in Rome. The young man was leaving for Munich the following day.

Tom carefully avoided the American residents of Rome who might expect him to come to their parties and ask them to his in return, though he loved to chat with Americans and Italians in the Café Greco and in the students' restaurants in the Via Margutta. He told his name only to an Italian painter named Carlino, whom he met in a Via Margutta tavern, told him also that he painted and was studying with a painter called Di Massimo. If the police ever investigated Dickie's activities in Rome, perhaps long after Dickie had disappeared and become Tom Ripley again, this one Italian painter could be relied upon to say that he knew Dickie Greenleaf had been painting in Rome in January. Carlino had never heard of Di Massimo, but Tom described him so vividly that Carlino would probably never forget him.

He felt alone, yet not at all lonely. It was very much like the feeling on Christmas Eve in Paris, a feeling that everyone was watching him, as if he had an audience made up of the entire world, a feeling that kept him on his mettle, because to make a mistake would be catastrophic. Yet he felt absolutely confident he would not make a mistake. It gave his existence a peculiar, delicious atmosphere of purity, like that, Tom thought, which a fine actor probably feels when he plays an important role on a stage with the conviction that the role he is playing could not be played better by anyone else. He was himself and yet not himself. He felt blameless and free, despite the fact that he consciously controlled every move he made. But he no longer felt tired after several hours of it, as he had at first. He had no need to relax when he was alone. Now, from the moment when he got out of bed and went to brush his teeth, he was Dickie, brushing his teeth with his right elbow jutted out, Dickie rotating the eggshell on his spoon for the last bite.

Dickie invariably putting back the first tie he pulled off the rack and selecting a second. He had even produced a painting in Dickie's manner.

By the end of January Tom thought that Fausto must have come and gone through Rome, though Marge's last letters had not mentioned him. Marge wrote, care of the American Express, about once a week. She asked if he needed any socks or a muffler, because she had plenty of time to knit, besides working on her book. She always put in a funny anecdote about somebody they knew in the village, just so Dickie wouldn't think she was eating her heart out for him, though obviously she was, and obviously she wasn't going to leave for the States in February without making another desperate try for him in person, Tom thought, hence the investments of the long letters and the knitted socks and muffler which Tom knew were coming, even though he hadn't replied to her letters. Her letters repelled him. He disliked even touching them, and after he glanced through them he tore them up and dropped them into the garbage.

He wrote finally:

I'm giving up the idea of an apartment in Rome for the time being. Di Massimo is going to Sicily for several months, and I may go with him and go on somewhere from there. My plans are vague, but they have the virtue of freedom and they suit my present mood.

Don't send me any socks, Marge. I really don't need a thing. Wish you much luck with 'Mongibello'.

He had a ticket for Majorca – by train to Naples, then the boat from Naples to Palma over the night of January thirty-first and February first. He had bought two new suitcases from Gucci's, the best leather goods store in Rome, one a large, soft suitcase of antelope hide, the other a neat tan canvas with brown leather straps. Both bore Dickie's initials. He had thrown the shabbier of his own two suitcases away, and the remaining one he kept in a closet of his apartment, full of his own clothes, in case of an emergency. But Tom was not expecting any emergencies. The scuttled boat in San Remo had never been found. Tom looked through the papers every day for something about it.

While Tom was packing his suitcases one morning his door-bell rang. He supposed it was a solicitor of some kind, or a mistake. He had no name on his door-bell, and he had told the superintendent that he did not want his name on the door-bell because he didn't like people to drop in on him. It rang for the second time, and Tom still ignored it, and went on with his lackadaisical packing. He loved to pack, and he took a long time about it, a whole day or two days, laying Dickie's clothes affectionately into suitcases, now and then trying on a good-looking shirt or a jacket in front of the mirror. He was standing in front of the mirror, buttoning a blue-and-white seahorse-patterned sport shirt of Dickie's that he had never worn, when there came a knock at his door.

It crossed his mind that it might be Fausto, that it would be just like Fausto to hunt him down in Rome and try to surprise him. That was silly, he told himself. But his hands were cool with sweat as he went to the door. He felt faint, and the absurdity of his faintness, plus the danger of keeling over and being found prostrate on the floor, made him wrench the door open with both hands, though he opened it only a few inches.

'Hello!' the American voice said out of the semi-darkness of the hall. 'Dickie? It's Freddie!'

Tom took a step back, holding the door open. 'He's— Won't you come in? He's not here right now. He should be back in a little later.'

Freddie Miles came in, looking around. His ugly, freckled face gawked in every direction. How in hell had he found the place, Tom wondered. Tom slipped his rings off quickly and pocketed them. And what else? He glanced around the room.

'You're staying with him?' Freddie asked with that wall-eyed stare that made his face look idiotic and rather scared.

'Oh, no. I'm just staying here for a few hours,' Tom said, casually removing the seahorse shirt. He had another shirt on under it. 'Dickie's out for lunch. Otello's, I think he said. He should be back around three at the latest.' One of the Buffis must have let Freddie in, Tom thought, and told him which bell to press, and told him Signor Greenleaf was in, too. Freddie had probably said he was an old friend of Dickie's. Now he would have to get Freddie out of the house without running into Signora Buffi downstairs, because she always sang out, 'Buon giorno, Signor Greenleaf!'

'I met you in Mongibello, didn't I?' Freddie asked. 'Aren't you Tom? I thought you were coming to Cortina.'

'I couldn't make it, thanks. How was Cortina?'

'Oh, fine. What happened to Dickie?'

'Didn't he write to you? He decided to spend the winter in Rome. He told me he'd written to you.'

'Not a word – unless he wrote to Florence. But I was in Salzburg, and he had my address.' Freddie half sat on Tom's long table, rumpling the green silk runner. He smiled. 'Marge told me he'd moved to Rome, but she didn't have any address except the American Express. It was only by the damnedest luck I found his apartment. I ran into somebody at the Greco last night who just happened to know his address. What's this idea of—'

'Who?' Tom asked. 'An American?'

'No, an Italian fellow. Just a young kid.' Freddie was looking at Tom's shoes. 'You've got the same kind of shoes Dickie and I have. They wear like iron, don't they? I bought my pair in London eight years ago.'

They were Dickie's grain-leather shoes. 'These came from America.' Tom said. 'Can I offer you a drink or would you rather try to catch Dickie at Otello's? Do you know where it is? There's not much use in your waiting, because he generally takes till three with his lunches. I'm going out soon myself.'

Freddie had strolled towards the bedroom and stopped, looking at the suitcases on the bed. 'Is Dickie leaving for somewhere or did he just get here?' Freddie asked, turning.

'He's leaving. Didn't Marge tell you? He's going to Sicily for a while.'

'When?'

'Tomorrow. Or late tonight, I'm not quite sure.'

'Say, what's the matter with Dickie lately?' Freddie asked, frowning. 'What's the idea of all the seclusion?'

'He says he's been working pretty hard this winter,' Tom said in an offhand tone. 'He seems to want privacy, but as far as I know he's still on good terms with everybody, including Marge.'

Freddie smiled again, unbuttoning his big polo coat. 'He's not going to stay on good terms with me if he stands me up a few more times. Are you sure he's on good terms with Marge? I got the idea from her that they'd had a quarrel. I thought maybe that was why they didn't go to Cortina.' Freddie looked at him expectantly.

'Not that I know of.' Tom went to the closet to get his jacket, so that Freddie would know he wanted to leave, then realized just in time that the grey flannel jacket that matched his trousers might be recognizable as Dickie's, if Freddie knew Dickie's suit. Tom reached for a jacket of his own and for his own overcoat that were hanging at the extreme left of the closet. The shoulders of the overcoat looked as if the coat had been on a hanger for weeks, which it had. Tom turned around and saw Freddie staring at the silver identification bracelet on his left wrist. It was Dickie's bracelet, which Tom had never seen him wearing, but had found in Dickie's stud box. Freddie was looking at it as if he had seen it before. Tom put on his overcoat casually.

Freddie was looking at him now with a different expression, with a little surprise. Tom knew what Freddie was thinking. He stiffened, sensing danger. You're not out of the woods yet, he told himself. You're not out of the house yet.

'Ready to go?' Tom asked.

'You do live here, don't you?'

'No!' Tom protested, smiling. The ugly, freckle-blotched face stared at him from under the garish thatch of red hair. If they could only get out without running into Signora Buffi downstairs, Tom thought. 'Let's go.'

'Dickie's loaded you up with all his jewellery, I see.'

Tom couldn't think of a single thing to say, a single joke to make. 'Oh, it's a loan,' Tom said in his deepest voice. 'Dickie got tired of wearing it, so he told me to wear it for a while.' He meant the identification bracelet, but there was also the silver clip on his tie, he realized, with the G on it. Tom had bought the tieclip himself. He could feel the belligerence growing in Freddie Miles as surely as if his huge body were generating a heat that he could feel across the room. Freddie was the kind of ox who might beat up somebody he thought was a pansy, especially if the conditions were as propitious as these. Tom was afraid of his eyes.

'Yes, I'm ready to go,' Freddie said grimly, getting up. He walked to the door and turned with a swing of his broad shoulders. 'That's the Otello not far from the Inghilterra?'

'Yes,' Tom said. 'He's supposed to be there by one o'clock.' Freddie nodded. 'Nice to see you again,' he said unpleasantly, and closed the door.

Tom whispered a curse. He opened the door slightly and listened to the quick *tap-tap – tap-tap* of Freddie's shoes descending the stairs. He wanted to make sure Freddie got out without speaking to one of the Buffis again. Then he heard Freddie's 'Buon giorno, signora.' Tom leaned over the stairwell. Three storeys down, he could see part of Freddie's coat-sleeve. He was talking in Italian with Signora Buffi. The woman's voice came more clearly.

'. . . only Signor Greenleaf,' she was saying. 'No, only one. . . . Signor Chi? . . . No, signor. . . . I do not think he has gone out today at all, but I could be wrong!' She laughed.

Tom twisted the stair rail in his hands as if it were Freddie's neck. Then Tom heard Freddie's footsteps running up the stairs. Tom stepped back into the apartment and closed the door. He could go on insisting that he didn't live here, that Dickie was at Otello's, or that he didn't know where Dickie was, but Freddie wouldn't stop now until he had found Dickie. Or Freddie would drag him downstairs and ask Signora Buffi who he was.

Freddie knocked on the door. The knob turned. It was locked. Tom picked up a heavy glass ashtray. He couldn't get his hand across it, and he had to hold it by the edge. He tried to think just for two seconds more: wasn't there another way out? What would he do with the body? He couldn't think. This was the only way out. He opened the door with his left hand. His right hand with the ashtray was drawn back and down.

Freddie came into the room. 'Listen, would you mind telling—'

The curved edge of the ashtray hit the middle of his forehead. Freddie looked dazed. Then his knees bent and he went down like a bull hit between the eyes with a hammer. Tom kicked the door shut. He slammed the edge of the ashtray into the back of Freddie's neck. He hit the neck again and again, terrified that Freddie might be only pretending and that one of his huge arms might suddenly circle his legs and pull him down. Tom struck his head a glancing blow, and blood came. Tom cursed himself. He ran and got a towel from the bathroom and put it under Freddie's head. Then he felt Freddie's wrist for a pulse. There was one, faint, and it seemed to flutter away as he touched it as if the pressure of his own fingers stilled it. In the next second it was gone. Tom listened for any sound behind the door. He imagined Signora Buffi standing behind the door with the hesitant smile she always had when she felt she was interrupting. But there wasn't any sound. There hadn't been any loud sound, he thought, either from the ashtray or when Freddie fell. Tom looked down at Freddie's mountainous form on the floor and felt a sudden disgust and a sense of helplessness.

It was only twelve-forty, hours until dark. He wondered if Freddie had people waiting for him anywhere? Maybe in a car downstairs? He searched Freddie's pockets. A wallet. The American passport in the inside breast pocket of the overcoat. Mixed Italian and some other kind of coins. A keycase. There were two car keys on a ring that said FIAT. He searched the wallet for a licence. There it was, with all the particulars: FIAT 1400 nero – convertible – 1955. He could find it if it was in the neighbourhood. He searched every pocket, and the pockets in the buff-coloured vest, for a garage ticket, but he found none. He went to the front window, then nearly smiled because it was so simple: there stood the black convertible across the street almost directly in front of the house. He could not be sure, but he thought there was no one in it.

He suddenly knew what he was going to do. He set about arranging the room, bringing out the gin and vermouth bottles from his liquor cabinet and on second thought the pernod because it smelled so much stronger. He set the bottles on the long table and mixed a martini in a tall glass with a couple of ice cubes in it, drank a little of it so that the glass would be soiled, then poured some of it into another glass, took it over to Freddie and crushed his limp fingers around it and carried it back to the table. He looked at the wound, and found that it had stopped bleeding or was stopping and had not run through the towel on to the floor. He propped Freddie up against the wall, and poured some straight gin from the bottle down his throat. It didn't go down very well, most of it went on to his shirtfront, but Tom didn't think the Italian police would actually make a blood test to see how drunk Freddie had been. Tom let his eyes rest absently on Freddie's limp, messy face for a moment, and his stomach contracted sickeningly and he quickly looked away. He mustn't do that again. His head had begun ringing as if he were going to faint.

That'd be a fine thing, Tom thought as he wobbled across the room towards the window, to faint now! He frowned at the black car down below, and breathed the fresh air in deeply. He wasn't going to faint, he told himself. He knew exactly what he was going to do. At the last minute, the pernod, for both of them. Two other glasses with their fingerprints and pernod. And the ashtrays must be full. Freddie smoked Chesterfields. Then the Appian Way. One of those dark places behind the tombs. There weren't any streetlights for long stretches on the Appian Way. Freddie's wallet would be missing. Objective: robbery.

He had hours of time, but he didn't stop until the room was ready, the dozen lighted Chesterfields and the dozen or so Lucky Strikes burnt down and stabbed out in the ashtrays, and a glass of pernod broken and only half cleaned up from the bathroom tiles, and the curious thing was that as he set his scene so carefully, he pictured having hours more time to clean it up – say between nine this evening when the body might be found, and midnight, when the police just might decide he was worth questioning, because somebody just might have known that Freddie Miles was going to call on Dickie Greenleaf today – and he knew that he *would* have it all cleaned up by eight o'clock, probably, because according to the story he was going to tell, Freddie would have left his house by seven (as indeed Freddie was going to leave his house by seven), and Dickie Greenleaf was a fairly tidy young man, even with a few drinks in him. But the point of the messy house was that the messiness substantitated merely for his own benefit the story that he was going to tell, and that therefore he had to believe himself.

And he would still leave for Naples and Palma at ten-thirty tomorrow morning, unless for some reason the police detained him. If he saw in the newspaper tomorrow morning that the body had been found, and the police did not try to contact him, it was only decent that he should volunteer to tell them that Freddie Miles had been at his house until late afternoon, Tom thought. But it suddenly occurred to him that a doctor might be able to tell that Freddie had been dead since noon. And he couldn't get Freddie out now, not in broad daylight. No, his only hope was that the body wouldn't be found for so many hours that a doctor couldn't tell exactly how long he had been dead. And he must try to get out of the house without *anybody* seeing him – whether he could carry Freddie down with a fair amount of ease like a passed-out drunk or not – so that if he had to make any statement, he could say that Freddie left the house around four or five in the afternoon.

He dreaded the five- or six-hour wait until nightfall so much that for a few moments he thought he *couldn't* wait. That mountain on the floor! And he hadn't wanted to kill him at all. It had been so unnecessary, Freddie and his stinking, filthy suspicions. Tom was trembling, sitting on the edge of a chair cracking his knuckles. He wanted to go out and take a walk, but he was afraid to leave the body lying there. There had to be noise, of course, if he and Freddie were supposed to be talking and drinking all afternoon. Tom turned the radio on to a station that played dance music. He could have a drink, at least. That was part of the act. He made another couple of martinis with ice in the glass. He didn't even want it, but he drank it.

The gin only intensified the same thoughts he had had. He stood looking down at Freddie's long, heavy body in the polo coat that was crumpled under him, that he hadn't the energy or the heart to straighten out, though it annoyed him, and thinking how sad, stupid, clumsy, dangerous and unnecessary his death had been, and how brutally unfair to Freddie. Of course, one could loathe Freddie, too. A selfish, stupid bastard who had sneered at one of his best friends – Dickie certainly was one of his best friends – just because he suspected him of sexual deviation. Tom laughed at that phrase 'sexual deviation'. Where was the sex? Where was the deviation? He looked at Freddie and said low and bitterly: 'Freddie Miles, you're a victim of your own dirty mind.'

16

HE WAITED AFTER all until nearly eight, because around seven there were always more people coming in and out of the house than at other times. At ten to eight, he strolled downstairs to make sure that Signora Buffi was not pottering around in the hall and that her door was not open, and to make sure there really was no one in Freddie's car, though he had gone down in the middle of the afternoon to look at the car and see if it was Freddie's. He tossed Freddie's polo coat into the back seat. He came back upstairs, knelt down and pulled Freddie's arm around his neck, set his teeth, and lifted. He staggered, jerking the flaccid weight higher on his shoulder. He had lifted Freddie earlier that afternoon, just to see if he could, and he had seemed barely able to walk two steps in the room with Freddie's pounds pressing his own feet against the floor, and Freddie was exactly as heavy now, but the difference was that he knew he had to get him out now. He let Freddie's feet drag to relieve some of his weight, managed to pull his door shut with his elbow, then began to descend the stairs. Half-way down the first flight, he stopped, hearing someone come out of an apartment on the second floor. He waited until the person had gone down the stairs and out the front door, then recommenced his slow, bumping descent. He had pulled a hat of Dickie's well down over Freddie's head so that the blood-stained hair would not show. On a mixture of gin and pernod, which he had been drinking for the last hour, Tom had gotten himself to a precisely calculated state of intoxication in which he thought he could move with a certain nonchalance and smoothness and at the same time be courageous and even foolhardy enough to take chances without flinching. The first chance, the worst thing that could happen, was that he might simply collapse under Freddie's weight before he got him to the car. He had sworn that he would not stop to rest going down the stairs. He didn't. And nobody else came out of any of the apartments, and nobody came in the front door. During the hours upstairs, Tom had imagined so tortuously everything that might happen – Signora Buffi or her husband coming out of their apartment just as he reached the bottom of the stairs, or himself fainting so that both he and Freddie would be discovered sprawled on the stairs together, or being unable to pick Freddie up again if he had to put him down to rest – imagined it all with such intensity, writhing upstairs in his apartment, that to have descended all the stairs without a single one of his imaginings happening made him feel he was gliding down under a magical protection of some kind, with ease in spite of the mass on his shoulder.

He looked out of the glass of the two front doors. The street looked normal: a man was walking on the opposite sidewalk, but there was always someone walking on one sidewalk or the other. He opened the first door with one hand, kicked it aside and dragged Freddie's feet through. Between the doors, he shifted Freddie to the other shoulder, rolling his head under Freddie's body, and for a second a certain pride went through him at his own strength, until the ache in his relaxing arm staggered him with its pain. The arm was too tired even to circle Freddie's body. He set his teeth harder and staggered down the four front steps, banging his hip against the stone newel post.

A man approaching him on the sidewalk slowed his steps as if he were going to stop, but he went on.

If anyone came over, Tom thought, he would blow such a breath of pernod in his face there wouldn't be any reason to ask what was the matter. Damn them, damn them, damn them, he said to himself as he jolted down the kerb. Passers-by, innocent passers-by. Four of them now. But only two of them so much as glanced at him, he thought. He paused a moment for a car to pass. Then with a few quick steps and a heave he thrust Freddie's head and one shoulder through the open window of the car, far enough in that he could brace Freddie's body with his own body while he got his breath. He looked around, under the glow of light from the streetlamp across the street, into the shadows in front of his own apartment house.

At that instant the Buffis' youngest boy ran out of the door and down the sidewalk without looking in Tom's direction. Then a man crossing the street walked within a yard of the car with only a brief and faintly surprised look at Freddie's bent figure, which did look almost natural now, Tom thought, practically as if Freddie were only leaning into the car talking to someone, only he really *didn't* look quite natural, Tom knew. But that was the advantage of Europe, he thought. Nobody helped anybody, nobody meddled. If this had been America—

'Can I help you?' a voice asked in Italian.

'Ah, no, no, grazie,' Tom replied with drunken good cheer. 'I know where he lives,' he added in mumbled English.

The man nodded, smiling a little, too, and walked on. A tall thin man in a thin overcoat, hatless, with a moustache. Tom hoped he wouldn't remember. Or remember the car.

Tom swung Freddie out on the door, pulled him around the door and on to the car seat, came around the car and pulled Freddie into the seat beside the driver's seat. Then he put on the pair of brown leather gloves he had stuck into his overcoat pocket. He put Freddie's key into the dashboard. The car started obediently. They were off. Down the hill to the Via Veneto, past the American Library, over to the Piazza Venezia, past the balcony on which Mussolini used to stand to make his speeches, past the gargantuan Victor Emmanuel Monument and through the Forum, past the Colosseum, a grand tour of Rome that Freddie could not appreciate at all. It was just as if Freddie were sleeping beside him, as sometimes people did sleep when you wanted to show them scenery.

The Via Appia Antica stretched out before him, grey and ancient in the soft lights of its infrequent lamps. Black fragments of tombs rose up on either side of the road, silhouetted against the still not quite dark sky. There was more darkness than light. And only a single car ahead, coming this way. Not many people chose to take a ride on such a bumpy, gloomy road after dark in the month of January. Except perhaps lovers. The approaching car passed him. Tom began to look around for the right spot. Freddie ought to have a handsome tomb to lie behind, he thought. There was a spot ahead with three or four trees near the edge of the road and doubtless a tomb behind them or part of a tomb. Tom pulled off the road by the trees and shut off his lights. He waited a moment, looking at both ends of the straight, empty road.

Freddie was still as limp as a rubber doll. What was all this about rigor mortis? He dragged the limp body roughly now, scraping the face in the dirt, behind the last tree and behind the little remnant of tomb that was only a four-feet-high, jagged arc of wall, but which was probably a remnant of the tomb of a patrician, Tom thought, and quite enough for this pig. Tom cursed his ugly weight and kicked him suddenly in the chin. He was tired, tired to the point of crying, sick of the sight of Freddie Miles, and the moment when he could turn his back on him for the last time seemed never to come. There was still the God-damned coat! Tom went back to the car to get it. The ground was hard and dry, he noticed as he walked back, and should not leave any traces of his steps. He flung the coat down beside the body and turned away quickly and walked back to the car on his numb, staggering legs, and turned the car around towards Rome again.

As he drove, he wiped the outside of the car door with his gloved hand to get the fingerprints off, the only place he had touched the car before he put his gloves on, he thought. On the street that curved up to the American Express, opposite the Florida nightclub, he parked the car and got out and left it with the keys in the dashboard. He still had Freddie's wallet in his pocket, though he had transferred the Italian money to his own billfold and had burnt a Swiss twenty-franc note and some Austrian schilling notes in his apartment. Now he took the wallet out of his pocket, and as he passed a sewer grate he leaned down and dropped it in.

There were only two things wrong, he thought as he walked towards his house: robbers would logically have taken the polo coat, because it was a good one, and also the passport, which was still in the overcoat pocket. But not every robber was logical, he thought, maybe especially an Italian robber. And not every murderer was logical, either. His mind drifted back to the conversation with Freddie. ' . . . *an Italian fellow. Just a young kid* . . . ' Somebody had followed him home at some time, Tom thought, because he hadn't told *anybody* where he lived. It shamed him. Maybe two or three delivery boys might know where he lived, but a delivery boy wouldn't be sitting in a place like the Café Greco. It shamed him and made him shrink inside his overcoat. He imagined a dark, panting young face following him home, staring up to see which window had lighted up after he had gone in. Tom hunched in his overcoat and walked faster as if he were fleeing a sick, passionate pursuer.

17

TOM WENT OUT before eight in the morning to buy the papers. There was nothing. They might not find him for days, Tom thought. Nobody was likely to walk around an unimportant tomb like the one he had put Freddie behind. Tom felt quite confident of his safety, but physically he felt awful. He had a hangover, the terrible, jumpy kind that made him stop half-way in everything he began doing, even stop half-way in brushing his teeth to go and see if his train really left at ten-thirty or at ten-forty-five. It left at ten-thirty.

He was completely ready by nine, dressed and with his overcoat and raincoat out on the bed. He had even spoken to Signora Buffi to tell her he would be gone for at least three weeks and possibly longer. Signora Buffi had behaved just as usual, Tom thought, and had not mentioned his American visitor yesterday. Tom tried to think of something to ask her, something quite normal in view of Freddie's questions yesterday, that would show him what Signora Buffi really thought about the questions, but he couldn't think of anything, and decided to let well enough alone. Everything was fine. Tom tried to reason himself out of the hangover, because he had had only the equivalent of three martinis and three pernods at most. He knew it was a matter of mental suggestion, and that he had a hangover because he had intended to pretend that he had been drinking a great deal with Freddie. And now when there was no need of it, he was still pretending, uncontrollably.

The telephone rang, and Tom picked it up and said 'Pronto', sullenly.

'Signor Greenleaf?' asked the Italian voice.

'Sì.'

'Qui parla la stazione polizia numero ottantatre. Lei è un amico di un' americano chi se chiama Fred-derick Mee-lays?'

'Frederick Miles? Sì,' Tom said.

The quick, tense voice stated that the corpse of Fred-derick Mee-lays had been found that morning on the Via Appia Antica, and that Signor Mee-lays had visited him at some time yesterday, was that not so?

'Yes, that is so.'

'At what time exactly?'

'From about noon to – perhaps five or six in the afternoon, I am not quite sure.'

'Would you be kind enough to answer some questions? . . . No, it is not necessary that you trouble yourself to come to the station. The interrogator will come to you. Will eleven o'clock this morning be convenient?'

'I'll be very glad to help if I can,' Tom said in a properly excited voice, 'but can't the interrogator come now? It is necessary for me to leave the house at ten o'clock.'

The voice made a little moan and said it was doubtful, but they would try it. If they could not come before ten o'clock, it was very important that he should not leave the house.

'Va bene,' Tom said acquiescently, and hung up.

Damn them! He'd miss his train *and* his boat now. All he wanted to do was get out, leave Rome and leave his apartment. He started to go over what he would tell the police. It was all so simple, it bored him. It was the absolute truth. They had had drinks, Freddie had told him about Cortina, they had talked a lot, and then Freddie had left, maybe a little high but in a very good mood. No, he didn't know where Freddie had been going. He had supposed Freddie had a date for the evening.

Tom went into the bedroom and put a canvas, which he had begun a few days ago, on the easel. The paint on the palette was still moist because he had kept it under water in a pan in the kitchen. He mixed some more blue and white and began to add to the greyish-blue sky. The picture was still in Dickie's bright reddish-browns and clear whites – the roofs and walls of Rome out of his window. The sky was the only departure, because the winter sky of Rome was so gloomy, even Dickie would have painted it greyish-blue instead of blue, Tom thought. Tom frowned, just as Dickie frowned when he painted.

The telephone rang again. 'God damn it!' Tom muttered, and went to answer it. 'Pronto!'

'Pronto! Fausto!' the voice said. 'Come sta?' And the familiar bubbling, juvenile laugh.

'Oh-h! Fausto! Bene, grazie! Excuse me'; Tom continued in Italian in Dickie's laughing, absent voice, 'I've been trying to paint – trying.' It was calculated to be possibly the voice of Dickie after having lost a friend like Freddie, and also the voice of Dickie on an ordinary morning of absorbing work.

'Can you have lunch?' Fausto asked. 'My train leaves at four-fifteen for Milano.'

Tom groaned, like Dickie. 'I'm just taking off for Naples. Yes, immediately, in twenty minutes!' If he could escape Fausto now, he thought, he needn't let Fausto know that the police had called him at all. The news about Freddie wouldn't be in the papers until noon or later.

'But I'm here! In Roma! Where's your house? I'm at the railroad station!' Fausto said cheerfully, laughing.

'Where'd you get my telephone number?'

'Ah! allora, I called up information. They told me you didn't give the number out, but I told the girl a long story about a lottery you won in Mongibello. I don't know if she believed me, but I made it sound very important. A house and a cow and a well and even a refrigerator! I had to call her back three times, but finally she gave it to me. Allora, Deekie, where are you?'

'That's not the point. I'd have lunch with you if I didn't have this train, but—'

'Va bene, I'll help you carry your bags! Tell me where you are and I'll come over with a taxi for you!'

'The time's too short. Why don't I see you at the railroad station in about half an hour? It's the ten-thirty train for Naples.'

'Okay!'

'How is Marge?'

'Ah – innamorata di te,' Fausto said, laughing. 'Are you going to see her in Naples?'

'I don't think so. I'll see you in a few minutes, Fausto. Got to hurry. Arrivederch.'

''Rivederch, Deekie! Addio!' He hung up.

When Fausto saw the papers this afternoon, he would understand why he hadn't come to the railroad station, otherwise Fausto would just think they had missed each other somehow. But Fausto probably would see the papers by noon, Tom thought, because the Italian papers would play it up big – the murder of an American on the Appian Way. After the interview with the police, he would take another train to Naples – after four o'clock, so Fausto wouldn't be still around the station – and wait in Naples for the next boat to Majorca.

He only hoped that Fausto wouldn't worm the address out of information, too, and decide to come over before four o'clock. He hoped Fausto wouldn't land here just when the police were here.

Tom shoved a couple of suitcases under the bed, and carried the other to a closet and shut the door. He didn't want the police to think he was just about to leave town. But what was he so nervous about? They probably hadn't any clues. Maybe a friend of Freddie's had known that Freddie was going to try to see him yesterday, that was all. Tom picked up a brush and moistened it in the turpentine cup. For the benefit of the police, he wanted to look as if he was not too upset by the news of Freddie's death to do a little painting while he waited for them, though he was dressed to go out, because he had said he intended to go out. He was going to be a friend of Freddie's, but not too close a friend.

Signora Buffi let the police in at ten-thirty. Tom looked down the stairwell and saw them. They did not stop to ask her any questions. Tom went back into his apartment. The spicy smell of turpentine was in the room.

There were two: an older man in the uniform of an officer, and a younger man in an ordinary police uniform. The older man greeted him politely and asked to see his passport. Tom produced it, and the officer looked sharply from Tom to the picture of Dickie, more sharply than anyone had ever looked at it before, and Tom braced himself for a challenge, but there was none. The officer handed him the passport with a little bow and a smile. He was a short, middle-aged man who looked like thousands of other middle-aged Italians, with heavy grey-and-black eyebrows and a short, bushy grey-and-black moustache. He looked neither particularly bright nor stupid.

'How was he killed?' Tom asked.

'He was struck on the head and in the neck by some heavy instrument,' the officer replied, 'and robbed. We think he was drunk. Was he drunk when he left your apartment yesterday afternoon?'

'Well – somewhat. We had both been drinking. We were drinking martinis and pernod.'

The officer wrote it down in his tablet, and also the time that Tom said Freddie had been there, from about twelve until about six.

The younger policeman, handsome and blank of face, was strolling around the apartment with his hands behind him, bending close to the easel with a relaxed air as if he were alone in a museum.

'Do you know where he was going when he left?' the officer asked.

'No, I don't.'

'But you thought he was able to drive?'

'Oh, yes. He was not too drunk to drive or I would have gone with him.'

The officer asked another question that Tom pretended not quite to grasp. The officer asked it a second time, choosing different words, and exchanged a smile with the younger officer. Tom glanced from one to the other of them, a little resentfully. The officer wanted to know what his relationship to Freddie had been. ·

'A friend,' Tom said. 'Not a very close friend. I had not seen or heard from him in about two months. I was terribly upset to hear about the disaster this morning.' Tom let his anxious expression make up for his rather primitive vocabulary. He thought it did. He thought the questioning was very perfunctory, and that they were going to leave in another minute or so. 'At exactly what time was he killed?' Tom asked.

The officer was still writing. He raised his bushy eyebrows. 'Evidently just after the signor left your house, because the doctors believe that he had been dead at least twelve hours, perhaps longer.'

'At what time was he found?'

'At dawn this morning. By some workmen who were walking along the road.'

'Dio mio!' Tom murmured.

'He said nothing about making an excursion yesterday to the Via Appia when he left your apartment?'

'No,' Tom said.

'What did you do yesterday after Signor Mee-lays left?'

'I stayed here,' Tom said, gesturing with open hands as Dickie would have done, 'and then I had a little sleep, and later I went out for a walk around eight or eight-thirty.' A man who lived in the house, whose name Tom didn't know, had seen him come in last night at about a quarter to nine, and they had said good evening to each other.

'You took a walk alone?'

'Yes.'

'And Signor Mee-lays left here alone? He was not going to meet anybody that you know of?'

'No. He didn't say so.' Tom wondered if Freddie had had friends with him at his hotel, or wherever he had been staying. Tom hoped that the police wouldn't confront him with any of Freddie's friends who might know Dickie. Now his name – Richard Greenleaf – would be in the Italian newspapers, Tom thought, and also his address. He'd have to move. It was hell. He cursed to himself. The police officer saw him, but it looked like a muttered curse against the sad fate that had befallen Freddie, Tom thought.

'So—' the officer said, smiling, and closed his tablet.

'You think it was—' Tom tried to think of the word for hoodlum '—violent boys, don't you? Are there any clues?'

'We are searching the car for fingerprints now. The murderer may have been somebody he picked up to give a ride to. The car was found this morning in the vicinity of the Piazza di Spagna. We should have some clues before tonight. Thank you very much, Signor Greenleaf.'

'Di niente! If I can be of any further assistance—'

The officer turned at the door. 'Shall we be able to reach you here for the next few days, in case there are any more questions?'

Tom hesitated. 'I was planning to leave for Majorca tomorrow.'

'But the questions may be, who is such-and-such a person who is a suspect,' the officer explained. 'You may be able to tell us who the person is in relation to the deceased.' He gestured.

'All right. But I do not think I knew Signor Miles that well. He probably had closer friends in the city.'

'Who?' The officer closed the door and took out his tablet.

'I don't know,' Tom said. 'I only know he must have had several friends here, people who knew him better than I did.'

'I am sorry, but we still must expect you to be in reach for the next couple of days,' he repeated quietly, as if there were no question of Tom's arguing about it, even if he was an American. 'We shall inform you as soon as you may go. I am sorry if you have made travel plans. Perhaps there is still time to cancel them. Good day, Signor Greenleaf.'

'Good day.' Tom stood there after they had closed the door. He could move to a hotel, he thought, if he told the police what hotel it was. He didn't want Freddie's friends or any friends of Dickie's calling on him after they saw his address in the newspapers. He tried to assess his behaviour from the polizia's point of view. They hadn't challenged him on anything. He had not acted horrified at the news of Freddie's death, but that jibed with the fact that he was not an especially close friend of Freddie's, either. No, it wasn't bad, except that he had to be on tap.

The telephone rang, and Tom didn't answer it, because he had a feeling that it was Fausto calling from the railroad station. It was eleven-five, and the train for Naples would have departed. When the phone stopped ringing, Tom picked it up and called the Inghilterra. He reserved a room, and said he would be there in about half an hour. Then he called the police station – he remembered that it was number eighty-three – and after nearly ten minutes of difficulties because he couldn't find anyone who knew or cared who Richard Greenleaf was, he succeeded in leaving a message that Signor Richard Greenleaf could be found at the Albergo Inghilterra, in case the police wanted to speak to him.

He was at the Inghilterra before an hour was up. His three suitcases, two of them Dickie's and one his own, depressed him: he had packed them for such a different purpose. And now this!

He went out at noon to buy the papers. Every one of the papers had it: AMERICANO MURDERED ON THE VIA APPIA ANTICA . . . SHOCKING MURDER OF RICCISSIMO AMER-ICANO FREDERICK MILES LAST NIGHT ON THE VIA APPIA . . . VIA APPIA MURDER OF AMERICANO WITHOUT CLUES . . . Tom read every word. There really were no clues, at least not yet, no tracks, no fingerprints, no suspects. But every paper carried the name Herbert Richard Greenleaf and gave his address as the place where Freddie had last been seen by anybody. Not one of the papers implied that Herbert Richard Greenleaf was under suspicion, however. The papers said that Miles had apparently had a few drinks and the drinks, in typical Italian journalistic style, were all enumerated and ran from americanos through Scotch whisky, brandy, champagne, even grappa. Only gin and pernod were omitted.

Tom stayed in his hotel room over the lunch hour, walking the floor and feeling depressed and trapped. He telephoned the travel office in Rome that had sold him his ticket to Palma, and tried to cancel it. He would have twenty per cent of his money back, they said. There was not another boat to Palma for about five days.

Around two o'clock his telephone rang urgently.

'Hello,' Tom said in Dickie's nervous, irritable tone.

'Hello, Dick. This is Van Houston.'

'Oh-h,' Tom said, as if he knew him, yet the single word conveyed no excess of surprise or warmth.

'How've you been? It's been a long time, hasn't it?' The hoarse, strained voice asked.

'Certainly has. Where are you?'

'At the Hassler. I've been going over Freddie's suitcases with the police. Listen, I want to see you. What was the matter with Freddie yesterday? I tried to find you all last evening, you know, because Freddie was supposed to be back at the hotel by six. I didn't have your address. What happened yesterday?'

'I wish I knew! Freddie left the house around six. We both had taken on quite a lot of martinis, but he looked capable of driving or naturally I wouldn't have let him go off. He said he had his car downstairs. I can't imagine what happened, except that he picked up somebody to give them a lift, and they pulled a gun on him or something.'

'But he wasn't killed by a gun. I agree with you somebody must have forced him to drive out there, or be blotted out, because he'd have had to get clear across town to get to the Appian Way. The Hassler's only a few blocks from where you live.'

'Did he ever black out before? At the wheel of a car?'

'Listen, Dickie, can I see you? I'm free now, except that I'm not supposed to leave the hotel today.'

'Neither am I.'

'Oh, come on. Leave a message where you are and come over.'

'I can't, Van. The police are coming over in about an hour and I'm supposed to be here. Why don't you call me later? Maybe I can see you tonight.'

'All right. What time?'

'Call me around six.'

'Right. Keep your chin up, Dickie.'

'You too.'

'See you,' the voice said weakly.

Tom hung up. Van had sounded as if he were about to cry at the last. 'Pronto?' Tom said, clicking the telephone to get the hotel operator. He left a message that he was not in to anybody except the police, and that they were to let nobody up to see him. Positively no one.

After that the telephone did not ring all afternoon. At about eight, when it was dark, Tom went downstairs to buy the evening papers. He looked around the little lobby and into the hotel bar whose door was off the main hall, looking for anybody who might be Van. He was ready for anything, ready even to see Marge sitting there waiting for him, but he saw no one who looked even like a police agent. He bought the evening papers and sat in a little restaurant a few streets away, reading them. Still no clues. He learned that Van Houston was a close friend of Freddie's, aged twenty-eight, travelling with him from Austria to Rome on a holiday that was to have ended in Florence, where both Miles and Houston had residences, the papers said. They had questioned three Italian youths, two of them eighteen and one sixteen, on suspicion of having done the 'horrible deed', but the youths had been later released. Tom was relieved to read that no fingerprints that could be considered fresh or usable had been found on Miles' 'bellissima Fiat 1400 convertible'.

Tom ate his costoletta di vitello slowly, sipped his wine, and glanced through every column of the papers for the last-minute items that were sometimes put into Italian papers just before they went to press. He found nothing more on the Miles case. But on the last page of the last newspaper he read:

BARCA AFFONDATA CON MACCHIE DI SANGUE TRO-VATA NELL' ACQUA POCA FONDO VICINO SAN REMO

He read it rapidly, with more terror in his heart than he had felt when he had carried Freddie's body down the stairs, or when the police had come to question him. This was like a nemesis, like a nightmare come true, even the wording of the headline. The boat was described in detail and it brought the scene back to him, Dickie sitting in the stern at the throttle, Dickie smiling at him, Dickie's body sinking through the water with its wake of bubbles. The text said that the stains were believed to be bloodstains, not that they were. It did not say what the police or anybody else intended to do about them. But the police would do something, Tom thought. The boatkeeper could probably tell the police the very day the boat was lost. The police could then check the hotels for that day. The Italian boatkeeper might even remember that it was two Americans who had not come back with the boat. If the police bothered to check the hotel registers around that time, the name Richard Greenleaf would stand out like a red flag. In which case, of course, it would be Tom Ripley who would be missing, who might have been murdered that day. Tom's imagination went in several directions: suppose they searched for Dickie's body and found it? It would be assumed to be Tom Ripley's now. Dickie would be

PATRICIA HIGHSMITH

suspected of murder. Ergo, Dickie would be suspected of
Freddie's murder, too. Dickie would become overnight 'a
murderous type'. On the other hand, the Italian boatkeeper
might not remember the day that one of his boats had not been
brought back. Even if he did remember, the hotels might not
be checked. The Italian police just might not be that interested.
Might, might, *might* not.

Tom folded up his papers, paid his check, and went out.

He asked at the hotel desk if there were any messages for
him.

'Si, signor. Questo e questo e questo—' The clerk laid them
out on the desk before him like a card player laying down a
winning straight.

Two from Van. One from Robert Gilbertson. (Wasn't there
a Robert Gilberston in Dickie's address book? Check on that.)
One from Marge. Tom picked it up and read its Italian carefully: Signorina Sherwood had called at three-thirty-five P.M.
and would call again. The call was long distance from
Mongibello.

Tom nodded, and picked them up. 'Thanks very much.' He
didn't like the looks of the clerk behind the desk. Italians were
so damned curious!

Upstairs he sat hunched forward in an armchair, smoking
and thinking. He was trying to figure out what would logically
happen if he did nothing, and what he could make happen by
his own actions. Marge would very likely come up to Rome.
She had evidently called the Rome police to get his address. If
she came up, he would have to see her as Tom, and try to
convince her that Dickie was out for a while, as he had with
Freddie. And if he failed – Tom rubbed his palms together
nervously. He mustn't see Marge, that was all. Not now with
the boat affair brewing. Everything would go haywire if he saw
her. It'd be the end of everything! But if he could only sit tight,
nothing at all would happen. It was just this moment, he
thought, just this little crisis with the boat story and the

unsolved Freddie Miles murder, that made things so difficult. But absolutely nothing would happen to him, if he could keep on doing and saying the right things to everybody. Afterwards it could be smooth sailing again. Greece, or India. Ceylon. Some place far, far away, where no old friend could possibly come knocking on his door. What a fool he had been to think he could stay in Rome! Might as well have picked Grand Central Station, or put himself on exhibition in the Louvre!

He called the Stazione Termini, and asked about the trains for Naples tomorrow. There were four or five. He wrote down the times for all of them. It would be five days before a boat left from Naples for Majorca, and he would sit the time out in Naples, he thought. All he needed was a release from the police, and if nothing happened tomorrow he should get it. They couldn't hold a man forever, without even any grounds for suspicion, just in order to throw an occasional question at him! He began to feel he would be released tomorrow, that it was absolutely logical that he should be released.

He picked up the telephone again, and told the clerk that if Miss Marjorie Sherwood called again, he would accept the call. If she called again, he thought, he could convince her in two minutes that everything was all right, that Freddie's murder didn't concern him at all, that he had moved to a hotel just to avoid annoying telephone calls from total strangers and yet still be within reach of the police in case they wanted him to identify any suspects they picked up. He would tell her that he was flying to Greece tomorrow or the next day, so there was no use in her coming to Rome. As a matter of fact, he thought, he could fly to Palma from Rome. He hadn't even thought of that before.

He lay down on the bed, tired, but not ready to undress, because he felt that something else was going to happen tonight. He tried to concentrate on Marge. He imagined her at this moment sitting in Giorgio's, or treating herself to a long, slow Tom Collins in the Miramare bar, and debating whether to call him up again. He could see her troubled eyebrows, her tousled hair as she sat brooding about what might be happening in Rome. She would be alone at the table, not talking to anyone. He saw her getting up and going home, taking a suitcase and catching the noon bus tomorrow. He was there on the road in front of the post office, shouting to her not to go, trying to stop the bus, but it pulled away...

The scene dissolved in swirling yellow-greyness, the colour of the sand in Mongibello. Tom saw Dickie smiling at him, dressed in the corduroy suit that he had worn in San Remo. The suit was soaking wet, the tie a dripping string. Dickie bent over him, shaking him. 'I swam!' he said. 'Tom, wake up! I'm all right! I swam! I'm alive!' Tom squirmed away from his touch. He heard Dickie laugh at him, Dickie's happy, deep laugh. '*Tom!*' The timbre of the voice was deeper, richer, *better* than Tom had even been able to make it in his imitations. Tom pushed himself up. His body felt leaden and slow, as if he were trying to raise himself out of deep water.

'*I swam!*' Dickie's voice shouted, ringing and ringing in Tom's ears as if he heard it through a long tunnel.

Tom looked around the room, looking for Dickie in the yellow light under the bridge lamp, in the dark corner by the tall wardrobe. Tom felt his own eyes stretched wide, terrified, and though he knew his fear was senseless, he kept looking everywhere for Dickie, below the half-drawn shades at the window, and on the floor on the other side of the bed. He hauled himself up from the bed, staggered across the room, and opened a window. Then the other window. He felt drugged. *Somebody put something in my wine*, he thought suddenly. He knelt below the window, breathing the cold air in, fighting the grogginess as if it were something that was going to overcome him if he didn't exert himself to the utmost. Finally he went into the bathroom and wet his face at the basin. The grogginess was going away. He knew he hadn't been drugged. He had let his imagination run away with him. He had been out of control.

He drew himself up and calmly took off his tie. He moved as Dickie would have done, undressed himself, bathed, put his pyjamas on and lay down in bed. He tried to think about what Dickie would be thinking about. His mother. Her last letter had enclosed a couple of snapshots of herself and Mr. Greenleaf sitting in the living-room having coffee, the scene he remembered from the evening he had had coffee with them after dinner. Mrs. Greenleaf had said that Herbert had taken the pictures himself by squeezing a bulb. Tom began to compose his next letter to them. They were pleased that he was writing more often. He must set their minds at rest about the Freddie affair, because they knew of Freddie. Mrs. Greenleaf had asked about Freddie Miles in one of her letters. But Tom was listening for the telephone while he tried to compose the letter, and he couldn't really concentrate.

THE FIRST THING he thought of when he woke up was Marge. He reached for the telephone and asked if she had called during the night. She had not. He had a horrible premonition that she was coming up to Rome. It shot him out of bed, and then as he moved in his routine of shaving and bathing, his feeling changed. Why should he worry so much about Marge? He had always been able to handle her. She couldn't be here before five or six, anyway, because the first bus left Mongibello at noon, and she wasn't likely to take a taxi to Naples.

Maybe he would be able to leave Rome this morning. At ten o'clock he would call the police and find out.

He ordered caffe latte and rolls sent up to his room, and also the morning papers. Very strangely, there was not a thing in any of the papers about either the Miles case or the San Remo boat. It made him feel odd and frightened, with the same fear he had had last night when he had imagined Dickie standing in the room. He threw the newspapers away from him into a chair.

The telephone rang and he jumped for it obediently. It was either Marge or the police. 'Pronto?'

'Pronto. There are two signori of the police downstairs to see you, signore.'

'Very well. Will you tell them to come up?'

A minute later he heard their footsteps in the carpeted hall. It was the same older officer as yesterday, with a different younger policeman.

'Buon giorno,' said the officer politely, with his little bow.

'Buon giorno,' Tom said. 'Have you found anything new?'

'No,' said the officer on a questioning note. He took the chair that Tom offered him, and opened his brown leather briefcase. 'Another matter has come up. You are also a friend of the American Thomas Reepley?'

'Yes,' Tom said.

'Do you know where he is?'

'I think he went back to America about a month ago.'

The officer consulted his paper. 'I see. That will have to be confirmed by the United States Information Department. You see, we are trying to find Thomas Reepley. We think he may be dead.'

'Dead? Why?'

The officer's lips under his bushy iron-grey moustache compressed softly between each statement so that they seemed to be smiling. The smile had thrown Tom off a little yesterday, too. 'You were with him on a trip to San Remo in November, were you not?'

They had checked the hotels. 'Yes.'

'Where did you last see him? In San Remo?'

'No. I saw him again in Rome.' Tom remembered that Marge knew he had gone back to Rome after Mongibello, because he had said he was going to help Dickie get settled in Rome.

'When did you last see him?'

'I don't know if I can give you the exact date. Something like two months ago, I think. I think I had a postcard from – from Genoa from him, saying that he was going to go back to America.'

'You think?'

'I know I had,' Tom said. 'Why do you think he is dead?'

The officer looked at his form paper dubiously. Tom glanced at the younger policeman, who was leaning against the bureau with his arms folded, staring impersonally at him.

'Did you take a boat ride with Thomas Reepley in San Remo?'

'A boat ride? Where?'

'In a little boat? Around the port?' the officer asked quietly, looking at Tom.

'I think we did. Yes, I remember. Why?'

'Because a little boat has been found sunken with some kind of stains on it that may be blood. It was lost on November twenty-fifth. That is, it was not returned to the dock from which it was rented. November twenty-fifth was the day you were in San Remo with Signor Reepley.' The officer's eyes rested on him without moving.

The very mildness of the look offended Tom. It was dishonest, he felt. But Tom made a tremendous effort to behave in the proper way. He saw himself as if he were standing apart from himself and watching the scene. He corrected even his stance, and made it more relaxed by resting a hand on the end post of the bed. 'But nothing happened to us on that boat ride. There was no accident.'

'Did you bring the boat back?'

'Of course.'

The officer continued to eye him. 'We cannot find Signor Reepley registered in any hotel after November twenty-fifth.'

'Really? – How long have you been looking?'

'Not long enough to search every little village in Italy, but we have checked the hotels in the major cities. We find you registered at the Hassler on November twenty-eighth to thirtieth, and then—'

'Tom didn't stay with me in Rome – Signor Ripley. He went to Mongibello around that time and stayed for a couple of days.'

'Where did he stay when he came up to Rome?'

'At some small hotel. I don't remember which it was. I didn't visit him.'

'And where were you?'

'When?'

'On November twenty-sixth and twenty-seventh. That is, just after San Remo.'

'In Forte dei Marmi,' Tom replied. 'I stopped off there on the way down. I stayed at a pension.'

'Which one?'

Tom shook his head. 'I don't recall the name. A very small place.' After all, he thought, through Marge he could prove that Tom was in Mongibello, alive, after San Remo, so why should the police investigate what pension Dickie Greenleaf had stayed at on the twenty-sixth and twenty-seventh? Tom sat down on the side of his bed. 'I do not understand yet why you think Tom Ripley is dead.'

'We think *somebody* is dead,' the officer replied, 'in San Remo. Somebody was killed in that boat. That was why the boat was sunk – to hide the bloodstains.'

Tom frowned. 'They are sure they are bloodstains?'

The officer shrugged.

Tom shrugged, too. 'There must have been a couple of hundred people renting boats that day in San Remo.'

'Not so many. About thirty. It's quite true, it could have been any one of the thirty – or any pair of the fifteen,' he added with a smile. 'We don't even know all their names. But we are beginning to think Thomas Reepley is missing.' Now he looked off at a corner of the room, and he might have been thinking of something else, Tom thought, judging from his expression. Or was he enjoying the warmth of the radiator beside his chair?

Tom recrossed his legs impatiently. What was going on in the Italian's head was obvious: Dickie Greenleaf had twice been on the scene of a murder, or near enough. The missing Thomas Ripley had taken a boat ride November twenty-fifth with Dickie Greenleaf. Ergo— Tom straightened up, frowning. 'Are you saying that you do not believe me when I tell you that I saw Tom Ripley in Rome around the first of December?'

'Oh, no, I didn't say that, no indeed!' The officer gestured placatingly. 'I wanted to hear what you would say about your – your travelling with Signor Reepley after San Remo, because we cannot find him.' He smiled again, a broad, conciliatory smile that showed yellowish teeth.

Tom relaxed with an exasperated shrug. Obvious that the Italian police didn't want to accuse an American citizen outright of murder. 'I'm sorry that I can't tell you exactly where he is right now. Why don't you try Paris? Or Genoa? He'd always stay in a small hotel, because he prefers them.'

'Have you got the postcard that he sent you from Genoa?'

'No, I haven't,' Tom said. He ran his fingers through his hair, as Dickie sometimes did when he was irritated. He felt better, concentrating on being Dickie Greenleaf for a few seconds, pacing the floor once or twice.

'Do you know any friends of Thomas Reepley?'

Tom shook his head. 'No, I don't even know him very well, at least not for a very long time. I don't know if he has many friends in Europe. I think he said he knew someone in Faenza. Also in Florence. But I don't remember their names.' If the Italian thought he was protecting Tom's friends from a lot of police questioning by not giving their names, then let him, Tom thought.

'Va bene, we shall inquire,' the officer said. He put his papers away. He had made at least a dozen notations on them.

'Before you go,' Tom said in the same nervous, frank tone, 'I want to ask when I can leave the city. I was planning to go to Sicily. I should like very much to leave today if it is possible. I intend to stay at the Hotel Palma in Palermo. It will be very simple for you to reach me if I am needed.'

'Palermo,' the officer repeated. 'Ebbene, that may be possible. May I use the telephone?'

Tom lighted an Italian cigarette and listened to the officer asking for Capitano Anlicino, and then stating quite impassively that Signor Greenleaf did not know where Signor Reepley was, and that he might have gone back to America, or he might be in Florence or Faenza in the opinion of Signor Greenleaf. 'Faenza,' he repeated carefully, 'vicino Bologna.'

When the man had got that, the officer said Signor Greenleaf wished to go to Palermo today. 'Va bene. Benone.' The officer turned to Tom, smiling. 'Yes, you may go to Palermo today.'

'Benone. Grazie.' He walked with the two to the door. 'If you find where Tom Ripley is, I wish you would let me know, too,' he said ingenuously.

'Of course! We shall keep you informed, signore. Buon giorno!'

Alone, Tom began to whistle as he repacked the few things he had taken from his suitcases. He felt proud of himself for having proposed Sicily instead of Majorca, because Sicily was still Italy and Majorca wasn't, and naturally the Italian police would be more willing to let him leave if he stayed in their territory. He had thought of that when it had occurred to him that Tom Ripley's passport did not show that he had been to France again after the San Remo–Cannes trip. He remembered he had told Marge that Tom Ripley had said he was going up to Paris and from there back to America. If they ever questioned Marge as to whether Tom Ripley was in Mongibello after San Remo, she might also add that he later went to Paris. And if he ever had to become Tom Ripley again, and show his passport to the police, they would see that he hadn't been to France again after the Cannes trip. He would just have to say that he had changed his mind after he told Dickie that, and had decided to stay in Italy. That wasn't important.

Tom straightened up suddenly from a suitcase. Could it all be a trick, really? Were they just letting him have a little more rope in letting him go to Sicily, apparently unsuspected? A sly little bastard, that officer. He'd said his name once. What was it? Ravini? Roverini? Well, what could be the advantage of letting him have a little more rope? He'd told them exactly where he was going. He had no intention of trying to run away from anything. All he wanted was to get out of Rome. He was frantic to get out! He threw the last items into his suitcase and slammed the lid down and locked it.

The phone again! Tom snatched it up. 'Pronto?'

'Oh, Dickie—!' breathlessly.

It was Marge and she was downstairs, he could tell from the sound. Flustered, he said in Tom's voice, 'Who's this?'

'Is this Tom?'

'Marge! Well, hello! Where are you?'

'I'm downstairs. Is Dickie there? Can I come up?'

'You can come up in about five minutes,' Tom said with a laugh. 'I'm not quite dressed yet.' The clerks always sent people to a booth downstairs, he thought. The clerks wouldn't be able to overhear them.

'Is Dickie there?'

'Not at the moment. He went out about half an hour ago, but he'll be back any minute. I know where he is, if you want to find him.'

'Where?'

'At the eighty-third police station. No, excuse me, it's the eighty-seventh.'

'Is he in any trouble?'

'No, just answering questions. He was supposed to be there at ten. Want me to give you the address?' He wished he hadn't started talking in Tom's voice: he could so easily have pretended to be a servant, some friend of Dickie's, anybody, and told her that Dickie was out for hours.

Marge was groaning. 'No-o. I'll wait for him.'

'Here it is!' Tom said as if he had found it. 'Twenty-one Via Perugia. Do you know where that is?' Tom didn't, but he was going to send her in the opposite direction from the American Express, where he wanted to go for his mail before he left town.

'I don't want to go,' Marge said. 'I'll come up and wait with you, if it's all right.'

'Well, it's—' He laughed, his own unmistakable laugh that Marge knew well. 'The thing is, I'm expecting somebody any minute. It's a business interview. About a job. Believe it or not, old believe-it-or-not Ripley's trying to put himself to work.'

'Oh,' said Marge, not in the least interested. 'Well, how is Dickie? Why does he have to talk to the police?'

'Oh, just because he had some drinks with Freddie that day. You saw the papers, didn't you? The papers make it ten times more important than it was for the simple reason that the dopes haven't got any clues at all about anything.'

'How long has Dickie been living here?'

'Here? Oh, just overnight. I've been up north. When I heard about Freddie, I came down to Rome to see him. If it hadn't been for the police, I'd never have found him!'

'You're telling me! I went to the police in desperation! I've been so worried, Tom. He might at least have phoned me – at Giorgio's or somewhere—'

'I'm awfully glad you're in town, Marge. Dickie'll be tickled pink to see you. He's been worried about what you might think of all this in the papers.'

'Oh, has he?' Marge said disbelievingly, but she sounded pleased.

'Why don't you wait for me in Angelo's? It's that bar right down the street in front of the hotel going towards the Piazza di Spagna steps. I'll see if I can sneak out and have a drink or a coffee with you in about five minutes, okay?'

'Okay. But there's a bar right here in the hotel.'

'I don't want to be seen by my future boss in a bar.'

'Oh, all right. Angelo's?'

'You can't miss it. On the street straight in front of the hotel. Bye-bye.'

He whirled around to finish his packing. He really was finished except for the coats in the closet. He picked up the telephone and asked for his bill to be prepared, and for somebody to carry his luggage. Then he put his luggage in a neat heap for the bellboys and went down via the stairs. He wanted to see if Marge was still in the lobby, waiting there for him, or possibly still there making another telephone call. She couldn't have been downstairs waiting when the police were here, Tom thought. About five minutes had passed between the time the police left and Marge called up. He had put on a hat to conceal his blonder hair, a raincoat which was new, and he wore Tom Ripley's shy, slightly frightened expression.

She wasn't in the lobby. Tom paid his bill. The clerk handed him another message: Van Houston had been here. The message was in his own writing, dated ten minutes ago.

Waited for you half an hour. Don't you ever go out for a walk? They won't let me up. Call me at the Hassler.

Van

Maybe Van and Marge had run into each other, if they knew each other, and were sitting together in Angelo's now.

'If anybody else asks for me, would you say that I've left the city?' Tom said to the clerk.

'Va bene, signore.'

Tom went out to his waiting taxi. 'Would you stop at the American Express, please?' he asked the driver.

The driver did not take the street that Angelo's was on. Tom relaxed and congratulated himself. He congratulated himself above all on the fact that he had been too nervous to stay in his apartment yesterday and had taken a hotel room. He never could have evaded Marge in his apartment. She had the address from the newspapers. If he had tried the same trick, she would have insisted on coming up and waiting for Dickie in the apartment. Luck was with him!

He had mail at the American Express – three letters, one from Mr. Greenleaf.

'How are you today?' asked the young Italian girl who had handed him his mail.

She'd read the papers, too, Tom thought. He smiled back at her naïvely curious face. Her name was Maria. 'Very well, thanks, and you?'

As he turned away, it crossed his mind that he could never use the Rome American Express as an address for Tom Ripley. Two or three of the clerks knew him by sight. He was using the Naples American Express for Tom Ripley's mail now, though he hadn't claimed anything there or written them to forward anything, because he wasn't expecting anything important for Tom Ripley, not even another blast from Mr. Greenleaf. When things cooled off a little, he would just walk into the Naples American Express some day and claim it with Tom Ripley's passport, he thought.

He couldn't use the Rome American Express as Tom Ripley, but he had to keep Tom Ripley with him, his passport and his clothes in order for emergencies like Marge's telephone call this morning. Marge had come damned close to being right in the room with him. As long as the innocence of Dickie Greenleaf was debatable in the opinion of the police, it was suicidal to think of leaving the country as Dickie, because if he had to switch back suddenly to Tom Ripley, Ripley's passport would not show that he had left Italy. If he wanted to leave Italy – to take Dickie Greenleaf entirely away from the police – he would have to leave as Tom Ripley, and re-enter later as Tom Ripley and become Dickie again once the police investigations were over. That was a possibility.

It seemed simple and safe. All he had to do was weather the next few days.

19

THE BOAT APPROACHED Palermo harbour slowly and tentatively, nosing its white prow gently through the floating orange peels, the straw and the pieces of broken fruit crates. It was the way Tom felt, too, approaching Palermo. He had spent two days in Naples, and there had been nothing of any interest in the papers about the Miles case and nothing at all about the San Remo boat, and the police had made no attempt to reach him that he knew of. But maybe they had just not bothered to look for him in Naples, he thought, and were waiting for him in Palermo at the hotel.

There were no police waiting for him on the dock, anyway. Tom looked for them. He bought a couple of newspapers, then took a taxi with his luggage to the Hotel Palma. There were no police in the hotel lobby, either. It was an ornate old lobby with great marble supporting columns and big pots of palms standing around. A clerk told him the number of his reserved room, and handed a bellboy the key. Tom felt so much relieved that he went over to the mail counter and asked boldly if there was any message for Signor Richard Greenleaf. The clerk told him there was not.

Then he began to relax. That meant there was not even a message from Marge. Marge would undoubtedly have gone to the police by now to find out where Dickie was. Tom had imagined horrible things during the boat trip: Marge beating him to Palermo by plane, Marge leaving a message for him at the Hotel Palma that she would arrive on the next boat. He had even looked for Marge on the boat when he got aboard in Naples.

Now he began to think that perhaps Marge had given Dickie up after this episode. Maybe she'd caught on to the idea that Dickie was running away from her and that he wanted to be with Tom, alone. Maybe that had even penetrated *her* thick skull. Tom debated sending her a letter to that effect as he sat in his deep warm bath that evening, spreading soapsuds luxuriously up and down his arms. Tom Ripley ought to write the letter, he thought. It was about time. He would say that he'd wanted to be tactful all this while, that he hadn't wanted to come right out with it on the telephone in Rome, but that by now he had the feeling she understood, anyway. He and Dickie were very happy together, and that was that. Tom began to giggle merrily, uncontrollably, and squelched himself by slipping all the way under the water, holding his nose.

Dear Marge, he would say. I'm writing this because I don't think Dickie ever will, though I've asked him to many times. You're much too fine a person to be strung along like this for so long...

He giggled again, then sobered himself by deliberately concentrating on the little problem that he hadn't solved yet: Marge had also probably told the Italian police that she had talked to Tom Ripley at the Inghilterra. The police were going to wonder where the hell he went to. The police might be looking for him in Rome now. The police would certainly look for Tom Ripley around Dickie Greenleaf. It was an added danger – if they were, for instance, to think that he was Tom Ripley now, just from Marge's description of him, and strip him and search him and find both his and Dickie's passports. But what had he said about risks? Risks were what made the whole thing fun. He burst out singing:

> *Papa non vuole, Mama ne meno,*
> *Come faremo far' l'amor'?*

He boomed it out in the bathroom as he dried himself. He sang in Dickie's loud baritone that he had never heard, but he felt sure Dickie would have been pleased with his ringing tone.

He dressed, put on one of his new non-wrinkling travelling suits, and strolled out into the Palermo dusk. There across the plaza was the great Norman-influenced cathedral he had read about, built by the English archbishop Walter-of-the-Mill, he remembered from a guidebook. Then there was Siracusa to the south, scene of a mighty naval battle between the Latins and the Greeks. And Dionysius' Ear. And Taormina. And Etna! It was a big island and brand-new to him. Sicilia! Stronghold of Giuliano! Colonized by the ancient Greeks, invaded by Norman and Saracen! Tomorrow he would commence his tourism properly, but this moment was glorious, he thought as he stopped to stare at the tall, towered cathedral in front of him. Wonderful to look at the dusty arches of its façade and to think of going inside tomorrow, to imagine its musty, sweetish smell, composed of the uncounted candles and incense-burnings of hundreds and hundreds of years. Anticipation! It occurred to him that his anticipation was more pleasant to him than his experiencing. Was it always going to be like that? When he spent evenings alone, handling Dickie's possessions, simply looking at his rings on his own fingers, or his woollen ties, or his black alligator wallet, was that experiencing or anticipation?

Beyond Sicily came Greece. He definitely wanted to see Greece. He wanted to see Greece as Dickie Greenleaf with Dickie's money, Dickie's clothes, Dickie's way of behaving with strangers. But would it happen that he couldn't see Greece as Dickie Greenleaf? Would one thing after another come up to thwart him – murder, suspicion, *people*? He hadn't wanted to murder, it had been a necessity. The idea of going to Greece, trudging over the Acropolis as Tom Ripley, American tourist, held no charm for him at all. He would as soon not go. Tears came in his eyes as he stared up at the campanile of the cathedral, and then he turned away and began to walk down a new street.

There was a letter for him the next morning, a fat letter from Marge. Tom squeezed it between his fingers and smiled. It was what he had expected, he felt sure, otherwise it wouldn't have been so fat. He read it at breakfast. He savoured every line of it along with his fresh warm rolls and his cinnamon-flavoured coffee. It was all he could have expected, and more.

. . . If you really *didn't* know that I had been by your hotel, that only means that Tom didn't tell you, which leaves the same conclusion to be drawn. It's pretty obvious now that you're running out and can't face me. Why don't you admit that you can't live without your little chum? I'm only sorry, old boy, that you didn't have the courage to tell me this before and *outright.* What do you think I am, a small-town hick who doesn't know about such things? *You're* the only one who's acting small-town! At any rate, I hope my telling you what you hadn't the courage to tell me relieves your conscience a little bit and lets you hold your head up. There's nothing like being proud of the person you love, is there! Didn't we once talk about this?

Accomplishment Number Two of my Roman holiday is informing the police that Tom Ripley is with you. They seemed in a perfect tizzy to find him. (I wonder why? What's he done now?) I also informed the police in my best Italian that you and Tom are inseparable and how they could have found you and still missed *Tom*, I could not imagine.

Changed my boat and I'll be leaving for the States around the end of March, after a short visit to Kate in Munich, after which I presume our paths will never cross again. No hard feelings, Dickie boy. I'd just given you credit for a lot more guts.

Thanks for all the wonderful memories. They're like something in a museum already or something preserved in amber, a little unreal, as you must have felt yourself always to me. Best wishes for the future,

Marge

Ugh! That corn at the end! Ah, Clabber Girl! Tom folded the letter and stuck it into his jacket pocket. He glanced at the two doors of the hotel restaurant, automatically looking for police. If the police thought that Dickie Greenleaf and Tom Ripley were travelling together, they must have checked the Palermo hotels already for Tom Ripley, he thought. But he hadn't noticed any police watching him, or following him. Or maybe they'd given the whole boat scare up, since they were sure Tom Ripley was alive. Why on earth should they go on with it? Maybe the suspicion against Dickie in San Remo and in the Miles murder, too, had already blown over. Maybe.

He went up to his room and began a letter to Mr. Greenleaf on Dickie's portable Hermes. He began by explaining the Miles affair very soberly and logically, because Mr. Greenleaf would probably be pretty alarmed by now. He said that the police had finished their questioning and that all they conceivably might want now was for him to try to identify any suspects they might find, because the suspect might be a mutual acquaintance of his and Freddie's.

The telephone rang while he was typing. A man's voice said that he was a Tenente Somebody of the Palermo police force.

'We are looking for Thomas Phelps Ripley. Is he with you in your hotel?' he asked courteously.

'No, he is not,' Tom replied.

'Do you know where he is?'

'I think he is in Rome. I saw him just three or four days ago in Rome.'

'He has not been found in Rome. You do not know where he might have been going from Rome?'

'I'm sorry, I haven't the slightest idea,' Tom said.

'Peccato,' sighed the voice, with disappointment. 'Grazie tante, signor.'

'Di niente.' Tom hung up and went back to his letter.

The dull yards of Dickie's prose came out more fluently now than Tom's own letters ever had. He addressed most of the letter to Dickie's mother, told her the state of his wardrobe, which was good, and his health, which was also good, and asked if she had received the enamel triptych he had sent her from an antique store in Rome a couple of weeks ago. While he wrote, he was thinking of what he had to do about Thomas Ripley. The quest was apparently very courteous and luke-warm, but it wouldn't do to take wild chances. He shouldn't have Tom's passport lying right in a pocket of his suitcase, even if it was wrapped up in a lot of old income tax papers of Dickie's so that it wasn't visible to a custom inspector's eyes. He should hide it in the lining of the new antelope suitcase, for instance, where it couldn't be seen even if the suitcase were emptied, yet where he could get at it on a few minutes' notice if he had to. Because some day he might have to. There might come a time when it would be more dangerous to be Dickie Greenleaf than to be Tom Ripley.

Tom spent half the morning on the letter to the Greenleafs. He had a feeling that Mr. Greenleaf was getting restless and impatient with Dickie, not in the same way that he had been impatient when Tom had seen him in New York, but in a much more serious way. Mr. Greenleaf thought his removal from Mongibello to Rome had been merely an erratic whim, Tom knew. Tom's attempt to make his painting and studying in Rome sound constructive had really been a failure. Mr. Greenleaf had dismissed it with a withering remark: something about his being sorry that he was still torturing himself with painting at all, because he should have learned by now that it took more than beautiful scenery or a change of scene to make a painter. Mr. Greenleaf had also not been much impressed by the interest Tom had shown in the Burke-Greenleaf folders that Mr. Greenleaf had sent him. It was a far cry from what Tom had expected by this time: that he would have Mr. Greenleaf eating out of his hand, that he would have made up for all Dickie's negligence and unconcern for his parents in the past, and that he could ask Mr. Greenleaf for some extra money and get it. He couldn't possibly ask Mr. Greenleaf for money now.

Take care of yourself, moms [he wrote]. Watch out for those colds. [She had said she'd had four colds this winter, and had spent Christmas propped up in bed, wearing the pink woollen shawl he had sent her as one of his Christmas presents.] If you'd been wearing a pair of those wonderful woollen socks you sent me, you never would have caught the colds. I haven't had a cold this winter, which is something to boast about in a European winter. . . . Moms, can I send you anything from here? I enjoy buying things for you . . .

20

FIVE DAYS PASSED, calm, solitary but very agreeable days in which he rambled about Palermo, stopping here and there to sit for an hour or so in a café or a restaurant and read his guidebooks and the newspapers. He took a carrozza one gloomy day and rode all the way to Monte Pelligrino to visit the fantastic tomb of Santa Rosalia, the patron saint of Palermo, depicted in a famous statue, which Tom had seen pictures of in Rome, in one of those states of frozen ecstasy that are given other names by psychiatrists. Tom found the tomb vastly amusing. He could hardly keep from giggling when he saw the statue: the lush, reclining female body, the groping hands, the dazed eyes, the parted lips. It was all there but the actual sound of the panting. He thought of Marge. He visited a Byzantine palace, the Palermo library with its paintings and old cracked manuscripts in glass cases, and studied the formation of the harbour, which was carefully diagrammed in his guidebook. He made a sketch of a painting by Guido Reni, for no particular purpose, and memorized a long inscription by Tasso on one of the public buildings. He wrote letters to Bob Delancey and to Cleo in New York, a long letter to Cleo describing his travels, his pleasures, and his multifarious acquaintances with the convincing ardour of Marco Polo describing China.

But he was lonely. It was not like the sensation in Paris of being alone yet not alone. He had imagined himself acquiring a bright new circle of friends with whom he would start a new life with new attitudes, standards, and habits that would be far better and clearer than those he had had all his life. Now he realized that it couldn't be. He would have to keep a distance from people, always. He might acquire the different standards and habits, but he could never acquire the circle of friends – not unless he went to Istanbul or Ceylon, and what was the use of acquiring the kind of people he would meet in those places? He was alone, and it was a lonely game he was playing. The friends he might make were most of the danger, of course. If he had to drift about the world entirely alone, so much the better: there was that much less chance that he would be found out. That was one cheerful aspect of it, anyway, and he felt better having thought of it.

He altered his behaviour slightly, to accord with the role of a more detached observer of life. He was still courteous and smiling to everyone, to people who wanted to borrow his newspaper in restaurants and to clerks he spoke to in the hotel, but he carried his head even higher and he spoke a little less when he spoke. There was a faint air of sadness about him now. He enjoyed the change. He imagined that he looked like a young man who had had an unhappy love affair or some kind of emotional disaster, and was trying to recuperate in a civilized way, by visiting some of the more beautiful places on the earth.

That reminded him of Capri. The weather was still bad, but Capri was Italy. That glimpse he had had of Capri with Dickie had only whetted his appetite. Christ, had Dickie been a bore *that* day! Maybe he should hold out until summer, he thought, hold the police off until then. But even more than Greece and the Acropolis, he wanted one happy holiday in Capri, and to hell with culture for a while. He had read about Capri in winter – wind, rain, and solitude. But still Capri! There was Tiberius' Leap and the Blue Grotto, the plaza without people but still the plaza, and not a cobblestone changed. He might even go today. He quickened his steps towards his hotel. The lack of tourists hadn't detracted from the Côte d'Azur. Maybe he could fly to Capri. He had heard of a seaplane service from Naples to Capri. If the seaplane wasn't running in February, he could charter it. What was money for?

'Buon giorno! Come sta?' He greeted the clerk behind the desk with a smile.

'A letter for you, signore. Urgentissimo,' the clerk said, smiling, too.

It was from Dickie's bank in Naples. Inside the envelope was another envelope from Dickie's trust company in New York. Tom read the letter from the Naples bank first.

10 Feb. 19——

Most esteemed signor:

It has been called to our attention by the Wendell Trust Company of New York, that there exists a doubt whether your signature of receipt of your remittance of five hundred dollars of January last is actually your own. We hasten to inform you so that we may take the necessary action.

We have already deemed it proper to inform the police, but we await your confirmation of the opinion of our Inspector of Signatures and of the Inspector of Signatures of the Wendell Trust Company of New York. Any information you may be able to give will be most appreciated, and we urge you to communicate with us at your earliest possible convenience.

> Most respectfully and obediently yours,
> Emilio di Braganzi
> Segretario Generale della Banca di Napoli

P.S. In the case that your signature is in fact valid, we urge you despite this to visit our offices in Naples as soon as possible in order to sign your name again for our permanent records. We enclose a letter to you sent in our care from the Wendell Trust Company.

Tom ripped open the trust company's letter.

5 Feb. 19——

Dear Mr. Greenleaf:

Our Department of Signatures has reported to us that in its opinion your signature of January on your regular monthly

187

remittance, No. 8747, is invalid. Believing this may for some reason have escaped your notice, we are hastening to inform you, so that you may confirm the signing of the said cheque or confirm our opinion that the said cheque has been forged. We have called this to the attention of the Bank of Naples also.

Enclosed is a card for our permanent signature file which we request you to sign and return to us.

Please let us hear from you as soon as possible.

Sincerely,
Edward T. Cavanach
Secretary

Tom wet his lips. He'd write to both banks that he was not missing any money at all. But would that hold them off for long? He had signed three remittances, beginning in December. Were they going to go back and check on all his signatures now? Would an expert be able to tell that all three signatures were forged?

Tom went upstairs and immediately sat down at the typewriter. He put a sheet of hotel stationery into the roller and sat there for a moment, staring at it. They wouldn't rest with this, he thought. If they had a board of experts looking at the signatures with magnifying glasses and all that, they probably would be able to tell that the three signatures were forgeries. But they were such damned good forgeries, Tom knew. He'd signed the January remittance a little fast, he remembered, but it wasn't a bad job or he never would have sent it off. He would have told the bank he lost the remittance and would have had them send him another. Most forgeries took months to be discovered, he thought. Why had they spotted this one in four weeks? Wasn't it because they were checking on him in every department of his life, since the Freddie Miles murder and the San Remo boat story? They wanted to see him personally in the Naples bank. Maybe some of the men there knew Dickie by sight. A terrible, tingling panic went over his shoulders and down his legs. For a moment he felt weak and helpless, too weak to move. He saw himself confronted by a dozen policemen, Italian and American, asking him where Dickie Greenleaf was, and being unable to produce Dickie Greenleaf or tell them where he was or prove that he existed. He imagined himself trying to sign H. Richard Greenleaf under the eyes of a dozen handwriting experts, and going to pieces suddenly and not being able to write at all. He brought his hands up to the typewriter keys and forced himself to begin. He addressed the letter to the Wendell Trust Company of New York.

12 Feb. 19——

Dear Sirs:

    In regard to your letter concerning my January remittance:

    I signed the cheque in question myself and received the money in full. If I had missed the cheque, I should of course have informed you at once.

    I am enclosing the card with my signature for your permanent record as you requested.

Sincerely,
H. Richard Greenleaf

He signed Dickie's signature several times on the back of the trust company's envelope before he signed his letter and then the card. Then he wrote a similar letter to the Naples bank, and promised to call at the bank within the next few days and sign his name again for their permanent record. He marked both envelopes 'Urgentissimo', went downstairs and bought stamps from the porter and posted them.

Then he went out for a walk. His desire to go to Capri had vanished. It was four-fifteen in the afternoon. He kept walking, aimlessly. Finally, he stopped in front of an antique shop window and stared for several minutes at a gloomy oil painting of two bearded saints descending a dark hill in moonlight. He went into the shop and bought it for the first price the man quoted to him. It was not even framed, and he carried it rolled up under his arm back to his hotel.

21

83 Stazione Polizia
Roma
14 Feb. 19——

Most esteemed Signor Greenleaf:

YOU ARE URGENTLY requested to come to Rome to answer some important questions concerning Thomas Ripley. Your presence would be most appreciated and would greatly expedite our investigations.

Failure to present yourself within a week will cause us to take certain measures which will be inconvenient both to us and to you.

Most respectfully yours,
Cap. Enrico Farrara

So they were still looking for Tom. But maybe it meant that something had happened on the Miles case, too, Tom thought. The Italians didn't summon an American in words like these. That last paragraph was a plain threat. And of course they knew about the forged cheque by now.

He stood with the letter in his hand, looking blankly around the room. He caught sight of himself in the mirror, the corners of his mouth turned down, his eyes anxious and scared. He looked as if he were trying to convey the emotions of fear and shock by his posture and his expression, and because the way he looked was involuntary and real, he became suddenly twice as frightened. He folded the letter and pocketed it, then took it out of his pocket and tore it to bits.

He began to pack rapidly, snatching his robe and pyjamas from the bathroom door, throwing his toilet articles into the leather kit with Dickie's initials that Marge had given him for Christmas. He stopped suddenly. He had to get rid of Dickie's belongings, all of them. Here? Now? Should he throw them overboard on the way back to Naples?

The question didn't answer itself, but he suddenly knew what he had to do, what he was going to do when he got back to Italy. He would not go anywhere near Rome. He could go straight up to Milan or Turin, or maybe somewhere near Venice, and buy a car, secondhand, with a lot of mileage on it. He'd say he'd been roaming around Italy for the last two or three months. He hadn't heard anything about the search for Thomas Ripley. Thomas Reepley.

He went on packing. This was the end of Dickie Greenleaf, he knew. He hated becoming Thomas Ripley again, hated being nobody, hated putting on his old set of habits again, and feeling that people looked down on him and were bored with him unless he put on an act for them like a clown, feeling incompetent and incapable of doing anything with himself except entertaining people for minutes at a time. He hated going back to himself as he would have hated putting on a shabby suit of clothes, a grease-spotted, unpressed suit of clothes that had not been very good even when it was new. His tears fell on Dickie's blue-and-white-striped shirt that lay uppermost in the suitcase, starched and clean and still as new-looking as when he had first taken it out of Dickie's drawer in Mongibello. But it had Dickie's initials on the pocket in little red letters. As he packed he began to reckon up defiantly the things of Dickie's that he could still keep because they had no initials, or because no one would remember that they were Dickie's and not his own. Except maybe Marge would remember a few, like the new blue leather address book that Dickie had written only a couple of addresses in, and that Marge had very likely given to him. But he wasn't planning to see Marge again.

Tom paid his bill at the Palma, but he had to wait until the next day for a boat to the mainland. He reserved the boat ticket in the name of Greenleaf, thinking that this was the last time he would ever reserve a ticket in the name of Greenleaf, but that maybe it wouldn't be, either. He couldn't give up the idea that it might all blow over. Just might. And for that reason it was senseless to be despondent. It was senseless to be despondent, anyway, even as Tom Ripley. Tom Ripley had never really been despondent, though he had often looked it. Hadn't he learned something from these last months? If you wanted to be cheerful, or melancholic, or wistful, or thoughtful, or courteous, you simply had to *act* those things with every gesture.

A very cheerful thought came to him when he awoke on the last morning in Palermo: he could check all Dickie's clothes at the American Express in Venice under a different name and reclaim them at some future time, if he wanted to or had to, or else never claim them at all. It made him feel much better to know that Dickie's good shirts, his studbox with all the cufflinks and the identification bracelet and his wrist-watch would be safely in storage somewhere, instead of at the bottom of the Tyrrhenian Sea or in some ashcan in Sicily.

So, after scraping the initials off Dickie's two suitcases, he sent them, locked, from Naples to the American Express Company, Venice, together with two canvases he had begun painting in Palermo, in the name of Robert S. Fanshaw, to be stored until called for. The only things, the only revealing things, he kept with him were Dickie's rings, which he put into the bottom of an ugly little brown leather box belonging to Thomas Ripley, that he had somehow kept with him for years everywhere he travelled or moved to, and which was otherwise filled with his own interesting collection of cufflinks, collar pins, odd buttons, a couple of fountain-pen points, and a spool of white thread with a needle stuck in it.

Tom took a train from Naples up through Rome, Florence, Bologna, and Verona, where he got out and went by bus to the town of Trento about forty miles away. He did not want to buy a car in a town as big as Verona, because the police might notice his name when he applied for his licence plates, he thought. In Trento he bought a secondhand cream-coloured Lancia for the equivalent of about eight hundred dollars. He bought it in the name of Thomas Ripley, as his passport read, and took a hotel room in that name to wait the twenty-four hours until his licence plates should be ready. Six hours later nothing had happened. Tom had been afraid that even this small hotel might recognize his name, that the office that took care of the applications for plates might also notice his name, but by noon the next day he had his plates on his car and nothing had happened. Neither was there anything in the papers about the quest for Thomas Ripley, or the Miles case, or the San Remo boat affair. It made him feel rather strange, rather safe and happy, and as if perhaps all of it were unreal. He began to feel happy even in his dreary role as Thomas Ripley. He took a pleasure in it, overdoing almost the old Tom Ripley reticence with strangers, the inferiority in every duck of his head and wistful, side-long glance. After all, would anyone, *anyone*, believe that such a character had ever done a murder? And the only murder he could possibly be suspected of was Dickie's in San Remo, and they didn't seem to be getting very far on that. Being Tom Ripley had one compensation, at least: it relieved his mind of guilt for the stupid, unnecessary murder of Freddie Miles.

He wanted to go straight to Venice, but he thought he should spend one night doing what he intended to tell the police he had been doing for several months: sleeping in his car on a country road. He spent one night in the back seat of the Lancia, cramped and miserable, somewhere in the neighbourhood of Brescia. He crawled into the front seat at dawn with such a painful crick in his neck he could hardly turn his head sufficiently to drive, but that made it authentic, he thought, that would make him tell the story better. He bought a guide-book of Northern Italy, marked it up appropriately with dates, turned down corners of its pages, stepped on its covers and broke its binding so that it fell open at Pisa.

The next night he spent in Venice. In a childish way Tom had avoided Venice simply because he expected to be disappointed in it. He had thought only sentimentalists and American tourists raved over Venice, and that at best it was only a town for honeymooners who enjoyed the inconvenience of not being able to go anywhere except by a gondola moving at two miles an hour. He found Venice much bigger than he had supposed, full of Italians who looked like Italians anywhere else. He found he could walk across the entire city via the narrow streets and bridges without setting foot in a gondola, and that the major canals had a transportation system of motor launches just as fast and efficient as the subway system, and that the canals did not smell bad, either. There was a tremendous choice of hotels, from the Gritti and the Danieli, which he had heard of, down to crummy little hotels and pensions in back alleys so off the beaten track, so removed from the world of police and American tourists, that Tom could imagine living in one of them for months without being noticed by anybody. He chose a hotel called the Costanza, very near the Rialto bridge, which struck the middle between the famous luxury hotels and the obscure little hostelries on the back streets. It was clean, inexpensive, and convenient to points of interest. It was just the hotel for Tom Ripley.

Tom spent a couple of hours pottering around in his room, slowly unpacking his old familiar clothes, and dreaming out of the window at the dusk falling over the Canale Grande. He imagined the conversation he was going to have with the police before long. . . . Why, I haven't any idea. I saw him in Rome. If you've any doubt of that, you can verify it with Miss Marjorie Sherwood. . . . Of course I'm Tom Ripley! (He would give a laugh.) I can't understand what all the fuss is about! . . . San Remo? Yes, I remember. We brought the boat back after an hour . . . . Yes, I came back to Rome after Mongibello, but I didn't stay more than a couple of nights. I've been roaming around the north of Italy. . . . I'm afraid I haven't any idea where he is, but I saw him about three weeks ago. . . . Tom got up from the windowsill smiling, changed his shirt and tie for the evening, and went out to find a pleasant restaurant for dinner. A good restaurant, he thought. Tom Ripley could treat himself to something expensive for once. His billfold was so full of long ten- and twenty-thousand-lire notes it wouldn't bend. He had cashed a thousand dollars' worth of traveller's cheques in Dickie's name before he left Palermo.

He bought two evening newspapers, tucked them under his arm and walked on, over a little arched bridge, through a long street hardly six feet wide full of leather shops and men's shirt shops, past windows glittering with jewelled boxes that spilled out necklaces and rings like the boxes Tom had always imagined that treasures spilled out of in fairy tales. He liked the fact that Venice had no cars. It made the city human. The streets were like veins, he thought, and the people were the blood, circulating everywhere. He took another street back and crossed the great quadrangle of San Marco's for the second time. Pigeons everywhere, in the air, in the light of shops – even at night, pigeons walking along under people's feet like sightseers themselves in their own home town! The chairs and tables of the cafés spread across the arcade into the plaza itself, so that people and pigeons had to look for little aisles through them to get by. From either end of the plaza blaring phonographs played in disharmony. Tom tried to imagine the place in summer, in sunlight, full of people tossing handfuls of grain up into the air for the pigeons that fluttered down for it. He entered another little lighted tunnel of a street. It was full of restaurants, and he chose a very substantial and respectable-looking place with white tablecloths and brown wooden walls, the kind of restaurants which experience had taught him by now concentrated on food and not the passing tourist. He took a table and opened one of his newspapers.

And there it was, a little item on the second page:

POLICE SEARCH FOR MISSING AMERICAN
Dickie Greenleaf, Friend of the Murdered Freddie Miles, Missing After Sicilian Holiday

Tom bent close over the paper, giving it his full attention, yet he was conscious of a certain sense of annoyance as he read it, because in a strange way it seemed silly, silly of the police to be so stupid and ineffectual, and silly of the newspaper to waste space printing it. The text stated that H. Richard ('Dickie') Greenleaf, a close friend of the late Frederick Miles, the American murdered three weeks ago in Rome, had disappeared after presumably taking a boat from Palermo to Naples. Both the Sicilian and Roman police had been alerted and were keeping a vigilantissimo watch for him. A final paragraph said that Greenleaf had just been requested by the Rome police to answer questions concerning the disappearance of Thomas Ripley, also a close friend of Greenleaf. Ripley had been missing for about three months, the paper said.

Tom put the paper down, unconsciously feigning so well the astonishment that anybody might feel on reading in a newspaper that he was 'missing', that he didn't notice the waiter trying to hand him the menu until the menu touched his hand. This was the time, he thought, when he ought to go straight to the police and present himself. If they had nothing against him — and what could they have against Tom Ripley? — they wouldn't likely check as to when he had bought the car. The newspaper item was quite a relief to him, because it meant that the police really had not picked up his name at the bureau of automobile registration in Trento.

He ate his meal slowly and with pleasure, ordered an espresso afterwards, and smoked a couple of cigarettes as he thumbed through his guidebook on Northern Italy. By then he had had some different thoughts. For example, why should he have seen an item this small in the newspaper? And it was in only one newspaper. No, he oughtn't to present himself until he had seen two or three such items, or one big one that would logically catch his attention. They probably would come out with a big item before long: when a few days passed and Dickie Greenleaf still had not appeared, they would begin to suspect that he was hiding away because he had killed Freddie Miles and possibly Tom Ripley, too. Marge might have told the police she spoke with Tom Ripley two weeks ago in Rome, but the police hadn't seen him yet. He leafed through the guidebook, letting his eyes run over the colourless prose and statistics while he did some more thinking.

He thought of Marge, who was probably winding up her house in Mongibello now, packing for America. She'd see in the papers about Dickie's being missing, and Marge would blame him, Tom knew. She'd write to Dickie's father and say that Tom Ripley was a vile influence, at the very least. Mr. Greenleaf might decide to come over.

What a pity he couldn't present himself as Tom Ripley and quiet them down about that, then present himself as Dickie Greenleaf, hale and hearty, and clear up that little mystery, too!

He might play up Tom a little more, he thought. He could stoop a little more, he could be shyer than ever, he could even wear horn-rimmed glasses and hold his mouth in an even sadder, droopier manner to contrast with Dickie's tenseness. Because some of the police he might talk to might be the ones who had seen him as Dickie Greenleaf. What was the name of that one in Rome? Rovassini? Tom decided to rinse his hair again in a stronger solution of henna, so that it would be even darker than his normal hair.

He looked through all the papers a third time for anything about the Miles case. Nothing.

22

THE NEXT MORNING there was a long account in the most important newspaper, saying in only a small paragraph that Thomas Ripley was missing, but saying very boldly that Richard Greenleaf was 'exposing himself to suspicion of participation' in the murder of Miles, and that he must be considered as evading the 'problem', unless he presented himself to be cleared of suspicion. The paper also mentioned the forged cheques. It said that the last communication from Richard Greenleaf had been his letter to the Bank of Naples, attesting that no forgeries had been committed against him. But two experts out of three in Naples said that they believed Signor Greenleaf's January and February cheques were forgeries, concurring with the opinion of Signor Greenleaf's American bank, which had sent photostats of his signatures back to Naples. The newspaper ended on a slightly facetious note: 'Can anybody commit a forgery against himself? Or is the wealthy American shielding one of his friends?'

To hell with them, Tom thought. Dickie's own handwriting changed often enough: he had seen it on an insurance policy among Dickie's papers, and he had seen it in Mongibello, right in front of his eyes. Let them drag out everything he had signed in the last three months, and see where it got them! They apparently hadn't noticed that the signature on his letter from Palermo was a forgery, too.

The only thing that really interested him was whether the police had found anything that actually incriminated Dickie in the murder of Freddie Miles. And he could hardly say that that really interested him, personally. He bought *Oggi* and *Epoca* at a news stand in the corner of San Marco's. They were tabloid-sized weeklies full of photographs, full of anything from murder to flagpole-sitting, anything spectacular that was happening anywhere. There was nothing in them yet about the missing Dickie Greenleaf. Maybe next week, he thought. But they wouldn't have any photographs of him in them, anyway. Marge had taken pictures of Dickie in Mongibello, but she had never taken one of him.

On his ramble around the city that morning he bought some rimmed glasses at a shop that sold toys and gadgets for practical jokers. The lenses were of plain glass. He visited San Marco's cathedral and looked all around inside it without seeing anything, but it was not the fault of the glasses. He was thinking that he had to identify himself, immediately. It would look worse for him, whatever happened, the longer he put it off. When he left the cathedral he inquired of a policeman where the nearest police station was. He asked it sadly. He felt sad. He was not afraid, but he felt that identifying himself as Thomas Phelps Ripley was going to be one of the saddest things he had ever done in his life.

'*You* are Thomas Reepley?' the captain of police asked, with no more interest than if Tom had been a dog that had been lost and was now found. 'May I see your passport?'

Tom handed it to him. 'I don't know what the trouble is, but when I saw in the papers that I am believed missing—' It was all dreary, dreary, just as he had anticipated. Policemen standing around blank-faced, staring at him. 'What happens now?' Tom asked the officer.

'I shall telephone to Rome,' the officer answered calmly, and picked up the telephone on his desk.

There was a few minutes' wait for the Rome line, and then, in an impersonal voice, the officer announced to someone in Rome that the American, Thomas Reepley, was in Venice. More inconsequential exchanges, then the officer said to Tom, 'They would like to see you in Rome. Can you go to Rome today?'

Tom frowned. 'I wasn't planning to go to Rome.'

'I shall tell them,' the officer said mildly, and spoke into the telephone again.

Now he was arranging for the Rome police to come to him. Being an American citizen still commanded certain privileges, Tom supposed.

'At what hotel are you staying?' the officer asked.

'At the Costanza.'

The officer gave this piece of information to Rome. Then he hung up and informed Tom politely that a representative of the Rome police would be in Venice that evening after eight o'clock to speak to him.

'Thank you,' Tom said, and turned his back on the dismal figure of the officer writing on his form sheet. It had been a very boring little scene.

Tom spent the rest of the day in his room, quietly thinking, reading, and making further small alterations in his appearance. He thought it quite possible that they would send the same man who had spoken to him in Rome, Tenente Rovassini or whatever his name was. He made his eyebrows a trifle darker with a lead pencil. He lay around all afternoon in his brown tweed suit, and even pulled a button off the jacket. Dickie had been rather on the neat side, so Tom Ripley was going to be notably sloppy by contrast. He ate no lunch, not that he wanted any, anyway, but he wanted to continue losing the few pounds he had added for the role of Dickie Greenleaf. He would make himself thinner than he had even been before as Tom Ripley. His weight on his own passport was one hundred and fifty-five. Dickie's was a hundred and sixty-eight, though they were the same height, six feet one and one-half.

At eight-thirty that evening his telephone rang, and the switchboard operator announced that Tenente Roverini was downstairs.

'Would you have him come up, please?' Tom said.

Tom went to the chair that he intended to sit in, and drew it still farther back from the circle of light cast by the standing lamp. The room was arranged to look as if he had been reading and killing time for the last few hours – the standing lamp and a tiny reading lamp were on, the counterpane was not smooth, a couple of books lay open face down, and he had even begun a letter on the writing table, a letter to Aunt Dottie.

The tenente knocked.

Tom opened the door in a languid way. 'Buona sera.'

'Buona sera. Tenente Roverini della Polizia Romana.' The tenente's homely, smiling face did not look the least surprised or suspicious. Behind him came another tall, silent young police officer – not another, Tom realized suddenly, but the one who had been with the tenente when Tom had first met Roverini in the apartment in Rome. The officer sat down in the chair Tom offered him, under the light. 'You are a friend of Signor Richard Greenleaf?' he asked.

'Yes.' Tom sat down in the other chair, an armchair that he could slouch in.

'When did you last see him and where?'

'I saw him briefly in Rome, just before he went to Sicily.'

'And did you hear from him when he was in Sicily?' The tenente was writing it all down in the notebook that he had taken from his brown briefcase.

'No, I didn't hear from him.'

'Ah-hah,' the tenente said. He was spending more time looking at his papers than at Tom. Finally, he looked up with a friendly, interested expression. 'You did not know when you were in Rome that the police wanted to see you?'

'No. I did not know that. I cannot understand why I am said to be missing.' He adjusted his glasses, and peered at the man.

'I shall explain later. Signor Greenleaf did not tell you in Rome that the police wanted to speak to you?'

'No.'

'Strange,' he remarked quietly, making another notation. 'Signor Greenleaf knew that we wanted to speak to you. Signor Greenleaf is not very co-operative.' He smiled at Tom.

Tom kept his face serious and attentive.

'Signor Reepley, where have you been since the end of November?'

'I have been travelling. I have been mostly in the north of Italy.' Tom made his Italian clumsy, with a mistake here and there, and with quite a different rhythm from Dickie's Italian.

'Where?' The tenente gripped his pen again.

'Milano, Torino, Faenza – Pisa—'

'We have inquired at the hotels in Milano and Faenza, for example. Did you stay all the time with friends?'

'No, I – slept quite often in my car.' It was obvious that he hadn't a great deal of money, Tom thought, and also that he was the kind of young man who would prefer to rough it with a guidebook and a volume of Silone or Dante, than to stay in a fancy hotel. 'I am sorry that I did not renew my permiso di soggiorno,' Tom said contritely. 'I did not know that it was such a serious matter.' But he knew that tourists in Italy almost never took the trouble to renew their soggiorno, and stayed for months after stating on entering the country that they intended to be there for only a few weeks.

'*Permesso* di soggiorno,' the tenente said in a tone of gentle, almost paternal correction.

'Grazie.'

'May I see your passport?'

Tom produced it from his inside jacket pocket. The tenente studied the picture closely, while Tom assumed the faintly anxious expression, the faintly parted lips, of the passport photograph. The glasses were missing from the photograph, but his hair was parted in the same manner, and his tie was tied in the same loose, triangular knot. The tenente glanced at the few stamped entries that only partially filled the first two pages of the passport.

PATRICIA HIGHSMITH

'You have been in Italy since October second, except for the short trip to France with Signor Greenleaf?'

'Yes.'

The tenente smiled, a pleasant Italian smile now, and leaned forward on his knees. 'Ebbene, this settles one important matter – the mystery of the San Remo boat.'

Tom frowned. 'What is that?'

'A boat was found sunken there with some stains that were believed to be bloodstains. Naturally, when you were missing so far as we knew, immediately after San Remo—' He threw his hands out and laughed. 'We thought it might be advisable to ask Signor Greenleaf what had happened to you. Which we did. The boat was missed the same day that you two were in San Remo!' He laughed again.

Tom pretended not to see the joke. 'But did not Signor Greenleaf tell you that I went to Mongibello after San Remo? I did some –' he groped for a word '– little labours for him.'

'Benone!' Tenente Roverini said, smiling. He loosened his brass-buttoned overcoat comfortably, and rubbed a finger back and forth across the crisp, bushy moustache. 'Did you also know Fred-derick Mee-lays?' he asked.

Tom gave an involuntary sigh, because the boat incident was apparently closed. 'No. I only met him once when he was getting off the bus in Mongibello. I never saw him again.'

'Ah-hah,' said the tenente, taking this in. He was silent a minute, as if he had run out of questions, then he smiled. 'Ah Mongibello! A beautiful village, is it not? My wife comes from Mongibello.'

'Ah, indeed!' Tom said pleasantly.

'Si. My wife and I went there on our honeymoon.'

'A most beautiful village,' Tom said. 'Grazie.' He accepted the Nazionale that the tenente offered him. Tom felt that this was perhaps a polite Italian interlude, a rest between rounds. They were surely going to get into Dickie's private life, the

204

forged cheques and all the rest. Tom said seriously in his plodding Italian, 'I have read in a newspaper that the police think that Signor Greenleaf may be guilty of the murder of Freddie Miles, if he does not present himself. Is it true that they think he is guilty?'

'Ah, no, no, no!' the tenente protested. 'But it is imperative that he present himself! Why is he hiding from us?'

'I don't know. As you say – he is not very co-operative,' Tom commented solemnly. 'He was not enough co-operative to tell me in Rome that the police wanted to speak with me. But at the same time – I cannot believe it is possible that he killed Freddie Miles.'

'*But* – you see, a man has said in Rome that he saw two men standing beside the car of Signor Mee-lays across the street from the house of Signor Greenleaf, and that they were both drunk or –' he paused for effect, looking at Tom '– perhaps one man was dead, because the other was holding him up beside the car! Of course, we cannot say that the man who was being supported was Signor Mee-lays or Signor Greenleaf,' he added, 'but if we could find Signor Greenleaf, we could at least ask him if he was so drunk that Signor Mee-lays had to hold him up!'

He laughed. 'Yes.'

'It is a very serious matter.'

'Yes, I can see that.'

'You have absolutely no idea where Signor Greenleaf might be at this moment?'

'No. Absolutely no.'

The tenente mused. 'Signor Greenleaf and Signor Mee-lays had no quarrel that you know of?'

'No, but—'

'But?'

Tom continued slowly, doing it just right. 'I know that Dickie did not go to a ski party that Freddie Miles had invited him to. I remember that I was surprised that he had not gone. He did not tell me why.'

'I know about the ski party. In Cortina d'Ampezzo. Are you sure there was no woman involved?'

Tom's sense of humour tugged at him, but he pretended to think this one over carefully. 'I do not think so.'

'What about the girl, Marjorie Sherwood?'

'I suppose it is *possible*,' Tom said, 'but I do not think so. I am perhaps not the person to answer questions about Signor Greenleaf's personal life.'

'Signor Greenleaf never talked to you about his affairs of the heart?' the tenente asked with a Latin astonishment.

He could lead them on indefinitely, Tom thought. Marge would back it up, just by the emotional way she would react to questions about Dickie, and the Italian police could never get to the bottom of Signor Greenleaf's emotional involvements. He hadn't been able to himself! 'No,' Tom said. 'I cannot say that Dickie ever talked to me about his most personal life. I know he is very fond of Marjorie.' He added, 'She also knew Freddie Miles.'

'How well did she know him?'

'Well—' Tom acted as if he might say more if he chose.

The tenente leaned forward. 'Since you lived for a time with Signor Greenleaf in Mongibello, you are perhaps in a position to tell us about Signor Greenleaf's attachments in general. They are most important.'

'Why don't you speak to Signorina Sherwood?' Tom suggested.

'We have spoken to her in Rome – before Signor Greenleaf disappeared. I have arranged to speak to her again when she comes to Genoa to embark for America. She is now in Munich.'

Tom waited, silent. The tenente was waiting for him to contribute something more. Tom felt quite comfortable now. It was going just as he had hoped in his most optimistic moments: the police held nothing against him at all, and they suspected him of nothing. Tom felt suddenly innocent and strong, as free of guilt as his old suitcase from which he had carefully scrubbed the *Deponimento* sticker from the Palermo baggage room. He said in his earnest, careful, Ripley-like way, 'I remember that Marjorie said for a while in Mongibello that she would *not* go to Cortina, and later she changed her mind. But I do not know why. If that could mean anything—'

'But she never went to Cortina.'

'No, but only because Signor Greenleaf did not go, I think. At least, Signorina Sherwood likes him so much that she would not go alone on a holiday after she expected to go on the holiday with him.'

'Do you think they had a quarrel, Signors Mee-lays and Greenleaf, about Signorina Sherwood?'

'I cannot say. It is possible. I know that Signor Miles was very fond of her, too.'

'Ah-hah.' The tenente frowned, trying to figure all that out. He glanced up at the younger policeman, who was evidently listening, though, from his immobile face, he had nothing to contribute.

What he had said gave a picture of Dickie as a sulking lover, Tom thought, unwilling to let Marge go to Cortina to have some fun, because she liked Freddie Miles too much. The idea of anybody, Marge especially, liking that wall-eyed ox in preference to Dickie made Tom smile. He turned the smile into an expression of non-comprehension. 'Do you actually think Dickie is running away from something, or do you think it is an accident that you cannot find him?'

'Oh, no. This is too much. First, the matter of the cheques. You perhaps know about that from the newspapers.'

'I do not completely understand about the cheques.'

The officer explained. He knew the dates of the cheques and the number of people who believed they were forged. He explained that Signor Greenleaf had denied the forgeries. 'But when the bank wishes to see him again about a forgery against himself, and also the police in Rome wish to see him again about the murder of his friend, and he suddenly vanishes—' The tenente threw out his hands. 'That can only mean that he is running away from us.'

'You don't think someone may have murdered *him*?' Tom said softly.

The officer shrugged, holding his shoulders up under his ears for at least a quarter of a minute. 'I do not think so. The facts are not like that. Not quite. Ebbene – we have checked by radio every boat of any size with passengers which has left from Italy. He has either taken a small boat, and it must have been as small as a fishing boat, or else he is hiding in Italy. Or of course, anywhere else in Europe, because we do not ordinarily take the names of people leaving our country, and Signor Greenleaf had several days in which to leave. In any case, he is hiding. In any case, he acts guilty. *Something* is the matter.'

Tom stared gravely at the man.

'Did you ever *see* Signor Greenleaf sign any of those remittances? In particular, the remittances of January and February?'

'I saw him sign one of them,' Tom said. 'But I am afraid it was in December. I was not with him in January and February. —Do you seriously suspect that he might have killed Signor Miles?' Tom asked again, incredulously.

'He has no actual alibi,' the officer replied. 'He says he was taking a walk after Signor Mee-lays departed, but nobody saw him taking the walk.' He pointed a finger at Tom suddenly. '*And* – we have learned from the friend of Signor Mee-lays, Signor Van Houston, that Signor Mee-lays had a difficult time finding Signor Greenleaf in Rome – as if Signor Greenleaf were trying to hide from him. Signor Greenleaf might have been angry with Signor Mee-lays, though, according to Signor Van Houston, Signor Mee-lays was not at all angry with Signor Greenleaf!'

'I see,' Tom said.

'Ecco,' the tenente said conclusively. He was staring at Tom's hands.

Or at least Tom imagined that he was staring at his hands. Tom had his own ring on again, but did the tenente possibly notice some resemblance? Tom boldly thrust his hand forward to the ashtray and put out his cigarette.

'Ebbene,' the tenente said, standing up. 'Thank you so much for you help, Signor Reepley. You are one of the very few people from whom we can find out about Signor Greenleaf's personal life. In Mongibello, the people he knew are extremely quiet. An Italian trait, alas! You know, afraid of the police.' He chuckled. 'I hope we can reach you more easily the next time we have questions to ask you. Stay in the cities a little more and in the country a little less. Unless, of course, you are addicted to our countryside.'

'I am!' Tom said heartily. 'In my opinion, Italy is the most beautiful country of Europe. But if you like, I shall keep in touch with you in Rome so you will always know where I am. I am as much interested as you in finding my friend.' He said it as if his innocent mind had already forgotten the possibility that Dickie could be a murderer.

The tenente handed him a card with his name and the address of his headquarters in Rome. He bowed. 'Grazie tante, Signor Reepley. Buona sera!'

'Buona sera,' Tom said.

The younger policeman saluted him as he went out, and Tom gave him a nod and closed the door.

He could have flown – like a bird, out of the window, with spread arms! The idiots! All around the thing and never guessing it! Never guessing that Dickie was running from the forgery questions because he wasn't Dickie Greenleaf in the first place! The one thing they were bright about was that Dickie Greenleaf might have killed Freddie Miles. But Dickie Greenleaf was dead, dead, deader than a doornail and he, Tom Ripley, was safe! He picked up the telephone.

'Would you give me the Grand Hotel, please,' he said in Tom Ripley's Italian. 'Il ristorante, per piacere. —Would you reserve a table for one for nine-thirty? Thank you. The name is Ripley. R-i-p-l-e-y.'

Tonight he was going to have a dinner. And look out at the moonlight on the Grand Canal. And watch the gondolas drifting as lazily as they ever drifted for any honeymooner, with the gondoliers and their oars silhouetted against the moonlit water. He was suddenly ravenous. He was going to have something luscious and expensive to eat – whatever the Grand Hotel's speciality was, breast of pheasant or petto di pollo, and perhaps cannelloni to begin with, creamy sauce over delicate pasta, and a good valpolicella to sip while he dreamed about his future and planned where he went from here.

He had a bright idea while he was changing his clothes: he ought to have an envelope in his possession, on which should be written that it was not to be opened for several months to come. Inside it should be a will signed by Dickie, bequeathing him his money and his income. Now that was an idea.

23

Venice

28 Feb. 19——

Dear Mr. Greenleaf:

I THOUGHT UNDER the circumstances you would not take it
amiss if I wrote you whatever personal information I have in regard to
Richard – I being one of the last people, it seems, who saw him.

I saw him in Rome around 2 February at the Inghilterra Hotel. As
you know, this was only two or three days after the death of Freddie
Miles. I found Dickie upset and nervous. He said he was going to
Palermo as soon as the police finished their questioning him in regard
to Freddie's death, and he seemed eager to get away, which was
understandable, but I wanted to tell you that there was a certain
depression underlying all this that troubled me much more than his
obvious nervousness. I had the feeling he would try to do something
violent – perhaps to himself. I knew also that he didn't want to see his
friend Marjorie Sherwood again, and he said he would try to avoid
her if she came up from Mongibello to see him because of the Miles
affair. I tried to persuade him to see her. I don't know if he did. Marge
has a soothing effect on people, as perhaps you know.

What I am trying to say is that I feel Richard may have killed
himself. At the time of this writing he has not been found. I certainly
hope he will be before this reaches you. It goes without saying that I
am sure Richard had nothing to do, directly or indirectly, with
Freddie's death, but I think the shock of it and the questioning that
followed did do something to upset his equilibrium. This is a depres-
sing message to send to you and I regret it. It may be all completely
unnecessary and Dickie may be (again understandably, according to
his temperament) simply in hiding until these unpleasantnesses blow

over. But as the time goes on, I begin to feel more uneasy myself. I thought it my duty to write you this, simply by way of letting you know....

Munich
3 March, 19—

Dear Tom:

Thanks for your letter. It was very kind of you. I've answered the police in writing, and one came up to see me. I won't be coming by Venice, but thanks for your invitation. I am going to Rome day after tomorrow to meet Dickie's father, who is flying over. Yes, I agree with you that it was a good idea for you to write to him.

I am so bowled over by all this, I have come down with something resembling undulant fever, or maybe what the Germans call Foehn, but with some kind of virus thrown in. Literally unable to get out of bed for four days, otherwise I'd have gone to Rome before now. So please excuse this disjointed and probably feeble-minded letter which is such a bad answer to your very nice one. But I did want to say I don't agree with you at all that Dickie might have committed suicide. He just isn't the type, though I know all you're going to say about people never acting like they're going to do it, etc. No, anything else but this for Dickie. He might have been murdered in some back alley of Naples – or even Rome, because who knows whether he got up to Rome or not after he left Sicily? I can also imagine him running out on obligations to such an extent that he'd be *hiding* now. I think that's what he's doing.

I'm glad you think the forgeries are a mistake. Of the bank, I mean. So do I. Dickie has changed so much since November, it could easily have changed his handwriting, too. Let's hope something's happened by the time you get this. Had a wire from Mr. Greenleaf about Rome – so must save all my energy for that.

Nice to know your address finally. Thanks again for your letter, your advice, and invitations.

Best,
Marge

P.S. I didn't tell you my *good* news. I've got a publisher interested in 'Mongibello'! Says he wants to see the whole thing before he can give me a contract, but it really sounds hopeful! Now if I can only finish the damn thing!

M.

She had decided to be on good terms with him, Tom supposed. She'd probably changed her tune about him to the police, too.

Dickie's disappearance was stirring up a great deal of excitement in the Italian press. Marge, or somebody, had provided the reporters with photographs. There were pictures in *Epoca* of Dickie sailing his boat in Mongibello, pictures of Dickie in *Oggi* sitting on the beach in Mongibello and also on Giorgio's terrace, and a picture of Dickie and Marge – 'girl friend of both il sparito Dickie and il assassinato Freddie' – smiling, with their arms around each other's shoulders, and there was even a businesslike portrait of Herbert Greenleaf, Sr. Tom had gotten Marge's Munich address right out of a newspaper. *Oggi* had been running a life story of Dickie for the past two weeks, describing his school years as 'rebellious' and embroidering his social life in America and his flight to Europe for the sake of his art to such an extent that he emerged as a combination of Errol Flynn and Paul Gauguin. The illustrated weeklies always gave the latest police reports, which were practically nil, padded with whatever theorizing the writers happened to feel like concocting that week. A favourite theory was that he had run off with another girl – a girl who might have been signing his remittances – and was having a good time, incognito, in Tahiti or South America or Mexico. The police were still combing Rome and Naples and Paris, that was all. No clues as to Freddie Miles' killer, and nothing about Dickie Greenleaf's having been seen carrying Freddie Miles, or vice versa, in front of Dickie's house. Tom wondered why they were holding that back from the newspapers. Probably because they couldn't write it up without subjecting themselves to charges of libel by Dickie. Tom was gratified to find himself described as 'a loyal friend' of the missing Dickie Greenleaf, who had volunteered everything he knew as to Dickie's character and habits, and who was as bewildered by his disappearance as anybody else. 'Signor Ripley, one of the young well-to-do American visitors in Italy,' said *Oggi*, 'now lives in a palazzo overlooking San Marco in Venice.' That pleased Tom most of all. He cut out that write-up.

Tom had not thought of it as a 'palace' before, but of course it was what the Italians called a palazzo – a two-storey house of formal design more than two hundred years old, with a main entrance on the Grand Canal approachable only by gondola, with broad stone steps descending into the water, and iron doors that had to be opened by an eight-inch-long key, besides the regular doors behind the iron doors which also took an enormous key. Tom used the less formal 'back door' usually, which was on the Viale San Spiridione, except when he wanted to impress his guests by bringing them to his home in a gondola. The back door – itself fourteen feet high like the stone wall that enclosed the house from the street – led into a garden that was somewhat neglected but still green, and which boasted two gnarled olive trees and a birdbath made of an ancient-looking statue of a naked boy holding a wide shallow bowl. It was just the garden for a Venetian palace, slightly run down, in need of some restoration which it was not going to get, but indelibly beautiful because it had sprung into the world so beautiful more than two hundred years ago. The inside of the house was Tom's ideal of what a civilized bachelor's home should look like, in Venice, at least: a checkerboard black-and-white marble floor downstairs extending from the formal foyer into each room, pink-and-white marble floor upstairs, furniture that did not resemble furniture at all but an embodiment of cinquecento music played on hautboys, recorders, and violas da gamba. He had his servants – Anna and Ugo, a young Italian couple who had worked for an American in Venice before, so that they knew the difference between a Bloody Mary and a crème de menthe frappé – polish the carved fronts of the armoires and chests and chairs until they seemed alive with dim lustrous lights that moved as one moved around them. The only thing faintly modern was the bathroom. In Tom's bedroom stood a gargantuan bed, broader than it was long. Tom decorated his bedroom with a series of panoramic pictures of Naples from 1540 to about 1880, which he found at an antique store. He had given his undivided attention to decorating his house for more than a week. There was a sureness in his taste now that he had not felt in Rome, and that his Rome apartment had not hinted at. He felt surer of himself now in every way.

His self-confidence had even inspired him to write to Aunt Dottie in a calm, affectionate and forbearing tone that he had never wanted to use before, or had never before been able to use. He had inquired about her flamboyant health, about her little circle of vicious friends in Boston, and had explained to her why he liked Europe and intended to live here for a while, explained so eloquently that he had copied that section of his letter and put it into his desk. He had written this inspired letter one morning after breakfast, sitting in his bedroom in a new silk dressing-gown made to order for him in Venice, gazing out of the window now and then at the Grand Canal and the Clock Tower of the Piazza San Marco across the water. After he had finished the letter he had made some more coffee and on Dickie's own Hermes he had written Dickie's will, bequeathing him his income and the money he had in various banks, and had signed it Herbert Richard Greenleaf, Jr. Tom thought it better not to add a witness, lest the banks or Mr. Greenleaf challenge him to the extent of demanding to know who the witness was, though Tom had thought of making up an Italian name, presumably someone Dickie might have called into his apartment in Rome for the purpose of witnessing the will. He would just have to take his chances on an unwitnessed will, he thought, but Dickie's typewriter was so in need of repair that its quirks were as recognizable as a particular handwriting, and he had heard that holograph wills required no witness. But the signature was perfect, exactly like the slim, tangled signature on Dickie's passport. Tom practised for half an hour before he signed the will, relaxed his hands, then signed a piece of scrap paper, then the will, in rapid succession. And he would defy anybody to prove that the signature on the will wasn't Dickie's. Tom put an envelope into the typewriter and addressed it To Whom It May Concern, with a notation that it was not to be opened until June of this year. He tucked it into a side pocket of his suitcase, as if he had been carrying it there for some time and hadn't bothered unpacking it when he moved into the house. Then he took the Hermes Baby in its case downstairs and dropped it into the little inlet of the canal, too narrow for a boat, which ran from the front corner of his house to the garden wall. He was glad to be rid of the typewriter, though he had been unwilling to part with it until now. He must have known, subconsciously, he thought, that he was going to write the will or something else of great importance on it, and that was the reason why he had kept it.

Tom followed the Italian newspapers and the Paris edition of the *Herald-Tribune* on the Greenleaf and Miles cases with the anxious concern befitting a friend of both Dickie and Freddie. The papers were suggesting by the end of March that Dickie might be dead, murdered by the same man or men who had been profiting by forging his signature. A Rome paper said that one man in Naples now held that the signature on the letter from Palermo, stating that no forgeries had been committed against him, was also a forgery. Others, however, did not concur. Some man on the police force, not Roverini, thought that the culprit or culprits had been 'intimo' with Greenleaf, that they had had access to the bank's letter and had had the audacity to reply to it themselves. 'The mystery is,' the officer was quoted, 'not only who the forger was but how he gained access to the letter, because the porter of the hotel remembers putting the registered bank letter into Greenleaf's hands. The hotel porter also recalls that Greenleaf was always alone in Palermo. . . .'

More hitting around the answer without ever hitting it. But Tom was shaken for several minutes after he read it. There remained only one more step for them to take, and wasn't somebody going to take it today or tomorrow or the next day? Or did they really already know the answer, and were they just trying to put him off guard – Tenente Roverini sending him personal messages every few days to keep him abreast of what was happening in the search for Dickie – and were they going to pounce on him one day soon with every bit of evidence they needed?

It gave Tom the feeling that he was being followed, especially when he walked through the long, narrow street to his house door. The Viale San Spiridione was nothing but a functional slit between vertical walls of houses, without a shop in it and with hardly enough light for him to see where he was going, nothing but unbroken housefronts and the tall, firmly locked doors of the Italian house gates that were flush with the walls. Nowhere to run to if he were attacked, no house door to duck into. Tom did not know who would attack him, if he were attacked. He did not imagine police, necessarily. He was afraid of nameless, formless things that haunted his brain like the Furies. He could go through San Spiridione comfortably only when a few cocktails had knocked out his fear. Then he walked through swaggering and whistling.

He had his pick of cocktail parties, though in his first two weeks in his house he went to only two. He had his choice of people because of a little incident that had happened the first day he had started looking for a house. A rental agent, armed with three huge keys, had taken him to see a certain house in San Stefano parish, thinking it would be vacant. It had not only been occupied but a cocktail party had been in progress, and the hostess had insisted on Tom and the rental agent, too, having a cocktail by way of making amends for their inconvenience and her remissness. She had put the house up for rent a month ago, had changed her mind about leaving, and had neglected to inform the rental agency. Tom stayed for a drink, acted his reserved, courteous self, and met all her guests, who he supposed were most of the winter colony of Venice and rather hungry for new blood, judging from the way they welcomed him and offered their assistance in finding a house. They recognized his name, of course, and the fact that he knew Dickie Greenleaf raised his social value to a degree that surprised even Tom. Obviously they were going to invite him everywhere and quiz him and drain him of every last little detail to add some spice to their dull lives. Tom behaved in a reserved but friendly manner appropriate for a young man in his position – a sensitive young man, unused to garish publicity, whose primary emotion in regard to Dickie was anxiety as to what had happened to him.

He left that first party with the addresses of three other houses he might look at (one being the one he took) and invitations to two other parties. He went to the party whose hostess had a title, the Contessa Roberta (Titi) della Latta-Cacciaguerra. He was not at all in the mood for parties. He seemed to see people through a mist, and communication was slow and difficult. He often asked people to repeat what they had said. He was terribly bored. But he could use them, he thought, to practise on. The naïve questions they asked him ('Did Dickie drink a lot?' and 'But he *was* in love with Marge, wasn't he?' and 'Where do you *really* think he went?') were good practice for the more specific questions Mr. Greenleaf was going to ask him when he saw him, if he ever saw him. Tom began to be uneasy about ten days after Marge's letter, because Mr. Greenleaf had not written or telephoned him from Rome. In certain frightened moments, Tom imagined that the police had told Mr. Greenleaf that they were playing a game

with Tom Ripley, and had asked Mr. Greenleaf not to talk
to him.

Each day he looked eagerly in his mailbox for a letter from
Marge or Mr. Greenleaf. His house was ready for their arrival.
His answers to their questions were ready in his head. It was like
waiting interminably for a show to begin, for a curtain to rise.
Or maybe Mr. Greenleaf was so resentful of him (not to mention possibly being actually suspicious) that he was going to
ignore him entirely. Maybe Marge was abetting him in that. At
any rate, he couldn't take a trip until *something* happened. Tom
wanted to take a trip, the famous trip to Greece. He had bought
a guidebook of Greece, and he had already planned his itinerary
over the islands.

Then, on the morning of April fourth, he got a
telephone call from Marge. She was in Venice, at the railroad
station.

'I'll come and pick you up!' Tom said cheerfully. 'Is Mr.
Greenleaf with you?'

'No, he's in Rome. I'm alone. You don't have to pick me
up. I've only got an overnight bag.'

'Nonsense!' Tom said, dying to do something. 'You'll never
find the house by yourself.'

'Yes, I will. It's next to della Salute, isn't it? I take the
motoscafo to San Marco's, then take a gondola across.'

She knew, all right. 'Well, if you insist.' He had just thought
that he had better take one more good look around the house
before she got here. 'Have you had lunch?'

'No.'

'Good! We'll lunch together somewhere. Watch your step
on the motoscafo!'

They hung up. He walked soberly and slowly through the
house, into both large rooms upstairs, down the stairs and
through his living-room. Nothing, anywhere, that belonged
to Dickie. He hoped the house didn't look too plush. He took a
silver cigarette box, which he had bought only two days ago

and had had initialled, from the living-room table and put it in the bottom drawer of a chest in the dining-room.

Anna was in the kitchen, preparing lunch.

'Anna, there'll be one more for lunch,' Tom said. 'A young lady.'

Anna's face broke into a smile at the prospect of a guest. 'A young American lady?'

'Yes. An old friend. When the lunch is ready, you and Ugo can have the rest of the afternoon off. We can serve ourselves.'

'Va bene,' Anna said.

Anna and Ugo came at ten and stayed until two, ordinarily. Tom didn't want them here when he talked with Marge. They understood a little English, not enough to follow a conversation perfectly, but he knew both of them would have their ears out if he and Marge talked about Dickie, and it irritated him.

Tom made a batch of martinis, and arranged the glasses and a plate of canapés on a tray in the living-room. When he heard the door knocker, he went to the door and swung it open.

'Marge! Good to see you! Come in!' He took the suitcase from her hand.

'How are you, Tom? My!— Is all this yours?' She looked around her, and up at the high coffered ceiling.

'I rented it. For a song,' Tom said modestly. 'Come and have a drink. Tell me what's new. You've been talking to the police in Rome?' He carried her topcoat and her transparent raincoat to a chair.

'Yes, and to Mr. Greenleaf. He's very upset – naturally.' She sat down on the sofa.

Tom settled himself in a chair opposite her. 'Have they found anything new? One of the police officers there has been keeping me posted, but he hasn't told me anything that really matters.'

'Well, they found out that Dickie cashed over a thousand dollars' worth of traveller's cheques before he left Palermo. *Just* before. So he must have gone off somewhere with it, like

Greece or Africa. He couldn't have gone off to kill himself after just cashing a thousand dollars, anyway.'

'No,' Tom agreed. 'Well, that sounds hopeful. I didn't see that in the papers.'

'I don't think they put it in.'

'No. Just a lot of nonsense about what Dickie used to eat for breakfast in Mongibello,' Tom said as he poured the martinis.

'Isn't it awful! It's getting a little better now, but when Mr. Greenleaf arrived, the papers were at their worst. Oh, thanks!' She accepted the martini gratefully.

'How is he?'

Marge shook her head. 'I feel so sorry for him. He keeps saying the American police could do a better job and all that, and he doesn't know any Italian, so that makes it twice as bad.'

'What's he doing in Rome?'

'Waiting. What can any of us do? I've postponed my boat again. —Mr. Greenleaf and I went to Mongibello, and I questioned everyone there, mostly for Mr. Greenleaf's benefit, of course, but they can't tell us anything. Dickie hasn't been back there since November.'

'No.' Tom sipped his martini thoughtfully. Marge was optimistic, he could see that. Even now she had that energetic buoyancy that made Tom think of the typical Girl Scout, that look of taking up a lot of space, of possibly knocking something over with a wild movement, of rugged health and vague untidiness. She irritated him intensely suddenly, but he put on a big act, got up and patted her on the shoulder, and gave her an affectionate peck on the cheek. 'Maybe he's sitting in Tangiers or somewhere living the life of Riley and waiting for all this to blow over.'

'Well, it's damned inconsiderate of him if he is!' Marge said, laughing.

'I certainly didn't mean to alarm anybody when I said what I did about his depression. I felt it was a kind of duty to tell you and Mr. Greenleaf.'

'I understand. No, I think you were right to tell us. I just don't think it's true.' She smiled her broad smile, her eyes glowing with an optimism that struck Tom as completely insane.

He began asking her sensible, practical questions about the opinions of the Rome police, about the leads that they had (they had none worth mentioning), and what she had heard on the Miles case. There was nothing new on the Miles case, either, but Marge did know about Freddie and Dickie's having been seen in front of Dickie's house around eight o'clock that night. She thought the story was exaggerated.

'Maybe Freddie was drunk, or maybe Dickie just had an arm around him. How could anybody tell in the dark? Don't tell me Dickie murdered him!'

'Have they any concrete clues at all that would make them think Dickie killed him?'

'Of course not!'

'Then why don't the so-and-so's get down to the business of finding out who really did kill him? And also where Dickie is?'

'*Ecco!*' Marge said emphatically. 'Anyway, the police are sure now that Dickie at least got from Palermo to Naples. A steward remembers carrying his bags from his cabin to the Naples dock.'

'Really,' Tom said. He remembered the steward, too, a clumsy little oaf who had dropped his canvas suitcase, trying to carry it under one arm. 'Wasn't Freddie killed hours after he left Dickie's house?' Tom asked suddenly.

'No. The doctors can't say exactly. And it seems Dickie didn't have an alibi, of course, because he was undoubtedly alone. Just more of Dickie's bad luck.'

'They don't actually *believe* Dickie killed him, do they?'

'They don't say it, no. It's just in the air. Naturally, they can't make rash statements right and left about an American citizen, but as long as they haven't any suspects and Dickie's disappeared— Then also his landlady in Rome said that Freddie came down to ask her who was living in Dickie's apartment or something like that. She said Freddie looked angry, as if they'd been quarrelling. She said he asked if Dickie was living alone.'

Tom frowned. 'I wonder why?'

'I can't imagine. Freddie's Italian wasn't the best in the world, and maybe the landlady got it wrong. Anyway, the mere fact that Freddie was angry about something looks bad for Dickie.'

Tom raised his eyebrows. 'I'd say it looked bad for Freddie. Maybe Dickie wasn't angry at all.' He felt perfectly calm, because he could see that Marge hadn't smelled out anything about it. 'I wouldn't worry about that unless something concrete comes out of it. Sounds like nothing at all to me.' He refilled her glass. 'Speaking of Africa, have they inquired around Tangiers yet? Dickie used to talk about going to Tangiers.'

'I think they've alerted the police everywhere. I think they ought to get the French police down here. The French are terribly good at things like this. But of course they can't. This is Italy,' she said with the first nervous tremor in her voice.

'Shall we have lunch here?' Tom asked. 'The maid is functioning over the lunch hour and we might as well take advantage of it.' He said it just as Anna was coming in to announce that the lunch was ready.

'Wonderful!' Marge said. 'It's raining a little, anyway.'

'Pronta la collazione, signore,' Anna said with a smile, staring at Marge.

Anna recognized her from the newspaper pictures, Tom saw. 'You and Ugo can go now if you like, Anna. Thanks.'

Anna went back into the kitchen – there was a door from the kitchen to a little alley at the side of the house, which the servants used – but Tom heard her pottering around with the coffee maker, stalling for another glimpse, no doubt.

'And Ugo?' Marge said. 'Two servants, no less?'

'Oh, they come in couples around here. You may not believe it, but I got this place for fifty dollars a month, not counting heat.'

'I don't believe it! That's practically like Mongibello rates!'

'It's true. The heating's fantastic, of course, but I'm not going to heat any room except my bedroom.'

'It's certainly comfortable here.'

'Oh, I opened the whole furnace for your benefit,' Tom said, smiling.

'What happened? Did one of your aunts die and leave you a fortune?' Marge asked, still pretending to be dazzled.

'No, just a decision of my own. I'm going to enjoy what I've got as long as it lasts. I told you that job I was after in Rome didn't pan out, and here I was in Europe with only about two thousand dollars to my name, so I decided to live it up and go home – broke – and start over again.' Tom had explained to her in his letter that the job he had applied for had been selling hearing aids in Europe for an American company, and he hadn't been able to face it, and the man who had interviewed him, he said, hadn't thought him the right type, either. Tom had also told her that the man had appeared one minute after he spoke to her, which was why he had been unable to keep his appointment with her in Angelo's that day in Rome.

'Two thousand dollars won't last you long at this rate.'

She was probing to see if Dickie had given him anything, Tom knew. 'It will last till summer,' Tom said matter-of-factly. 'Anyway, I feel I deserve it. I spent most of the winter going around Italy like a gypsy on practically no money, and I've had about enough of that.'

'Where *were* you this winter?'

'Well, not with Tom. I mean, not with Dickie,' he said laughing, flustered at his slip of the tongue. 'I know you probably thought so. I saw about as much of Dickie as you did.'

'Oh, come on now,' Marge drawled. She sounded as if she were feeling her drinks.

Tom made two or three more martinis in the pitcher. 'Except for the trip to Cannes and the two days in Rome in February, I haven't seen Dickie at all.' It wasn't quite true, because he had written her that 'Tom was staying' with Dickie in Rome for several days after the Cannes trip, but now that he was face to face with Marge he found he was ashamed of her knowing, or thinking, that he had spent so much time with Dickie, and that he and Dickie might be guilty of what she had accused Dickie of in her letter. He bit his tongue as he poured their drinks, hating himself for his cowardice.

During lunch – Tom regretted very much that the main dish was cold roast beef, a fabulously expensive item on the Italian market – Marge quizzed him more acutely than any police officer on Dickie's state of mind while he was in Rome. Tom was pinned down to ten days spent in Rome with Dickie after the Cannes trip, and was questioned about everything from Di Massimo, the painter Dickie had worked with, to Dickie's appetite and the hour he got up in the morning.

'How do you think he felt about *me*? Tell me honestly. I can take it.'

'I think he was worried about you,' Tom said earnestly. 'I think – well, it was one of those situations that turn up quite often, a man who's terrified of marriage to begin with—'

'But I never asked him to marry me!' Marge protested.

'I know, but—' Tom forced himself to go on, though the subject was like vinegar in his mouth. 'Let's say he couldn't face the responsibility of your caring so much about him. I think he wanted a more casual relationship with you.' That told her everything and nothing.

Marge stared at him in that old, lost way for a moment, then rallied bravely and said, 'Well, all that's water under the bridge by now. I'm only interested in what Dickie might have done with himself.'

Her fury at his apparently having been with Dickie all winter was water under the bridge, too, Tom thought, because she hadn't wanted to believe it in the first place, and now she didn't have to. Tom asked carefully, 'He didn't happen to write to you when he was in Palermo?'

Marge shook her head. 'No. Why?'

'I wanted to know what kind of state you thought he was in then. Did you write to him?'

She hesitated. 'Yes – matter of fact, I did.'

'What kind of a letter? I only ask because an unfriendly letter might have had a bad effect on him just then.'

'Oh – it's hard to say what kind. A fairly friendly letter. I told him I was going back to the States.' She looked at him with wide eyes.

Tom enjoyed watching her face, watching somebody else squirm as they lied. That had been the filthy letter in which she said she had told the police that he and Dickie were always together. 'I don't suppose it matters then,' Tom said, with sweet gentleness, sitting back.

They were silent a few moments, then Tom asked her about her book, who the publisher was, and how much more work she had to do. Marge answered everything enthusiastically. Tom had the feeling that if she had Dickie back and her book published by next winter, she would probably just explode with happiness, make a loud, unattractive *ploop!* and that would be the end of her.

'Do you think I should offer to talk to Mr. Greenleaf, too?' Tom asked. 'I'd be glad to go to Rome—' Only he wouldn't be so glad, he remembered, because Rome had simply too many people in it who had seen him as Dickie Greenleaf. 'Or do you think he would like to come here? I could put him up. Where's he staying in Rome?'

'He's staying with some American friends who have a big apartment. Somebody called Northup in Via Quattro

Novembre. I think it'd be nice if you called him. I'll write the address down for you.'

'That's a good idea. He doesn't like me, does he?'

Marge smiled a little. 'Well, frankly, no. I think he's a little hard on you, considering. He probably thinks you sponged off Dickie.'

'Well, I didn't. I'm sorry the idea didn't work out about my getting Dickie back home, but I explained all that. I wrote him the nicest letter I could about Dickie when I heard he was missing. Didn't that help any?'

'I think it did, but— Oh, I'm terribly sorry, Tom! All over this wonderful tablecloth!' Marge had turned her martini over. She daubed at the crocheted tablecloth awkwardly with her napkin.

Tom came running back from the kitchen with a wet cloth. 'Perfectly all right,' he said, watching the wood of the table turn white in spite of his wiping. It wasn't the tablecloth he cared about, it was the beautiful table.

'I'm so sorry,' Marge went on protesting.

Tom hated her. He suddenly remembered her bra hanging over the windowsill in Mongibello. Her underwear would be draped over his chairs tonight, if he invited her to stay here. The idea repelled him. He deliberately hurled a smile across the table at her. 'I hope you'll honour me by accepting a bed for the night. Not mine,' he added, laughing, 'but I've got two rooms upstairs and you're welcome to one of them.'

'Thanks a lot. All right, I will.' She beamed at him.

Tom installed her in his own room – the bed in the other room being only an outsized couch and not so comfortable as his double bed – and Marge closed her door to take a nap after lunch. Tom wandered restlessly through the rest of the house, wondering whether there was anything in his room that he ought to remove. Dickie's passport was in the lining of a suitcase in his closet. He couldn't think of anything else. But women had sharp eyes, Tom thought, even Marge. She might snoop around. Finally he went into the room while she was still asleep and took the suitcase from the closet. The floor squeaked, and Marge's eyes fluttered open.

'Just want to get something out of here,' Tom whispered. 'Sorry.' He continued tiptoeing out of the room. Marge probably wouldn't even remember, he thought, because she hadn't completely waked up.

Later he showed Marge all around the house, showed her the shelf of leather-bound books in the room next to his bedroom, books that he said had come with the house, though they were his own, bought in Rome and Palermo and Venice. He realized that he had had about ten of them in Rome, and that one of the young police officers with Roverini had bent close to them, apparently studying their titles. But it was nothing really to worry about, he thought, even if the same police officer were to come back. He showed Marge the front entrance of the house, with its broad stone steps. The tide was low and four steps were bared now, the lower two covered with thick wet moss. The moss was a slippery, long-filament variety, and hung over the edges of the steps like messy dark-green hair. The steps were repellent to Tom, but Marge thought them very romantic. She bent over them, staring at the deep water of the canal. Tom had an impulse to push her in.

'Can we take a gondola and come in this way tonight?' she asked.

'Oh sure.' They were going out to dinner tonight, of course. Tom dreaded the long Italian evening ahead of them, because they wouldn't eat until ten, and then she'd probably want to sit in San Marco's over espressos until two in the morning.

Tom looked up at the hazy, sunless Venetian sky, and watched a gull glide down and settle on somebody else's front steps across the canal. He was trying to decide which of his new Venetian friends he would telephone and ask if he could bring Marge over for a drink around five o'clock. They would all be delighted to meet her, of course. He decided on the Englishman Peter Smith-Kingsley. Peter had an Afghan, a piano, and a well-equipped bar. Tom thought Peter would be best because Peter never wanted anybody to leave. They could stay there until it was time for them to go to dinner.

TOM CALLED Mr. Greenleaf from Peter Smith-Kingsley's house at about seven o'clock. Mr. Greenleaf sounded friendlier than Tom had expected, and sounded pitifully hungry for the little crumbs Tom gave him about Dickie. Peter and Marge and the Franchettis – an attractive pair of brothers from Trieste whom Tom had recently met – were in the next room and able to hear almost every word he said, so Tom did it better than he would have done it completely alone, he felt.

'I've told Marge all I know,' he said, 'so she'll be able to tell you anything I've forgotten. I'm only sorry that I can't contribute anything of real importance for the police to work on.'

'These police!' Mr. Greenleaf said gruffly. 'I'm beginning to think Richard is dead. For some reason the Italians are reluctant to admit he might be. They act like amateurs – or old ladies playing at being detectives.'

Tom was shocked at Mr. Greenleaf's bluntness about Dickie's possibly being dead. 'Do *you* think Dickie might have killed himself, Mr. Greenleaf?' Tom asked quietly.

Mr. Greenleaf sighed. 'I don't know. I think it's possible, yes. I never thought much of my son's stability, Tom.'

'I'm afraid I agree with you,' Tom said. 'Would you like to talk to Marge? She's in the next room.'

'No, no, thanks. When's she coming back?'

'I think she said she'd be going back to Rome tomorrow. If you'd possibly like to come to Venice, just for a slight rest, Mr. Greenleaf, you're very welcome to stay at my house.'

But Mr. Greenleaf declined the invitation. It wasn't necessary to bend over backwards, Tom realized. It was as if he were really inviting trouble, and couldn't stop himself. Mr. Greenleaf thanked him for his telephone call and said a very courteous good night.

Tom went back into the other room. 'There's no more news from Rome,' he said dejectedly to the group.

'Oh.' Peter looked disappointed.

'Here's for the phone call, Peter,' Tom said, laying twelve hundred lire on top of Peter's piano. 'Thanks very much.'

'I have an idea,' Pietro Franchetti began in his English-accented English. 'Dickie Greenleaf has traded passports with a Neapolitan fisherman or maybe a Roman cigarette pedlar, so that he can lead the quiet life he always wanted to. It so happens that the bearer of the Dickie Greenleaf passport is not so good a forger as he thought he was, and he had to disappear suddenly. The police should find a man who can't produce his proper carta d'identità, find out who he is, then look for a man with his name, who will turn out to be Dickie Greenleaf!'

Everybody laughed, and Tom loudest of all.

'The trouble with that idea,' Tom said, 'is that lots of people who knew Dickie saw him in January and February—'

'*Who?*' Pietro interrupted with that irritating Italian belligerence in conversation that was doubly irritating in English.

'Well, I did, for one. Anyway, as I was going to say, the forgeries now date from December, according to the bank.'

'Still, it's an idea,' Marge chirruped, feeling very good on her third drink, lolling back on Peter's big chaise-longue. 'A very Dickie-like idea. He probably would have done it right after Palermo, when he had the bank forgery business on top of everything else. I don't believe those forgeries for one minute. I think Dickie'd changed so much that his handwriting changed.'

'I think so, too,' Tom said. 'The bank isn't unanimous, anyway, in saying they're all forged. America's divided about it, and Naples fell right in with America. Naples never would have noticed a forgery if the U.S. hadn't told them about it.'

'I wonder what's in the papers tonight?' Peter asked brightly, pulling on the slipperlike shoe that he had half taken off because it probably hurt. 'Shall I go out and get them?'

But one of the Franchettis volunteered to go, and dashed out of the room. Lorenzo Franchetti was wearing a pink embroidered waistcoat, all' inglese, and an English-made suit and heavy-soled English shoes, and his brother was dressed in much the same way. Peter, on the other hand, was dressed in Italian clothes from head to foot. Tom had noticed, at parties and at the theatre, that if a man was dressed in English clothes he was bound to be an Italian, and vice versa.

Some more people arrived just as Lorenzo came back with the papers – two Italians and two Americans. The papers were passed around. More discussion, more exchanges of stupid speculation, more excitement over today's news: Dickie's house in Mongibello had been sold to an American for twice the price he originally asked for it. The money was going to be held by a Naples bank until Greenleaf claimed it.

The same paper had a cartoon of a man on his knees, looking under his bureau. His wife asked, 'Collar button?' And his answer was, 'No, I'm looking for Dickie Greenleaf.'

Tom had heard that the Rome music halls were taking off the search in skits, too.

One of the Americans who had just come in, whose name was Rudy something, invited Tom and Marge to a cocktail party at his hotel the following day. Tom started to decline, but Marge said she would be delighted to come. Tom hadn't thought she would be here tomorrow, because she had said something at lunch about leaving. The party would be deadly, Tom thought. Rudy was a loud-mouthed, crude man in flashy clothes who said he was an antique dealer. Tom manœuvred himself and Marge out of the house before she accepted any more invitations that might be further into the future.

Marge was in a giddy mood that irritated Tom throughout their long five-course dinner, but he made the supreme effort and responded in kind – like a helpless frog twitching from an electric needle, he thought – and when she dropped the ball, he picked it up and dribbled it a while. He said things like, 'Maybe Dickie's suddenly found himself in his painting, and he's gone away like Gauguin to one of the South Sea Islands.' It made him ill. Then Marge would spin a fantasy about Dickie and the South Sea Islands, making lazy gestures with her hands. The worst was yet to come, Tom thought: the gondola ride. If she dangled those hands in the water, he hoped a shark bit them off. He ordered a dessert that he hadn't room for, but Marge ate it.

Marge wanted a private gondola, of course, not the regular ferry-service gondola that took people over ten at a time from San Marco's to the steps of Santa Maria della Salute, so they engaged a private gondola. It was one-thirty in the morning. Tom had a dark-brown taste in his mouth from too many espressos, his heart was fluttering like bird wings, and he did not expect to be able to sleep until dawn. He felt exhausted, and lay back in the gondola's seat about as languidly as Marge, careful to keep his thigh from touching hers. Marge was still in ebullient spirits, entertaining herself now with a monologue about the sunrise in Venice, which she had apparently seen on some other visit. The gentle rocking of the boat and the rhythmic thrusts of the gondolier's oar made Tom feel slightly sickish. The expanse of water between the San Marco boat stop and his steps seemed interminable.

The steps were covered now except for the upper two, and the water swept just over the surface of the third step, stirring its moss in a disgusting way. Tom paid the gondolier mechanically, and was standing in front of the big doors when he realized he hadn't brought the keys. He glanced around to see if he could climb in anywhere, but he couldn't even reach a window ledge from the steps. Before he even said anything, Marge burst out laughing.

'You didn't bring the key! Of all things, stuck on the door-step with the raging waters around us, and no key!'

Tom tried to smile. Why the hell should he have thought to bring two keys nearly a foot long that weighed as much as a couple of revolvers? He turned and yelled to the gondolier to come back.

'Ah!' the gondolier chuckled across the water. 'Mi dispiace, signor! Deb' ritornare a San Marco! Ho un appuntamento!' He kept on rowing.

'We have no keys!' Tom yelled in Italian.

'Mi dispiace, signore!' replied the gondolier. 'Mandarò un altro gondoliere!'

Marge laughed again. 'Oh, some other gondolier'll pick us up. Isn't it beautiful?' She stood on tiptoe.

It was not at all a beautiful night. It was chilly, and a slimy little rain had started falling. He might get the ferry gondola to come over, Tom thought, but he didn't see it. The only boat he saw was the motoscafo approaching the San Marco pier. There was hardly a chance that the motoscafo would trouble to pick them up, but Tom yelled to it, anyway. The motoscafo, full of lights and people, went blindly on and nosed in at the wooden pier across the canal. Marge was sitting on the top step with her arms around her knees, doing nothing. Finally, a lowslung motor-boat that looked like a fishing boat of some sort slowed down, and someone yelled in Italian: 'Locked out?'

'We forgot the keys!' Marge explained cheerfully.

But she didn't want to get into the boat. She said she would wait on the steps while Tom went around and opened the street door. Tom said it might take fifteen minutes or more, and she would probably catch a cold there, so she finally got in. The Italian took them to the nearest landing at the steps of the Santa Maria della Salute church. He refused to take any money for his trouble, but he accepted the rest of Tom's pack of American cigarettes. Tom did not know why, but he felt more frightened that night, walking through San Spiridione with Marge, than if he had been alone. Marge, of course, was not affected at all by the street, and talked the whole way.

25

TOM WAS AWAKENED very early the next morning by the banging of his door knocker. He grabbed his robe and went down. It was a telegram, and he had to run back upstairs to get a tip for the man. He stood in the cold living-room and read it.

CHANGED MY MIND. WOULD LIKE TO SEE YE.
ARRIVING 11.45 A.M.

H. GREENLEAF

Tom shivered. Well, he had expected it, he thought. But he hadn't, really. He dreaded it. Or was it just the hour? It was barely dawn. The living-room looked grey and horrible. That 'YE' gave the telegram such a creepy, archaic touch. Generally Italian telegrams had much funnier typographical errors. And what if they'd put 'R'. or 'D.' instead of the 'H.'? How would he be feeling then?

He ran upstairs and got back into his warm bed to try to catch some more sleep. He kept wondering if Marge would come in or knock on his door because she had heard that loud knocker, but he finally decided she had slept through it. He imagined greeting Mr. Greenleaf at the door, shaking his hand firmly, and he tried to imagine his questions, but his mind blurred tiredly and it made him feel frightened and uncomfortable. He was too sleepy to form specific questions and answers, and too tense to get to sleep. He wanted to make coffee and wake Marge up, so he would have someone to talk to, but he couldn't face going into that room and seeing the underwear and garter belts strewn all over the place, he absolutely *couldn't*.

It was Marge who woke him up, and she had already made coffee downstairs, she said.

'What do you think?' Tom said with a big smile. 'I got a telegram from Mr. Greenleaf this morning and he's coming at noon.'

'He *is*? When did you get the telegram?'

'This morning early. If I wasn't dreaming.' Tom looked for it. 'Here it is.'

Marge read it. ' "Would like to see ye," ' she said, laughing a little. 'Well, that's nice. It'll do him good, I hope. Are you coming down or shall I bring the coffee up?'

'I'll come down,' Tom said, putting on his robe.

Marge was already dressed in slacks and a sweater, black corduroy slacks, well-cut and made to order, Tom supposed, because they fitted her gourdlike figure as well as pants possibly could. They prolonged their coffee drinking until Anna and Ugo arrived at ten with milk and rolls and the morning papers. Then they made more coffee and hot milk and sat in the living-room. It was one of the mornings when there was nothing in the papers about Dickie or the Miles case. Some mornings were like that, and then the evening papers would have something about them again, even if there was no real news to report, just by way of reminding people that Dickie was still missing and the Miles murder was still unsolved.

Marge and Tom went to the railroad station to meet Mr. Greenleaf at eleven forty-five. It was raining again, and so windy and cold that the rain felt like sleet on their faces. They stood in the shelter of the railroad station, watching the people come through the gate, and finally there was Mr. Greenleaf, solemn and ashen. Marge rushed forward to kiss him on the cheek, and he smiled at her.

'Hello, Tom!' he said heartily, extending his hand. 'How're you?'

'Very well, sir, And you?'

Mr. Greenleaf had only a small suitcase, but a porter was carrying it and the porter rode with them on the motoscafo, though Tom said he could easily carry the suitcase himself. Tom suggested they go straight to his house, but Mr. Greenleaf wanted to instal himself in a hotel first. He insisted.

'I'll come over as soon as I register. I thought I'd try the Gritti. Is that anywhere near your place?' Mr. Greenleaf asked.

'Not too close, but you can walk to San Marco's and take a gondola over,' Tom said. 'We'll come with you, if you just want to check in. I thought we might all have lunch together — unless you'd rather see Marge by yourself for a while.' He was the old self-effacing Ripley again.

'Came here primarily to talk to you!' Mr. Greenleaf said.

'Is there any news?' Marge asked.

Mr. Greenleaf shook his head. He was casting nervous, absent-minded glances out the windows of the motoscafo, as if the strangeness of the city compelled him to look at it, though nothing of it was registering. He had not answered Tom's question about lunch. Tom folded his arms, put a pleasant expression on his face, and did not try to talk any more. The boat's motor made quite a roar, anyway. Mr. Greenleaf and Marge were talking very casually about some people they knew in Rome. Tom gathered that Marge and Mr. Greenleaf got along very well, though Marge had said she had not known him before she met him in Rome.

They went to lunch at a modest restaurant between the Gritti and the Rialto, which specialized in seafoods that were always displayed raw on a long counter inside. One of the plates held varieties of the little purple octopuses that Dickie had liked so much, and Tom said to Marge, nodding towards the plates as they passed, 'Too bad Dickie isn't here to enjoy some of those.'

Marge smiled gaily. She was always in a good mood when they were about to eat.

Mr. Greenleaf talked a little more at lunch, but his face kept its stony expression, and he still glanced around as he spoke, as if he hoped that Dickie would come walking in at any moment. No, the police hadn't found a blessed thing that could be called a clue, he said, and he had just arranged for an American private detective to come over and try to clear the mystery up.

It made Tom swallow thoughtfully – he, too, must have a lurking suspicion, or illusion, perhaps, that American detectives were better than the Italian – but then the evident futility of it struck him as it was apparently striking Marge, because her face had gone long and blank suddenly.

'That may be a very good idea,' Tom said.

'Do you think much of the Italian police?' Mr. Greenleaf asked him.

'Well – actually, I do,' Tom replied. 'There's also the advantage that they speak Italian and they can get around everywhere and investigate all kinds of suspects. I suppose the man you sent for speaks Italian?'

'I really don't know. I don't know,' Mr. Greenleaf said in a flustered way, as if he realized he should have demanded that, and hadn't. 'The man's name is McCarron. He's said to be very good.'

He probably didn't speak Italian, Tom thought. 'When is he arriving?'

'Tomorrow or the next day. I'll be in Rome tomorrow to meet him if he's there.' Mr. Greenleaf had finished his vitello alla parmigiana. He had not eaten much.

'Tom has the most beautiful house!' Marge said, starting in on her seven-layer rum cake.

Tom turned his glare at her into a faint smile.

The quizzing, Tom thought, would come at the house, probably when he and Mr. Greenleaf were alone. He knew Mr. Greenleaf wanted to talk to him alone, and therefore he proposed coffee at the restaurant where they were before Marge could suggest having it at home. Marge liked the coffee that his filter pot made. Even so, Marge sat around with them in the living-room for half an hour after they got home. Marge was incapable of sensing anything, Tom thought. Finally Tom frowned at her facetiously and glanced at the stairs, and she got the hint, clapped her hand over her mouth and announced that she was going up to have a wee nap. She was in her usual invincibly merry mood, and she had been talking to Mr. Greenleaf all during lunch as if of *course* Dickie wasn't dead, and he mustn't, mustn't worry so much because it wasn't good for his digestion. As if she still had hopes of being his daughter-in-law one day, Tom thought.

Mr. Greenleaf stood up and paced the floor with his hands in his jacket pockets, like an executive about to dictate a letter to his stenographer. He hadn't commented on the plushness of the house, or even much looked at it, Tom noticed.

'Well, Tom,' he began with a sigh, 'this is a strange end, isn't it?'

'End?'

'Well, you living in Europe now, and Richard—'

'None of us has suggested yet that he might have gone back to America,' Tom said pleasantly.

'No. That couldn't be. The immigration authorities in America are much too well alerted for that.' Mr. Greenleaf continued to pace, not looking at him. 'What's your real opinion as to where he may be?'

'Well, sir, he could be hiding out in Italy – very easily if he doesn't use a hotel where he has to register.'

'Are there any hotels in Italy where one doesn't have to register?'

'No, not officially. But anyone who knows Italian as well as Dickie might get away with it. Matter of fact, if he bribed some little innkeeper in the south of Italy not to say anything, he could stay there even if the man knew his name was Richard Greenleaf.'

'And is that your idea of what he may be doing?' Mr. Greenleaf looked at him suddenly, and Tom saw that pitiful expression he had noticed the first evening he had met him.

'No, I— It's possible. That's all I can say about it.' He paused. 'I'm sorry to say it Mr. Greenleaf, but I think there's a possibility that Dickie is dead.'

Mr. Greenleaf's expression did not change. 'Because of that depression you mentioned in Rome? What exactly did he say to you?'

'It was his general mood.' Tom frowned. 'The Miles thing had obviously shaken him. He's the sort of man— He really does hate publicity of any kind, violence of any kind.' Tom licked his lips. His agony in trying to express himself was genuine. 'He did say if one more thing happened, he would blow his top – or he didn't know what he would do. Also for the first time, I felt he wasn't interested in his painting. Maybe it was only temporary, but up until then I'd always thought Dickie had his painting to go to, whatever happened to him.'

'Does he really take his painting so seriously?'

'Yes, he does,' Tom said firmly.

Mr. Greenleaf looked off at the ceiling again, his hands behind him. 'A pity we can't find this Di Massimo. He might know something. I understand Richard and he were going to go together to Sicily.'

'I didn't know that,' Tom said. Mr. Greenleaf had got that from Marge, he knew.

'Di Massimo's disappeared, too, if he ever existed. I'm inclined to think Richard made him up to try to convince me he was painting. The police can't find a painter called Di Massimo on their – their identity lists or whatever it is.'

'I never met him,' Tom said. 'Dickie mentioned him a couple of times. I never doubted his identity – or his actuality.' He laughed a little.

'What did you say before about "if one more thing happened to him"? What else had happened to him?'

'Well, I didn't know then, in Rome, but I think I know what he meant now. They'd questioned him about the sunken boat in San Remo. Did they tell you about that?'

'No.'

'They found a boat in San Remo, scuttled. It seems the boat was missed on the day or around the day Dickie and I were there, and we'd taken a ride in the same kind of boat. They were the little motor-boats people rented there. At any rate, the boat was scuttled, and there were stains on it that they thought were bloodstains. They happened to find the boat just after the Miles murder, and they couldn't find *me* at that time, because I was travelling around the country, so they asked Dickie where I was. I think for a while, Dickie must have thought they suspected him of having murdered me!' Tom laughed.

'Good lord!'

'I only know this, because a police inspector questioned me about it in Venice just a few weeks ago. He said he'd questioned Dickie about it before. The strange thing is that I didn't know I was being looked for – not very seriously, but still being looked for – until I saw it in the newspaper in Venice. I went to the police station here and presented myself.' Tom was still smiling. He had decided days ago that he had better narrate all this to Mr. Greenleaf, if he ever saw him, whether Mr. Greenleaf had heard about the San Remo boat incident or not. It was better than having Mr. Greenleaf learn about it from the police, and be told that he had been in Rome with Dickie at a time when he should have known that the police were looking for him. Besides, it fitted in with what he was saying about Dickie's depressed mood at that time.

'I don't quite understand all this,' Mr. Greenleaf said. He was sitting on the sofa, listening attentively.

'It's blown over now, since Dickie and I are both alive. The reason I mention it at all is that Dickie knew I was being looked for by the police, because they had asked him where I was. He may not have known exactly where I was at the first interview with the police, but he did know at least that I was still in the country. But even when I came to Rome and saw him, he didn't tell the police he'd seen me. He wasn't going to be that co-operative, he wasn't in the mood. I know this because at the very time Marge talked to me in Rome at the hotel, Dickie was out talking to the police. His attitude was, let the police find me themselves, he wasn't going to tell them where I was.'

Mr. Greenleaf shook his head, a kind of fatherly, mildly impatient shake of the head, as if he could easily believe it of Dickie.

'I think that was the night he said, if one more thing happened to him— It caused me a little embarrassment when I was in Venice. The police probably thought I was a moron for not knowing before that I was being looked for, but the fact remains I didn't.'

'Hm-m,' Mr. Greenleaf said uninterestedly.

Tom got up to get some brandy.

'I'm afraid I don't agree with you that Richard committed suicide,' Mr. Greenleaf said.

'Well, neither does Marge. I just said it's a possibility. I don't even think it's the most likely thing that's happened.'

'You don't? What do you think is?'

'That he's hiding,' Tom said. 'May I offer you some brandy, sir? I imagine this house feels pretty chilly after America.'

'It does, frankly.' Mr. Greenleaf accepted his glass.

'You know, he could be in several other countries besides Italy, too,' Tom said. 'He could have gone to Greece or France or anywhere else after he got back to Naples, because no one was looking for him until days later.'

'I know, I know,' Mr. Greenleaf said tiredly.

26

TOM HAD HOPED Marge would forget about the cocktail party invitation of the antique dealer at the Danieli, but she didn't. Mr. Greenleaf had gone back to his hotel to rest around four o'clock, and as soon as he had gone Marge reminded Tom of the party at five o'clock.

'Do you really want to go?' Tom asked. 'I can't even remember the man's name.'

'Maloof. M-a-l-o-o-f,' Marge said. 'I'd like to go. We don't have to stay long.'

So that was that. What Tom hated about it was the spectacle they made of themselves, not one but two of the principals in the Greenleaf case, conspicuous as a couple of spotlighted acrobats at a circus. He felt – he knew – they were nothing but a pair of names that Mr. Maloof had bagged, guests of honour that had actually turned up, because certainly Mr. Maloof would have told everybody today that Marge Sherwood and Tom Ripley were attending his party. It was unbecoming, Tom felt. And Marge couldn't excuse her giddiness simply by saying that she wasn't worried a bit about Dickie's being missing. It even seemed to Tom that Marge guzzled the martinis because they were free, as if she couldn't get all she wanted at his house, or as if he wasn't going to buy her several more when they met Mr. Greenleaf for dinner.

Tom sipped one drink slowly and managed to stay on the other side of the room from Marge. He was the friend of Dickie Greenleaf, when anybody began a conversation by asking him if he was, but he knew Marge only slightly.

'Miss Sherwood is my house guest,' he said with a troubled smile.

'Where's Mr. Greenleaf? Too bad you didn't bring him.' Mr. Maloof said, sidling up like an elephant with a huge Manhattan in a champagne glass. He wore a checked suit of loud English tweed, the kind of pattern, Tom supposed, the English made, reluctantly, especially for such Americans as Rudy Maloof.

'I think Mr. Greenleaf is resting,' Tom said. 'We're going to see him later for dinner.'

'Oh,' said Mr. Maloof. 'Did you see the papers tonight?' This last politely, with a respectfully solemn face.

'Yes, I did,' Tom replied.

Mr. Maloof nodded, without saying anything more. Tom wondered what inconsequential item he could have been going to report if he had said he hadn't read the papers. The papers tonight said that Mr. Greenleaf had arrived in Venice and was staying at the Gritti Palace. There was no mention of a private detective from America arriving in Rome today, or that one was coming at all, which made Tom question Mr. Greenleaf's story about the private detective. It was like one of those stories told by someone else, or one of his own imaginary fears, which were never based on the least fragment of fact and which, a couple of weeks later, he was ashamed that he *could* have believed. Such as that Marge and Dickie were having an affair in Mongibello, or were even on the brink of having an affair. Or that the forgery scare in February was going to ruin him and expose him if he continued in the role of Dickie Greenleaf. The forgery scare had blown over, actually. The latest was that seven out of ten experts in America had said that they did not believe the cheques were forged. He could have signed another remittance from the American bank, and gone on forever as Dickie Greenleaf, if he hadn't let his imaginary fears get the better of him. Tom set his jaw. He was still listening with a fraction of his brain to Mr. Maloof, who was trying to sound intelligent and serious by describing his expedition to the islands of Murano and Burano that morning. Tom set his jaw, frowning, listening, and concentrating doggedly on his own life. Perhaps he should believe Mr. Greenleaf's story about the private detective coming over, until it was disproven, but he would not let it rattle him or cause him to betray fear by so much as the blink of an eye.

Tom made an absent-minded reply to something Mr. Maloof had said, and Mr. Maloof laughed with inane good cheer and drifted off. Tom followed his broad back scornfully with his eyes, realizing that he had been rude, was being rude, and that he ought to pull himself together, because behaving courteously even to this handful of second-rate antique dealers and bric-à-brac and ashtray buyers – Tom had seen the samples of their wares spread out on the bed in the room where they had put their coats – was part of the business of being a gentleman. But they reminded him too much of the people he had said good-bye to in New York, he thought, that was why they got under his skin like an itch and made him want to run.

Marge was the reason he was here, after all, the only reason. He blamed *her*. Tom took a sip of his martini, looked up at the ceiling, and thought that in another few months his nerves, his patience, would be able to bear even people like this, if he ever found himself with people like this again. He had improved, at least, since he left New York, and he would improve still more. He stared up at the ceiling and thought of sailing to Greece, down the Adriatic from Venice, into the Ionian Sea to Crete. That was what he would do this summer. June. *June.* How sweet and soft the word was, clear and lazy and full of sunshine! His reverie lasted only a few seconds, however. The loud, grating American voices forced their way into his ears again, and sank like claws into the nerves of his shoulders and his back. He moved involuntarily from where he stood, moved towards Marge. There were only two other women in the room, the horrible wives of a couple of the horrible businessmen, and Marge, he had to admit, was better-looking than either of them, but her voice, he thought, was worse, like theirs only worse.

He had something on the tip of his tongue to say about their leaving, but, since it was unthinkable for a man to propose leaving, he said nothing at all, only joined Marge's group and smiled. Somebody refilled his glass. Marge was talking about Mongibello, telling them about her book, and the three grey-templed, seamy-faced, bald-headed men seemed to be entranced with her.

When Marge herself proposed leaving a few minutes later, they had a ghastly time getting clear of Maloof and his cohorts, who were a little drunker now and insistent that they *all* get together for dinner, and Mr. Greenleaf, too.

'That's what Venice is for – a good time!' Mr. Maloof kept saying idiotically, taking the opportunity to put his arm around Marge and maul her a little as he tried to make her stay, and Tom thought it was a good thing that he hadn't eaten yet because he would have lost it right then. 'What's Mr. Greenleaf's number? Let's call him up!' Mr. Maloof weaved his way to the telephone.

'I think we'd better get out of here!' Tom said grimly into Marge's ear. He took a hard, functional grip on her elbow and steered her towards the door, both of them nodding and smiling good-bye as they went.

'What's the *matter*?' Marge asked when they were in the corridor.

'Nothing. I just thought the party was getting out of hand,' Tom said, trying to make light of it with a smile. Marge was a little high, but not too high to see that something was the matter with him. He was perspiring. It showed on his forehead, and he wiped it. 'People like that get me down,' he said, 'talking about Dickie all the time, and we don't even know them and I don't want to. They make me ill.'

'Funny. Not a soul talked to me about Dickie or even mentioned his name. I thought it was much better than yesterday at Peter's house.'

Tom lifted his head as he walked and said nothing. It was the class of people he despised, and why say that to Marge, who was of the same class?

They called for Mr. Greenleaf at his hotel. It was still early for dinner, so they had apéritifs at a café in a street near the Gritti. Tom tried to make up for his explosion at the party by being pleasant and talkative during dinner. Mr. Greenleaf was in a good mood, because he had just telephoned his wife and found her in very good spirits and feeling much better. Her doctor had been trying a new system of injections for the past ten days, Mr. Greenleaf said, and she seemed to be responding better than to anything they had tried before.

It was a quiet dinner. Tom told a clean, mildly funny joke, and Marge laughed hilariously. Mr. Greenleaf insisted on paying for the dinner, and then said he was going back to his hotel because he didn't feel quite up to par. From the fact that he carefully chose a pasta dish and ate no salad, Tom thought that he might be suffering from the tourist's complaint, and he wanted to suggest an excellent remedy, obtainable in every drugstore, but Mr. Greenleaf was not quite the person one could say a thing like that to, even if they had been alone.

Mr. Greenleaf said he was going back to Rome tomorrow, and Tom promised to give him a ring around nine o'clock the next morning to find out which train he had decided on. Marge was going back to Rome with Mr. Greenleaf, and she was agreeable to either train. They walked back to the Gritti – Mr. Greenleaf with his taut face-of-an-industrialist under his grey homburg looking like a piece of Madison Avenue walking through the narrow, zigzagging streets – and they said good night.

'I'm terribly sorry I didn't get to spend more time with you,' Tom said.

'So am I, my boy. Maybe some other time.' Mr. Greenleaf patted his shoulder.

Tom walked back home with Marge in a kind of glow. It had all gone awfully well, Tom thought. Marge chattered to him as they walked, giggling because she had broken a strap of her bra and had to hold it up with one hand, she said. Tom was thinking of the letter he had received from Bob Delancey this afternoon, the first word he'd gotten from Bob except one postcard ages ago, in which Bob had said that the police had questioned everybody in his house about an income tax fraud of a few months ago. The defrauder, it seemed, had used the address of Bob's house to receive his cheques, and had gotten the cheques by the simple means of taking the letters down from the letterbox edge where the postman had stuck them. The postman had been questioned, too, Bob had said, and remembered the name George McAlpin on the letters. Bob seemed to think it was rather funny. He described the reactions of some of the people in the house when they were questioned by the police. The mystery was, who took the letters addressed to George McAlpin? It was very reassuring. That income tax episode had been hanging over his head in a vague way, because he had known there would be an investigation at some time. He was glad it had gone this far and no further. He couldn't imagine how the police would ever, could ever, connect Tom Ripley with George McAlpin. Besides, as Bob had remarked, the defrauder had not even tried to cash the cheques.

He sat down in the living-room to read Bob's letter again when he got home. Marge had gone upstairs to pack her things and to go to bed. Tom was tired too, but the anticipation of freedom tomorrow, when Marge and Mr. Greenleaf would be gone, was so pleasant to relish he would not have minded staying up all night. He took his shoes off so he could put his feet up on the sofa, lay back on a pillow, and continued reading Bob's letter. 'The police think it's some outsider who dropped by occasionally to pick up his mail, because none of the dopes in this house look like criminal types . . . .' It was strange to read about the people he knew in New York, Ed and Lorraine, the newt-brained girl who had tried to stow herself away in his cabin the day he sailed from New York. It was strange and not at all attractive. What a dismal life they led, creeping around New York, in and out of subways, standing in some dingy bar on Third Avenue for their entertainment, watching television, or even if they had enough money for a Madison Avenue bar or a good restaurant now and then, how dull it all was compared to the worst little trattoria in Venice with its tables of green salads, trays of wonderful cheeses, and its friendly waiters bringing you the best wine in the world! 'I certainly do envy you sitting there in Venice in an old palazzo!' Bob wrote. 'Do you take a lot of gondola rides? How are the girls? Are you getting so cultured you won't speak to any of us when you come back? How long are you staying, anyway?'

Forever, Tom thought. Maybe he'd never go back to the States. It was not so much Europe itself as the evenings he had spent alone, here and in Rome, that made him feel that way. Evenings by himself simply looking at maps, or lying around on sofas thumbing through guidebooks. Evenings looking at his clothes — his clothes and Dickie's — and feeling Dickie's rings between his palms, and running his fingers over the antelope suitcase he had bought at Gucci's. He had polished the suitcase with a special English leather dressing, not that it needed polishing because he took such good care of it, but for its protection. He loved possessions, not masses of them, but a select few that he did not part with. They gave a man self-respect. Not ostentation but quality, and the love that cherished the quality. Possessions reminded him that he existed, and made him enjoy his existence. It was as simple as that. And wasn't that worth something? He existed. Not many people in the world knew how to, even if they had the money. It really didn't take money, masses of money, it took a certain security. He had been on the road to it, even with Marc Priminger. He had appreciated Marc's possessions, and they were what had attracted him to the house, but they were not his own, and it had been impossible to make a beginning at acquiring anything of his own on forty dollars a week. It would have taken him the best years of his life, even if he had economized stringently, to buy the things he wanted. Dickie's money had given him only an added momentum on the road he had been travelling. The money gave him the leisure to see Greece, to collect Etruscan pottery if he wanted to (he had recently read an interesting book on that subject by an American living in Rome), to join art societies if he cared to and to donate to their work. It gave him the leisure, for instance, to read his Malraux tonight as late as he pleased, because he did not have to go to a job in the morning. He had just bought a two-volume edition of Malraux's *Psychologie de l'Art* which he was now reading, with great pleasure, in French with the aid of a dictionary. He thought he might nap for a while, then read some in it, whatever the hour. He felt cosy and drowsy, in spite of the espressos. The curve of the sofa corner fitted his shoulders like somebody's arm, or rather fitted it better than somebody's arm. He decided he would spend the night here. It was more comfortable than the sofa upstairs. In a few minutes he might go up and get a blanket.

'Tom?'

He opened his eyes. Marge was coming down the stairs, barefoot. Tom sat up. She had his brown leather box in her hand.

'I just found Dickie's rings in here,' she said rather breathlessly.

'Oh. He gave them to me. To take care of.' Tom stood up.

'When?'

'In Rome, I think.' He took a step back, struck one of his shoes and picked it up, mostly in an effort to seem calm.

'What was he going to do? Why'd he give them to you?'

She'd been looking for thread to sew her bra, Tom thought. Why in hell hadn't he put the rings somewhere else, like in the lining of that suitcase? 'I don't really know,' Tom said. 'A whim or something. You know how he is. He said if anything ever happened to him, he wanted me to have his rings.'

Marge looked puzzled. 'Where was he going?'

'To Palermo. Sicily.' He was holding the shoe in both hands in a position to use the wooden heel of it as a weapon. And how he would do it went quickly through his head: hit her with the shoe, then haul her out by the front door and drop her into the canal. He'd say she'd fallen, slipped on the moss. And she was such a good swimmer, he'd thought she could keep afloat.

Marge stared down at the box. 'Then he *was* going to kill himself.'

'Yes – if you want to look at it that way, the rings— They make it look more likely that he did.'

'Why didn't you say anything about it before?'

'I think I absolutely forgot them. I put them away so they wouldn't get lost and I never thought of looking at them since the day he gave them to me.'

'He either killed himself or changed his identity – didn't he?'

'Yes.' Tom said it sadly and firmly.

'You'd better tell Mr. Greenleaf.'

'Yes, I will. Mr. Greenleaf and the police.'

'This practically *settles* it,' Marge said.

Tom was wringing the shoe in his hands like a pair of gloves now, yet still keeping the shoe in position, because Marge was staring at him in a funny way. She was still thinking. Was she kidding him? Did she know now?

Marge said earnestly, 'I just can't imagine Dickie ever being without his rings,' and Tom knew then that she hadn't guessed the answer, that her mind was miles up some other road.

He relaxed then, limply, sank down on the sofa and pretended to busy himself with putting on his shoes. 'No,' he agreed, automatically.

'If it weren't so late, I'd call Mr. Greenleaf now. He's probably in bed, and he wouldn't sleep all night if I told him, I know.'

Tom tried to push a foot into the second shoe. Even his fingers were limp, without strength. He racked his brain for something sensible to say. 'I'm sorry I didn't mention it sooner,' he brought out in a deep voice. 'It was just one of those—'

'Yes, it makes it kind of silly at this point for Mr. Greenleaf to bring a private detective over, doesn't it?' Her voice shook.

Tom looked at her. She was about to cry. This was the very first moment, Tom realized, that she was admitting to herself that Dickie could be dead, that he probably was dead. Tom went towards her slowly. 'I'm sorry, Marge. I'm sorry above all that I didn't tell you sooner about the rings.' He put his arm around her. He fairly had to, because she was leaning against him. He smelled her perfume. The Stradivari, probably. 'That's one of the reasons I felt sure he'd killed himself – at least that he might have.'

'Yes,' she said in a miserable, wailing tone.

She was not crying, actually, only leaning against him with her head rigidly bent down. Like someone who has just heard the news of a death, Tom thought. Which she had.

'How about a brandy?' he said tenderly.

'No.'

'Come over and sit on the sofa.' He led her towards it.

She sat down, and he crossed the room to get the brandy. He poured brandy into two inhalers. When he turned around, she was gone. He had just time to see the edge of her robe and her bare feet disappear at the top of the stairs.

She preferred to be by herself, he thought. He started to take a brandy up to her, then decided against it. She was probably beyond the help of brandy. He knew how she felt. He carried the brandies solemnly back to the liquor cabinet. He had meant to pour only one back, but he poured them both back, and then let it go and replaced the bottle among the other bottles.

He sank down on the sofa again, stretched a leg out with his foot dangling, too exhausted now even to remove his shoes. As tired as after he had killed Freddie Miles, he thought suddenly, or as after Dickie in San Remo. He had come so close! He remembered his cool thoughts of beating her senseless with his shoe heel, yet not roughly enough to break the skin anywhere, of dragging her through the front hall and out of the doors with the lights turned off so that no one would see them, and his quickly invented story, that she had evidently slipped, and thinking she could surely swim back to the steps, he hadn't jumped in or shouted for help until— In a way, he had even imagined the exact words that he and Mr. Greenleaf would say to each other afterwards, Mr. Greenleaf shocked and astounded, and he himself just as apparently shaken, but only apparently. Underneath he would be as calm and sure of himself as he had been after Freddie's murder, because his story would be unassailable. Like the San Remo story. His stories were good because he imagined them intensely, so intensely that he came to believe them.

For a moment he heard his own voice saying: ' . . . I stood there on the steps calling to her, thinking she'd come up any second, or even that she might be playing a trick on me . . . . But I wasn't *sure* she'd hurt herself, and she'd been in such good humour standing there a moment before . . . .' He tensed himself. It was like a phonograph playing in his head, a little drama taking place right in the living-room that he was unable to stop. He could see himself standing with the Italian police and Mr. Greenleaf by the big doors that opened to the front hall. He could see and hear himself talking earnestly. And being believed.

But what seemed to terrify him was not the dialogue or his hallucinatory belief that he had done it (he knew he hadn't), but the memory of himself standing in front of Marge with the shoe in his hand, imagining all this in a cool, methodical way.

And the fact that he had done it twice before. Those two other times were *facts*, not imagination. He could say he hadn't wanted to do them, but he had done them. He didn't want to be a murderer. Sometimes he could absolutely forget that he had murdered, he realized. But sometimes – like now – he couldn't. He had surely forgotten for a while tonight, when he had been thinking about the meaning of possessions, and why he liked to live in Europe.

He twisted on to his side, his feet drawn up on the sofa. He was sweating and shaking. What was happening to him? What had happened? Was he going to blurt out a lot of nonsense tomorrow when he saw Mr. Greenleaf, about Marge falling into the canal, and his screaming for help and jumping in and not finding her? Even with Marge standing there with them, would he go berserk and spill the story out and betray himself as a maniac?

He had to face Mr. Greenleaf with the rings tomorrow. He would have to repeat the story he had told to Marge. He would have to give it details to make it better. He began to invent. His mind steadied. He was imagining a Roman hotel room, Dickie and he standing there talking, and Dickie taking off both his rings and handing them to him. Dickie said: 'It's just as well you don't tell anybody about this . . . .'

27

MARGE CALLED Mr. Greenleaf at eight-thirty the next morning to ask how soon they could come over to his hotel, she had told Tom. But Mr. Greenleaf must have noticed that she was upset. Tom heard her starting to tell him the story of the rings. Marge used the same words that Tom had used to her about the rings – evidently Marge had believed him – but Tom could not tell what Mr. Greenleaf's reaction was. He was afraid this piece of news might be just the one that would bring the whole picture into focus, and that when they saw Mr. Greenleaf this morning he might be in the company of a policeman ready to arrest Tom Ripley. This possibility rather offset the advantage of his not being on the scene when Mr. Greenleaf heard about the rings.

'What did he say?' Tom asked when Marge had hung up.

Marge sat down tiredly on a chair across the room. 'He seems to feel the way I do. He said it himself. It looks as if Dickie meant to kill himself.'

But Mr. Greenleaf would have a little time to think about it before they got there, Tom thought. 'What time are we due?' Tom asked.

'I told him about nine-thirty or before. As soon as we've had some coffee. The coffee's on now.' Marge got up and went into the kitchen. She was already dressed. She had on the travelling suit that she had worn when she arrived.

Tom sat up indecisively on the edge of the sofa and loosened his tie. He had slept in his clothes on the sofa, and Marge had awakened him when she had come down a few minutes ago. How he had possibly slept all night in the chilly room he didn't know. It embarrassed him. Marge had been amazed to find him there. There was a crick in his neck, his back, and his right shoulder. He felt wretched. He stood up suddenly. 'I'm going upstairs to wash,' he called to Marge.

He glanced into his room upstairs and saw that Marge had packed her suitcase. It was lying in the middle of the floor, closed. Tom hoped that she and Mr. Greenleaf were still leaving on one of the morning trains. Probably they would, because Mr. Greenleaf was supposed to meet the American detective in Rome today.

Tom undressed in the room next to Marge's, then went into the bathroom and turned on the shower. After a look at himself in the mirror he decided to shave first, and he went back to the room to get his electric razor which he had removed from the bathroom, for no particular reason, when Marge arrived. On the way back he heard the telephone ring. Marge answered it. Tom leaned over the stairwell, listening.

'Oh, that's fine,' she said. 'Oh, that doesn't matter if we don't. . . . Yes, I'll tell him. . . . All right, we'll hurry. Tom's just washing up. . . . Oh, less than an hour. Bye-bye.'

He heard her walking towards the stairs, and he stepped back because he was naked.

'Tom?' she yelled up. 'The detective from America just got here! He just called Mr. Greenleaf and he's coming from the airport!'

'Fine!' Tom called back, and angrily went into the bedroom. He turned the shower off, and plugged his razor into the wall outlet. Suppose he'd been under the shower? Marge would have yelled up, anyway, simply assuming that he would be able to hear her. He would be glad when she was gone, and he hoped she left this morning. Unless she and Mr. Greenleaf decided to stay to see what the detective was going to do with him. Tom knew that the detective had come to Venice especially to see him, otherwise he would have waited to see Mr. Greenleaf in Rome. Tom wondered if Marge realized that too. Probably she didn't. That took a minimum of deduction.

Tom put on a quiet suit and tie, and went down to have coffee with Marge. He had taken his shower as hot as he could bear it, and he felt much better. Marge said nothing during the coffee except that the rings should make a great difference both to Mr. Greenleaf and the detective, and she meant that it should look to the detective, too, as if Dickie had killed himself. Tom hoped she was right. Everything depended on what kind of man the detective would be. Everything depended on the first impression he made on the detective.

It was another grey, clammy day, not quite raining at nine o'clock, but it had rained, and it would rain again, probably towards noon. Tom and Marge caught the gondola from the church steps to San Marco, and walked from there to the Gritti. They telephoned up to Mr. Greenleaf's room. Mr. Greenleaf said that Mr. McCarron was there, and asked them to come up.

Mr. Greenleaf opened his door for them. 'Good morning,' he said. He pressed Marge's arm in a fatherly way. 'Tom—'

Tom came in behind Marge. The detective was standing by the window, a short chunky man of about thirty-five. His face looked friendly and alert. Moderately bright, but only moderately, was Tom's first impression.

'This is Alvin McCarron,' Mr. Greenleaf said. 'Miss Sherwood and Mr. Tom Ripley.'

They all said, 'How do you do?'

Tom noticed a brand-new briefcase on the bed with some papers and photographs lying around it. McCarron was looking him over.

'I understand you're a friend of Richard's?' he asked.

'We both are,' Tom said.

They were interrupted for a minute while Mr. Greenleaf saw that they were all seated. It was a good-sized, heavily furnished room with windows on the canal. Tom sat down in an armless chair upholstered in red. McCarron had installed himself on the bed, and was looking through his sheaf of papers. There were a few photostated papers, Tom saw, that looked like pictures of Dickie's cheques. There were also several loose photographs of Dickie.

'Do you have the rings?' McCarron asked, looking from Tom to Marge.

'Yes,' Marge said solemnly, getting up. She took the rings from her handbag and gave them to McCarron.

McCarron held them out in his palm to Mr. Greenleaf. 'These are his rings?' he asked, and Mr. Greenleaf nodded after only a glance at them, while Marge's face took on a slightly affronted expression as if she were about to say, '*I* know his rings just as well as Mr. Greenleaf and probably better.' McCarron turned to Tom. 'When did he give them to you?' he asked.

'In Rome. As nearly as I can remember, around February third, just a few days after the murder of Freddie Miles,' Tom answered.

The detective was studying him with his inquisitive, mild brown eyes. His lifted eyebrows put a couple of wrinkles in the thick-looking skin of his forehead. He had wavy brown hair, cut very short on the sides, with a high curl above his forehead, in a rather cute college-boy style. One couldn't tell a thing from that face, Tom thought; it was trained. 'What did he say when he gave them to you?'

'He said that if anything happened to him he wanted me to have them. I asked him what he thought was going to happen to him. He said he didn't know, but something might.' Tom paused deliberately. 'He didn't seem more depressed at that particular moment than a lot of other times I'd talked to him, so it didn't cross my mind that he was going to kill himself. I knew he intended to go away, that was all.'

'Where?' asked the detective.

'To Palermo, he said.' Tom looked at Marge. 'He must have given them to me the day you spoke to me in Rome – at the

Inghilterra. That day or the day before. Do you remember the date?'

'February second,' Marge said in a subdued voice.

McCarron was making notes. 'What else?' he asked Tom. 'What time of day was it? Had he been drinking?'

'No. He drinks very little. I think it was early afternoon. He said it would be just as well if I didn't mention the rings to anybody, and of course I agreed. I put the rings away and completely forgot about them, as I told Miss Sherwood – I suppose because I'd so impressed on myself that he didn't want me to say anything about them.' Tom spoke straightfor- wardly, stammering a little, inadvertently, just as anybody might stammer under the circumstances, Tom thought.

'What did you do with the rings?'

'I put them in an old box that I have – just a little box I keep odd buttons in.'

McCarron regarded him for a moment in silence, and Tom took the moment to brace himself. Out of that placid yet alert Irish face could come anything, a challenging question, a flat statement that he was lying. Tom clung harder in his mind to his own facts, determined to defend them unto death. In the silence, Tom could almost hear Marge's breathing, and a cough from Mr. Greenleaf made him start. Mr. Greenleaf looked remarkably calm, almost bored. Tom wondered if he had fixed up some scheme with McCarron against him, based on the rings story?

'Is he the kind of man to lend you the rings for luck for a short time? Had he ever done anything else like that?' McCarron asked.

'No,' Marge said before Tom could answer.

Tom began to breathe more easily. He could see that McCarron didn't know yet what he should make out of it. McCarron was waiting for him to answer. 'He had lent me certain things before,' Tom said. 'He'd told me to help myself to his ties and jackets now and then. But that's quite a different matter from the rings, of course.' He had felt a compulsion to say that, because Marge undoubtedly knew about the time Dickie had found him in his clothes.

'I can't imagine Dickie without his rings,' Marge said to McCarron. 'He took the green one off when he went swimming, but he always put it right on again. They were just like part of his dressing. That's why I think he was either intending to kill himself or he meant to change his identity.'

McCarron nodded. 'Had he any enemies that you know of?'

'Absolutely none,' Tom said. 'I've thought of that.'

'Any reason you can think of why he might have wanted to disguise himself, or assume another identity?'

Tom said carefully, twisting his aching neck, '*Possibly* – but it's next to impossible in Europe. He'd have had to have a different passport. Any country he'd have entered, he would have had to have a passport. He'd have had to have a passport even to get into a hotel.'

'You told me he might not have had to have a passport,' Mr. Greenleaf said.

'Yes, I said that about small hotels in Italy. It's a remote possibility, of course. But after all this publicity about his disappearance, I don't see how he could still be keeping it up,' Tom said. 'Somebody would surely have betrayed him by this time.'

'Well, he left with his passport, obviously,' McCarron said, 'because he got into Sicily with it and registered at a big hotel.'

'Yes,' Tom said.

McCarron made notes for a moment, then looked up at Tom. 'Well, how do you see it, Mr. Ripley?'

McCarron wasn't nearly finished, Tom thought. McCarron was going to see him alone later. 'I'm afraid I agree with Miss Sherwood that it looks as if he's killed himself, and it looks as if he intended to all along. I've said that before to Mr. Greenleaf.'

McCarron looked at Mr. Greenleaf, but Mr. Greenleaf said nothing, only looked expectantly at McCarron. Tom had the feeling that McCarron was now inclined to think that Dickie was dead, too, and that it was a waste of time and money for him to have come over.

'I just want to check these facts again,' McCarron said, still plodding on, going back to his papers. 'The last time Richard was seen by anyone is February fifteenth, when he got off the boat in Naples, coming from Palermo.'

'That's correct,' Mr. Greenleaf said. 'A steward remembers seeing him.'

'But no sign of him at any hotel after that, and no communications from him since.' McCarron looked from Mr. Greenleaf to Tom.

'No,' Tom said.

McCarron looked at Marge.

'No,' Marge said.

'And when was the last time you saw him, Miss Sherwood?'

'On November twenty-third, when he left for San Remo,' Marge said promptly.

'You were then in Mongibello?' McCarron asked, pronouncing the town's name with a hard 'g', as if he had no knowledge of Italian, or at least no relationship to the spoken language.

'Yes,' Marge said. 'I just missed seeing him in Rome in February, but the last time I saw him was in Mongibello.'

Good old Marge! Tom felt almost affectionate towards her – underneath everything. He had begun to feel affectionate this morning, even though she had irritated him. 'He was trying to avoid everyone in Rome,' Tom put in. 'That's why, when he first gave me the rings, I thought he was on some tack of getting away from everyone he had known, living in another city, and just vanishing for a while.'

'Why, do you think?'

Tom elaborated, mentioning the murder of his friend Freddie Miles, and its effect on Dickie.

'Do you think Richard knew who killed Freddie Miles?'

'No. I certainly don't.'

McCarron waited for Marge's opinion.

'No,' Marge said, shaking her head.

'Think a minute,' McCarron said to Tom. 'Do you think that might have explained his behaviour? Do you think he's avoiding answering the police by hiding out now?'

Tom thought for a minute. 'He didn't give me a single clue in that direction.'

'Do you think Dickie was afraid of something?'

'I can't imagine of what,' Tom said.

McCarron asked Tom how close a friend Dickie had been of Freddie Miles, whom else he knew who was a friend of both Dickie and Freddie, if he knew of any debts between them, any girl friends – 'Only Marge that I know of,' Tom replied, and Marge protested that she wasn't a *girl* friend of Freddie's, so there couldn't possibly have been any *rivalry* over her – and could Tom say that he was Dickie's best friend in Europe?

'I wouldn't say that,' Tom answered. 'I think Marge Sherwood is. I hardly know any of Dickie's friends in Europe.'

McCarron studied Tom's face again. 'What's your opinion about these forgeries?'

'Are they forgeries? I didn't think anybody was sure.'

'I don't think they are,' Marge said.

'Opinion seems to be divided,' McCarron said. 'The experts don't think the letter he wrote to the bank in Naples is a forgery, which can only mean that if there is a forgery somewhere, he's covering up for someone. Assuming there is a forgery, do you have any idea who he might be trying to cover up for?'

Tom hesitated a moment, and Marge said, 'Knowing him, I can't imagine him covering up for anyone. Why should he?'

McCarron was staring at Tom, but whether he was debating his honesty or mulling over all they had said to him, Tom couldn't tell. McCarron looked like a typical American automobile salesman, or any other kind of salesman, Tom thought –

cheerful, presentable, average in intellect, able to talk baseball with a man or pay a stupid compliment to a woman. Tom didn't think too much of him, but, on the other hand, it was not wise to underestimate one's opponent. McCarron's small, soft mouth opened as Tom watched him, and he said, 'Would you mind coming downstairs with me for a few minutes, Mr. Ripley, if you've still got a few minutes?'

'Certainly,' Tom said, standing up.

'We won't be long,' McCarron said to Mr. Greenleaf and Marge.

Tom looked back from the door, because Mr. Greenleaf had gotten up and was starting to say something, though Tom didn't listen. Tom was suddenly aware that it was raining, that thin, grey sheets of rain were slapping against the window-panes. It was like a last glimpse, blurred and hasty – Marge's figure looking small and huddled across the big room, Mr. Greenleaf doddering forward like an old man, protesting. But the comfortable room was the thing, and the view across the canal to where his house stood – invisible now because of the rain – which he might never see again.

Mr. Greenleaf was asking, 'Are you – you are coming back in a few minutes?'

'Oh, yes,' McCarron answered with the impersonal firm-ness of an executioner.

They walked towards the elevator. Was this the way they did it? Tom wondered. A quiet word in the lobby. He would be handed over to the Italian police, and then McCarron would return to the room just as he had promised. McCarron had brought a couple of the papers from his briefcase with him. Tom stared at an ornamental vertical moulding beside the floor number panel in the elevator: an egg-shaped design framed by four raised dots, egg-shape, dots, all the way down. *Think of some sensible, ordinary remark to make about Mr. Greenleaf, for instance*, Tom said to himself. He ground his teeth. If he only wouldn't start sweating now. He hadn't started yet, but maybe it would break out all over his face when they reached the lobby. McCarron was hardly as tall as his shoulder. Tom turned to him just as the elevator stopped, and said grimly, baring his teeth in a smile, 'Is this your first trip to Venice?'

'Yes,' said McCarron. He was crossing the lobby. 'Shall we go in here?' He indicated the coffee bar. His tone was polite.

'All right,' Tom said agreeably. The bar was not crowded, but there was not a single table that would be out of earshot of some other table. Would McCarron accuse him in a place like this, quietly laying down fact after fact on the table? He took the chair that McCarron pulled out for him. McCarron sat with his back to the wall.

A waiter came up. 'Signori?'

'Coffee,' McCarron said.

'Cappuccino,' Tom said. 'Would you like a cappuccino or an espresso?'

'Which is the one with milk? Cappuccino?'

'Yes.'

'I'll have that.'

Tom gave the order.

McCarron looked at him. His small mouth smiled on one side. Tom imagined three or four different beginnings: 'You killed Richard, didn't you? The rings are just too much, aren't they?' Or 'Tell me about the San Remo boat, Mr. Ripley, in detail.' Or simply, leading up quietly, 'Where were you on February fifteenth, when Richard landed in . . . Naples? All right, but where were you living then? Where were you living in January, for instance? . . . Can you prove it?'

McCarron was saying nothing at all, only looking down at his plump hands now, and smiling faintly. As if it had been so absurdly simple for him to unravel, Tom thought, that he could hardly force himself to put it into words.

At a table next to them four Italian men were babbling away like a madhouse, screeching with wild laughter. Tom wanted to edge away from them. He sat motionless.

Tom had braced himself until his body felt like iron, until sheer tension created defiance. He heard himself asking, in an incredibly calm voice, 'Did you have time to speak to Tenente Roverini when you came through Rome?' and at the same time he asked it, he realized that he had even an objective in the question: to find out if McCarron had heard about the San Remo boat.

'No, I didn't,' McCarron said. 'There was a message for me that Mr. Greenleaf would be in Rome today, but I'd landed in Rome so early, I thought I'd fly over and catch him – and also talk to you.' McCarron looked down at his papers. 'What kind of a man is Richard? How would you describe him as far as his personality goes?'

Was McCarron going to lead up to it like this? Pick out more little clues from the words he chose to describe him? Or did he only want the objective opinion that he couldn't get from Dickie's parents? 'He wanted to be a painter,' Tom began, 'but he knew he'd never be a very good painter. He tried to act as if he didn't care, and as if he were perfectly happy and leading exactly the kind of life he wanted to lead over here in Europe.' Tom moistened his lips. 'But I think the life was beginning to get him down. His father disapproved, as you probably know. And Dickie had got himself into an awkward spot with Marge.'

'How do you mean?'

'Marge was in love with him, and he wasn't with her, and at the same time he was seeing her so much in Mongibello, she kept on hoping—' Tom began to feel on safer ground, but he pretended to have difficulty in expressing himself. 'He never actually discussed it with me. He always spoke very highly of Marge. He was very fond of her, but it was obvious to every-body – Marge too – that he never would marry her. But Marge never quite gave up. I think that's the main reason Dickie left Mongibello.'

McCarron listened patiently and sympathetically, Tom thought. 'What do you mean never gave up? What did she do?'

Tom waited until the waiter had set down the two frothy cups of cappuccino and stuck the tab between them under the sugar bowl. 'She kept writing to him, wanting to see him, and at the same time being very tactful, I'm sure, about not intruding on him when he wanted to be by himself. He told me all this in Rome when I saw him. He said, after the Miles murder, that he certainly wasn't in the mood to see Marge, and he was afraid that she'd come up to Rome from Mongibello when she heard of all the trouble he was in.'

'Why do you think he was nervous after the Miles murder?' McCarron took a sip of the coffee, winced from the heat or the bitterness, and stirred it with the spoon.

Tom explained. They'd been quite good friends, and Freddie had been killed just a few minutes after leaving his house.

'Do you think Richard might have killed Freddie?' McCarron asked quietly.

'No, I don't.'

'Why?'

'Because there was no reason for him to kill him – at least no reason that I happen to know of.'

'People usually say, because so-and-so wasn't the type to kill anybody,' McCarron said. 'Do you think Richard was the type who could have killed anyone?'

Tom hesitated, seeking earnestly for the truth. 'I never thought of it. I don't know what kind of people are apt to kill somebody. I've seen him angry—'

'When?'

Tom described the two days in Rome, when Dickie, he said, had been angry and frustrated because of the police questioning, and had actually moved out of his apartment to avoid phone calls from friends and strangers. Tom tied this in with a growing frustration in Dickie, because he had not been progressing as he had wanted to in his painting. He depicted Dickie as a stubborn, proud young man, in awe of his father and therefore determined to defy his father's wishes, a rather erratic fellow who was generous to strangers as well as to his friends, but who was subject to changes of mood – from sociability to sullen withdrawal. He summed it up by saying that Dickie was a very ordinary young man who liked to think he was extraordinary. 'If he killed himself,' Tom concluded, 'I think it was because he realized certain failures in himself – inadequacies. It's much easier for me to imagine him a suicide than a murderer.'

'But I'm not so sure that he didn't kill Freddie Miles. Are you?'

McCarron was perfectly sincere. Tom was sure of that. McCarron was even expecting him to defend Dickie now, because they had been friends. Tom felt some of his terror leaving him, but only some of it, like something melting very slowly inside him. 'I'm not sure,' Tom said, 'but I just don't believe that he did.'

'I'm not sure either. But it would explain a lot, wouldn't it?'

'Yes,' Tom said. 'Everything.'

'Well, this is only the first day of work,' McCarron said with an optimistic smile. 'I haven't even looked over the report in Rome. I'll probably want to talk to you again after I've been to Rome.'

Tom stared at him. It seemed to be over. 'Do you speak Italian?'

'No, not very well, but I can read it. I do better in French, but I'll get along,' McCarron said, as if it were not a matter of much importance.

It was very important, Tom thought. He couldn't imagine McCarron extracting everything that Roverini knew about the Greenleaf case solely through an interpreter. Neither would McCarron be able to get around and chat with people like Dickie Greenleaf's landlady in Rome. It was most important. 'I talked with Roverini here in Venice a few weeks ago,' Tom said. 'Give him my regards.'

'I'll do that.' McCarron finished his coffee. 'Knowing Dickie, what places do you think he would be likely to go if he wanted to hide out?'

Tom squirmed back a little on his chair. This was getting down to the bottom of the barrel, he thought. 'Well, I know he likes Italy best. I wouldn't bet on France. He also likes Greece. He talked about going to Majorca at some time. All of Spain is a possibility, I suppose.'

'I see,' McCarron said, sighing.

'Are you going back to Rome today?'

McCarron raised his eyebrows. 'I imagine so, if I can catch a few hours' sleep here. I haven't been to bed in two days.'

He held up very well, Tom thought. 'I think Mr. Greenleaf was wondering about the trains. There are two this morning and probably some more in the afternoon. He was planning to leave today.'

'We can leave today.' McCarron reached for the check. 'Thanks very much for your help, Mr. Ripley. I have your address and phone number, in case I have to see you again.'

They stood up.

'Mind if I go up and say good-bye to Marge and Mr. Greenleaf?'

McCarron didn't mind. They rode up in the elevator again. Tom had to check himself from whistling. *Papa non vuole* was going around in his head.

Tom looked closely at Marge as they went in, looking for signs of enmity. Marge only looked a little tragic, he thought. As if she had recently been made a widow.

'I'd like to ask you a few questions alone, too, Miss Sherwood,' McCarron said. 'If you don't mind,' he said to Mr. Greenleaf.

'Certainly not. I was just going down to the lobby to buy some newspapers,' Mr. Greenleaf said.

McCarron was carrying on. Tom said good-bye to Marge and to Mr. Greenleaf, in case they were going to Rome today and he did not see them again. He said to McCarron, 'I'd be very glad to come to Rome at any time, if I can be of any help. I expect to be here until the end of May, anyway.'

'We'll have something before then,' McCarron said with his confident Irish smile.

Tom went down to the lobby with Mr. Greenleaf.

'He asked me the same questions all over again,' Tom told Mr. Greenleaf, 'and also my opinion of Richard's character.'

'Well, what is your opinion?' Mr. Greenleaf asked in a hopeless tone.

Whether he was a suicide or had run away to hide himself would be conduct equally reprehensible in Mr. Greenleaf's eyes, Tom knew. 'I told him what I think is the truth,' Tom said, 'that he's capable of running away and also capable of committing suicide.'

Mr. Greenleaf made no comment, only patted Tom's arm. 'Good-bye, Tom.'

'Good-bye,' Tom said. 'Let me hear from you.'

Everything was all right between him and Mr. Greenleaf, Tom thought. And everything would be all right with Marge, too. She had swallowed the suicide explanation, and that was the direction her mind would run in from now on, he knew.

Tom spent the afternoon at home, expecting a telephone call, one telephone call at least from McCarron, even if it was not about anything important, but none came. There was only a call from Titi, the resident countess, inviting him for cocktails that afternoon. Tom accepted.

Why should he expect any trouble from Marge, he thought. She never had given him any. The suicide was an idée fixe, and she would arrange everything in her dull imagination to fit it.

28

MCCARRON CALLED TOM the next day from Rome, wanting the names of everyone Dickie had known in Mongibello. That was apparently all that McCarron wanted to know, because he took a leisurely time getting them all, and checking them off against the list that Marge had given him. Most of the names Marge had already given him, but Tom went through them all, with their difficult addresses – Giorgio, of course, Pietro the boatkeeper, Fausto's Aunt Maria whose last name he didn't know though he told McCarron in a complicated way how to get to her house, Aldo the grocer, the Cecchis, and even old Stevenson, the recluse painter who lived just outside the village and whom Tom had never even met. It took Tom several minutes to list them all, and it would take McCarron several days to check on them, probably. He mentioned everybody but Signor Pucci, who had handled the sale of Dickie's house and boat, and who would undoubtedly tell McCarron, if he hadn't learned it through Marge, that Tom Ripley had come to Mongibello to arrange Dickie's affairs. Tom did not think it very serious, one way or the other, if McCarron did know that he had taken care of Dickie's affairs. And as to people like Aldo and Stevenson, McCarron was welcome to all he could get out of them.

'Anyone in Naples?' McCarron asked.

'Not that I know of.'

'Rome?'

'I'm sorry, I never saw him with any friends in Rome.'

'Never met this painter – uh – Di Massimo?'

'No. I saw him once,' Tom said, 'but I never met him.'

'What does he look like?'

'Well, it was just on a street corner. I left Dickie as he was going to meet him, so I wasn't very close to him. He looked about five feet nine, about fifty, greyish-black hair – that's about all I remember. He looked rather solidly built. He was wearing a light-grey suit, I remember.'

'Hm-m – okay,' McCarron said absently, as if he were writing all that down. 'Well, I guess that's about all. Thanks very much, Mr. Ripley.'

'You're very welcome. Good luck.'

Then Tom waited quietly in his house for several days, just as anybody would do, if the search for a missing friend had reached its intensest point. He declined three or four invitations to parties. The newspapers had renewed their interest in Dickie's disappearance, inspired by the presence in Italy of an American private detective who had been hired by Dickie's father. When some photographers from *Europeo* and *Oggi* came to take pictures of him and his house, he told them firmly to leave, and actually took one insistent young man by the elbow and propelled him across the living-room towards the door. But nothing of any importance happened for five days – no telephone calls, no letters, even from Tenente Roverini. Tom imagined the worst sometimes, especially at dusk when he felt more depressed than at any other time of day. He imagined Roverini and McCarron getting together and developing the theory that Dickie could have disappeared in November, imagined McCarron checking on the time he had bought his car, imagined him picking up a scent when he found out that Dickie had not come back after the San Remo trip and that Tom Ripley had come down to arrange for the disposal of Dickie's things. He measured and remeasured Mr. Greenleaf's tired, indifferent good-bye that last morning in Venice, interpreted it as unfriendly, and imagined Mr. Greenleaf flying into a rage in Rome when no results came of all the efforts to find Dickie, and suddenly demanding a thorough investigation of

Tom Ripley, that scoundrel he had sent over with his own money to try to get his son home.

But each morning Tom was optimistic again. On the good side was the fact that Marge unquestioningly believed that Dickie had spent those months sulking in Rome, and she would have kept all his letters and she would probably bring them all out to show to McCarron. Excellent letters they were, too. Tom was glad he had spent so much thought on them. Marge was an asset rather than a liability. It was really a very good thing that he had put down his shoe that night that she had found the rings.

Every morning he watched the sun, from his bedroom window, rising through the winter mists, struggling upward over the peaceful-looking city, breaking through finally to give a couple of hours of actual sunshine before noon, and the quiet beginning of each day was like a promise of peace in the future. The days were growing warmer. There was more light, and less rain. Spring was almost here, and one of these mornings, one morning finer than these, he would leave the house and board a ship for Greece.

On the evening of the sixth day after Mr. Greenleaf and McCarron had left, Tom called him in Rome. Mr. Greenleaf had nothing new to report, but Tom had not expected anything. Marge had gone home. As long as Mr. Greenleaf was in Italy, Tom thought, the papers would carry something about the case every day. But the newspapers were running out of sensational things to say about the Greenleaf case.

'And how is your wife?' Tom asked.

'Fair. I think the strain is telling on her, however. I spoke to her again last night.'

'I'm sorry,' Tom said. He ought to write her a nice letter, he thought, just a friendly word while Mr. Greenleaf was away and she was by herself. He wished he had thought of it before.

Mr. Greenleaf said he would be leaving at the end of the week, via Paris, where the French police were also carrying on the search. McCarron was going with him, and if nothing happened in Paris they were both going home. 'It's obvious to me or to anybody,' Mr. Greenleaf said, 'that he's either dead or deliberately hiding. There's not a corner of the world where the search for him hasn't been publicized. Short of Russia, maybe. My God, he never showed any liking for that place, did he?'

'Russia? No, not that I know of.'

Apparently Mr. Greenleaf's attitude was that Dickie was either dead or to hell with him. During that telephone call, the to-hell-with-him attitude seemed to be uppermost.

Tom went over to Peter Smith-Kingsley's house that same evening. Peter had a couple of English newspapers that his friends had sent him, one with a picture of Tom ejecting the *Oggi* photographer from his house. Tom had seen it in the Italian newspapers too. Pictures of him on the streets of Venice and pictures of his house had also reached America. Bob and Cleo both had airmailed him photographs and write-ups from New York tabloids. They thought it was all terribly exciting.

'I'm good and sick of it,' Tom said. 'I'm only hanging around here to be polite and to help if I can. If any more reporters try to crash my house, they're going to get it with a shotgun as soon as they walk in the door.' He really was irritated and disgusted, and it sounded in his voice.

'I quite understand,' Peter said. 'I'm going home at the end of May, you know. If you'd like to come along and stay at my place in Ireland, you're more than welcome. It's deadly quiet there, I can assure you.'

Tom glanced at him. Peter had told him about his old Irish castle and had shown him pictures of it. Some quality of his relationship with Dickie flashed across his mind like the memory of a nightmare, like a pale and evil ghost. It was because the same thing could happen with Peter, he thought, Peter the upright, unsuspecting, naïve, generous good fellow – except that he didn't look enough like Peter. But one evening, for Peter's amusement, he had put on an English accent and had imitated Peter's mannerisms and his way of jerking his head to one side as he talked, and Peter had thought it hilariously funny. He shouldn't have done that, Tom thought now. It made Tom bitterly ashamed, that evening and the fact that he had thought even for an instant that the same thing that had happened with Dickie could happen with Peter.

'Thanks,' Tom said. 'I'd better stay by myself for a while longer. I miss my friend Dickie, you know. I miss him terribly.' He was suddenly near tears. He could remember Dickie's smiles that first day they began to get along, when he had confessed to Dickie that his father had sent him. He remembered their crazy first trip to Rome. He remembered with affection even that half-hour in the Carlton Bar in Cannes, when Dickie had been so bored and silent, but there had been a reason why Dickie had been bored, after all: he had dragged Dickie there, and Dickie didn't care for the Côte d'Azur. If he'd only gotten his sightseeing done all by himself, Tom thought, if he only hadn't been in such a hurry and so greedy, if he only hadn't misjudged the relationship between Dickie and Marge so stupidly, or had simply waited for them to separate of their own volition, then none of this would have happened, and he *could* have lived with Dickie for the rest of his life, travelled and lived and enjoyed living for the rest of his life. If he only hadn't put on Dickie's clothes that day—

'I understand, Tommie boy, I really do,' Peter said, patting his shoulder.

Tom looked up at him through distorting tears. He was imagining travelling with Dickie on some liner back to America for Christmas holidays, imagining being on as good terms with Dickie's parents as if he and Dickie had been brothers. 'Thanks,' Tom said. It came out a childlike 'blub'.

'I'd really think something was the matter with you if you didn't break down like this,' Peter said sympathetically.

29

Venice

3 June, 19—

Dear Mr. Greenleaf:

WHILE PACKING A suitcase today, I came across an envelope that Richard gave me in Rome, and which for some unaccountable reason I had forgotten until now. On the envelope was written 'Not to be opened until June' and, as it happens, it is June. The envelope contained Richard's will, and he leaves his income and possessions to me. I am as astounded by this as you probably are, yet from the wording of the will (it is typewritten) he seems to have been in possession of his senses.

I am only bitterly sorry I did not remember having the envelope, because it would have proven much earlier that Dickie intended to take his own life. I put it into a suitcase pocket, and then I forgot it. He gave it to me on the last occasion I saw him, in Rome, when he was so depressed.

On second thought, I am enclosing a photostat copy of the will so that you may see it for yourself. This is the first will I have even seen in my life, and I am absolutely unfamiliar with the usual procedure. What should I do?

Please give my kindest regards to Mrs. Greenleaf and realize that I sympathize deeply with you both, and regret the necessity of writing this letter. Please let me hear from you as soon as possible. My next address will be:

c/o American Express

Athens, Greece

Most sincerely yours,

Tom Ripley

In a way it was asking for trouble, Tom thought. It might start a new investigation of the signatures, on the will and also the remittances, one of the relentless investigations that insurance companies and probably trust companies also launched when it was a matter of money out of their own pockets. But that was the mood he was in. He had bought his ticket for Greece in the middle of May, and the days had grown finer and finer, making him more and more restless. He had taken his car out of the Fiat garage in Venice and had driven over the Brenner to Salzburg and Munich, down to Trieste and over to Bolzano, and the weather had held everywhere, except for the mildest, most springlike shower in Munich when he had been walking in the Englischer Garten, and he had not even tried to get under cover from it but had simply kept on walking, thrilled as a child at the thought that this was the first German rain that had ever fallen on him. He had only two thousand dollars in his own name, transferred from Dickie's bank account and saved out of Dickie's income, because he hadn't dared to withdraw any more in so short a time as three months. The very chanciness of trying for all of Dickie's money, the peril of it, was irresistible to him. He was so bored after the dreary, eventless weeks in Venice, when each day that went by had seemed to confirm his personal safety and to emphasize the dullness of his existence. Roverini had stopped writing to him. Alvin McCarron had gone back to America (after nothing more than another inconsequential telephone call to him from Rome), and Tom supposed that he and Mr. Greenleaf had concluded that Dickie was either dead or hiding of his own will, and that further search was useless. The newspapers had stopped printing anything about Dickie for want of anything to print. Tom had a feeling of emptiness and abeyance that had driven him nearly mad until he made the trip to Munich in his car. When he came back to Venice to pack for Greece and to close his house, the sensation had been worse: he was about to go to Greece, to those ancient heroic islands, as little Tom

Ripley, shy and meek, with a dwindling two-thousand-odd in his bank, so that he would practically have to think twice before he bought himself even a book on Greek art. It was intolerable.

He had decided in Venice to make his voyage to Greece an heroic one. He would see the islands, swimming for the first time into his view, as a living, breathing, courageous individual – not as a cringing little nobody from Boston. If he sailed right into the arms of the police in Piraeus, he would at least have known the days just before, standing in the wind at the prow of a ship, crossing the wine-dark sea like Jason or Ulysses return-ing. So he had written the letter to Mr. Greenleaf and mailed it three days before he was to sail from Venice. Mr. Greenleaf would probably not get the letter for four or five days, so there would be no time for Mr. Greenleaf to hold him in Venice with a telegram and make him miss his ship. Besides, it looked better from every point of view to be casual about the thing, not to be reachable for another two weeks until he got to Greece, as if he were so unconcerned as to whether he got the money or not, he had not let the fact of the will postpone even a little trip he had planned to make.

Two days before his sailing, he went to tea at the house of Titi della Latta-Cacciaguerra, the countess he had met the day he had started looking for a house in Venice. The maid showed him into the living-room, and Titi greeted him with the phrase he had not heard for many weeks: 'Ah, ciao, Tomaso! Have you seen the afternoon paper? They have found Dickie's suitcases! And his paintings! Right here in the American Express in Venice!' Her gold earrings trembled with her excitement.

'*What?*' Tom hadn't seen the papers. He had been too busy packing that afternoon.

'Read it! Here! All his clothes deposited only in February! They were sent from Naples. Perhaps he is here in Venice!'

Tom was reading it. The cord around the canvases had come undone, the paper said, and in wrapping them again a clerk had discovered the signature of R. Greenleaf on the paintings.

Tom's hands began to shake so that he had to grip the sides of the paper to hold it steady. The paper said that the police were now examining everything carefully for fingerprints.

'Perhaps he is alive!' Titi shouted.

'I don't think – I don't see why this proves he is alive. He could have been murdered or killed himself after he sent the suitcases. The fact that it's under another name – Fanshaw—' He had the feeling the countess, who was sitting rigidly on the sofa staring at him, was startled by his nervousness, so he pulled himself together abruptly, summoned all his courage and said, 'You see? They're looking through everything for fingerprints. They wouldn't be doing that if they were sure Dickie sent the suitcases himself. Why should he deposit them under Fanshaw, if he expected to claim them again himself? His passport's even here. He packed his passport.'

'Perhaps he is hiding himself under the name of Fanshaw! Oh, caro mio, you need some tea!' Titi stood up. 'Giustina! Il te, per piacere, subitissimo!'

Tom sank down weakly on the sofa, still holding the newspaper in front of him. What about the knot on Dickie's body? Wouldn't it be just his luck to have that come undone now?

'Ah, carissimo, you are so pessimistic,' Titi said, patting his knee. 'This is good news! Suppose all the fingerprints are his? Wouldn't you be happy then? Suppose tomorrow, when you are walking in some little street of Venice, you will come face to face with Dickie Greenleaf, alias Signor Fanshaw!' She let out her shrill, pleasant laugh that was as natural to her as breathing.

'It says here that the suitcases contained everything – shaving kit, toothbrush, shoes, overcoat, complete equipment,' Tom said, hiding his terror in gloom. 'He couldn't be alive and leave all that. The murderer must have stripped his body and deposited his clothes there because it was the easiest way of getting rid of them.'

This gave even Titi pause. Then she said, 'Will you not be so downhearted until you know what the fingerprints are?

You are supposed to be off on a pleasure trip tomorrow. Ecco il te!'

The day after tomorrow, Tom thought. Plenty of time for Roverini to get his fingerprints and compare them with those on the canvases and in the suitcases. He tried to remember any flat surfaces on the canvas frames and on things in the suitcases from which fingerprints could be taken. There was not much, except the articles in the shaving kit, but they could find enough, in fragments and smears, to assemble ten perfect prints if they tried. His only reason for optimism was that they didn't have his fingerprints yet, and that they might not ask for them because he was not yet under suspicion. But if they already had Dickie's fingerprints from somewhere? Wouldn't Mr. Greenleaf send Dickie's fingerprints from America the very first thing, by way of checking? There could be any number of places they could find Dickie's fingerprints: on certain possessions of his in America, in the house in Mongibello—

'Tomaso! Take your tea!' Titi said, with another gentle press of his knee.

'Thank you.'

'You will see. At least this is a step toward the truth, what *really* happened. Now let us talk about something else, if it makes you so unhappy! Where do you go from Athens?'

He tried to turn his thoughts to Greece. For him, Greece was gilded, with the gold of warriors' armour and with its own famous sunlight. He saw stone statues with calm, strong faces, like the women on the porch of the Erechtheum. He didn't want to go to Greece with the threat of the fingerprints in Venice hanging over him. It would debase him. He would feel as low as the lowest rat that scurried in the gutters of Athens, lower than the dirtiest beggar who would accost him in the streets of Salonika. Tom put his face in his hands and wept. Greece was finished, exploded like a golden balloon.

Titi put her firm, plump arm around him. 'Tomaso, cheer up! Wait until you have reason to feel so downcast!'

'I can't see why you don't see that this is a bad sign!' Tom said desperately. 'I really don't!'

30

THE WORST SIGN of all was that Roverini, whose messages had been so friendly and explicit up to now, sent him nothing at all in regard to the suitcases and canvases having been found in Venice. Tom spent a sleepless night and then a day, of pacing his house while he tried to finish the endless little chores pertaining to his departure, paying Anna and Ugo, paying various tradesmen. Tom expected the police to come knocking on his door at any hour of the day or night. The contrast between his tranquil self-confidence of five days ago and his present apprehension almost tore him apart. He could neither sleep nor eat nor sit still. The irony of Anna's and Ugo's commiseration with him, and also of the telephone calls from his friends, asking him if he had any ideas as to what might have happened in view of the finding of the suitcases, seemed more than he could bear. Ironic, too, that he could let them know that he was upset, pessimistic, desperate even, and they thought nothing of it. They thought it was perfectly normal, because Dickie after all might have been murdered: everybody considered it very significant that all Dickie's possessions had been in the suitcases in Venice, down to his shaving kit and comb.

Then there was the matter of the will. Mr. Greenleaf would get it the day after tomorrow. By that time they might know that the fingerprints were not Dickie's. By that time they might have intercepted the *Hellenes*, and taken his own fingerprints. If they discovered that the will was a forgery, too, they would have no mercy on him. Both murders would come out, as naturally as ABC.

By the time he boarded the *Hellenes* Tom felt like a walking ghost. He was sleepless, foodless, full of espressos, carried along only by his twitching nerves. He wanted to ask if there was a radio, but he was positive there was a radio. It was a good-sized triple-deck ship with forty-eight passengers. He collapsed about five minutes after the stewards had brought his luggage into his cabin. He remembered lying face down on his bunk with one arm twisted under him, and being too tired to change his position, and when he awakened the ship was moving, not only moving but rolling gently with a pleasant rhythm that suggested a tremendous reserve of power and a promise of unending, unobstructable forward movement that would sweep aside anything in its way. He felt better except that the arm he had been lying on hung limply at his side like a dead member, and flopped against him when he walked through the corridor so that he had to grip it with the other hand to hold it in place. It was a quarter of ten by his watch, and utterly dark outside.

There was some kind of land on his extreme left, probably part of Yugoslavia, five or six little dim white lights, and otherwise nothing but black sea and black sky, so black that there was no trace of an horizon and they might have been sailing against a black screen, except that he felt no resistance to the steadily ploughing ship, and the wind blew freely on his forehead as if out of infinite space. There was no one around him on the deck. They were all below, eating their late dinner, he supposed. He was glad to be alone. His arm was coming back to life. He gripped the prow where it separated in a narrow V and took a deep breath. A defiant courage rose in him. What if the radioman were receiving at this very minute a message to arrest Tom Ripley? He would stand up just as bravely as he was standing now. Or he might hurl himself over the ship's gunwale – which for him would be the supreme act of courage as well as escape. Well, what if? Even from where he stood, he could hear the faint *beep-beep-beep* from the radio room at the top of the superstructure. He was not afraid. This was it. This was the way he had hoped he would feel, sailing to Greece. To look out at the black water all around him and not be afraid was almost as good as seeing the islands of Greece coming into view. In the soft June darkness ahead of him he could construct in imagination the little islands, the hills of Athens dotted with buildings, and the Acropolis.

There was an elderly Englishwoman on board the ship, travelling with her daughter who herself was forty, unmarried and so wildly nervous she could not even enjoy the sun for fifteen minutes in her deck-chair without leaping up and announcing in a loud voice that she was 'off for a walk'. Her mother, by contrast, was extremely calm and slow, she had some kind of paralysis in her right leg, which was shorter than the other so that she had to wear a thick heel on her right shoe and could not walk except with a cane – the kind of person who would have driven Tom insane in New York with her slowness and her unvarying graciousness of manner, but now Tom was inspired to spend hours with her in the deck-chair, talking to her and listening to her talk about her life in England and about Greece, when she had last seen Greece in 1926. He took her for slow walks around the deck, she leaning on his arm and apologizing constantly for the trouble she was giving him, but obviously she loved the attention. And the daughter was obviously delighted that someone was taking her mother off her hands.

Maybe Mrs. Cartwright had been a hellcat in her youth, Tom thought, maybe she was responsible for every one of her daughter's neuroses, maybe she had clutched her daughter so closely to her that it had been impossible for the daughter to lead a normal life and marry, and maybe she deserved to be kicked overboard instead of walked around the deck and listened to for hours while she talked, but what did it matter? Did the world always mete out just deserts? Had the world meted his out to him? He considered that he had been lucky beyond reason in escaping detection for two murders, lucky from the time he had assumed Dickie's identity until now. In the first part of his life fate had been grossly unfair, he thought, but the period with Dickie and afterwards had more than compensated for it. But something was going to happen now in Greece, he felt, and it couldn't be good. His luck had held just too long. But supposing they got him on the fingerprints, and on the will, and they gave him the electric chair – could that death in the electric chair equal in pain, or could death itself, at twenty-five, be so tragic, that he could not say that the months from November until now had not been worth it? Certainly not.

The only thing he regretted was that he had not seen all the world yet. He wanted to see Australia. And India. He wanted to see Japan. Then there was South America. Merely to look at the art of those countries would be a pleasant, rewarding life's work, he thought. He had learned a lot about painting, even in trying to copy Dickie's mediocre paintings. At the art galleries in Paris and Rome he had discovered an interest in paintings that he had never realized before, or perhaps that had not been in him before. He did not want to be a painter himself, but if he had money, he thought, his greatest pleasure would be to collect paintings that he liked, and to help young painters with talent who needed money.

His mind went off on such tangents as he walked with Mrs. Cartwright around the deck, or listened to her monologues that were not always interesting. Mrs. Cartwright thought him charming. She told him several times, days before they got to Greece, how much he had contributed to her enjoyment of the voyage, and they made plans as to how they would meet at a certain hotel in Crete on the second of July, Crete being the only place their itineraries crossed. Mrs. Cartwright was travelling by bus on a special tour. Tom acquiesced to all her suggestions, though he never expected to see her again once they got off the ship. He imagined himself seized at once and taken on board another ship, or perhaps a plane, back to Italy. No radio messages had come about him – that he knew of – but would they necessarily inform him if any had come? The ship's paper, a little one-page mimeographed sheet that appeared every evening at each place on the dinner tables, was entirely concerned with international political news, and would not have contained anything about the Greenleaf case even if something important had happened. During the ten-day voyage Tom lived in a peculiar atmosphere of doom and of heroic, unselfish courage. He imagined strange things: Mrs. Cartwright's daughter falling overboard and he jumping after her and saving her. Or fighting through the waters of a ruptured bulkhead to close the breach with his own body. He felt possessed of a preternatural strength and fearlessness.

When the boat approached the mainland of Greece Tom was standing at the rail with Mrs. Cartwright. She was telling him how the port of Piraeus had changed in appearance since she had seen it last, and Tom was not interested at all in the changes. It existed, that was all that mattered to him. It wasn't a mirage ahead of him, it was a solid hill that he could walk on, with buildings that he could touch – if he got that far.

The police were waiting on the dock. He saw four of them, standing with folded arms, looking up at the ship. Tom helped Mrs. Cartwright to the very last, boosted her gently over the kerb at the end of the gangplank, and said a smiling good-bye to her and her daughter. He had to wait under the R's and they under the C's to receive their luggage, and the two Cartwrights were leaving right away for Athens on their special bus.

With Mrs. Cartwright's kiss still warm and slightly moist on his cheek, Tom turned and walked slowly towards the policemen. No fuss, he thought, he'd just tell them himself who he was. There was a big newsstand behind the policemen, and he thought of buying a paper. Perhaps they would let him. The policemen stared back at him from over their folded arms as he approached them. They wore black uniforms with visored caps. Tom smiled at them faintly. One of them touched his cap and stepped aside. But the others did not close in. Now Tom was practically between two of them, right in front of the newsstand, and the policemen were staring forward again, paying no attention to him at all.

Tom looked over the array of papers in front of him, feeling dazed and faint. His hand moved automatically to take a familiar paper of Rome. It was only three days old. He pulled some lire out of his pocket, realized suddenly that he had no Greek money, but the newsdealer accepted the lire as readily as if he were in Italy, and even gave him back change in lire.

'I'll take these, too,' Tom said in Italian, choosing three more Italian papers and the Paris *Herald-Tribune*. He glanced at the police officers. They were not looking at him.

Then he walked back to the shed on the dock where the ship's passengers were awaiting their luggage. He heard Mrs. Cartwright's cheerful halloo to him as he went by, but he pretended not to have heard. Under the R's he stopped and opened the oldest Italian paper, which was four days old.

NO ONE NAMED ROBERT S. FANSHAW FOUND, DEPOSITOR OF GREENLEAF BAGGAGE

said the awkward caption on the second page. Tom read the long column below it, but only the fifth paragraph interested him:

The police ascertained a few days ago that the fingerprints on the suitcases and paintings are the same as the fingerprints found in Greenleaf's abandoned apartment in Rome. Therefore, it has been assumed that Greenleaf deposited the suitcases and the paintings himself. . . .

Tom fumbled open another paper. Here it was again:

. . . In view of the fact that the fingerprints on the articles in the suitcases are identical with those in Signor Greenleaf's apartment in

Rome, the police have concluded that Signor Greenleaf packed and dispatched the suitcases to Venice, and there is speculation that he may have committed suicide, perhaps in the water in a state of total nudity. An alternative speculation is that he exists at present under the alias of Robert S. Fanshaw or another alias. Still another possibility is that he was murdered, after packing or being made to pack his own baggage – perhaps for the express purpose of confusing the police inquiries through fingerprints . . .

In any case, it is futile to search for 'Richard Greenleaf' any longer, because, even if he is alive, he has not his 'Richard Greenleaf' passport . . . .

Tom felt shaky and lightheaded. The glare of sunlight under the edge of the roof hurt his eyes. Automatically he followed the porter with his luggage towards the customs counter, and tried to realize, as he stared down at his open suitcase that the inspector was hastily examining, exactly what the news meant. It meant he was not suspected at all. It meant that the fingerprints really had guaranteed his innocence. It meant not only that he was not going to jail, and not going to die, but that he was not suspected at all. He was free. Except for the will.

Tom boarded the bus for Athens. One of his table companions was sitting next to him, but he gave no sign of greeting, and couldn't have answered anything if the man had spoken to him. There would be a letter concerning the will at the American Express in Athens, Tom was sure. Mr. Greenleaf had had plenty of time to reply. Perhaps he had put his lawyers on to it right away, and there would be only a polite negative reply in Athens from a lawyer, and maybe the next message would come from the American police, saying that he was answerable for forgery. Maybe both messages were awaiting him at the American Express. The will could undo it all. Tom looked out of the window at the primitive, dry landscape. Nothing was registering on him. Maybe the Greek police were waiting for him at the American Express. Maybe the four men he had seen had not been police but some kind of soldiers.

The bus stopped. Tom got out, corralled his luggage, and found a taxi.

'Would you stop at the American Express, please?' he asked the driver in Italian, but the driver apparently understood 'American Express' at least, and drove off. Tom remembered when he had said the same words to the taxi driver in Rome, the day he had been on his way to Palermo. How sure of himself he'd been that day, just after he had given Marge the slip at the Inghilterra!

He sat up when he saw the American Express sign, and looked around the building for policemen. Perhaps the police were inside. In Italian, he asked the driver to wait, and the driver seemed to understand this too, and touched his cap. There was a specious ease about everything, like the moment just before something was going to explode. Tom looked around inside the American Express lobby. Nothing unusual. Maybe the minute he mentioned his name—

'Have you any letters for Thomas Ripley?' he asked in a low voice in English.

'Reepley? Spell it, if you please.'

He spelt it.

She turned and got some letters from a cubbyhole.

Nothing was happening.

'Three letters,' she said in English, smiling.

One from Mr. Greenleaf. One from Titi in Venice. One from Cleo, forwarded. He opened the letter from Mr. Greenleaf.

9 June, 19——

Dear Tom:

Your letter of 3 June received yesterday.

It was not so much of a surprise to my wife and me as you may have imagined. We were both aware that Richard was very fond of you, in spite of the fact he never went out of his way to tell us this in any of his letters. As you pointed out, this will does, unhappily, seem to indicate that Richard has taken his own life. It is a conclusion that we here have at last accepted – the only other chance being that Richard has assumed another name and for reasons of his own has chosen to turn his back on his family.

My wife concurs with me in the opinion that we should carry out Richard's preferences and the spirit of them, whatever he may have done with himself. So you have, insofar as the will is concerned, my personal support. I have put your photostat copy into the hands of my lawyers, who will keep you informed as to their progress in making over Richard's trust fund and other properties to you.

Once more, thank you for your assistance when I was overseas. Let us hear from you.

With best wishes
Herbert Greenleaf

Was it a joke? But the Burke-Greenleaf letterpaper in his hand felt authentic – thick and slightly pebbled and the letterhead engraved – and besides, Mr. Greenleaf wouldn't joke like this, not in a million years. Tom walked on to the waiting taxi. It was no joke. It was his! Dickie's money and his freedom. And the freedom, like everything else, seemed combined, his and Dickie's combined. He could have a house in Europe and a house in America too, if he chose. The money for the house in Mongibello was still waiting to be claimed, he thought suddenly, and he supposed he should send that to the Greenleafs, since Dickie put it up for sale before he wrote the will. He smiled, thinking of Mrs. Cartwright. He must take her a big box of orchids when he met her in Crete, if they had any orchids in Crete.

He tried to imagine landing in Crete – the long island, peaked with the dry, jagged lips of craters, the little bustle of excitement on the pier as his boat moved into the harbour, the small-boy porters, avid for his luggage and his tips, and he would have plenty to tip them with, plenty for everything and everybody. He saw four motionless figures standing on the imaginary pier, the figures of Cretan policemen waiting for him, patiently waiting with folded arms. He grew suddenly tense, and his vision vanished. Was he going to see policemen waiting for him on every pier that he ever approached? In Alexandria? Istanbul? Bombay? Rio? No use thinking about that. He pulled his shoulders back. No use spoiling his trip worrying about imaginary policemen. Even if there *were* policemen on the pier, it wouldn't necessarily mean—

'A donda, a donda?' the taxi driver was saying, trying to speak Italian for him.

'To a hotel, please,' Tom said. 'Il meglio albergo. Il meglio, il meglio!'